FATE AWAKENED

WEREWOLVES OF ULTERRA BOOK 1

JOCELYN MONTANA

H. DELANEY PUBLISHING

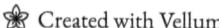 Created with Vellum

Map design by S.J. Primrose
Cover design by Merel Pierce Designs.

For my mom who gifted me with the love of reading.

And also for my dad, who always told me that he thought I was meant to be a writer.

GLOSSARY

Glossary of Terms

ala — An ancient being that can shift into a massive raven and wield large hail. Destructive and dangerous and guards the junction at the Shaking Mountain.

azhdaya — A two headed, wingless serpent. Lives on mountain tops and covets land. Tries to kill anyone that enters its territory.

bauk — An ogre like creature with tusks in the lower jaw and leathery skin. Smart and more difficult to kill than goblins. Like dark places and possessive over their hiding holes. Eat humans but more interested in feeding off those with magic. They keep them alive and drain them over and over to fuel their own brief bursts of magic. Can only be killed by a blow behind the knees, under the armpits, and under the ears.

brownie — Immortals about four feet tall that live in usually already occupied homes. If the owner of the home has offered them milk or other treats brownies love, they will usually willingly take care of the home and help those that live there.

Bodec Mountains — Jagged mountains in the northern section of the Kuls, outside the vae border.

cockatrice — Called the vultures of Peklo because they like to eat the dead. Resemble a cross between a rooster and lizard. Can fly and attack with their claws. About the size of a horse.

Coromesto — the main city of Trulo and magic is weaved openly into daily living.

Cursed (the) — All the immortals punished to leave Ulterra and live in Peklo forever.

Divoky Forest — The wild forest west of the Wide River.

dokkaebi — A clever variety of spawn that covets things like money and possessions. Resembles humans in appearance and will join villages to blend in.

enchanter — Can enchant objects, create draughts, and possibly influence humans and animals to do their bidding.

frior — The vulk term for someone who is their ally.

gloson — A swine-like beast standing ten feet high at the shoulder with a blue spine along its back and four eyes. The males have four tusks in the lower jaw.

goblin — Four-foot-tall spawn of the underworld with long hair. They like to live in the forest and prey upon unsuspecting passersby. Not usually very intelligent and competitive with other spawn.

Herskala Academy — The school for all magic-wielders in Trulo kingdom.

hzievda — A star.

incubus — Male variety of demon who can gain more energy and power through sexual activity.

jedak — An amphibian resembling a massive frog with long vines on its head. It disguises itself by sinking into the mud of the bog so the vines look harmless, but then it preys on passersby.

junctions — The crossing places between Peklo and Ulterra. There are only a few known crossing places, and each is guarded. No one may exit Peklo unless they allow it.

kon — A large variety of horse with wider hooves to manage the treacherous Ryba Mountains where they are native.

Krol — King of the vulk. A krol wears golden armbands on their biceps and has enhanced senses and strength. They are able to walk between Ulterra and Peklo and into the realms of the afterlife.

Kuls — All the way to the east, it covers all the land east of the Wide River.

leshak — Fifteen-foot-tall beings with an elk skull for a head and large elk antlers. They kill by consuming souls.

magicwielders — Usually humans, although on occasion a peltwalker is born with magical abilities. Almost always the gift is passed along genetically which has created strong magic families and alliances. A human with this ability has a longer life span.

There are three castes:
- sorcerer
- spellcaster
- enchanter

necromancer — Dark magic practitioner with a connection to death.

obol — A gold coin that makes up the main monetary system in Ulterra. It weighs 25 grams and shavings of gold can be combined to equal an obol when they weigh 25 grams.

Peklo — The underworld which resides below Ulterra. While physically below Ulterra, it is another realm and is separated by a barrier. Only set crossing points (junctions) allow crossing between Ulterra and Peklo, although the two realms sometimes shift against each other and pockets form which allows denizens of the underworld to break through.

peltwalker — A human looking species that can shift into an animal when they touch the specialized gifted pelt/feather of that animal. Some known clans are:
- lionwalkers
- wolfwalkers
- eaglewalkers

Piesok — The main city of Stok kingdom.

ravec — Giant insectoid creature that lives in Peklo and rarely leaves its dark holes. Spits bile to incapacitate its prey and pre-cook them.

Rohant — The eastern kingdom.

Ryba - A fishing village up in the north.

sorcerer — Innate magic users that can cast magic without using spells or a medium of any kind.

spawn — A group of creatures banned to the underworld that try to escape to prey upon humans. Refers to several different species — goblins, bauk, and dokkaebi.

spellcaster — Always have to use a spell or a medium like a crystal, rock or chalk diagram to cast magic.

Stok — The southern kingdom.

succubus — Female variety of demon who can gain more energy and power through sexual activity.

Trulo — The western kingdom.

Uit — Vulk swear word.

Ulterra — The upperworld consisting of one large landmass, several islands, and a surrounding sea.

vae — A supernatural species that lives in the Kuls, looks mostly human, and has magic abilities.

vedogon — A dangerous and rare fish that is difficult to catch and has lethal spines along its back.

Vieska — The smallest village inside Rohant.

vulk — Werewolves. Current pack members are:
1.   Hans

2. Juri
3. Kyril
4. Ayren
5. Thane
6. Danyr (Dan)
7. Troyan (Troy)
8. Blazh
9. Finn

Wailing Trail — The only known way in and out of Rohant. A treacherous path through the mountains.

wyvern — Dragon-like serpent with the ability to fly.

zorzye — A species of human-looking supernatural beings with the ability to wield light.

Zuby Mountains — The high mountains of the southern Kuls.

Map of Ulterra

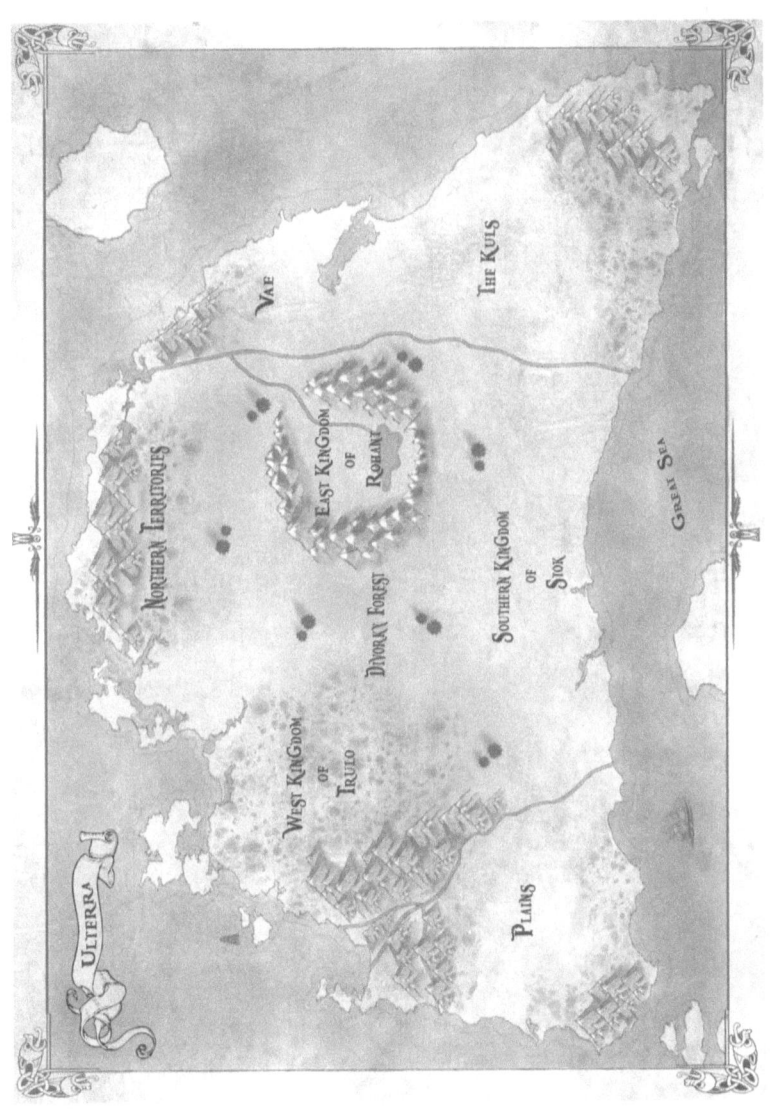

AN UNWELCOME SCENT wafted on one thin wisp of a breeze over the door sill into Hans's den. It crept like a hungry tongue, licking down the throat of the dark entryway until it swirled into the cavernous living room.

The vulk sat in silent darkness as he sat every evening, staring at his empty hearth and ignoring the vacant chair next to him. When the scent reached him, he jerked his head up. *Sulfur.* The stench of rotten eggs ... and brimstone.

Snarling, Hans stood and stretched to his full height. His claws lengthened. Brimstone meant it was time to hunt. If spawn from Peklo—the underworld—entered his territory, they died.

He strode toward the door, and the thick blanket of dust over the furniture swirled sluggishly into the air before settling back in place. Hans yanked the stone door open and homed in on the location of the sulfur. About five miles away, to the west, near the human kingdom of Rohant.

The odor was faint but definitely in his territory. Good. He hadn't sunk his claws into spawn in several months. For the few brief moments when he stood over a dead spawn, the darkness inside him, fueled by one hundred years of fury and grief, lifted. During those fleeting minutes, he felt like his old self again. The one before ...

He growled and stepped forward. No. He didn't think about the past.

The cool inky shadows of the forest embraced him like a lover, his fur so dark he wasn't visible unless he chose. Both moons hung low and full in the sky, washing the trees with pale light. His vision adjusted into gradients of gray and revealed his forest as clearly as the light of day. Grass, dead and bent to receive winter, crumpled under his feet with each step, but he rocked his weight soundlessly, padding like a silent specter.

He hadn't ventured into this part of the forest for decades, but he didn't glance around him. *Kill the spawn and return to his den.* To his solitude.

The scent strengthened, sharp and powerful, with a hint of—he halted, and fury punched through him. His claws lengthened to their full six inches, and red tinged his vision. It wasn't only brimstone in the air. All spawn wore the sulfurous scent of the underworld wrapped around them like a blanket, but that wasn't the only odor drifting on the air. A richer, charred stench joined it. A scent distinct and well-known to him.

A magicwielder was with them.

He should have known. The earth hadn't shaken tonight. The only way spawn entered Ulterra was if a tremor in the earth brushed the two realms together and formed a pocket, or rift, creating a portal up to Ulterra. Or if those with magic thinned the barrier and created a portal. No quaking earth meant magic intervention.

If a magicwielder was involved, things were more complicated, and more likely, the spawn weren't *near* the kingdom of Rohant but in it. Mingling with the humans. Taking easy prey.

What was surprising, though, was a magicwielder daring

to enter his lands after he'd banned them one hundred years ago. Did they really think he'd forgiven? Or forgotten? He hadn't. He thought about what their kind had done every day. What he'd lost.

He bared his teeth. It had been many years since he'd walked among the humans. If he could shift to a human form, like a peltwalker, it would be easier, but he had one form. The one told in stories to scare children. The humans knew a vulk owned these woods but knowing and seeing were two different things.

Amusing, really. Vulk kept the real monsters away. Only a vulk had the strength and power to close a rift, and only a vulk dedicated his life to killing spawn and keeping Ulterra safe. But humans didn't write stories about that.

He leaped forward, his claws digging into the grass. The trees thinned as he left the heart of the forest and descended into Rohant. His territory included the entire kingdom, the ring of mountains around it, and a swath of Divorky Forest beyond.

He scanned the bowl of the valley before him, swiveling his head to find the exact location of the scent. Rohant spread below, with flickers of human firelight from the villages scattered between the flanks of the mountains. To the north, where the palace sat, was a blaze of torches and fires from the guardhouses, but the scent wasn't that way. It trailed away to his left, near the smallest village tucked against the smallest mountain. Inside that mountain lay a cave, one he'd used a few times. An ideal hiding spot, but not good enough to fool a vulk.

Blood pounded through his veins. Time to destroy the threat.

Townspeople crowded by the roaring fire, pints in hand, to hear the last remaining bard spin a yarn. Briony remained at the tavern bar with the bartender, Owen. Every time she shifted on her stool, the rough wooden seat snagged her wool britches. The leaves bore the first blush of crimson, but already her breath froze in the air, and she'd had to open her winter clothes chest. Now, with the crush of farmers nipping in after the first day of harvest and the fire roaring, she roasted.

The fug of the crowd mucked up the windows with condensation and added to the fire's heat. She plucked at her simple wool-lined white shirt, fanning a bit of breeze up her neck, and glanced at the bard. All the other summer peddlers and vendors had left for the season, and if he didn't join them, the pass through the mountains would close, and the weather would force him to stay until the mud cleared in the spring.

Winter came harsh and fast as the ring of mountains surrounding them breathed down snow and ice. It kept Rohant a kingdom apart from the rest of Ulterra, with the Wailing Road the only way in and out. Their small hamlet, Vieska, was nestled the farthest into the mountains. So far off the beaten path, it was surprising a bard dropped by at all. Although judging by the stack of gold coins on the table next to him, he'd done well, and perhaps his journey here was a savvy one.

The bard wore purple and white crushed velvet breeches and a matching vest over a puffed ivory shirt. He stroked the pointed front of his matching purple triangular hat. "How about a riveting tale from these parts? The Shadow of Death, maybe?"

Ruddy-faced farmers, their leathery skin chapped and tanned, glanced at each other and shrugged. A small girl sitting cross-legged on the floor in the front squeaked.

Owen leaned across the bar and nudged Briony with a rag somewhere between the color of milky tea and sludge. "You think his stories are as good as the ones you're reading down here all the time?"

Every summer, the book peddler cart, Only an Obol, arrived with the other vendors. She saved all year to buy a few new books, and when she finished reading them, Briony swapped her books into Vieska's lending library and retrieved new ones. As many as she could lay her hands on. Since Vieska had access to the book cart only once a year, everyone shared.

She raised a brow. "Am I ignoring you and your stimulating conversation too much?"

"Ayup. As your landlord, part of your rent is to listen to my stories." Owen was barrel-chested with a keg-like belly to match. A bit fitting since, in addition to running the tavern, he brewed its beer himself and believed beer went with every meal and every occasion. He rented out the small flat above the tavern, and once Briony had high enough weekly wages she'd moved in. The apartment had two rooms, and the noise of the bar below filtered into her bedroom late into the night, but it was all hers.

Her lips quirked. "As much as I love hearing the story about how you discovered the perfect variety of hops for your golden ale, which gets more riveting each time, I think I'll escape into my book adventures."

Owen's eyebrows waggled a bit the way they did whenever he teased her. "You don't have adventure enough patching people up at the surgery?"

She'd worked for the doctor since she was eleven, first as an unpaid apprentice, then as his assistant. "I'm patching up the aftereffects of other people's adventures. I want to live my own."

"Yeah, yeah." Owen nodded toward the fireplace. "Anyway, I think your story's starting."

The bard rocked back on his heels and grinned. "All of Ulterra knows the woods of Rohant are the darkest. If you wander into the Divorky Forest, especially late at night, chances are great you won't return home because while the shadow of death stalks us all until we breathe our last breath, in Rohant, he actually walks here among you. Maybe some of you have even seen him?"

A few farmers frowned and drank.

"Yes, these are the woods of a great beast. A werewolf. Or in the ancient tongue, a vulk. Beware them all, but especially the Shadow of Death."

Now with a captive audience, the bard puffed his chest out, waving his arm with a flourish. "Darker than a moonless night, you may think a human is stalking through the forest, for he lurks on two legs, but when he gets close, you won't see the limbs and muscles of a man but the fur and features of a wolf. Teeth sharper than nails. Claws are so lethal you won't feel them as they slice through you. And far, far larger than any man. Run into him, and you won't ever be seen again."

The bard flexed his fingers into claws, and the little girl jumped.

"Tone it down." Ivan, the butcher, nodded toward the girl on the floor. "I don't want her waking up screaming all night."

Widowed two years ago, Ivan had started coming round the doctor's surgery weekly to chat with Briony. Her boss, Doc Tucless, wasn't pleased to be woken from his chair in the back to treat patients while Ivan kept her preoccupied. Behind his back, the entire town called him Doc Toothless. The man had a mouth like a tortoise—all gums.

Doc grinned and greeted Ivan like he was thrilled to see him. Ivan had enormous arms from cutting meat all day, so Doc didn't dare tell him to shoo, and also, Ivan gave him a nice discount on steaks.

However, after Ivan sauntered away, he'd hiss to her the butcher only wanted a tup and she should tell him to leave her alone and focus on work. Doc relished pointing out Ivan was no fool—he'd never marry her. Besides being too old at twenty-eight, Briony wasn't a Vieskan, and she brought no land to a marriage. Why would Ivan want *her* when he could marry one of the young daughters with land for his expanding cattle herds?

All that mattered in Vieska was land and lineage. Briony had neither, and she'd only recently paid off her apprentice debt to Doc Toothless and earned her own money. If Ivan was considering marriage, she should be grateful for his attention. His father's family traced back to one of the founding families, a long line of butchers. Since Ivan took over the business, though, he'd started buying his own cattle, intent on becoming a landowner and gaining the prestige that came along with it. Prestige that would extend to her if they married.

The bard flung his arms out. "Don't worry, child," he said to Ivan's young daughter. "If you stay here in Vieska, you're safe. Now, let me tell the tale of the Shadow of Death and the vae king—"

The tavern door slammed open and crisp night air gusted in. Two royal guards shouldered through the door, struggling to squeeze their bulk through the entrance. Their heads tucked right into their shoulders, and the green and white tunics of the royal livery stretched across their squat frames so tightly the seams threatened to burst.

In the twenty-two years since she'd arrived in town, the king had only stopped by once to place his seal on kegs of Owen's beer destined for an inter-kingdom beer competition. Why were palace guards here tonight?

They scanned the room, their beady, heavy-lidded small eyes landing on her. "You. Come with us." Which one spoke? Neither of their lips moved much, and the words were more grunts than speech.

"What? Me?"

One of them grunted and jerked his thumb over his shoulder. "Get in the coach."

The tavern was still, every patron frozen and staring at her.

7

Searching their faces, Briony's mouth dropped open. This had to be a joke. "Why does the king want me?"

One tiny sliver of hope shone through the confusion. Last summer, she'd grown the rare krasa plant and made a cream from it. Originally intended as a treatment for burns, it sold like crazy in the weekly market after customers saw their wrinkles smooth. A peddler had taken some to sell for her last month. If the king had heard about it, this might be her chance to make a bit of extra gold.

"Not our business. Don't keep the king waiting."

Briony slid off her stool and grabbed her down jacket. No one had ever been carted off to the palace before. Her gaze met Ivan's, and he looked down.

Owen bustled around the bar and tossed his rag on a stool. "You can't come into my bar and take her away."

Before the guards replied, a snort came from the group by the fire as a petite woman with hair scraped back into a bun stepped forward. "Not surprising the king wants her. She probably got in trouble." Ah, Aunt Petra. Tucked amongst the crowd, her "aunt" hadn't been visible. If Briony had seen her, she would have gone upstairs. There was no way she was sharing a space with that woman.

Uncertainty flickered across Owen's face.

"It's alright," Briony said. "I'll go find out why the king wants to meet with me." She shot Owen a quick smile, slipped on her coat, and followed the guards outside.

The town square stretched ahead of her, the cobblestones glistening in the moonlight. Rimmed with solid yet dignified stone buildings bleached with age, only one archway led in and out. Despite its cloistered interior, townspeople and vendors filled the square on market day and during festivals.

Only the tavern was out of place. Still roofed with thatch instead of slate, its roofline appeared uneven and seemed to lean like one of its drunk patrons on the sedate building next to it. The guards led her across the square, where a coach stood with two dark horses in harnesses, steam rising off their sweating bodies into the cool night air.

She caught a glimpse of the royal crest on the door before one guard opened it, jumped inside, and grabbed her wrist. He yanked her off her feet, hauling her in after him.

"Hey! I'm coming with you. No need for that." She rubbed her wrist as she sat across from him. He banged on the wall, and the carriage took off with a clatter of hooves on stone, far faster than it should be, tossing her back against the seat. She yelped and grabbed the windowsill, and the guard across from her grinned.

The landscape raced past in a blur, and the coach bounced over rocky terrain. She scrabbled to remain seated as each jolt flung her in the air. Darkness pressed in, the light from the two moons obscured by thick trees overhead. Shouldn't they be on the main road through Rohant up to the palace? No dense forest grew along the route.

Her heart pounded, and her fingers dug into the plush siding of the coach. "Where are we going?"

No response. Farther and farther, the coach raced into the forest.

When the coach finally halted, she fell forward, and the guard grabbed her upper arm in an iron-like grip. Briony's stomach lurched, and she gagged. She'd caught a whiff of his stench as they sat in the cloistered carriage, but up close, he stank like he'd eaten eggs and then puked them up.

When the door opened, he pushed her ahead of him. She sucked in the fresh air and stepped down from the coach to find a man in a black hooded cloak waiting.

This was not the palace, and the squat man with a pug nose and a shaggy goat-like beard was not the king. The two guards flanked her so closely that their plumes of breath puffed past her face.

"Why are we here? Who are you?"

Goat-beard didn't answer. He studied her, lifting his

lantern up to her face. The lantern and the light from the two full moons overhead revealed a dirt road littered with fallen leaves, their slight vegetal scent chasing away the unpleasant stench from the guards at her back. The road was more like a hunting path up into the mountains, with only two wheel tracks gouged into the dirt.

Why was she here?

"She's the right one." Goat-beard nodded to himself. "Can't be too many in Vieska with black hair and light eyes like that."

She scanned the forest. They hadn't traveled far, and they'd gone uphill, so they must be on the flank of one of the two mountains bordering Vieska. "If you don't tell me what the hell's going on, I'm hiking back home right now."

Two hands clamped on her shoulders, the fingers digging in.

She jerked, but there was no give. "Hey! Let me go!" The guard's hands tightened.

"You sure the spell worked, Hoyt?" asked one guard. "Why would the spell tell you to use some girl to keep a vulk busy? Ask the Dark Lady. Be sure, or she'll be angry."

Her pulse skyrocketed. Vulk? The bard in the tavern spoke the truth; a vulk was in this area. Even the hunters didn't dare go far into the Divorky Forest out of fear they'd anger him. He was a feral beast, cruel and ruthless, killing anyone and anything he deemed a threat. Or so the stories went.

Sweat beaded at her temple and ran down her neck. What the hell was going on? She needed to get out of here. Now.

"I can't ask her. Either I use the scrying bowl for the spell to see my steps, or I summon her. I can't do both at the same time. And if I break the order of the spell, I have to start all over again. I don't have enough energy stored for that."

Goat-beard—she thought they'd called him Hoyt—studied her. "I'm surprised too. The spell is supposed to summon something to weaken a vulk. I figured I'd need to conjure up some silver or craft a cage. What is some slip of a human compared to a vulk? Eh, no matter. As long as she keeps it distracted long enough for me to perform stage two, that's all that's important. Maybe the vulk play with their food?"

He shrugged, turned, and focused past her shoulder. His eyes sat back in his skull. Dark and fathomless. He raised his palm, and it glowed red. Briony yelped and shied back.

The two guards barked out a hoarse, coughing laugh and held her still.

Magic was forbidden in Rohant. By the king's decree, if magicwielders passed through, they weren't allowed to practice. A crack sounded, and an acrid stench singed her nose.

Briony looked over her shoulder. A narrow path lay visible, the branches swept aside, so the granite side of the mountain glinted clearly in a wash of moonlight. A door opened into the mountain's depths, revealing a dark passage.

What was this?

Both guards turned, and the grip on her shoulders loosened a fraction. It was enough. She twisted and slid free. Her boots kicked up leaves as she shot forward.

"Get her!" yelled Hoyt.

Ripping sounded behind her, but she didn't turn and look. She flew over the track, then ducked to the right into the forest. Needles and leaves lay slick and slippery, and she skidded, arms wheeling, as she slid down a slope. A hand clamped down on her wrist and jerked her backward, spinning her to the ground.

She kicked but faltered mid-swing and screamed.

A creature with the tattered remnants of a tunic around his neck grinned down at her. Large tusks protruded from his jutting lower jaw, and his skin was leathery gray. The rotten egg smell swirled stronger.

A bauk.

A second bauk, similar but with squashed ears, joined

11

them. This couldn't be real. The ogre-like monsters were tales to keep children from wandering off. Not real.

The second bauk's rheumy yellow eyes narrowed, and he bared his flat bone-grinding teeth. "I think she's scared."

The one holding her grunted and jerked her to her feet. He plucked her from the ground and tossed her over his shoulder. She kicked, the toe of her boots hitting stomach and ribs, and her fists flailed against his back, but he didn't flinch. "Good. Fear sweetens the meat. If Hoyt screwed up and the vulk don't eat 'er, I will."

"If the spell don't work, there's no chow. The Dark Lady will be mad."

"Not with us."

This had to be a dream. Wake up. Wake up! Men didn't turn into monsters from nightmares before her eyes. Creatures that discussed *eating* her.

They passed the coach, and Hoyt trotted up next to them. "Get her inside and keep her still while I see what the spell needs me to do next."

Her stomach heaved, and she struggled not to be sick. Cold sweat slicked across her skin. As they carried her into the passageway, cool air and darkness engulfed her.

2

THE BAUK CARRIED Briony down the passage, past torches burning in sconces along the walls, revealing wet, dripping rock. It was warm and stuffy, with a musty basement smell oozing up from the dirt floor. The guard kicked a door open and hunched down to enter a small room. Torchlight revealed a dirt floor. A wooden chair and a low table with a pewter bowl were the only pieces of furniture.

Her captor slung her into the chair and wrenched her arms behind her back as one hand circled her wrists in a punishing grip. His skin was like cracked leather.

"I don't care if you do work for the king. You have no right to keep me here." She eyed the second guard, who slammed the door shut after Hoyt entered and stood to block the only exit. Would the king have these ... things working for him? He'd outlawed magic, so he was unlikely to employ the magicwielder either.

Hoyt waved a glowing hand over the bowl, and the surface flickered to life with swirls of color. The angle wasn't right for her to see, but Hoyt studied it, nodding. His back was to her, his arms jerking in sharp twitchy motions. "You really think I'd deign to work for a king?"

"Deign?"

He didn't turn around. "No. I bow to a much more powerful leader. One who taught me powerful enchantments. Like those that made these bauk look like guards and turned my old cart into a royal coach. Well, royal looking enough to fool someone like you." He laughed. "Didn't you wonder why a royal coach didn't have gold inlaid over every surface? Or why a king would want *you*? You're pretty enough, but you have no elegance, no manners, and you wear breeches and a linen shirt like some kind of mine worker. Your hands are so rough, if you pleasured the king's royal member with them, he'd be so chafed he wouldn't be able to sit a horse."

The king's pale, cruel-looking face flashed to mind, and she blanched. It was no insult to be overlooked there. "Fashion criticism from a grown man wandering around the woods in a cape? Is it a cape, or did you steal your granny's nightshirt? And is that supposed to be a beard? You don't know any spells to make it fill out?"

Hoyt spun on his heel, holding a steel syringe, the kind used to force-feed medicine into animals. The tip still glowed a faint red, and one fat droplet of a milky substance leaked out as he held it pointed upward with two fingers on the grips and his thumb on the plunger. Had he just ... crafted that from thin air?

"Well, I can't say I feel bad about making you drink this serum now." He glanced up at the guard behind her. "Swallow it, or I force it down. Your choice."

Fingers squeezed painfully around her wrists, mashing the bones together. A small whimper escaped before she bit it back. "What is that going to do?"

"No idea. I get a step to perform, and I do it." He waved the syringe back and forth. "My spell work is good, but I'm not speedy. This concoction is supposed to give me at least a half-hour once the vulk arrives so I can prepare the next bit.

Maybe you consume this, and the vulk takes his time, giving you a little longer to live before munching on you. Open."

The bauk grabbed her chin.

She jerked. "Get your hands off me. I'll take it."

Hoyt nodded, and the scraping fingers with their putrid stench dropped away.

Steel clinked against her upper teeth, the cold metal tube scraping against her tongue. The serum squirted out in a torrent and burst against the back of her throat. She choked and fought to swallow it. Sickly sweet, like cordial, it was thick and tough to get down. Hoyt depressed the plunger, and she gulped the last swallow.

Warmth spread from her belly through her limbs, a gentle licking heat. The light from the torches seemed brighter. The tang of the dirt floor strengthened as she inhaled. Her skin tingled, as if anticipating someone was about to run their hands across it.

Like a snapped bowstring, a pluck of lust bloomed in her lower stomach. She bit back a moan. The warmth continued to surge, rising from a simmer to a slow boil. The fabric of her shirt brushed against her neck, and she broke into goose-bumps. She squirmed, and the bodice of her undershirt scraped across her breasts, releasing another jolt of lust.

She barely noticed Hoyt back at the bowl, waving his arm. The room, the guards, and the hand around her wrist were all there, but there was something far more pressing she needed. She thrashed in her seat, and a hand clamped on her shoulder to keep her in place. The touch burned like ice, and bile rose in her throat.

Hoyt frowned. "This is unexpected. Take her into the cave. I have to conjure a bench to strap her to."

Both guards dragged her back into the dark hallway and descended farther. Their touch was like sandpaper on her skin. Wrong. Her stomach lurched like she was going to lose her dinner again. An ache throbbed between her thighs. No one here could soothe it. They couldn't give her what she needed. She jerked hard and whimpered.

Bruising hands clutched harder and hauled her forward.

At the end of the corridor, one guard grunted, and with a squeal of metal on rock, a door pushed outward, splashing warm light into the hall.

They shoved her the last few steps into a cavern, well-lit by torches. Stalagmites rimmed the perimeter, casting reaching shadows along the craggy walls, and stalactites dripped from the high ceiling like icicles. The circular space magnified the sound of water trickling nearby.

Hoyt strode forward, his palms glowing red. His arms rose in front of him and flailed in intricate patterns as he murmured in a strange language under his breath. In the center of the cave rose a piece of wooden furniture, out of place in the natural setting. It looked like a padded two-level bench with black leather restraints on it.

Restraints. If they tied her down, there was no way she'd break free. No way she'd cool the burning need ripping through her.

Briony yelled and squirmed, but they dragged her like she weighed nothing, her boots scraping on the stone floor.

"Strip her and tie her down. Hurry. I'm sure the vulk's on his way. This one is known for hating magic. He's vicious." Hoyt gave her a quick, appraising glance up and down. "That looks like some kind of breeding bench. Not what I expected, but whatever distracts it."

"What the hell is wrong with you? Let me out of here." Briony thrashed, trying to twist away.

"They're beasts, you know. When they breed, they knot. You'd better hope he kills you."

Briony's brain hiccuped. Knot?

She'd learned about knotting the past summer when one of the lending library books featured the peltwalker clans of the northern territories. Peltwalkers shifted into animals—

lion, wolf, eagle—and the book hinted that those who shifted into wolves knotted during mating. Whispered speculation spread like wildfire through the town. Even old ladies held up zucchinis at the market and wondered how a knot swelled at the base of a man's member to seal a mating pair together during sex.

Briony gulped.

Hoyt waved his hand. "I'll need to come back when he's fully distracted, but how will I know the best time to return?" He tapped his chin with a finger and looked at Briony. She knew he wasn't asking for input. "Better set an alert so I'll know when conditions are perfect, even if there's a slight chance he'll smell it." After a few muttered incantations, a brief flare of reddish light appeared, and her hair ruffled as a gust of air blew through the cave. "Good. That should work."

As he scuttled away, he muttered, "A half-hour. All I need is a half-hour."

The bauk guard raised a hand with its short, spiked claws. "I cut off your clothes."

"No! I'll do it." His flesh brushing against hers? No.

Her stomach churned. Underneath her fear, need lapped through her veins. She wanted powerful hands to caress up her back, dig into her waist, and pull her close. But only the *right* hands with a touch that would make her melt and soothe the ache begging for relief.

The bauk halted, but he kept his claws raised. "Start."

She knelt to untie her boots and scanned the cave without moving her head. One side of the cave was darker than the others—it had to be where the mouth was. Could she run for it again? The two guards were fast, and their strength was scary.

Both of them crowded closer as if reading her mind.

Her pulse skyrocketed. She didn't have a chance. Her fingers stabbed at the knots. Knots. She had to get out of here before a vulk wanted to ... play with her.

Her hands shook so hard she couldn't get them under control. The warmth from before, the flaring need, faded as pure terror swept over her. It took her several tries to loosen the laces. Without glancing at either guard, she released the toggles of her jacket and slipped her shirt and britches off. At her undergarments, she froze.

"Hurry up," said the shorter guard. "We eat humans. No interest in looking."

She gulped, glanced at their awful teeth, and shuddered.

Taking a deep breath, she shed the rest of her clothes. "Just tie a rope to my leg. You don't have to strap me down."

They didn't answer.

The squat one pushed her forward, bent her over the higher part of the bench, and tightened a strap around her waist. The lower part of the bench was split into two, and the leaner bauk wrestled one arm onto each fork and fastened leather restraints around her upper arms and wrists. It left her rounded, her feet still on the floor, her head and chest lying on the padding, and her arms below and slightly in front of her. When the one behind her tried to spread her legs and buckle them into place, she kicked him hard in the chest. It was like hitting a wall, and he let out his low, choppy laugh.

He snagged her knee, and his fingers bit like iron rings into her flesh as he pulled the leather into place. Briony panted, immobilized, except for her head. Burning built behind her eyelids. She was helpless—she couldn't rip free and race out of here.

She bit back a sob. No. She wasn't showing these assholes anything. Besides, she didn't cry. She hadn't since she was eleven years old.

The guards studied her one last time as if critiquing their work. They spoke to each other in an oily guttural language that reminded her of dead, rotting things. Her skin crawled.

With a shrug, they trudged back the way they'd entered,

slamming the door behind them. It blended so perfectly into the rich umber walls not even a seam showed.

Shit, she was in a cave, exposed and vulnerable. Dangling like a lure. She jerked hard, then studied the bindings at her wrists. Could she loosen them?

Heat caressed her skin like a hand smoothing down her bare back, and she stopped struggling. Similar to the room she'd just left, the cavern was warm—balmy even—but this waft of warmth was something else. It whispered through her, coiled low in her stomach, and pumped through her veins, an insistent force surging back into place.

Desire. Need.

Her breasts pressed against the leather and began to ache. Each inhale teased her lips, whispering across them. They wanted more attention. A nibble, a kiss. She'd never felt *air* trickle past her lips like this before.

What the hell had the magicwielder given her? Her head was muzzy. It was difficult to focus and remember her fear. Recall why she didn't want to wait here for the vulk. Another roil of lust swept through her, concentrating between her legs. Moisture dribbled down her thighs.

The torches flickered, and a faint breath of wind puffed from the dark side of the cave. A cool lick over her heated skin. A tiny scratching sound, a hint of claws on stone, and she froze.

There was a change in the air, the same way it got quiet and heavy before a violent storm. Her skin prickled. She wasn't alone in the cave any longer. Slowly, she raised her head and peered forward.

A slight scuff, and he stepped into the torchlight.

She wasn't sure what she'd expected, but her breath hitched in her chest. The vulk was eight feet tall at least, standing on two legs like a man. Although his facial features were wolf-like, with long ears and a muzzle, he was no wolf. His limbs were muscular and defined like a human with his broad, powerful shoulders and chest, and massive thighs. Hair, so dark it seemed to absorb the shadows, grew thicker around his neck and face but was more of a dusting along his thick arms and legs.

The Shadow of Death was here. In the cave with her.

Scarlet eyes trained on her, and he bared his teeth and snarled. Low and menacing, it ripped through the cave, and she cowered, her eyes still on his, shrinking as small as possible on her bench with a small whimper. He crouched and stepped forward, his lethal nails elongating.

He was going to kill her. She squeezed her eyes shut and tensed, hoping it would end quickly.

3

A FEMALE PUMPING out arousal drenched the cave with need so potent it slapped him in the face. Hans inhaled deeply. Lust, a honeyed vanilla, thickened his cock and all traces of sulfur vanished. But there was something else. Not the intense hit of her desire, but her true fragrance, an ethereal cloud of mountain laurel, sweet and fresh.

Before the incident, his favorite place was up along the slope of the mountain behind his den, in a small meadow, protected from the wind. There he'd bask in the sun and watch the eagles float on the thermals over Rohant. It was the closest to peace and contentment he'd ever known. Mountain laurel ran wild there and filled the air with their sweet perfume, and as the same fragrance washed over him now, it brought with it the same echoes of warmth and drowsy calm.

He'd come here to maim. Kill. But the fury howling through his blood changed into a different kind of hunger. As he drew another deep breath, the insistent pull of her desire coated his tongue. Did humans have heats? Because this one demanded his attention. Still, he remained motionless.

This human wasn't the magicwielder he'd sought here, or

she'd reek of brimstone from casting magic. So there was still a threat here. He stepped back, trying to clear his nose and ignore the human bent over in front of him. He'd witnessed what happened when a vulk became clouded by a female. Disaster. Misery.

He snarled again, and his hands fisted.

The woman with violet-blue eyes, too large for her face, peered up at him and trembled. The delicate, flowery scent faded as her fear grew. He didn't like that.

He hummed deep in his throat, somewhere between a growl and a purr. A noise he'd never made before. Where had that come from? Her lips parted, and she stopped shaking.

Until his nose lay buried in the curve of her throat, he didn't even realize he'd gone to her side. But here was where that sweet fragrance was strongest. He wanted to drink her in.

His gaze fell to a black strap cinching her arm to the bench. With a growl, he yanked away and surveyed her. What the hell? Females joined with him willingly. They didn't need to be pinned down.

His vision turned red, and he growled again as his claws extruded like six-inch lances. The female whimpered and screwed her eyes shut.

He ripped through the bindings, taking care not to nick her delicate skin. Her skin was a soft golden color, like the throat of a newborn fawn, and when his knuckles brushed against it—smooth. Soft.

As his path led him behind her to remove the ties at her waist and her legs, he dragged in a ragged breath. The urge to rut, to mate after all this time, surged hard. And she lay spread before him.

He swallowed and ripped the leather straps free.

She pushed herself back and stood, flexing her wrists, then turned, revealing the most beautiful female he'd ever seen. Average height, her head reached his chest, and her curves fell precisely right. Her hair was as dark as his, escaping the

22

binding at her neck to tumble free. But what he liked best was she gazed up at him without fear.

"Thanks." She rubbed her arms. "I don't know if you can understand me."

Vulk-kind only spoke to other vulk or their allies. It was verboten to reveal their ability to speak, especially to humans. So, he remained silent, stepped back, and jerked his chin towards the exit.

THE WAY to the mouth of the cave was clear. The vulk had even taken a step back to let her leave. His eyes weren't red any longer but a vivid, piercing blue. A luminous, stunning blue she'd only seen in chunks of ice when the icebergs floated down from the north into the small lake near Vieska. An impossible color to replicate. Until now. These eyes were intelligent. Human. His gaze locked on hers, and she forgot to breathe. His chest wasn't rising or falling, so she didn't think he did either.

She took a step, but it wasn't toward the exit.

Only a foot away from the great beast, Briony placed her palms on his stomach, the ridges of his muscles like rock under his fur. He shuddered.

This massive creature and her touch made him shake. She trailed her hands upward over the light spray of hair along his chest. A whiff of pine and fresh mountain air swirled off him. She leaned closer and drew it deep into her lungs. This was what the urge inside her pushed her to search for. This exact scent. Him.

A rumble rose from his chest. A silky note. Hypnotic. Like it was calling to her. An answering tingle stirred between her legs, and her fingers curled. The power of him, the primitive, primal strength, was breathtaking.

He still hadn't moved. Hadn't responded to her touch. A

pair of leather trousers, cut off below the knees, slung low on his hips. It didn't strike her as odd that he wore clothing.

The tingle turned to a rippling fire, sizzling through her blood. She forgot where she was, what had happened. All she needed was for him to respond. Touch her. This was what she wanted. His touch. Only his.

She lowered her hand and unclasped his trousers, pushing them down until they pooled at his feet, and she gasped. Free from restraint, he jutted forward high and proud. Flushed red, it was at least a foot long and thick as her wrist. The bottom few inches flared slightly. Under her gaze, the flesh there throbbed and swelled a fraction, promising more.

What would it feel like to be filled with that? She couldn't tear her gaze away. Far too big. Too thick.

He dipped his head and dragged his mouth along her shoulder and up her neck. Teeth nibbled under her ear, and her head fell back.

"Yes." Had she said that aloud? When he drew back, his eyes had turned completely black. In one quick motion, he spun her around.

Unrestrained, she leaned willingly over the bench. It bent her at the perfect height for his attention.

Hands stroked down her back, followed by nibbles next to her spine, and she pressed into them, sighing. She expected the sting of claws but didn't care. His touch soothed the prickling of her skin and stoked the fire building inside. She wanted, needed more. She could run naked back to her village, but no one there would be able to satisfy this ache. None of the few tepid lovers in her past gave her real pleasure. She'd never wanted them like this. It had to be him. Only him.

There were no claws. Either he sheathed them, or he kept them at bay. As his hands traced over the dip of her lower back, the simmer of heat erupted, and she moaned and arched, flexing and presenting herself to him.

Hot breath fanned her inner thighs, and for a moment, nothing happened. Her heart hammered so loud it drowned out any other noise in the cave.

A tongue shoved deep inside her with a long, rich hum, and she jolted. Warm, curling in a wave motion, it glided over a spot that uncoiled a whip of pleasure. She cried out—maybe she said the word werewolf—but she wasn't sure. The long organ withdrew and skated over her outer lips, over another spot begging for attention, then penetrated again. Her core fluttered as he delved once more and dragged his tongue over that same spot. Sparks lit up inside her. Lulled by the short hums vibrating from his throat as he lapped, attuned to every movement of his tongue, she panted and floated away on the ecstasy mounting with every sweep.

Her back bowed to give him better access, and slicks of liquid dripped down her thighs. His pace increased. Rapid, greedy laves. He stopped teasing and demanded. She crested with a yell and shut her eyes as explosions of color danced along her vision. Her nails dug deep crescents into the padding.

The vulk continued to devour, to push his tongue deeper. Too much. With a whine, she shook her head and swung her hips from side to side.

A quick reprimanding growl, short and snappy, and one of his hands gripped her waist, holding her still.

There was no break. He tasted. Teased. Outside, inside. Drew her to the precipice again. When she shuddered into another body curling release, he hummed a pleasured note, and the tonguing ceased.

Ridged muscle and the smooth hair of his chest flowed over her back as he mounted her. While back claws scrambled on the stone floor, his hands landed near her face, the claws curled over the end of the bench, and he lowered, warm and wide, a dominating presence above her.

A frisson of panic alarmed the back of her mind. What the hell was she doing? He was much taller than her, and she'd seen what he was working with. They'd never fit.

He shifted over her, and his length slid up her thigh and angled into place. She moaned and rubbed her cheek against his neck. She didn't want him to stop.

In one surge, he pushed inside. Pleasure with an edge of pain erupted at the contact. Prepared though she was, he was too thick. She grabbed the padded bench and held on as he thrust and tried to burrow deeper. She scrabbled, and her hips bucked. He made that soft humming sound, and it was like a caress. She relaxed, her grip on the bench loosening. When he eased out, then sank forward again, he glided more easily into her.

"Oh. That's—" Words failed, and she ended on a moan.

He pumped faster, filling her as he worked himself inside. So good. She crooned, and her back arched in pleasure. His breath hitched, and he raked his teeth down her neck. Another thrust and the muscles of his arms flexed as his claws bit deep, splintering the wood. He surged forward. A tug, a brief flash of pain, another hard pump, and he buried himself to the root.

Briony panted under him and squirmed. This wasn't possible. Yet she molded around him as if they were supposed to fit together. She shivered.

He nuzzled her and chuffed his own pleasure in her ear, neither of them moving. Then he reared back and began ploughing deep.

Each long stroke worked spots inside she didn't know existed. Slow and forceful, over and over. Every glide teased out her pleasure, stoked her toward her peak, but didn't quite let her tip over. She whimpered and moaned, but he only rumbled in her ear and kept the same tormenting pace.

It could have been hours, it could have been minutes, but eventually, his breathing turned ragged, and his growl became dark and sensual. Primal. His pace quickened, and she snapped her hips to meet his.

Something jarred against her entrance with every thrust. He'd thickened at his base. She tensed and writhed. How would he fit that inside her? He already filled her completely.

Warmth lashed over the nape of her neck as he licked, then a scrape of his teeth. She stopped wriggling, her limbs slackening. Each of his breaths rasped against her neck in strangled gasps. His hips pumped in short nudges as he worked his swollen knot inside. Pressing. Insisting. Until, with one last jerk, he filled her.

Intense pressure coupled with a slight burn, and Briony cried out. He'd tied her to him. Demanded she take all. And even though it ached, she wanted this exquisite fullness.

Slowly, he rocked deeper to catch into position, locking into place behind her pubic bone. All soreness faded, and pleasure blossomed. She groaned.

The great vulk trembled and dropped his head near hers. He grew warm, so warm inside her that she felt every inch of him as he surged in his release. But he didn't stop moving. He curled his hips, pressing them into her in small circles, and spirals of intense bliss shot through her. Throbbing vibration and greedy hips ... that was all it took.

Briony exploded and cried out. Every muscle clenched as she spasmed. She came. And came. Milked him deeper. Demanded more. Dissolved into mush and uttered incoherent sounds.

He leaned forward, rooted deeper, and she bucked again, driving him to follow her into another climax, another torrent of seed bathing her insides.

It didn't stop. When she recovered from one orgasm, she hungered for another, and he was happy to drive her to another peak, chasing it with his own. Each time she found her pleasure, he rumbled small notes of satisfaction in her ear.

Eventually, the haze faded, and they both sank to the

bench, still joined. The vulk relaxed, half on top of her, his warm body spreading across her back. All she wanted was to burrow closer to that warmth. Have his scent coat every inch of her skin.

<Mine.> The deep, commanding voice reverberated in her thoughts. Was he speaking to her? Was that possible?

4

WHAT THE HELL JUST HAPPENED? The female underneath Hans rested her cheek on her arms and stared up at him, those stunning eyes drowsy and sated, her mouth pink and delicate, the lower lip marked with tiny bites where she'd worried it with her teeth. What did he do now? He'd never knotted anyone before. His past partners wanted their pleasure fast. They weren't interested in lying together and caressing. Since vulk didn't do affection, he wasn't interested in holding them either.

Yet tonight, there wasn't a flicker of a question that he'd have her under him like this. Content, filled, and as close to him as possible. Right now, it was hard to remember anything existed other than her.

He dropped his head and nuzzled up her neck to her jaw. She sighed and leaned into his touch. Shifting to one side, one of her hands fluttered off the bench, rose toward his face, and faltered. He closed the distance to nestle into her palm, and her fingers went to the back of his neck and stroked.

Something softened in his chest. Dislodged and stirred to life the empty husk that normally sat there. He purred. It broke from his throat, raspy and gruff. This wasn't a vulk noise. Vulk snarled. Growled. They didn't rumble in contentment. Or hum. He paused, and she stopped trailing her fingers up and down his neck.

Nope, he didn't want her to stop. Hans purred again, deep and rich. Got used to the way it vibrated in his throat.

She sighed and melted against him. He liked her like this.

She cooed and moaned sleepily. "Werewolf. Vulk."

Hans frowned. The little female said that many times when she came, but he wanted her to call out his real name.

He brushed his lips at her neck again and licked along the slope of her shoulder with the tip of his tongue. Did she like that?

She shivered. He did it again.

There was a flash of light, and he jerked his head up. Translucent and gold, a symbol floated in the air before them. Four lines intersected through a circle, creating a diamond, or a sort of star, in the center.

It shimmered once, then sang out in a clear tone,

"First, a rune will bind,
But only a bite permanently entwines.
With true love, it must be done,

Or two will never be one.

The vulk they call Shadow,
Content to always be solo.
Return to the great decision of the past,
And decide if that choice should last.

The lightwielder was betrayed,
By those who should have stayed.
To give away her heart,
Everything may fall apart.

It isn't a decision made lightly,
The bonds weave tightly.
Two souls chosen by fate,
Have only a month's time to gain their mate."

THE SYMBOL SHIMMERED AGAIN and dissolved, but two streaks of gold shot forward, one straight into his chest. He reared back, slipping free of her body. His heartbeat pounded in his ears, and his chest twinged.

He stared downward. In the center of his chest lay a small tattoo in gold of the same symbol from the air. With a growl, he rubbed at it and covered it with his fur. What trickery was this? There was no odor to it. No magic. But strange symbols didn't appear out of the blue and speak.

He growled. He'd come to the cave because he'd scented magic, softened for this female, and look what happened? Hans had dropped his guard to play bed games and lost his head. *He should know better. Should know* much, much better. A threat was present, and he'd ignored it.

The female slid from the bench and stood in front of him, her finger tracing the mark on her own chest. "What is this?" She seemed genuinely confused about what happened, about this symbol on their chests, but humans were tricky. Devious.

"I don't know. Didn't you do this?"

She skittered and fell sideways. He swooped forward and caught her before she hit the ground.

"You can talk? Why didn't you say something before?"

"My mouth was busy, and I don't speak to humans." He still had his arm around her waist and didn't feel like releasing her.

Her eyes narrowed. "Why not?"

"Tough to have a conversation when they're running away in terror." True, but he'd also never wanted to break the vulk rule about speaking to humans before. He tilted his head to the side and studied her. She scowled at him, unafraid and unconcerned she was naked in his arms. The corner of his mouth twitched.

"What's your name?"

"Briony. What's yours?" Her face softened when she asked, and he drew her closer. The pulse in her throat jumped.

"Hans." He glanced at the symbol in delicate gold on her chest. "Did you make that mark appear in the air?"

"No, of course not."

CRASH!

He whirled, tucking Briony behind him. A door stood open, and a magicwielder holding something glowing red in his hands raced forward, flanked by two bauk.

Interesting. Large, tough beasts, bauk weren't an easy kill, and they didn't show in Ulterra often. They preferred the perpetual mist and darkness of Peklo.

The magicwielder wore a black cloak with an insignia over the chest. Hans had tangled with this kind before. Not a magicwielder—a necromancer. Those who meddled with the dark side of magic and death.

He snarled. His claws lanced out, and he crouched.

The necromancer yelled and tossed the object in his hands into the air. It didn't fall back to the ground; instead, it spun with a whirring noise. It had a vaguely oblong shape. A dart? An arrow?

A vulk's skin was resistant to magic, most spells bouncing right off, but this? He'd never seen anything like it before. The object in the air plunged straight for him, and Hans dove to the left and rolled. The arrow pivoted midair and re-aimed.

What? Magic didn't do that. Hans leaped to his feet. In a blur of red, the missile launched at his chest, far faster than he'd thought possible. He spun, but it was too late.

Right before it hit, he twisted, and it smashed into his right ribs.

He roared, more in surprise than pain. The magic pierced his usually impenetrable vulk hide and burrowed deep. An icy chill shot through him. Vision blurring, he staggered sideways, slipped, and fell to the floor.

There was a high-pitched scream. "What did you do to him?"

"What do you care, girlie?" The necromancer loomed over him, his hands glowing red, and he turned to look at Briony. "You're lucky you're still alive. A vulk only lives to kill. They don't care about anything else." He reached into his black robes and pulled out a long knife and small flask. Hans jerked and snarled. Strained to rise to his feet. Nothing. His muscles seized, no longer under his control. Fury shot through him, but he barely felt it over the cold enveloping him. Icy fingers wrapped around his chest so tightly that he had to suck in air in quick gasps. What the hell happened?

Sulfur plumed, and bile rose in his throat as the necromancer muttered a few words. Hans struggled and strained to move an arm. A finger. Wanting to take this asshole's head off in one clean swipe. But he couldn't move. Couldn't even flick a claw.

The knife slashed and bit deep into his forearm. Warm blood gushed, and the necromancer stooped and held the flask against Hans's skin, filling it up. "I've succeeded. The Dark

Lady can return." The man smiled, revealing yellowed teeth, then turned away toward the cave's center.

The cave and the figures in it blended as his vision dulled, but he could still make out Briony crouched by the bench. She'd pulled her clothes toward her and was tugging them on. Her gaze met his, then flicked toward the bauk. The necromancer and the bauk huddled near him, leaving the mouth of the cave clear. None of them were interested in her; if she ran, she could escape.

<Get out of here.> He willed her to understand by glancing at the exit. Even as he hoped she'd seek safety, the new bond in his chest screamed not to let her get far. Not to let her out of his sight. *She's mine.*

Her chin jerked a fraction upward, and she shook her head.

Chanting filled the cave as the necromancer spoke in the arcane language of magicwielders. Wind whipped through the cave, and the necromancer raised his arms and tilted the flask of Hans's blood. The instant the liquid dripped onto the ground, thick black fog billowed through the cave, crowding out the torchlight. The room was milky darkness. A crack boomed and echoed through the space.

Warmth spread against his side as a smaller body slid next to him. "What did they do to you? Let me see. I can heal you." Briony's hands roamed his body with gentle, searching fingers. If he wasn't frozen to the floor and in the middle of a magic hell storm, he'd enjoy it. Trying to see through the fog and battle his dimming vision was like looking through a dirty window, but he could still make out Briony's face hovering over his chest and the way she pursed her lips as she sought his injury.

She'd stayed to help him.

Something stirred deep inside, where he'd thought nothing existed. "Run." It was hard to breathe, never mind speak, but he gasped out the words. "Get out of here."

"Hush."

She found the place along his ribs where the arrow hit and hissed. As she pressed her palm hard against his side, a streak of pain squeezed all the air out of his lungs. Her hand warmed, and he took an easy gulp of air. Another. The vice around his chest eased—he could breathe again.

Even with his senses clouded from whatever the necromancer hit him with, there was no scent of magic as she bent over him and healed him, so she wasn't a magicwielder working a spell. How was she doing this?

Her face grew pinched and pale, and she bit her lip. His vision cleared, and when he tried to flex his claws, they moved. Briony panted and slumped forward. She trembled, and the warmth of her hand on his side faded. She brought her lips to his ear. "I don't know what he shot you with," she whispered between chattering teeth. "It's not a normal wound, and I can't heal it completely, but I helped for now."

His strength hadn't fully returned, but it was good enough. Briony, however, shivered despite the cave's warmth. He wrapped his arm around her and pulled her close. "When I move, I want you to stay down, no matter what I do. And when I say run, you run."

"If I ran before, you'd still be a paralyzed lump on the floor."

"This time, listen. If you get hit with magic, you die. If it hits me, it doesn't bother me much. Well, usually." His ribs still ached.

Her fingers tightened on his fur. "Those creatures might try to eat me," she said.

"I'll keep them away while I get the necromancer to burn out his magic. I estimate he's almost through his magical stores with all the power he's using. When he's tapped out, we move."

A flash of green light filled the cavern, followed by bitter laughter. "Finally, I'm back in Ulterra. Where my magic works again." The fog had settled down to ankle height, and a statuesque, tall figure stood above its murk. Her back was to Hans, with brown hair down to her shoulders and an intricately patterned green dress sweeping the floor. She tossed her head. "The underworld really is hell."

He froze. Impossible. He'd witnessed her death one hundred years ago. Seen her fall into the depths of Peklo, never to return. He was the one who'd sent her there.

She turned, an older woman with a thin face, dark eyes, and hard lines around the mouth. Morana. Her lips curled into a small smile as she scanned Hans. "Good job, Hoyt. I wasn't sure your skill was high enough to get that spell right." She raised her arms, and her long sleeves slipped back, revealing a glowing green bracelet on each wrist. It looked more like rope, twisting, cutting into her flesh, and twining farther up her arm.

"Thank you, my lady." The necromancer's voice cracked. He was right to be afraid. What a stupid idiot to summon Morana from whatever hole she'd landed in.

How had she survived? She was a magicwielder, but she was a mortal peltwalker. Only cursed immortals or spawn survived in Peklo, and she was neither.

"When we raise our king from the abyss, you will be rewarded," Morana said.

Hoyt bowed.

Morana turned to Hans. "The great black vulk. We meet again. And you're down there on the floor, and I'm up here. Exactly how it should be." She strode closer, her skirts swooshing across the stone with each step. "The time of the vulk having dominion over Ulterra is over. A new king and queen are here."

Her gaze dropped to Briony at his side when she drew closer. "What is this human doing here?"

"I needed her for the spell," called the necromancer.

Morana shrugged. "Get rid of her."

Flipping to his feet, Hans barreled into her and knocked her sideways. With one swipe, he slashed his claws through Morana's neck. They ripped through her flesh without a spray of fresh blood. No torn muscle or bone. As he stared at her neck, the gouges healed immediately until no wound remained.

Morana blasted his chest with green light, and he flew several steps backward. She raised her arms, the rope bracelets flashing a deeper green on her wrists. She smiled.

Hans dove for Briony and rolled with her toward the back of the cave. At least she'd listened and stayed down. Balls of green light blasted a few inches from where she'd lain and plumed into a fiery flare.

"You idiot, Hoyt. I knew you'd fail," Morana screamed. "If you did the spell right, the vulk would be dead now." She rounded on the necromancer. He scrambled backward and babbled a spell, but it was too late. Green light hit him in the chest, lifting him off his feet, and he slammed into the far wall. With an ominous crunch, the necromancer slid to the ground.

Morana whirled toward the two bauk and pointed at Hans. "Attack him. I don't care what you do with the human." The bauk pounced.

Hans snarled and pushed Briony behind him.

A bauk had tough, almost impermeable skin except for three places: underneath their ears, in their armpits, and the back of their knees. He would have tackled them to the ground because it was easier to pin and stab that way, but he wasn't taking the chance of Morana getting a shot at Briony.

He kicked, and his hind claws caught one in the side of his head. Right where he needed to. The bauk's knees buckled, and it crashed to the ground. Black, thick blood oozed over the cave floor, releasing its horrid stench of maggoty meat.

Green light shot past his face, and he pulled Briony to him and whirled.

The last bauk lunged, his teeth gnashing a few inches from

Briony's arm. She shrieked and clutched Hans. Her terror threaded into his chest, and he felt her heartbeat skyrocket. He wasn't sure how he could feel her inside his chest, but he did.

His vision went red.

Snarling, he pounced, grabbed the bauk's head, and twisted. As its spine cracked, it screamed. His claws sank deep for the kill with one quick stab into its neck. Bauk handled.

Morana hissed. She was only a few feet away, her hands raised. "I have to do everything myself." She walked forward, hands in front of her, green stirring at her wrists.

They needed to get out of here. Morana's magic wasn't faltering. With the magic she'd cast, she should be drained by now. Magicwielder magic required building up spark stores, but she didn't appear concerned at all.

He hauled Briony backward as a slash of green light buzzed past her chest. Certainly a death blast.

His vision went red. He wanted to pummel Morana to a pulp. Take out every shred of his rage on her head. Exact his vengeance.

Briony clutched his waist, and he paused. He didn't know the significance of the glowing bracelets and how the magicwielder had an unending supply of magic. What if Morana kept healing, unable to die? It was only a matter of time before she hit Briony with her magic. If he was the only one in the cave, he'd stay until he was certain Morana was dead, but he wasn't alone.

Morana focused on Briony and her hands glowed green.

"Change of plans." He picked Briony up and raced toward the exit. "Her magic isn't fading."

A blast slammed into his shoulder, and he fell forward. Right before he landed, he twisted, landing on his back and cushioning Briony to his chest.

Morana raced forward and dove at them, her hand reaching for his throat.

"No," Briony screamed. She threw her arm out and

smashed Morana across the face. Morana teetered sideways; her mouth open in shock.

Morana swung, green light gathering in her palm, but Briony grabbed Morana's arm, forcing it up and away from them. Her nails raked down Morana's wrist and over the bracelet.

An intense flash of green and white light blasted between the two women. Ozone burned the air. Morana screamed, and he sat up in time to see her fly across the cave in a shower of white sparks and hit the opposite wall. Hard. She slumped to the ground and didn't move.

Hans scrambled to his feet. "Now we run."

They raced toward the mouth of the cave, but Briony halted and scooped something off the floor. He paused for her. "Come on."

"Your trousers." She sprinted forward and tossed them at him.

"Who cares about trousers?"

"I do."

He flung them over his shoulder and grabbed her hand, intending to haul her next to him to run faster, but her hand was tiny and delicate, so he carefully wrapped it in his own. The same warmth from when they lay on the bench together stirred in the deep place inside him. "Hurry. We must get deep in my forest, where Morana can't track us."

Briony held up her fist. "Especially since I think she'll want this back." Clutched between her fingers hung one of Morana's bracelets.

5

THE AIR CHILLED, and the forest grew darker. Not that Briony could see worth a damn. Even the full moon's light didn't penetrate through the thick trees. They'd run for ages, Hans never letting go of her hand as he guided her around trees and over roots, his grip firm yet gentle.

She wanted his hand on hers. Wanted him close to feel his warmth and let his pine scent wash over her, especially after healing him. Healing always made her freeze.

Her chest pounded, and it wasn't only from running. A foreign sensation centered under the new mark on her chest and surrounded her heart. Its masculine presence nestled into place as if taking up permanent residence and seduced with small pulses of comforting warmth.

What did that symbol in the cave do to her? It felt like a thread wove her to Hans, and if he left her side, she'd flood with icy panic.

They slowed in a thick stand of pines with trunks so broad they dwarfed even Hans. Beneath them, a thick carpet of needles deadened their footsteps. The trees enclosed a small clearing, with just enough space between their branches to allow pale moonlight to reveal a hillock backed against one of the mighty mountains. A stream snaked next to it, the water burbling a low and quiet melody.

Hans dropped her hand and walked toward the mossy mound in front of the mountain. Her fingers twitched. They felt empty.

The muscles of his back and shoulders flexed, and with one heave, he hauled open a door at least fifteen feet high and two feet thick.

He turned, his hand resting on the stone door. "Coming in?"

She stared at the yawning darkness. Yet another hole in a mountain. This time, the lair of a beast called the Shadow of Death. A vulk. This entire evening had to be a bad dream. One she'd wake from at any moment.

Hans sighed, grabbed the trousers still dangling over his shoulder, and bent and tugged them on. "Better?"

She studied him for a moment. Hans wasn't the one trying to kill her. He'd licked her neck softly like a kiss. Shielded her from those monsters. Her face heated. He'd done a lot more than lick her neck.

The events of the night blurred together. Being hauled out of Vieska by monsters, experiencing pleasure with a stranger in a cave, then running for her life. What was real? What wasn't?

Kill her. That awful witch's words echoed in her head. There hadn't been a second's hesitation. Briony was nothing. Her hands fisted. Once again, she was a pawn tossed around with no agency over her life.

Briony stepped forward and ducked around Hans. She hadn't paused because she was afraid to go into his den with him. She'd paused because she wasn't.

She descended a smooth floor into vast darkness, and the thick door slammed shut behind her, cutting off the faint moonlight. The cool of the night chased them inside, mixing with a mineral tang similar to a warm cellar. It was just the two of them in here, no one else. No one could open that door except a vulk. She exhaled a long breath. *Safe.* Her shoulders relaxed from where they'd been bunched up around her ears.

Hans brushed past her. "Wait here."

Briony placed a hand on the wall. A clang and some rustling sounded a short distance in front of her. There was a flicker of flame, then a fire caught in a wide, arching hearth, revealing the room in front of her. Wide with lofty ceilings, it was sparse, with only two chairs before the fireplace.

The stone under her feet wasn't dugout mountain rock. Someone had taken the time to set polished granite stones to create a beautiful floor that was unmatched even in the wealthiest homes in Vieska. Crafted rock also created the intricate mantelpiece. When the fire flickered, it caught the threads of pyrite glinting like liquid silver. In places, claw marks gouged the wall, leaving it raw. Unfinished.

"You live here alone?"

"Yes. Sit." Hans gestured toward one chair.

Briony walked farther into the room instead. "You know, in the normal world, when you invite someone into your home, the host is a bit more welcoming and not so bossy." An archway to the right revealed a sliver of another room, and she walked toward it. A squat potbellied stove, gigantic table, and sink spread out in a kitchen and dining area, with exquisitely crafted cabinets. Cabinets that didn't have doors and gaped, their shelves bare. Dust coated everything. "You sure you live here? It looks abandoned."

Across from the front entryway stood two doors. One opened into a dark passageway, and the other remained closed. "Can I have a tour? I want to see a vulk's den."

"No tour. I didn't invite you over for tea. I brought you here to save your life. Sit."

She glared at him as she strode to the fireplace. "Who saved who? Those monsters would have killed you, or ..." she shuddered, "done more horrible stuff to you if I hadn't helped."

When she sat, she noticed light wood inset with warm red

in an intricate pattern along the seat back. Her chair was clean, but dust spread over the chair across from her, and Hans didn't sit in it.

He leaned against the mantel and crossed his arms. "They may have tried to kill me, but they would have failed."

"I guess you don't count that witch among your friends. Who is she? What's going on?"

Hans pushed off the wall and paced. "Her name is Morana. I killed her a hundred years ago. Well, I thought I did."

Briony studied him. "Guess she's a little miffed about that. What happened?"

He kept pacing. "It's a long story. I'm more interested in learning how she survived." There was a long silence. Guess the story wasn't getting told. "She isn't a witch." Hans stopped his pacing. "What do you know about magic?"

She shrugged. "It's forbidden in Rohant. If magicwielders have come through, I've never met one."

His eyes narrowed. "What about that healing trick you did? Wasn't that magic?"

She crossed her arms. "I want answers first. Tell me about magicwielders and why you said their magic would run out. And about Morana."

His stare was intense. Imperial. He sucked all the energy in the room toward him, but she didn't look away. The massive vulk across from her might be imposing, but she was certain he wouldn't hurt her. Especially if he had the same sensation in his chest, she had in hers. The one urging her to touch him and convince him to make that soft, soothing, purring sound again.

"You need anything? Food? Water?" His expression was inscrutable.

Her mouth fell open. "What? No, I'm okay. Besides, what could you have to eat around here? Dried up old carcasses?"

"I'm sure I could find something for your tiny teeth. Some small bones or soft, raw meat."

Was he serious? "I'm fine."

He returned to lean against the mantel. "There. I've fulfilled my host duties."

"That was an awful attempt." She couldn't decipher the way he stared at her. Curiosity? Annoyance? In some ways, his face reacted like a human's, but in others, it was foreign.

"How do I know you'll answer my questions if I answer yours first?" Hans asked. "Or tell me the truth?"

Briony crossed her arms. "You'll have to trust me."

He growled low in his throat. "You could have run, and you didn't. Why did you stay? Was it to ignite that symbol?"

Briony shot to her feet. "I have no idea what that symbol is."

His gaze bore into hers as the silence stretched between them. "All right, I'll tell you about magic." He practically snarled it as if annoyed he'd spoken first. "Magicwielders come in three varieties. You saw two tonight. A spellcaster is someone only able to wield magic if they use a medium, like a spell or a crystal."

She nodded. "Like the man in the cave." He'd used spells and the bowl of water to perform magic.

"Yes. Then you have sorcerers. They're rare and the most powerful because they create magic at will."

"And that's Morana?"

He rubbed his mouth, and his brow furrowed. "Morana didn't have that kind of skill before. She was an enchanter, the third kind. Someone who manipulates objects and people. They aren't often in battle but can inflict damage in other ways."

She'd entered a new world. A vulk, a storybook creature, stood a few feet away from her talking about magic. Even though they spoke about Morana, replays of how he'd touched her in the cave kept distracting her.

Her face grew hot. His touch was far more skilled and pleasurable than anything she'd experienced before. Was any of that experience real? Or was it the serum she'd taken?

A magic serum used by a spellcaster to manipulate her. Anger flashed, hot and bubbling to replace the memories of rolling pleasure, and Briony's hands fisted. "Could she have trained to get more skilled or something?"

"No. It doesn't work like that. Magicwielders are born with all the power they'll ever have. They learn how to use it and hoard their energy to spark it. Their energy drains fast when they're blasting magic like back in the cave, but Morana's didn't." He shook his head, claws clicking on the stone as he pivoted while pacing.

"That guy in the black cape, the spellcaster? He performed spell after spell, and he didn't seem drained."

Hans rubbed his head. "Some believe if they study the dark side of magic, they can become more powerful, and they won't tire as quickly. The spellcaster was one of those. They call themselves necromancers. It's all bullshit, though. They have the same magical abilities as any other magicwielder and the same limitations." But he frowned and appeared lost in thought.

"How do you know all this?"

He stared at her for a long moment. "It's important to know your enemy."

Strands of hair fell free from the binding at the nape of her neck, and she tucked it behind her ears. She sat back down. "They used me to get you to stay in the cave." She glanced at where the necromancer sliced through Hans's arm. No mark remained.

Briony told him how the monsters appeared as guards and took her from Vieska. When she got to the part about the necromancer forcing her to drink the serum in the syringe, Hans lunged forward to crouch in front of her.

He cupped the side of her face. "Are you sick? Do I need to get you help?"

She shook her head. "No. It made me ..." Briony cleared her throat and stared over his shoulder at the fire. "Hoyt, the necromancer, didn't know what the serum would do, but he needed a lure to keep you busy." *Focus on the nice flames. Good and high.* Her face burned again, but it wasn't from their heat. The words came out in a rush. "I guess the best distraction was to cause ... attraction ... between us. The kind that made me ..." She swallowed. "Usually, I like to exchange a few words with someone before I undress them." She'd done a lot more than undress him.

He dropped his hand and stood. "That's why you didn't run?"

She also wanted to ask if his desire was induced, but she bit her lip and remained silent. When she saw Hans, the cave, the necromancer, and the ogre creatures vanished until it was only the two of them. She'd noticed his form, noticed the scary claws, but she hadn't run. Instead, she'd touched him. Was it because of the serum? It wasn't coursing through her veins any longer, yet she'd run to him even now, to where it felt safe.

"Did the necromancer cause the symbol in the air?"

"No. Magicwielder magic has a scent, and there was none when the symbol appeared, so the necromancer didn't cast that." His face was impassive and unreadable. His gaze icy and guarded. "You feel better now? That stuff out of your system?"

She nodded.

His blue eyes blazed. "Maybe this is a human trick."

Arms crossed over her chest, and she narrowed her eyes. "Look, a few hours ago, I was in my village drinking in the tavern, like any other normal day. Ogres captured me, and some magic object appeared and bound us together. I didn't have anything to do with any of it." Her hand pressed against the mark over her heart. "Do you know what the symbol is or not?"

He thumbed the center of his chest, and a hint of gold peeked through his fur. "No."

"When the symbol showed up, the poem sang out, 'first a rune will bind.' Is that what it is? A rune?" Every word of the poem resounded in her head like it was being spoken aloud.

He shrugged. "Never heard of a rune, but that little poem? Dead wrong. It can't be about the two of us."

The lightwielder was betrayed by those that should have stayed.

Her hands fisted. Those lines struck close to home. What if this poem *was* about her? There was one memory …

She ran her hands through her hair. Nope. Not going there. She didn't dwell on the past because she couldn't change anything.

To give away her heart, everything might fall apart.

Well, about her or not, she'd never give her heart away. Never. No one stayed. No one was trustworthy.

Why couldn't she find normal true love? Why did she have a riddle? She was no romantic, but she'd thought maybe, just maybe, someone would look at her and want her without their love ever wavering. She'd never had someone love her, really love her. And she wanted that. Wanted a family. Children. A place where she woke up every day knowing she was wanted. Cherished.

"I mean, are you a lightwielder?" he asked. Apparently, he remembered each line of the poem, too.

Briony frowned. "I can heal, but there's no light involved. Actually, I can only heal at night, so I'd notice if there was light shining somewhere." She shrugged. It was strange but true. "And I'm not using magic. I mean, you said it smells, and I've never noticed anything like that. It's simply an ability I was born with."

He grunted. "It's magic. Yours just doesn't work like a magicwielder's."

She startled. "How do you know?"

"I've seen magic used by some immortals of Ulterra. Yours is similar."

Briony examined her hands. Had magic coursed through her all this time? "I'll be marched out of Vieska at the end of a pitchfork if the town learns I'm doing most of the healing by magic. I already hide I'm the one actually treating most of our patients, and not the doctor."

"Why?"

She shrugged. "They don't want to be treated by an outsider. Besides, I'm only a lowly assistant, not a proper doctor."

"You're not from Vieska?"

She stared into the fire again. "Not exactly."

"Where are you from?"

"It's a long story." She met his gaze and held it. That's right—she'd thrown his words back at him, and no, she wasn't discussing *her* story any further tonight either.

She replayed the poem in her head again. "Okay, maybe I'm using magic, but there's no light involved. I'm no lightwielder. But 'the vulk they call Shadow?' That's you."

He shrugged. "Maybe. Everything else it said was wrong, though. Especially the part about only having a month to become mates." He chuffed. "The vulk don't take mates."

Briony's mouth opened and closed a few times. A bitterness long nursed in her heart reared up, its taste sour. If somehow this poem was about the two of them, of course fate paired her with someone who would never be with her.

Her stomach clenched. Good. Better to know now.

She raised her chin. "Why not?"

"Our only loyalty is to our creed and our pack brothers. There's no space for anything else."

Her eyes narrowed. "Only brothers? What about female vulk? They aren't allowed in your little pack?"

"All vulk are male."

"What?" None of the stories ever mentioned that. "How do you make baby vulk?"

He shifted his weight from foot to foot. "The vulk and the peltwalker wolf clans are closely aligned. Under the right conditions, a vulk can have children with interested females. It's not common, but it's possible. We aren't compatible with anyone else."

From what she'd read in the book last year, peltwalkers lived in clans based on the animal they shifted into. The wolf clans shifted into actual wolves, not into werewolf form like Hans, and when they shifted, their minds were closer to the animal than the human.

Her face heated, and she stared at the fire so she didn't have to look at him. "Only peltwalkers can get pregnant? There's no chance with a human?" She hadn't considered pregnancy until this moment.

"Not at all."

She should feel relief at his words, but the twinge in her chest wasn't relief. She let out a breath. "Well, this was helpful. We only have more questions and no answers."

"We?"

Her eyes narrowed. "I'm part of this now. Morana tried to kill me, too." *The vulk they call Shadow, content to always walk solo.* Well, he wasn't solo right now, he was with her. The idea of him leaving her made a familiar sense of panic rise into her throat. She dug in her pocket and held up Morana's bracelet in her clenched fist. "And I have this."

His gaze remained steady on hers. "I have an idea about how to get some answers, but it involves traveling for days and sleeping on the ground. Most likely, Morana will chase us. On top of that, you'll be with me constantly. You really want to come along?"

49

6

HANS HELD HIS BREATH. He continued leaning against the hearth and turned his head to watch the fire. What if she wanted to leave? His hackles rose, and a savage instinct reared up from deep inside him. No. She stayed with him.

Hell, he'd caved and answered her questions. Him. One of the fiercest fighters, known for never backing down, couldn't stand it when she glared at him. And every time her large eyes met his, the suspicion he had about her trapping him with the symbol crumbled.

Two souls chosen by fate must choose to make each other their mate. Two *souls* chosen by fate? Not a chance. He ran his hand over his head. When he'd told Briony the poem was wrong, he'd meant it.

After a long pause, she said, "I'm coming with you." He let out a long breath and uncrossed his arms.

"I want to wash. Do vulk wash?"

He didn't look at her, only used his thumb and pointed behind him. "Even us beasties like to be clean. The closed door is the bathroom. There's a shower and a tub in there. We've had the fire going long enough that there's hot water."

She stood up. "How does this burrow have hot water? Vieska barely has hot water."

He pushed off the wall, and his lip rose up his eyetooth in irritation. "A burrow is for rabbits." Hans jerked his chin toward the fireplace. "I have a couple of water tanks next to the chimney shaft. They're layered with copper that also attaches to the flue. Light a fire and the tanks get hot and heat the hot water pipes through the house."

"Huh." A line formed between her brows, and she studied him strangely. "What about light in there? I don't see any gas lamps."

"Maybe your eyes will adjust to the dark." The corner of his mouth twitched. "Or I can go in and help you. Since you won't be able to see."

Her face flushed. It had done that a few times, and it fascinated him. "That won't be necessary."

He opened his palms. "Just being a good host." Striding past her to the closet, he rooted around until he found the lantern. There was a small chip on the glass's rim, but it wasn't broken, and a hunk of melted venison fat remained in its base. He lit it and gave it to her. "Count your bruises."

She was walking toward the bathroom, and she paused. "What? Why?"

"We'll pay Morana back for every injury."

Briony turned, and the lantern cast a rosy haze over her face. "Is that the vulk way?"

"No. It's mine." He stepped closer. "If what you say is true, they took you from your home and brought you into my battle. If they marred your skin, for every mark, we'll return it to Morana's head tenfold."

Her brow raised. "What about any bite marks I find?"

He stepped closer. "Those you should stroke with pleasure and remember how you got them."

The rosiness on her face was not only from the lantern before she turned and scurried into the bathroom.

. . .

HANS LEANED AGAINST HIS HEADBOARD, his hands behind his head. When she'd finished showering, she hadn't asked where to rest, and he hadn't offered his bed. Instead, she'd curled up on the chair by the fire.

Probably best.

Vulk dens were sacred and private. Even close friends rarely invited each other into their space, and his bedroom was his most intimate place. He could argue that he'd brought her here because it was the only safe place, but that wasn't true. There were plenty of other caves only he knew about where they could have holed up.

He rubbed his face. When he returned home, alone, after killing Morana, the hints of mountain laurel already filling his den would linger for weeks and tease him with her memory. He both wanted that scent on his bed and wanted to avoid endless nights of torture as her scent caused him to replay the memory of her under him in the cave.

Those wooden chairs didn't have any cushions.

He growled and lurched out of bed. His claws snicked on the floor as he paced his room.

He inhaled deeply, but an acrid, burned taste clung to his tongue and seared his nose like it had every time he'd tried to smell. The poison had singed his senses, making everything watery and indistinct.

He cursed in Vulk, "Uit."

A sudden zinging beat through his chest, like a small, panicked animal trying to run free. In one leap, he bounded from his bedroom into the main room. Briony was frightened. No, not frightened. Terrified.

Curled on the seat of the chair, her head lay on her arm, and her eyelids twitched. His gut lurched with an unfamiliar roil at the sight of her folded in such an uncomfortable position.

"Hey." She didn't wake.

He crouched in front of her and breathed deep. Damn this poison! No sulfur broke through over the rot coating his senses, but he couldn't be sure. There were ways to bewitch someone in dreams. Briony jerked and whimpered.

He ran the back of his knuckles over her cheek. "Wake up."

She gasped and shot up. "Where am I?"

"My den, remember?"

Her eyes widened, and her head swiveled as she scanned the room. She breathed rapidly, and he didn't think she focused on her surroundings.

"Oh yeah, the dark burrow." Her voice was small. "I never dream. I'm always so exhausted at night I collapse and sleep straight through to morning."

"But you had a nightmare tonight?"

She nodded. "It was all dark, but there was something after me. Something big, even taller than you. All I heard was this awful sucking sound. And I saw glowing green eyes." She put her hand in her pocket. "The same color as this."

She pulled out Morana's bracelet. Without being on Morana's arm, it lay in a coil, dull and gray. "Well, when it was lit up with magic."

He leaned closer and placed his palm on the back of the chair. "I don't think it's a good idea to keep that bracelet close to you."

She stared at it in her hand and finally nodded. With a scoot on the chair, she inched toward him. If he dropped his head a few inches, his mouth would be on her neck.

"I need to get things ready to leave tomorrow, and you're in the way sleeping out here." He didn't recognize his own voice. It was soft. Gentle.

"Where do you expect me to go, then? Outside?" She placed one hand on his arm and grabbed the lantern.

"That's not a bad idea. Are you a good screamer? You can

sit on top of the hillock and alert me if any danger arises. Like a living weathervane." He scooped her up, and she nestled against his chest, cradling the lantern.

"I'm not really the scream-for-help type."

When he entered his bedroom, he plucked the lantern from her hand, placed it on the bedside table, and cranked more fat into the flame to cast more light. Not that there was much for her to see, only his bed, nightstand, and a chest, but the lantern beat the dark back. He placed her on one side of the bed. "What type are you?"

She shrugged. "The figure-it-out-myself type. I think."

There were no blankets on his bed—he didn't need them—so he went to his closet, grabbed one, and tucked it around her.

She toyed with the edge. "This is a nice quilt. Where did you get it?"

"My mother," he answered automatically, then regretted it.

"Is she still alive? She'd be a peltwalker, right?"

He sighed. "Peltwalkers live much longer than humans, and my mother hasn't aged much. She lives with the wolf clan of Rohant. Do you have a family?"

"Not to speak of." Her lips pressed into a thin line and pressure twisted in his chest. Hans outlined the rune mark tattooed over his heart with a fingertip. This mark bound them together in ways he didn't understand. Earlier, he'd known she was scared, and now he knew her past pained her.

Would she pick up on his feelings, too? Good thing he rarely had any.

An urge to soothe her, to use his mouth, his hands, strum the soft noises she liked, surged through him. He didn't move.

The bed creaked as Briony surveyed the furniture, running her hands over the small table next to the bed, then examining the chest at the foot before twisting to examine the headboard.

"Where did you buy this furniture? Who makes vulk-sized stuff?"

"I made it."

"That's ... surprising."

He shrugged. "Why? Because of my claws?" If he couldn't use his claws to sculpt the wood, he filed them daily into stubs to hold the needed tools. They grew back almost immediately, so it was tough, but he'd managed.

She glanced at his hands. "No, I didn't think of that. I just figured you slept on the floor."

"Not if I can help it. Vulk dens are far nicer than those wooden fire traps you humans live in and far more comfortable." He crossed his arms. "The vulk are masters at sculpting stone and wood."

Briony glanced at the walls of his room where hunks of stone jutted out in places. He'd banged his elbow on them plenty of times. "Well, our homes may be above ground, but our walls are smooth."

His hands fisted. He wasn't about to explain why the stonework of his den was in its current state. "Get some rest, and I'll get our stuff ready."

Her fingers twisted the quilt. "Don't you sleep?"

"Not much, and not at night." Her mouth opened again, but he strode to the doorway. "We'll have to move fast to ensure Morana doesn't follow. You'll need your strength."

And he slipped out the door.

7

"GET UP AND GET DRESSED. We have to go."

Briony jolted upright. Almost the moment after he'd left the room, she'd fallen into a deep and dreamless sleep, lulled by the soft hints of Hans's pine smell all around her. Pine and the woodsy masculine scent that was his alone.

"What's wrong?"

Hans brought her boots and jacket over, and she slid out of bed to put them on. "The forest is uneasy, and it's best if we leave."

"I thought you said it was safe in your den?"

"From Morana, yes, but something else is going on."

She followed him into the living room, and he slung a massive pack onto his back. As he straightened, he winced.

"Your wound is acting up, isn't it? Do we have time for me to ...?" She didn't wait for an answer. She walked to his right side and lay her hands over his ribs. Briony inhaled sharply. The poison was worse than yesterday. It twisted through Hans, reaching and spreading from his ribs toward his heart and lungs. Like a worm burrowed in one spot and extending tendrils outward to attack slowly. She swallowed and poured energy into severing each strand. Her hands grew hot, and a bead of sweat formed on her brow.

As she leached off the poisonous roots, she grew colder, and her teeth chattered. Her vision swam. She'd never let herself heal this long before. A small lump of the worm remained, and she struggled to attack it, but the creeping chill wrapped around her.

Hans jerked her hand away, and she swayed. He rubbed her arms, and she slumped against him. "I can't get it all, so I need to keep checking this and beating it back."

"Why are you so cold?" He growled and tucked her against him as he helped her out of the den. She liked the weight of his arm around her. The warmth.

"My hands grow hot, and I go cold. It's like all my body heat goes away."

He squeezed her tighter to his side. "I don't like it. Are you alright?"

"I'll be fine, and I'll get warm again soon, but I can't heal for a bit." Warmth already spread through her from where she pressed against him—he was like an oven.

They exited the den and entered the clearing. The two moons still glistened in the sky, but the two suns tipped high enough over the horizon for dawn to break through the dense forest, shining a milky light over the landscape. A dense soupy fog swirled knee-high around the bases of the trees, emitting a sour, skunk-like stench.

The songbirds should be up making a ruckus. Yet the creaking of the trees as gusts of wind rattled them together was the only sound. The entire forest hunkered down like hunted prey, trembling and waiting.

Briony leaned closer to Hans, her breath pluming in the air.

An owl screamed a warning, and a twig snapped to their left. "We have two visitors," Hans said. He put his arm around her, but he didn't push her behind him like he had when he fought Morana.

Two vulk stepped around the trees into the small clearing. Both stood a couple of inches shorter than Hans but still massive and broad. They were dark charcoal gray, but one had a small patch of cream on his chest and wore tan trousers and a matching vest of a thick hide. The other wore sandy-colored shorts.

They called out to Hans in words she didn't understand. Vulk spoke another language?

Hans responded in the same language, and she studied him from the corner of her eye. Tense, but not angry.

Did he not like these vulk? Were they the reason the forest was uneasy?

"What's going on? Who are they?" she asked.

Hans sighed. "That's Juri," he gestured toward the vulk wearing the vest, "and the other is Kyril." Both glared at her. "This is Briony. She doesn't speak Vulk, so we'll switch to common tongue." There was a long pause, and the air grew frostier. Briony expected the other vulk to balk at Hans telling them what to do, but they only stared.

Juri shifted onto his heels. "Things are happening throughout Ulterra I thought you'd want to know about."

Kyril bared his teeth. "I told him we should take care of it ourselves because you wouldn't care, but he insisted."

Hans didn't say anything, and Briony studied his face for a reaction. Why wouldn't Hans care?

"There are more rifts than normal opening everywhere," Juri continued. "And all the spawn rush to the east. They don't hunt, and they seem to work together. They aren't fighting each other like they usually do."

"Aren't you killing them?" Hans asked flatly.

Kyril snarled. "As many as we can find, but the rifts occur two or three times a day, and there aren't enough vulk."

"They're all headed north of the vae border." Juri met Hans's gaze.

Briony started. Vae? She thought they only existed in fairy-tales. According to the old stories, they appeared to be human, yet had a touch of something ... other ... in the way they moved and had mysterious powers. In some tales, they were friendly, and in others, not so much.

"Where are you going?" Kyril pointed at the pack. "Why are you with a human?"

Tension spiked off Hans, and for many long moments, the only movement was the fog pooling around their legs. A thunderous rumbling off in the distance shook the ground. The watery dawn light in the clearing snuffed out.

Briony pointed overhead. "What is that?" Between the branches, the sky peeked through. Snaking across it, thick black clouds writhed and expanded far faster than any storm clouds she'd ever seen.

The hair on the back of her neck rose.

A screech pierced the forest. Something fist-sized crashed through the trees and pelted her shoulder hard. Briony cried out, and Hans swept her in front of him. A fist-sized ball of hail bounced to the ground.

Branches snapped as more rained down around them, and Briony grabbed Hans's arm and tugged. "Let's get back inside."

"No. It's an ala. Inside my den won't be safe." As if that explained it. Before she realized what he was going to do, Hans picked her up, crushed her against his chest, and sprinted into the forest.

Another screech and the tumult of clouds formed into a diaphanous raven, its wings at least a hundred feet wide. The branches overhead provided some cover, but hail still bounced off Hans's head and shoulders.

Fear raced up her spine, and she clutched at Hans.

Juri and Kyril raced at his side. "She won't follow us too

far from her mountain," Juri shouted to be heard over the rush of hail through the branches.

"Go for the pass," shouted Hans.

"Do you want me to take the human? You've gotten slow." Kyril wasn't out of breath.

Hans growled, tightening his grip, and he weaved more swiftly through the trees. As the trees whirred by, she couldn't believe this was slow for Hans.

A high-pitched screech and a taloned foot, scaly and black, ripped into the ground at their left. Briony screamed a warning and the three vulk leaped. Hans landed on his poisoned side, hitting the ground hard with a grunt, but he cushioned her, and she bounced painlessly against his chest. Where they'd been running moments ago, the ala tore an entire slope of pines out of the earth. Hans bounded to his feet and sprinted faster.

The ala tossed full-sized trees with trunks as wide as a carriage right at them. Trees snapped as they were hit, catapulting and rolling through the forest with an avalanche-like roar.

Hans tossed her over his shoulder, and she clung to the backpack as he sprang up into a tree to let rubble flood past below them. They kept racing, and the forest thinned to expose the steep cliffs of the mountainside.

They reached the forest's edge, and dizzying cliffs yawned below them. Briony broke out in a sweat, and her stomach dropped. Steep cliffs. Death. Mountains surrounded Rohant on all sides, with only one road in and out. This wasn't it. They were trapped.

The vulk didn't pause. They launched themselves over the side. Briony screamed and screwed her eyes shut, digging her fingernails into Hans's back. His muscles bunched and flexed, and wind rushed past her face, but she refused to look.

The thrashing wind vanished with one last echoing screech. Briony cracked an eyelid. They leaped down onto a trail cut into the mountains, with tall rock stretching high on either side and only a slim crack of sunlight above them. Hans placed her on her feet, his hands lingering at her waist.

Briony took a deep trembling breath. "Are we safe here?"

Hans turned to Juri. "What do you scent?"

A puzzled expression crossed Juri's face, and he squinted at Hans. "No more fog, and the ala is leaving."

Hans nodded. "That fog wasn't natural." His fur lay matted in spots, and she reached up and touched the wet smudge on his bicep. Her fingertips came away bloody. He'd been pelted by hail the entire time, yet she didn't have a single scratch.

"What's an ala?" she asked.

Hans rolled his shoulders. "An immortal who lives in the Shaking Mountain." It was the tallest peak in Rohant's mountain range. "She isn't an underworld spawn, but she isn't from the world of Ulterra, either. She's a guardian of one of the junctions—the passing places between Ulterra and Peklo—and prevents anyone from crossing in either direction. Mostly she stays on the underworld side, though. When I've seen her previously, it's been on friendlier terms."

"Why was she chasing us?" Briony laid her palm on the wound on Hans's arm, but he placed his own on top of hers.

"Don't bother. I don't want you to get cold again. I heal quickly. Even with ..." He glanced at the other two vulk. "I heal quickly." She didn't remove her hand, and neither did he. Her galloping heart calmed.

Juri pointed upward. "That may be why the ala chased us. She thinks we got them past her."

Briony squinted. She only saw a few vultures, or maybe hawks, circling high above the pass.

Hans sucked in a breath. "That would do it, and their appearance explains the brimstone fog. Someone created it to confuse her and get those beasts up from Peklo. No wonder she's angry." That someone had to be Morana. Who else?

"What are they?"

"Cockatrice. Picture a cross between a rooster and a giant lizard. Too small to pose a serious threat if they attack us, but intelligent enough to follow us and report back to whoever they're working with."

She watched them circling far above the pass and thought she could make out a long tail swiping behind each one. "Those things came from the underworld? I thought it was only a myth, not an actual place."

"A myth?" Kyril eyed her. "No. It's real. It's a dangerous realm full of the cursed ones and the beasts that thrive in the dark. Some want to remain down there, and some," he glanced up at the circling cockatrice, "want to escape to Ulterra. Don't humans know this?"

"We have tales about monsters." She glanced at Hans. "Like the Shadow of Death and the bauk, but the only mention of Peklo is as an imaginary world. Isn't it a nothing land?"

Juri scoffed. "No, it's not a nothing land. It's a replica of Ulterra, with the same mountains, the same rivers, but no sunlight, only a perpetual mist. It's directly below us but separate."

Briony had never read about this in her books from Only an Obol. She looked at the dirt under her boots. "Can you dig down to Peklo?"

"No. There is a barrier between the two realms except for the few places Ulterra and Peklo touch. Those are the junctions. There are a few we know of. One is the Shaking Mountain, where it punches so deep into the ground that it also enters Peklo. The junctions are always open, so guardians protect them to keep the real monsters from crossing up into Ulterra."

Kyril growled. "The two realms sometimes bump and form a temporary rift, like a pocket with a portal that spawn like to slither through. Vulk have no magic, but we have a power left to us from our great Wulf ancestor that allows us to close rifts. We kill anything that escapes." He turned away as if sorry he'd spoken.

Juri's voice took on a smooth, lilting tone. "Back when the earth was young, when humans were only a small clan by the Great Sea, all the species moved freely between both realms. Some creatures preferred the light, and some the dark, but they all got along until there was a schism, and it was clear that some trod a dark path and needed to be contained. That's when the Deciding War broke out. After the war ended, the junction guardians were put in place, and the spawn and the cursed were banished to Peklo."

"Juri's our bard," Kyril said.

Juri narrowed his eyes. "I know our history."

"The only time you're happy is if you're sitting at the fire telling tales. That makes you a bard."

Juri switched to Vulk and said something that made Kyril guffaw.

<Some things never change.>

"What did you say?" She stared up at Hans. They still stood only a few inches from each other.

"I didn't say anything."

Briony frowned. She'd definitely heard his voice.

"Let's get going." Hans ushered her forward.

It was warmer in the protected pass with no wind gusting. Water seeped through cracks in the slate stone walls and wet the rock, and out of one crevice, a small waterfall splashed down onto the floor. Hans stopped. "This water is pure. We can fill the canteens here."

"Where are we? Where are we going?"

"We're heading east toward the Wide River."

Juri put his head under the spout and drank while Hans knelt and took off his pack. Wiping his mouth, Juri stood. "Why?"

As he filled the canteens, Hans told Juri and Kyril about

the cave and Morana, although he was selective about what he shared. She was thankful he left out how they met—they didn't need to know about that—but he didn't tell them about the poison either, and she wasn't sure that was a good idea.

Kyril's lip curled up his eyetooth. "You're sure *she* wasn't part of it?"

"They attacked her too."

Briony had her mouth under the water, and she spluttered and straightened. No mention of their chat last night and his suspicions. Kyril's lip relaxed, but he didn't look convinced.

"What's your plan?" Juri asked.

"I'm going to Baba Yaga."

Juri rubbed his mouth. "It's always a risk to work with the Forest Mother, even for you."

Hans didn't respond.

Briony took another long drink and thought about the tales she'd read or heard as a child. None of them mentioned a Baba Yaga. The name Forest Mother seemed protective and helpful, but if Juri was worried about her ...

A chill trailed up her spine. What had she gotten herself into? She gulped, and the water went down wrong. She coughed, and the vulk stopped talking and stared at her. A great beginning.

Thirst slaked, Hans moved to his burlap backpack. It sat on the ground with thick leather straps and a canvas rolled and strapped to its top. She joined him and studied it. "I can carry something."

"This pack is built for a vulk and is about two hundred pounds." He raised a brow. "You think you can haul this on your back?"

Briony put her hands on her hips. "I'm scrappier than I look. Maybe not vulk level, but I can hold my own. I'm on my feet all day, and my legs are famously powerful. Back at school, the boys would sneak away during our outdoor breaks to compete at chicken fighting. It's this contest where you stand on a narrow log a few feet up in the air, and you have to knock your opponent into the mud with only your legs. You know," she flapped her arms, "like how roosters fight? No arms?"

Hans stared at her. No expression. "Like a chicken. Okay."

"Well, I made the boys let me fight too, and when I was twelve, I beat every single one of them. Some of those boys were fifteen and big." She jogged in place a few steps. "See? Strong legs." Tossing all the boys in the mud hadn't endeared her to them and hadn't helped her find many suitors when she grew up, but she didn't have much opportunity anyway.

"And here I thought, after living for one hundred and eighty-six years, I couldn't find humans any stranger." She goggled at him. He was *one hundred and eighty-six*? The corner of his mouth twitched. "Despite convincing me you can mimic poultry, I think I'll keep the pack." He topped off one of the round, metal canteens with water and tightened the cap. It sat in a linen pouch with a long strap, so hunters could sling it around them when they went out for the day. Hans handed it to her. "Here, great chicken hunter. Hold this for us." His arm snaked around her waist, and he pulled her close. A warm breath fanned her neck before he nibbled under her ear.

Half a second later, he was gone, striding ahead down the path with Juri. It was so fast; she wasn't even sure it had happened. "Chicken-*fighter* and you're really old," she called after him and hiked the canteen over her shoulder. "Unnatural to be that old, really." She took a long moment and let her heart rate settle. Why had she told him that stupid chicken-fighting story? When was the last time she'd even thought about that? She shook her head and followed down the path.

Kyril leaned against the cliff wall, his stony gaze trained on her. Waiting. When she reached him, he pushed off and joined her. He gestured with his thumb where Juri spoke quietly to Hans a short distance ahead of them. "Hans has spoken more to you in the last few minutes than he's said to Juri in the past century. And Juri was his best friend."

"But not anymore?"

Kyril growled, low and menacing. "Hans refuses to be around anyone. Even his pack. Why is he chatting with *you*?"

Her pulse skittered at the restrained fierceness of his growl, but she didn't lose a step. "I'm just lucky, I guess."

Kyril grunted. "Something's fishy about this. Hans wouldn't be with you if he wasn't forced somehow." Without waiting for a reply, he loped ahead of her.

She sighed and walked to the side of the pass, keeping a few steps between her and the vulk. Kyril was right. Hans wouldn't have asked her to join him if there was no serum and no rune. Although that also meant she'd be home, safe, back in Vieska. Right about now, she'd be cleaning the surgery before the morning patients arrived. Her lips formed in a tight smile. Doc Toothless would have to manage on his own today.

As they walked on, sweat dripped down her back, and she took off her coat and bundled it in Hans's pack. Juri took his vest off and slung it over his shoulder.

Kyril chuffed. "I said you'd get too hot."

Juri shrugged. "It's already snowing back home."

"Where's that?" Briony asked.

There was a pause, and she didn't think he would answer. "I live up in the Northern Territories. Where the ice doesn't melt."

Due to the severe weather, only the hardiest peddlers traveled that way. If the snow wasn't falling, wind and rain swept the landscape. However, many peltwalker clans in compact villages were strewn across the vast expanse of tundra. The peddlers that made it up there described the low-slung lodges with double walls to keep the cold out. She wanted to see it one day.

She turned to Kyril, walking slightly ahead of them. "What about you?"

"I live near Stok. Where it never snows. None of this icy weather bullshit." Stok, the glittering southern kingdom where buildings were crafted of sandstone, and the land was filled with rippling sand dunes and birds the colors of jewels.

"Your skin's gotten thin," Juri said. "The last time you visited me, you didn't stop bawling about the weather. And we had a gorgeous summer that year. Three entire days."

Kyril erupted in a torrent of Vulk, and Juri's jaws parted in a grin. It was odd to see such a savage being suddenly soften. Even his tawny-colored eyes warmed, the corners crinkling.

Hans remained silent, and when she turned to study him, she couldn't picture him ever grinning. There was an edge to him. A power that made him impressive but also remote. Inaccessible.

It was difficult to gauge how much time passed, but the path ahead of them widened as the mountains parted. They stood at the top of a gentle hill of short grass not yet dead and brown from a killing frost, sloping down to a forest of shaking golden aspens. From their higher vantage point, dips and rises of the forest spread before them, the gold melding into greens and touches of blue juniper as it sprawled down to what had to be the Wide River.

The water wasn't visible from here, only the slash of the river gorge and its imposing bank along the opposite side. Past the river, continuing east, the trees were a mass of green so dark they appeared almost black and murky as if the sun didn't reach that far. Humans didn't cross the river because there lay the Kuls, the wild terrain of Ulterra. If someone dared enter, no one ever heard from them again.

She was warm, but she shivered. A sinking feeling grew in the pit of her stomach, and she stared at the far-off bank.

"Where does Baba Yaga live?"

Hans walked forward. "The Kuls."

8

Briony squeaked, closed the distance between them, and clutched at his arm. "I can't go there."

She'd remained a few steps apart from him for most of the trip through the pass. Since he kept battling the urge to pick her up, pin her against the mountain, and taste her again, he'd let her have her space. Especially since he kept wondering how strong her chicken-fighter legs were. He wanted to run his hands over them to find out, then make them tremble with a few sweeps of his tongue.

His lips twitched. She'd tossed a bunch of older boys off logs. Like a vulk would. When the vulk spent time together as a pack, sometimes aggression built up, and they needed an outlet, so they sparred. No claws, no teeth. They didn't stand on logs, but he liked the idea.

He put his hand on her lower back and bit back a purr at having her close again. "It'll be fine in the Kuls. You'll be with me."

Juri caught his eye. "Caladin won't be happy if he sees you."

Hans snarled. "Cal can—" He glanced at Briony and decided not to say the rest aloud.

Juri grinned. "He's king now."

Hans grunted. "I didn't think the old king and queen would step down so soon. What happened?" Vae were immortal, so Caladin gaining the crown wouldn't be because of his parents' death. Or it was unlikely that was the case, anyway. He frowned. Their death wasn't something he wanted to consider. Back when he'd roamed Ulterra, the past king and queen invited him to stay in the vae realm for a time, and he'd liked them. For vae anyway.

Juri shrugged. "You know how the vae are. They guard their secrets as closely as we do. Who knows why they do anything?"

Briony's eyes widened. "Are we going to see the vae?"

"No. We're staying to the south. Their territory is in the north."

A small moonstone winked a flash of milky white, its domed face visible where it lay embedded in the grass. He paused and stared down at it. After eons, the markers for the old vulk roads remained. Hidden in plain sight, all vulk would notice a moonstone on the ground and know what it meant, but others would stride right past.

He scanned down the slope to the rocky banks of the gorge where the pack den lay hidden along the cliff face. "Are any vulk living in the den?"

Juri strolled over and stood next to him. "Only Ayren."

"Still?"

"He never claimed a territory. It probably never crossed his mind that he should. He was, what? Early twenties when the pack dissolved? Barely a vulk."

He grunted in reply. Being close to the den, seeing Juri and Kyril, and hearing them bicker like they always did, felt like old times. Except he kept glancing to his left, expecting to see—

No.

A slash of anger clawed through him. Blank darkness, his

constant companion, welled up. A void allowing him to push his memories aside and escape into rage and a welcome nothingness. Around him, the scenery dulled as he fisted his hands so hard his claws nearly broke the skin.

Briony's arm brushed against his, and his skin tingled. Some of the pressure twisting his insides loosened, and the tunnel vision, the gloom, lifted.

"You alright?"

He jerked his head in a nod.

Her fingers trailed against his palm. The sun returned, and birds chirped in the trees again. He'd stopped walking at some point, and it was only the two of them. Kyril and Juri waited a distance ahead. She rubbed her chest and frowned. "Are you sure? Something feels bad, and it isn't …" She jabbed with her thumb toward the wound on his ribs. "I'm all twitchy because I can feel something's not right with you."

Could she really feel what he felt?

A blanket of warmth threaded through his chest and spread through their bond. She was concerned for him. His hand drifted toward hers, and he stroked her palm. For the first time, the void didn't consume him.

Juri and Kyril stared, but he didn't care. "I was thinking about the past. Not anything good."

He stepped over the moonstone and continued toward the gorge, Briony at his side. A hawk swooped through the air, a crow chasing after it. The crow's angry chorus bounced through the trees as the birds disappeared into the aspens.

When they approached the gorge, another moonstone shone to the left, marking the way to the vulk den. "Any new vulk born that haven't taken their true form yet?" Hans asked Juri. One hundred years was a long time without adding to the pack numbers.

"No."

That meant the number of vulk remained at ten. No— nine—and none older than two hundred and fifty. Small numbers. Vulk were immortal with enhanced strength and healing, especially at night, but it was still possible to kill one. Tough, but possible. They'd lost the last of the older vulk, the ones with knowledge of the ancient ways, during the vicious Territory Wars when the humans discovered what silver weapons could do. The vulk won that war and destroyed all the silver weapons, but the cost was enormous.

One hundred years had passed, and still no children? "No one visits the wolfwalker females?"

"The clan in Rohant is in your territory, and your territory is off-limits." Juri raised a brow at him, and Hans glanced away.

"What about the clans up in the north?"

Juri shrugged. "Guess not."

"What happens if one of the wolf clan women becomes pregnant?" Briony asked. "Does she come live with you?"

Kyril scoffed. "No. The vulk walk alone or with their pack. Only. The wolfwalkers understand. The entire clan helps raise a vulk child until they reach maturity and take their vulk form. Then they leave their clan and join the pack." The wolf clans raised a vulk son like he was a prince, and a wolfwalker female who bore a vulk child earned great respect.

Briony stopped walking. "You abandon her? That's not right." None of the vulk responded, but they glanced at each other, then quickly away. Hans's mother never mentioned his father, and her sadness was palpable the few times he'd tried, even though she tried to hide it. When he joined the pack, he'd never met another black-furred vulk. If he'd tried to ask the previous pack Alpha who his father was, the Alpha would have torn his arm off. Asking about things like that was forbidden.

All these years, his mother never took another mate. When the two moons were full, he'd caught her in the past walking alone through the forest. She never said why, but he suspected she hoped his father would return. Watching her, he'd decided his liaisons with wolfwalker females would be brief and never involve children.

When they entered the aspens, Briony stopped and let out a small trill. Her face tilted upward as her gaze swept over the trees. "Look at this place."

"It's a forest." The autumn leaves were yellow, and the sun slanted through the branches over the ground, giving the place a golden hue. "I guess it's nice." He wouldn't have noticed if she hadn't pointed it out.

"Where are we crossing into the Kuls?" Juri asked.

"You and Kyril will meet up with Ayren and let the rest of the vulk know what's going on. Fan out and chase down spawn."

"That's it? We're on our own?" Kyril wasn't baring his teeth, but he was close.

Hans shrugged.

"No." Juri's gaze burned on his. "I'm going to the Kuls with you."

"No. Go with Kyril."

Kyril raised a brow. "You think you can give orders? Like an Alpha?"

"I'm *suggesting* what I know to be best." He crossed his arms. Briony coughed, but it seemed suspiciously laugh-like. "Besides, you need a pack. Supplies." In Ulterra, the vulk knew every cave, every hollow, and there was always a place to sleep when they traveled. In the Kuls—not so much.

"I'm going with you," Juri repeated. "The den has old packs and supplies. I'll get what I need."

Hans growled and opened his mouth.

Briony tugged on his arm. "Can I talk to you? Over there?" For a tiny human, she hauled him firmly away through the copse of aspens. "You want to go into the Kuls with poison in your system with only me? Kyril said you aren't running as fast, and you asked Juri to smell for you."

He growled again. "Juri is the pack tracker. He's got the best nose. That's the only reason I asked."

"Bullshit, Hans. I saw the funny way he looked at you. I'm guessing you *never* ask for help. Ever."

He scowled. Since when were humans as observant as a vulk?

Briony plowed on. "If something happens, if the poisoning gets worse, he's much stronger than I am, and he can help you if you keel over. Besides," she glanced up at the sky, "what about those cockatrice things? Where did they go? What if they come back? I'm not going if you don't bring him." Her chin jutted up. "Kyril said Juri is your best friend, and you haven't spoken to each other in ages. Bring him with us."

"Vulk don't keel over." If there were others around, he'd have to care about them again, be responsible for their life and death. Without them, he was stronger. More ruthless. Without vulnerability. The way vulk worked best. The whiff of mountain laurel floating off her skin overpowered the crushed leaves underfoot.

"Hans." Briony placed her hand on his stomach and his muscles clenched. She stared up at him. Trusting. Sweet.

He glanced at Juri, back stiff and arms crossed, turned away from them. With a sigh, he squared his shoulders and strode up to the pair. "We'll break at the gorge and have lunch." He turned to Juri. "Get what you need. We aren't waiting around long. Briony pointed out the cockatrices are missing. We need to get across the river fast." Briony joined him and shot him a brief, quick smile.

He'd caved again, but when she looked at him like that, he didn't mind.

9

DENUDED tree trunks lay like matchsticks along the rocky shore at the bottom of the gorge. Briony shifted to find a more comfortable spot on the one she sat on a few paces from where the river swept past, churning with foam. With its reddish bark, Douglas fir ran thick along either side of the river and shaded overhead.

Hans fished around in the pack and handed her hunks of dried meat. "Here. Eat." She and Hans waited for Juri to return from his trip to the pack den. Kyril had left with him, giving her a curt nod as a goodbye.

She was hungry enough to eat about anything, but the meat was good. A touch salty, but hints of dried garlic and pepper gave it a nice added flavor. "Not bad."

"Mine's better." Juri's claws scratched over rocks as he returned, a pack slung on his back. Either the den was close by, or she and Hans took a long time going down the cliff face. Maybe both. The narrow path down the gorge was built for goats, not people. She'd frozen completely, unable to take a single step while teetering on the edge. Surely, she'd die. Then Hans placed his hand on her lower back and tucked her against him. A wave of calm washed over her, and she could move. She hadn't looked down once, and Hans probably had heard her heart racing, it pounded so loudly, but she'd made it down. She knew Hans wouldn't let her fall.

"He protects his recipe like a dragon protects its hoard of gold," Hans said.

Juri shrugged and sat beside them. "It's just as valuable."

She wiped her brow, her appetite gone. "Are there dragons?" Nothing would surprise her.

The corner of Hans's mouth twitched. "We'll have to keep an eye out once we get into the Kuls."

Her eyes narrowed as she studied his face, but Hans began unraveling the canvas and wrapping it around the pack, refusing to look at her. Was he serious? "You know, humans don't go there because of stories about that place causing certain death. Tell me if there are dragons."

He kept his back to her. "You're with me, so you're fine. If you do what I say immediately, no questions, the dragons will stay away."

"Now I know you're full of shit." Her brow remained wrinkled, though. She really wasn't sure. All the stories about the Kuls spoke of awful things that happened to those who traveled there.

"You need to worry about the river first." Now he glanced up. "It's best if you strip for the swim. If you keep your clothes on, they'll weigh you down. And you'll be wet for the rest of the day. Naked is best." His expression read all innocence.

She glanced at Juri. "That's not going to happen."

"Juri won't look at you," Hans said something in Vulk, and Juri shuffled away toward the river, his back to them. Juri had his own pack wrapped in canvas, and he placed it in the water at his feet, where it bobbed at the surface. Briony turned away as he shucked his trousers and dove in.

"Nope. Not going to happen." She bent and began yanking off her boots. "You don't need to see me naked, either."

"I've already seen it."

Briony jerked upward and pointed at him. "No discussing that."

"Fine, I'll keep my eyes on the river. Change behind a tree."

She stripped to everything but her cotton underclothes and paused. Being naked with Hans in the cave, with hazy desire coursing through her veins, was one thing. Here in the light of day, was another. It would be miserable being damp the rest of the day, though.

Hans stood with his back to her, facing the river, his hand outstretched for her clothes.

Fine. She peeled the rest of her clothes off and handed them to him. Hans undressed, put their things in the pack, and waded into the water. "Come on, get on my back." He tossed their pack to Juri, and Juri swam forward.

A screech sounded overhead, and the hairs on her arms lifted. The birds fell silent, and the cry echoed through the trees. She didn't need to look up to know what animal made that sound.

"Hurry," Hans said. "In the water, they can dive at us, and I'll have to roll to swipe at them. Let's go before they get here."

Her pulse skyrocketed, and she clambered over the rocks, wincing as she stepped on sharp stones. She gritted her teeth, wrapped her arms and legs around Hans, and hung on as he leaned forward and sliced into the water.

Her lungs seized at the shock of the ice-cold river. Water crashed against them, the air filled with the rushing noise of its force as it tried to push them downstream, but Hans swam forward in fluid, powerful strokes. Juri already neared the far bank with their packs.

A shadow blocked the suns overhead. Two cockatrices floated above the gorge, their large, feathered wings etched sharply against the blue sky. As Hans described, they had vaguely rooster-like heads, but their bodies were scaled, and a long, forked serpent tail lashed back and forth beneath them. He hadn't mentioned they were much, much larger than a rooster. She'd expected vulture-sized creatures. These were horse-sized.

But they didn't dive. Only watched. She clung to Hans as he made it halfway across.

Another chilling screech and a third cockatrice shot into view from behind them. This one pulling something through the air behind it.

"It's Morana!" Briony had to shout to be heard over the current. "She's after us!" The cockatrice dove and Morana appeared in her open chariot, the walls waist-high, the brass glittering in the sunlight. One hand clutched the front, and the other hovered in the air, green light flowing forth.

Hans increased his pace.

The current reversed, drawing the water back with a sucking sound. A whooshing grew louder and louder. Briony scanned upstream. A wall of water headed straight for them.

"Hans!"

"I see it." His stroke lengthened, but it was too late. The wave crashed over them. Briony spun free and cartwheeled through the water.

The water churned and frothed. Punching deep, the waves pushed her farther down. Briony kicked but went nowhere. The water kept tumbling on top of her.

Which way was up? Her lungs burned. Air. She needed air.

She snagged on a boulder and grappled, her fingers slipping across the smooth stone until they found a crack and dug in. Briony twisted and got her feet under her. The pressure lessened as the current lightened.

Bubbles floated by her face. Upward. Toward air.

She kicked as hard as she could and followed their path, lungs screaming. Light shot through the murk. With one last desperate scissor of her legs, her head broke the surface. She gulped in air and pivoted, scanning for Hans and turning toward the far bank.

He bobbed about twenty feet downriver, swimming toward her, and she turned for the bank and swam as hard as she could toward Juri, standing with the packs on the narrow slip of beach. Her feet touched rocks, and she crawled out of the river, her arms, and legs a numb ache. Juri kept his face averted as he tossed her clothes to her.

Hans scrabbled onto the shore after her. "You alright?"

She nodded and held her clothes before her to shield her nudity.

"Why was I carrying you on my back like a sloth if you're a good swimmer?"

She shivered. "You ordered me to get on your back, remember?" Shading her eyes with her hand, she scanned the sky over the gorge. Clear. The water ran so high now it sloshed at the roots of the trees bordering the bank, and debris whipped along in the rapids. "Where is Morana?"

"Whatever she did to make that wave created a big wind gust," Juri said. "I saw the cockatrices blow backward across the river into the trees. Hard. If we're lucky, they're too injured to fly, and maybe Morana crashed, too."

Hans growled. "She doesn't seem to die easily."

Briony stared at the rushing water. "How are we going to return?" There was no way they'd cross back over to Ulterra.

"It should die back down. We can deal with that later."

She shivered violently and stepped behind some bushes for privacy. She released her hair and wrung it out. She should have cut it ages ago. It reached to the middle of her back, and she usually twisted it up, keeping it out of her face. If she didn't take care, it would turn to frizz and blow up to three times its normal size. She swiped the water from her limbs the best she could with the side of her palm, but it didn't whisk away everything.

Hans shook his arms out, ruffled the hair on his head, and then pulled his trousers on. "That's it? You're dry?"

"My hair is waterproof."

She stared at the hair on his chest. "That's convenient."

"You want help drying off?"

She scanned the sky. "Don't we need to get going?"

"We can take a minute. We're in the Kuls now, and the trees here are thick. If the cockatrice attack, they'll have to dive under the branches, bringing them close enough for me to drag them to the ground. Morana might risk it, but those cockatrice won't come close to a vulk." He frowned. "You're cold all the time. I don't like it."

She shivered so hard that her teeth rattled. "I'm not cold all the time, and it's no joy for me either."

"In one minute, I can have you dry and warm."

She didn't want to tug her clothes on over her damp skin, and the memory of his hands roaming her body flashed before her. Skilled, purposeful, *warm* hands she'd enjoyed. "Fine."

He walked around the bushes and dropped to one knee in front of her. She still clutched her clothes in front of her, and he reached around them to rub her back and arms in quick circles. Water dripped down her neck, and he leaned forward and chased it with his tongue.

"Oh." She wobbled, and her toes curled into the rocky soil. "Your tongue is really warm."

Water still glistened on her skin, and he used the tip of his tongue to lap it away. First along the flare of her collarbones, then in a slow trail up her neck. All the while rubbing his hands down her legs and back, rubbing the warmth back into her limbs.

Her lips parted on a sigh as he trailed up the front of her throat. He pulled back, studying her face, and brought her hands to his mouth. He nibbled along her fingers and then moved downward, licking the water away from her wrist and arm. As she watched him repeat the action with her other arm, she stopped shivering.

He dropped her hands, and she reached forward to brush his cheek.

Hans stood abruptly, and her hand fell to her side. "We should go now. I think you're dry enough to get your clothes on." He turned away and tossed the pack on his back.

Juri said something in Vulk and glanced her way. She quickly slipped into her underthings, pulled her breeches, socks, and shirt on, then laced her boots up in short, jerky motions. Why did they have to speak their secret language? She was part of this journey and wanted to know what was happening.

Scowling, she stomped to join them, and the three walked down the bank. She tripped over a rock, and Hans grabbed the back of her breeches, catching her right before she sprawled flat on her face.

He growled. "If you're tired, I'll carry you."

"I'm fine." She kicked a rock.

He pointed to his right. "Walk over there. It's flatter."

Her scowl deepened. "I like walking here. Stop telling me what to do."

Juri rumbled out a deep laugh. "He's the Alpha, which means he's the boss. He tells people what to do. It's sort of his thing."

Her step hitched. "What do you mean, he's the Alpha?"

Hans growled again. "He doesn't mean anything. You should focus on walking."

Juri's smile faded, and he turned his face away, the muscle of his jaw jumping. "The path out of the gorge is over here." Back stiff, he loped up a staircase cut roughly into the cliff side.

Annoyance shot from Hans so strongly that the bond in her chest twinged. What was that about?

Hans remained behind her, probably waiting for her to

stumble again, so she stomped so hard on each step the thud echoed in the narrow chasm. Other than insects and birds, it was the only noise.

As they neared the top, Briony studied the stone stairs cut out from the cliff beneath them. Based on the scat and overgrowth, only the local wildlife used it now, but someone took the time to create this once. A pale milky stone, about as large as her fist and perfectly round, lay in front of her boot. It winked as a polished contrast to the gritty slate. "Look at this stone."

"It's a moonstone. If you stop to look at everything in the Kuls, we might reach Baba Yaga next year." His growly, grumpy tone. Ever since Juri made the Alpha comment, Hans's mood had shifted. What did Juri mean? He hadn't said Hans was *an* Alpha; he'd said he was *the* Alpha, and now Hans was in major snarl mode.

"What's a moonstone?"

He sighed. "It's a gemstone that shines at night. Many think it's because they reflect the moon's light, but they shine even during storms when the moons are behind a cloud. You can use moonstones to light a path if you know where to collect them."

"Do you know where to find them?"

He gave her an icy glare. "Of course. Are your questions finished for the day? How do you have so many?"

As they caught up to Juri, waiting at the top of the stairs, she poked his arm. "You should put those stones in your den. Then it wouldn't be so dark in there all the time."

Juri's mouth dropped open. "*She* was in your den? I saw you in the clearing with her, but—" He shook his head then spoke directly to Briony. "Getting an invitation to a vulk's home is a high honor. Vulk dens are masterpieces, and suggesting improvements is like slapping him in the face. If you were another vulk, his claws would be at your throat."

She halted. "Masterpieces?" With a quick glance at Hans,

she cleared her throat. "I mean, there was some nice stonework on the floor, but it was a bit dark, so I probably didn't see it fully to appreciate it. Sorry."

"You haven't finished your den?" Juri spoke quietly, but the surprise still carried through.

"She doesn't know what she's talking about."

Annoyance shot through her. "It definitely looked unfinished. The walls weren't smooth."

Juri stared at Hans. "It's been over a century since you started working on it."

Hans walked past them without replying.

She was curious what Juri meant by over a century, but she wasn't about to ask Hans another question in his grumpy mood. And besides, they'd reached the crest of the gorge and stepped off the stairs.

The Kuls spread out before them. A dense canopy stretched overhead, so thick the sky wasn't visible. This was why it hadn't appeared that the sun penetrated this side of the river, and Hans said the cockatrice would have trouble attacking them.

The trees weren't a kind she'd seen anywhere else in Ulterra. The leaves blazed a deep green with a center stem of plum. The same rich plum color peeked out in the notches and crooks of the smooth bark. Each leaf was wider than even Hans's huge hand, and as they brushed against each other in a breeze she didn't feel, they chimed instead of rustled.

"What are these trees?" she asked Juri.

"A type of rowan."

She reached out to stroke the bark of one, and he grabbed her wrist. "Be careful. These trees are sentient, in their own way."

Hans bared his teeth. "Stay at my side." Another shot of irritation rippled over her, and her eyes narrowed. That face wouldn't get him anywhere.

Juri dropped her wrist, and she turned her back to them

both. "I can walk and avoid touching trees." There wasn't a path, but there was a way through the trees where the underbrush was clear, and that was how they proceeded. She shuffled closer to Juri. "What do you mean, sentient?" She wanted to speak to the non-snarling vulk. Even though the urge to run her hands up Hans's back and soothe him was so strong it made her fingers twitch, she wasn't dealing with his mercurial mood. Let him walk alone.

"You should only take the wood of a rowan if the tree has fallen because of natural causes or dropped a branch. Otherwise, you may be cursed."

"How?"

"Have you heard the tale of the Dark King and the thief?" She shook her head; she'd never read that in any of her fairy tale books.

As they trudged, Juri told her the tale, his voice changing to a low, melodic tone. She forgot where she was and what she was doing, gasping at the tense parts, laughing when his pitch altered to describe the plucky thief. She was so absorbed that the ache in the soles of her feet and the pinch in her calves dropped away. In the end, when the Dark King and the thief both sacrificed everything to defeat the curse of the Kuls, her eyes filled with tears.

Kyril was right. Juri was a bard.

By the time Juri finished his story, the light was fading fast, and the gloom of twilight swallowed up the path. They set the tents up in no time, had a fire roaring, and she'd removed her undergarments, washed them in the small trickle of a stream nearby, and hung them up to dry. It felt oddly intimate with only her shirt and breeches on. Juri disappeared and returned with two fat turkeys slung over his shoulder, and she helped him pluck them.

There was a brief argument about eating them raw—a violent no from her—and Hans created a spit for roasting. Sitting cross-legged and as close to the fire as she could without bursting into flames, her lids grew heavy. She stared at the fire instead of the two vulk across from her. All she wanted was food and to collapse into bed.

"How old are you?" Juri asked her.

"It's rude to ask someone their age."

Juri's brows shot up. "Not for a vulk. We wear our age proudly."

"What's it like living forever?"

Juri cocked his head. "Humans live a long time, too."

She guffawed. "Humans live to one hundred or so if they're lucky."

For the first time, Juri appeared flustered. "Not all the time. Up north where I live, there's a fishing village near me where a mix of peltwalkers, magicwielders, and humans live together." He bent his head and used a stick to poke at the fire. "There's a human female that I know doesn't have any pelt-walker or magicwielder blood who looks about the same age as you, but I know she's one hundred and eighty-six years old. The same age I am." He jerked his chin towards Hans. "The same age as both of us. We were born a few months apart."

Hans cocked his head. "This female lives in Ryba?"

Juri still studied the fire. "Yeah."

Briony looked from one vulk to the other. Juri fidgeted in his seat, and Hans's brows had risen. "Is there something the matter with Ryba?" she asked.

"It's where he grew up before becoming a vulk." Hans studied Juri. "You return and watch this human so closely you know her exact age?"

Juri still hadn't looked up. "I don't enter the village when I return to see my mother, but yeah, I look for the human to see how she's doing sometimes. I knew her from ... before. You know, before I joined the pack. She has her own boat and fishes with the larger fleets. And she's the only one that harvests the oysters on the good beds north of the town. She's fiercely territorial of them, I've seen her chase off others when they get too close." Sounded like Juri watched her more often than sometimes.

He whacked a burning log with his stick. "She should be first choice for a mate, yet she's always alone." His gaze met Briony's. "Do you have a mate?"

Hans growled, and his eyes glinted red. "That's a good question."

She glared at him. "No." How could he ask that? If she'd had a husband, she wouldn't have stayed for his attentions in the cave. And she certainly wouldn't be walking the Kuls with him.

"Why not?"

Her chin rose. "I'm not discussing this with you."

His lip rose over his eyetooth. "Why?"

"You didn't want to answer my questions earlier, and I don't feel like answering yours now."

Juri's eyes widened, and he ducked his head, but she thought he smiled. "She's not afraid of you."

Hans grunted.

Silence spread like a fourth companion, blanketing the rest of their time at the campfire until Briony stood. "I'm going to bed." She didn't wait for a response.

Briony kicked off her boots, opened the tent flap, and yawned. The waxed leather tent stretched wider and far longer than human tent so a vulk could stretch out flat. Inside, she could stand without her head hitting the top. Folded over one pallet on the ground lay the quilt. When did he pack that? That was ... considerate. A slight tug of warmth bloomed in her chest. She pulled it over her and fell instantly asleep.

10

"HEY, get up. Something's wrong with Hans."

Briony sat up, and it was all shadow. Her heart hammered as it took her a moment to remember where she was. A sliver of light shone where Juri cracked the tent flap.

She whipped the quilt off her legs. "What are you talking about?"

Juri held the flap open for her. "I can't wake him for his watch."

Pain sizzled in her chest so sharply she lost her breath. His pain. Kicking her boots out of the way, she ran to where Hans lay on his side by the fire. He twitched, his hair matting to his skin as sweat coated him. Icy fear slid down her spine. "We need to roll him. He's lying on the side I need to touch."

"Vulk don't sweat like this." Juri turned Hans to his back.

Damn fool vulk. She'd been tired and annoyed and hadn't asked about the poison, and he'd said nothing, of course. She pressed her hands over the wound, which was worse than yesterday. The worm—the poison—had malice. An intention. It held Hans in a weakened state, unable to fight, unable to move as it spread through his system.

Thank heavens it was still nighttime. She bit her lip so

hard she tasted blood. Time lost all meaning, and a cold sweat slicked her skin. As she removed the tendrils burrowing through him, she grew colder. So cold. Spots danced across her vision, and her hands shook, but she pushed on. Exhaustion rolled over her. It was difficult to concentrate, difficult to leach off the last few remnants.

There. She let out a breath she didn't know she'd been holding. Once again, she'd beaten it back until all that remained was a small germ-like husk, but it wasn't gone for good. It would continue to spread through Hans.

She slumped forward and put her hands on his chest. He still burned with fever, and his heat warmed her.

"He looks a little better," Juri said.

She jumped; she'd forgotten about Juri. "He's feverish. I've subdued the poison, but his body is still fighting it." As she spoke, her words slurred together.

"What poison?"

She wiped her brow and sat back. Her vision was returning to normal, and she wasn't shaking as hard. She described what the necromancer did in the cave and the poison stuck inside Hans.

Juri's jaw dropped. "Hans hasn't been weak a day in his life and never depends on anyone but himself. Needing your help must be torture."

After slightly hesitating, she ran her fingers over Hans's sharp cheekbone. Watching Hans lie still was wrong. He was virile and strong. Tension needled between her shoulder blades. It clawed and scratched like abrasive wool. *Get him back on his feet.*

Hans remained asleep, but he bared his teeth slightly, wrinkling his nose as her fingers grazed his face. His hands came off his chest and cradled her arm. With a soft, gentle motion, he rubbed her wrist.

"What's he doing?"

Juri's brow wrinkled, and he didn't answer.

Briony wiggled her arm free and stood with a wobble. "I'll keep him comfortable and work on his fever. I can keep watch if you want?"

He studied her. "Keep the fire high and stay within its light. It will keep most unfriendly beasts away, but there are still things prowling these woods that won't hesitate to kill you. If the forest goes silent or you hear anything strange, yell for me." His brow raised. "If something happens to Hans or me, you're as good as dead, so keep a good lookout."

Briony waved him off, and he turned and shuffled into his tent.

The small stream they'd used to cook and fill their canteens trickled close enough that it lay within the fire's light, so she rooted around in their pack until she found a scrap of fabric and wetted it.

She laid it on Hans's neck and lingered, her gaze drifting over his chest and torso. It was the first time she could study Hans up close. As well as touch him wherever she wanted.

With only the lightest stroke of her fingertips, she ran her hands up his chest. He was so ... massive. If he came to her tiny apartment above the tavern, the top of his head would hit the upper doorframe, and he'd have to slip sideways to get his shoulders through.

She shook her head. Hans wasn't coming to her tiny apartment.

Bolder, she petted his chest again. After all, she was a healer, and she was checking his breathing. That's all.

His chest rose and fell in smooth, regular movements. Being this close to him, she wanted to follow her hands up his chest with her entire body and coat herself in his pine scent with its wild, fierce edge.

As his fever faded, the heat of his skin cooled. But hers started to burn. What was a chill from using her magic rapidly turning to heat. No man warmed her inside like this. Well, Hans wasn't a man. Or awake. Licks of heat danced over her skin. An aching hunger throbbed between her legs. She bit back a moan.

There was no more serum swirling inside her, but this couldn't be natural, could it? The rune bound them together and created this attraction, but they weren't really destined. There was no future for them.

Her stomach twisted, and she sat back. Baba Yaga would confirm all this was fake when they met her. Probably even know how to release their bond. She pressed her lips together and squared her shoulders. Treat him like a patient. Act professional.

Mumbling something she couldn't understand, Hans opened his eyes. His gaze was unfocused, his eyes glassy until they found her. His arms snaked up and wrapped around her waist, hauling her on top of him, so her head tucked right above his heart.

"Hey!" She flailed, trying to roll away, but he cradled her against him. Firmly, but gently. "You need to let me go."

He purred. That same sultry rumble from the cave.

"Oh." She buried her face in his chest and, for a second, indulged her need to get closer and nestled. That purr was divine, and she wanted to live in it. Have it surround her always. The thrum got louder. Feverish Hans liked her response.

He wasn't awake and had no clue what he was doing, but oh, this was nice. He encircled her, warmed her, and she was safe. And her head fit perfectly on his chest where she could hear the beating of his heart.

She curled her hands in the sprinkle of fur on his chest, and peace washed over her.

He needed to let her back up. She was supposed to take care of him and keep watch. Right now, a dragon could crash into camp, and she wouldn't notice. Her lids grew heavy. Maybe a few more minutes. No one had ever cradled her like this. Not her parents. Definitely not her aunt. And not her few lovers. For once, someone held her like he treasured her.

She sighed and relaxed, her lids fluttering. He'd release her in a moment and never know this happened.

HANS WOKE AND GROANED. Had he battled a troll? Every muscle felt pummeled to shit. He lay on his back, and his chest was heavy. He glanced down. Briony sprawled on top of him, clasped tightly in his arms, asleep, while the fire sputtered. He held her like she was his. As if anyone who tried to take her from him would die. A kernel of pleasure unfurled. Briony was comfortable enough to sleep on him. Out of every man and every immortal in Ulterra, she lay with *him*.

Why were they out by the fire, though? Flashes of fevered dreams and aching muscles flickered.

Maybe he should wake her and ask, but as he watched her sleeping, noticed the way her long lashes dusted her cheek, how her perfect lips were a dusky pink, he didn't want to. For the first time in his life, he envied the peltwalkers' ability to shift into human form. What would it be like to kiss her and taste those lips? His blunt muzzle wasn't made for kissing. He could always use his tongue, but he wanted to seal his mouth on hers.

She burrowed her face into his chest and glued herself to him, her leg slipping between his, rubbing awfully close to ...

He groaned as his cock leaped to attention, more painfully hard than he'd ever felt it. His heart pounded, and he stared at her neck. He wanted to nibble a line up the delicate curve to wake her. When awake, she'd get on her stomach and part her legs for him, eager for him to strip her and ...

Uit! This was ridiculous. He fisted his hands until his palms stung. He was an Alpha—he had control. No. Not an Alpha, only Hans.

All vulk gained control as they aged, but anger and lust still sparked blood madness. Not for him, though. He was icy calm. Always. He was famous for it. That was why even in the cave, her arousal hadn't driven him into a maddened rut.

He wasn't rutting right now. The frenzied haze of the cave wasn't there. Yet still, every pulse of his heart whispered to *claim her. Take her.* Not only to make her body sing with pleasure but something deeper. Something he didn't understand.

No. That would never happen. Vulk didn't take a mate. Ever. It was impossible. He could give her nothing. It was verboten to share the secrets of the vulk. He couldn't tell her why the vulk always walked alone. It was best if he kept her at a distance.

His arms tightened, and he nestled her closer.

BIRDS CALLED, loud and insistent as they flitted through the forest for their morning feast. A gust of wind puffed against the leather side of the tent behind them, and it flapped once, hitting the ground with a small slap. He roused and stretched, Briony still clinging to him like a burr. What was the best way to wake her? Leaning forward, he nuzzled below her jaw. "Wake up."

She moaned, rubbed against him, and arousal plumed into the air.

Inside his head, he swore violently. There was no way she was awake. She had to be dreaming. His eyes narrowed. What if she dreamed of someone else? She'd said she had no mate, but perhaps a male courted her. She hadn't answered his questions last night.

A small whimper and her thigh skated over his cock. He thickened further, and his cock throbbed, practically ripping through his trousers.

Briony's head rose off his chest, and her eyes opened to meet his gaze directly. Her hair fell free of its restraint and tumbled over her shoulders. It was much longer than he'd expected, well down her back. He ran the ends through his fingers

"Oh, no." She glanced around. "I was supposed to keep watch, not fall asleep. Don't tell Juri."

"What happened last night?" he asked. It came out gruff. Not how he meant it to.

Her eyes narrowed. "You didn't tell me the poison was bothering you. It was much worse than before, and it took you under. I had to beat it back last night, and from now on, I check you regularly whether or not you like it." She jutted her chin out as if daring him to argue.

"Fine." He'd let her lay her hands on him whenever she wanted. Maybe she'd have to sleep on him again.

"Oh." She blinked. "Good."

"Is snoozing on top of patients a normal healing practice for humans?"

She huffed and pushed off his chest to sit up, a line forming between her brows. "I think we should get you to Baba Yaga fast. Whatever is left from the necromancer spell is getting worse. How long will it take to get to Baba Yaga?"

"Walking at your speed, it'll take about seven days, but if you can push it and walk long hours, including some at night, we can make it in six." She half straddled him, his hands still at her waist, but she hadn't tried to wriggle away. It seemed perfectly natural to have a conversation with her on top of him.

She nodded. "I can walk faster."

"Walk next to me. Not Juri."

An angry glare. "Juri told me stories. Are *you* going to do that?"

The same seething anger that sent his temper haywire yesterday twisted through him. Every moment she'd paid attention to Juri, watched Juri raptly with parted lips, he'd wanted to tear a tree out by its roots and throw it as far as he could.

"I don't tell stories." He sat up and seated her in front of him, close enough that their legs still touched. "But I'll let you ask as many questions as you want. And I'll answer."

"Oh, you mean have a conversation like normal people do?" She played with her hair, and her breasts quivered, reminding him she wore nothing under her shirt. She raised a brow. "What if I want to ask questions about you? Or the vulk?"

"I may not answer all of them." His lip curled upward a fraction. "But if I do, you have to answer my questions. No more saying it isn't any of my business." Now, he'd find out everything about her.

Briony twisted her hair back into a knot. "No grumps. No more growling and snarling."

"Fine."

Briony paused, her hands still in her hair, and studied him. "All right, I'll walk next to you. Are you jealous I talked to Juri instead of you?"

He stood. "That's absurd. Vulk don't get jealous." Frowning, Hans walked to their tent to pack it away.

As he broke down camp with Juri, her words kept replaying. *Are you jealous?* As Briony packed up across camp, he turned to Juri and asked in Vulk, "Do you think I acted jealous yesterday?"

Juri coughed and ran his hand over his face. "I thought you were going to hit me when I touched her wrist. And last night, when you were out of it, you rubbed the same wrist, putting your scent over mine. She didn't know what you were doing, but I did. A bit possessive, I'd say." Juri glanced at Briony, who kicked dirt over the fire. "She told me about the poison. How did she heal you? What's going on between you two?"

"I should have told you about the poison."

Juri paused as he tightened the straps on his backpack and glanced up, his brows raised in surprise.

Hans shrugged. "I don't know how she heals me. I don't think she does either. She can just ... heal."

"Is she really a human?"

Briony chose that moment to walk over. She held out the quilt rolled into a tube. "Here you go. To put in the pack." Her cheeks flushed. "Thank you for bringing this." She hadn't folded it up correctly for packing, but she'd tried. He took it and nodded.

Juri reached out and fingered the corner of the quilt. A grin broke across his face. "Your mother."

Per vulk law, life began the first day they turned into their true form. Vulk considered their transformation their actual birth, and everything before that moment, their twenty years as a human, was supposed to be forgotten. They were even supposed to walk away from their families.

Well, Hans had never been one to follow the rules.

His mother was his *mother*. Always. Even as a vulk, and during these past years, when he barely stirred from his den, he still saw her. Comforted her in what small ways he could. Not that he was capable of much.

"I guessed you and Zann still visited her. I knew I couldn't be the only one who still went back home. Zann used to say —" Juri's grin slipped, and he ducked his head. "Sorry Hans." He grabbed his pack and shuffled into the woods.

He stood frozen, the quilt slipping from his hands. Briony caught it and stuffed it into the pack. "Who's Zann?"

Zann. He hadn't heard his brother's name aloud in years. "He's dead." He pivoted away, unseeing, and it was like someone else performed the last few tasks at camp, and he watched from afar. Detached.

"Here." Briony handed him food wrapped in some cloth. "Breakfast."

"I'm fine."

"No, you aren't." Her chin thrust forward, and she ripped off a hunk of turkey meat and waved it in front of his mouth. "I'm your doctor, and you need to eat."

"Are you ordering a vulk around?"

She took a step closer. "I'm *suggesting* what I know to be best."

The corner of his mouth twitched, and mountain laurel swirled in the air. He brought his hands up to cradle the hand holding the food, his massive claw-tipped fingers obscene against her delicate skin, and he bent his head to pluck the bite from her fingers.

Her eyes widened, and her lips parted. The pulse under his fingertips jumped, but he knew it wasn't from fear. Briony didn't fear him.

Testing, he stroked his thumb up the paper-thin skin of her inner wrist. Her pulse skittered.

"I think you can feed yourself the rest." Her voice was breathy and strange, but she wasn't tugging to get away.

"True. But I like it better when you do it." Another stroke with his thumb, and this time her pupils flared. "Perhaps I need to return the favor." He'd feed her all her favorite things and get to brush her lips each time he brought his hand to her mouth.

A line creased Briony's brows. "That seems intimate. Like courting."

"Vulk don't court." He said it automatically, and the hazy expression dropped from her face. She slipped her hand free from his and stepped back.

She was right. Offering her food would be intimate. Especially since he'd be holding her while he fed her. "Wooing is a human thing," he said. "Although peltwalkers do it too. I think it's a waste of time."

Briony tossed her head and fastened the toggles on her coat. "Of course, you do."

He shouldered their pack. "Seemed like a lot of chasing,

and once they caught the person they wanted, they moved on to another. Maybe it's different with humans." The boys he'd grown up with, especially after they reached maturity, spent most of their time pursuing girls. He and his brother had other interests. Maybe it was being vulk and not having a future with the wolf clan, but it wasn't a priority to bed females.

An odd expression crossed her face. "No, it's similar."

"Real courtship should be different." He shrugged. "Not a chase, but showing the other person they have your complete focus. That all you want is them." His brows rose. "After she's decided I'm the one, I'd chase her. For real. Through the forest. And when I caught her, I wouldn't let go."

Briony swallowed hard, her delicate throat flexing. She gestured at the food still in his hand. "Well, if you invite a girl into your den and you want to hand feed her, you may want to consider stocking your kitchen with more than tiny bones and raw meat. It may be tough for a vulk to believe, but non-vulk like other foods than meat."

The corner of his mouth twitched. "I was kidding when I offered you that. I know what humans eat."

She shook her head. "No one will ever know when you're kidding. You have one face. Snarly."

The urge to laugh bubbled up, but he stifled it. "Come on. Juri's far ahead by now. We have to catch up if we want to cover a lot of ground today."

"You still have to answer my questions. You agreed."

He groaned, but really, a frisson of excitement rolled through him. She was so unexpected, and he was looking forward to her questions.

11

THE ROWAN TREES surrounding the path grew increasingly gnarled. While all the trees had a watchfulness in the Kuls, now it felt like unfriendly gazes pressed on her. Bird cries rang out, none of them familiar, and she never caught sight of them. Hazelnut bushes dotted between the trees, and their dropped nuts crunched underfoot. The forest felt empty, but she knew it wasn't. She'd catch movement out of the corner of her eye, but when she turned to look—nothing.

Briony turned her head. "Are the rowans the only trees in the Kuls? I haven't seen any others."

A gray squirrel, one of the few animals she'd seen, dug a small hole in the trail ahead of them, working to bury his stash. When they approached, the squirrel glanced up and scolded Hans shrilly.

Hans's gaze snapped to the ground with a growl. "What the hell?" He swooped in a black blur.

"No! Don't kill it!"

Hans turned, and the squirrel's head stuck out of the top of his hand. "Are you serious? A dead squirrel is the only good squirrel."

"No way! Squirrels are cute!"

With a massive sigh and a pained grimace, he knelt and let it go. The squirrel ran up the closest tree and clung to it, wailing loudly about its brush with death.

"You eat them?" she asked.

"Of course."

"But they have sweet little ears and bushy tails."

"This time of year, they also have a nice nutty flavor." The corner of his mouth twitched.

She'd noticed that twitch and had suspicions about it. Especially since whenever he did it, a warm bloom filled her chest from his side of the bond.

"Next squirrel that doesn't fear me," Hans ran a claw across his throat, "is a goner."

Better hope no more squirrels made stupid decisions. She smiled and pointed at the forest. "Time to answer my questions. Why only the one type of tree?"

"We're in the wilds of the Kuls, and here the rowan reigns. Closer to Baba Yaga, in the bog, you'll see others, and up in vae territory, there are many varieties of trees. Some like those in the rest of Ulterra, and some you won't find anywhere else."

"Plants too?"

"Yes. They have a flower that, when it blooms, is bigger than your head." He scowled and glanced away as if embarrassed he'd said that.

She stepped closer, their arms brushing against each other. "That must be beautiful. What are some of their other flowers?"

"Well, there are these tiny plants all over vae land. Only about this big." He held up his hand and showed her a span between his thumb and forefinger of a couple of inches. "They only bloom every twenty or thirty years. It's unpredictable. When they do, everywhere you look is a carpet of pink, and the air fills with golden pollen. The vae stop everything and hold a sacred festival to celebrate them."

"You've seen that?"

He nodded. "Once." He glanced down at her. "Why the interest in plants?"

"To raise extra money, I started raising krasa flowers. The surgery paid a small fortune to buy a salve made from their pods—it's great for burns and scars—and I figured, why not make it myself? Well, it works so well it smooths wrinkles away, too. Older women in town buy it and use it like crazy." She mimed smoothing the product over her face.

He stared at her. "Humans smear things on their faces?"

She ignored his question with a wave of her hand. How would she explain skincare to a vulk? "No one knows where the seeds originally came from, and few people can get them to grow. Maybe they're vae flowers?"

To raise a krasa plant, she nursed them indoors by the fire for weeks when they were tiny seeds in their pots. Then, as sproutlings, she treated them like babies, keeping them at the window and ensuring they luxuriated in warmth until they were large enough to be planted in the small patch of ground behind the tavern. If even a hint—a shiver—of frost or chill whispered over their delicate leaves while they were young, they wouldn't produce their exquisite flowers three months later. The tiny pods produced by those flowers were worth their weight in gold. Literally.

"Why do you want extra money?"

Her face grew hot, and she watched the trail ahead intently. "I want to leave Vieska. It isn't the place for me."

"Why?"

She explained the entrenched views of her village and the value they placed on land and old, established families. And how a newcomer didn't fit in easily.

He growled. "Perhaps I should remind the Vieskans why I'm the Shadow of Death. In other parts of Ulterra, your healing gifts would be treasured. That and your chicken-fighting skills."

She laughed. The first time she'd laughed since ... when?

"Oh, sure. I'd become famous for beating all the boys and be single forever. The male ego just loves being beaten."

His lips twitched. "You might be right. A vulk never allows himself to be defeated. But I might pretend to let you win."

"Oh really? Why's that?"

He gazed at her, and her breath hitched. His stare was intense. Heated. "If it made you smile. Besides, after every loss, I'd challenge you to fight me again the next day. That way, I'd see you all the time."

"Crafty." Her cheeks warmed, and she ducked her head.

They walked silently for a while, her mind drifting back to the flowers. All those pretty plants, and they weren't going into vae territory. "Why don't you get along with the vae? What are they like?"

"They sit around and play music instead of fighting, and they speak in riddles a lot. And the king of the vae, Caladin, and I ... had an altercation."

Briony halted mid-step. "Wait a minute. You met royalty, and you fought him?"

"He was only a princeling then."

She shook her head. "So? I mean, not everyone meets a future *king,* and you scrapped with him!"

Hans stared at her like she was daft. "Is this king thing supposed to matter?"

"Are you nuts? If I met the king of Rohant and hit him, he'd have his guards kill me instantly."

Hans growled. "I'd kill your king and all the guards before they touched you. Hit him all you want."

Briony dropped her gaze to the ground again, feeling warm all over. No one had ever defended her. "Oh."

"Now, I answered a personal question, so you must answer one of mine." Briony almost rolled her eyes at his tone. Hans had two ways of speaking. An imperial command or a bossy demand. There was also his soft, crooning voice when he held her close, but she rarely heard it. That one she craved.

"Go ahead."

"Why no mate?"

The question from last night. "Oh, well, I already told you about Vieska. I can't bring anything to a marriage, so I have no value. Although the town butcher, Ivan, seems interested right now."

His eyes glinted red. "Are you going to choose him?"

She shrugged. "I could stop working for the doctor, which would be nice. But I want something ... more." There was no way she was going to tell him she wanted real love. The kind that would both consume her and hold her close. If it existed, she wanted to find it, but based on her experience, she didn't think it did. "Next question."

"Tell me about working for this doctor." Briony explained about being first his apprentice and now his assistant.

"You chose this work?"

She studied the ground. "Not exactly. It's what I have to do," she said, expecting him to press and ask further questions. Ones she didn't want to talk about as she strolled many miles away from the surgery.

"The vulk have things they must do too."

They walked in silence for a stretch until he suddenly asked, "After I freed you in the cave, you stayed. Do you really believe it's because of drinking the serum?"

Her step hiccuped, and she stumbled. Hans reached out, his arm a blur, and steadied her. "Are we walking too fast? I *will* carry you today if you trip."

She shook her head. No, she just hadn't expected that question. It was the same one she kept asking herself. The memory of his presence in the cave washed over her. How she'd wanted to touch him, not flee. The way every part of her yearned for him. Only him.

"I want to know why you stayed." Now it was his soft,

silky voice. The one that was like a caress. They'd both stopped walking, and she hadn't noticed him closing the distance between them until he almost brushed against her.

"I liked your smell." She blurted it out and clapped her hand over her mouth.

"Did you?" He purred the words. "Do you still?"

"It's the only appealing thing about you." Did a vulk understand teasing?

Hans stepped closer and bent to whisper against her ear. "That's not true. You're supposed to answer my questions truthfully."

Briony's breath hitched, and she wanted to touch him, but she kept her hands at her sides. "You're right. I like how warm you are, too. Lying on you last night, you were like an oven even after the fever left. It was pleasant."

He growled, but it wasn't his angry one; it was a chiding one. Three days with him, and she'd already learned the nuances of his growls. His mouth brushed her neck. "I could point out the things I did in the cave that you also found *appealing*. Some of them I can perform right here."

She shivered. "That's probably a bad idea." But even to her ears, she didn't sound convincing.

The underbrush rustled, and Juri reappeared. "Why are you so slow? We need to move faster. The weather's turning."

12

HANS'S FUR stuck to his skin. Juri was right. The weather had turned for the worse and wasn't showing signs of improving. They'd finally reached the bog after a slog of six days with no break from the unceasing wet. Briony never complained, but they weren't able to talk much again because during the day, the rush of rainfall through the leaves made hearing difficult, and at night she was so exhausted from their increased pace that she hurried to bed after dinner.

The biting rain rolled through the forest, dripping from the leaves to plop into the sludgy murk of the bog pond. No ripples waved across its surface. No bubbles.

The rowan trees crouched like fat, potbellied men, their squat trunks above the bog, their roots burrowing into the water. Fog wove around them. Bright flashes of light green moss trailed from high in the canopy to dip below the motionless surface. Tiny lizards with long tails scuttled up and down and dove into the water with a plop, leaving no ripples in their wake as the three of them stepped onto the long, matted grass. A moonstone flashed under their feet; its pale light visible through the brown mire.

He tucked Briony under his arm. "Stay close and step

where I step. A wrong move here and the bog will keep you." He pointed at a thicket of vines a few steps from the path. One of its tendrils wrapped around the grayish lump of a dead swamp rat, and the stench of death wafted over them, overpowering the rot burping up underfoot. Unlike the rest of the bog, where moss or tall rush grasses blanketed everything, nothing grew near this. "It's feeding, so it won't bother us."

"What is that?"

As they stepped past, the vines rose from the ground as the fat bulb they attached to, covered in mud, rose from the ground. The vines twitched, and a crack split open horizontally, revealing a red, cavernous mouth with flat, grinding teeth, and it closed around half of the gray carcass and sucked. Muck squelched, and the mouth disappeared below again.

Briony squeaked and flattened against him. "I thought that was a plant!"

"No. It's a jedak. It's a sort of … amphibian, maybe? Kind of like giant frogs with no legs. It can't move much. Those vine things are its arms. Or hair." He shrugged. "A few of them live in here. Hopefully, that's the only one near the path."

A red flush blotched Briony's cheeks, and her hair stuck to her brow and temples from the rain. Or sweat. They'd pushed hard today, maybe too hard for her. Without asking, he picked her up. "I'll carry you. It's safer."

When she didn't argue, he knew she was tired or nervous. Not scared enough to create the flutter in his chest again, but enough that she didn't mind him carrying her.

It was the first chance he'd had to touch her in days. He curled her close and bit back a purr. She wrapped her arms around his neck, and he wobbled when her fingers brushed his nape. It was soothing and distracting, and if she kept it up, he'd topple into the bog, and they'd risk death mired in the muck.

There was no way he'd tell her to stop.

"What else lives in here?" Her fingers trailed up his neck

again. "One problem with carrying me is that it's easier for me to ask questions. You should think about that before you pick me up again."

He rubbed his jaw over the top of her head. "There are gloson in here. They look like wild boar but stand about ten feet at the shoulder. Their size means they can walk through here without getting stuck. They have a dull blue ridge on their backs. Except for the male. This time of year, it's breeding season, and his will be bright blue."

"What a showoff."

One corner of his lips twitched. "At least he'll be too busy finding his harem to bother us right now. They can be territorial even with a vulk."

Juri was a few paces ahead, and he looked back over his shoulder. "Good eating. Back years ago, I came to the deep Kuls to stalk this massive male. He even had a name by that point—Big Bluey. That bastard was so mean he didn't have any ladies willing to put up with him."

"Huh, a grumpy male." Briony stroked again. "Sounds familiar."

Hans chuffed and nipped her neck. Her fingers tightened, and she gasped.

He tucked her back in place like nothing happened. "As a tracker, Juri's the best hunter alive."

Juri shrugged, his pack sliding up and down. "I don't always hunt to kill. Sometimes finding rare or unknown animals is enough of a thrill. And it usually turns into a good story."

"What about Bluey?"

"Well—" Juri jerked to a halt, his hackles rising. "The bog waters are shifting. They're covering where we need to step."

Above the fetid stench of the bog, an ill breeze plumed with the fog, and Hans's hackles rose. The bog never made it easy on visitors. One earned the right to tread here or died. "Faster."

He sprang after Juri and leaped from one platform of matted grass to the next. There was still a distance before they reached the sturdy ground of Baba Yaga's clearing.

Wet grass tore beneath his hind claws as he dug in. The water rose, seeping over their toes. Only a motionless pool of bog stretched ahead of them, no ripples, no bubbles, with spiky tips of grass poking up like shards and decrepit, dead branches twisting toward the canopy as if begging for their brethren overhead to rescue them from their demise. No path showed any longer.

"I don't know where the next step is," Juri said.

Shit. A century had passed since he'd come this way, and he didn't remember the path either. Briony's heart pounded against his own chest. He turned to retreat and froze.

The water covered the path back, too.

What the hell did this place think it was doing? Trying to trap *him*? This bog knew him. In the past, he'd tread over every bit of the Kuls, even the wildest woods in the south. He was Hans Volak. He was a vulk whose blood lay entwined in the ancient vulk roads. Nothing barred him from them.

He perched Briony on the highest clump of grass between him and Juri. "Cover your ears."

Her eyes widened, but she clapped her hands over her ears. He peered through the brown murk at his feet and searched. The sludge closed around his ankles in thick, mucous-like glops. The dim white light may be almost lost, but it was still there.

He roared. Not a howl—he'd howled for days after Zann died and hadn't howled since.

A light twinkled below him. He drove his hand into the water and clutched the moonstone. His vision turned red, and he roared again. Under his palm, the moonstone warmed, its light spreading. The fog curled back on itself, and the mud bubbled. Other moonstone broke through the mud and lit halos of warm white light along the path ahead of them. Around each one, the bog roiled and steamed.

Wind swept through the trees, and rain splattered across his face. The air was fresh like the mountains.

The water receded.

Juri stood with his mouth hanging open. "How did you do that?"

Hans straightened and wiped his hand across his thigh. "This is an old vulk path. It's been here since time began. Nothing keeps us from our own path. It's clear now." He eyed his hands and turned to Briony. "I can carry you again, but I'm mucky."

Briony's eyes on his remained wide. "I'll walk."

With a nod, he tucked her against his side. Despite their size difference, she slotted into him like she belonged.

As Baba Yaga's hill rose into place, a jedak lashed a vine at Juri. With a snarl, Hans slashed and severed it in two. The jedak whined and jerked under the mud, clamping its vines together.

As they stepped onto Baba Yaga's island, his claws dug into solid earth, no more slippery mud. Crouched like a spider in the middle of a web, her hut was high inside a gnarled rowan. Instead of roots, the bottom ten feet of the trunk was stumpy and stunted and resembled chicken feet. Juri said the tree walked, but anytime Hans came to the bog, the tree was in the same place.

Light flickered from knots punched out in the bark to form windows. He shook his head. Somehow Baba Yaga controlled the rowan so completely it allowed a fire inside.

Needle-like prickles danced down his spine—the warning of Baba Yaga's magic. No sulfur here. Her power was something else.

"Look at this place. Who *is* Baba Yaga?" whispered Briony.

"I'll take the lead talking to her because she's dangerous. Anything she says can have many meanings, and if she offers you something, take care. Nothing is ever free, and you may not know the true cost until it's too late."

Did he really want to take Briony here? Baba Yaga would most likely tell them their binding was a mistake and after, Briony would return home. His steps slowed. He searched for a plausible reason to delay. Anything to keep Briony with him, keep her talking to him. Keep this feeling inside his chest for a few minutes longer.

As they approached, a door split open in the hut's side fifteen feet off the ground, and a branch sprouted beneath, growing wide and thick, creating a ramp as it lowered to the ground. The three of them took the first step together.

13

HER SOCKS SQUISHED inside her boots, squelching with each step, and rainwater streamed onto the amber-colored floor. Briony cast around for a floor mat, a towel, anything. No luck, only the smooth floor merging seamlessly into the wall and ceiling to create a hollow, like being inside an egg. A fire crackled across the room—its flames not burning the tree around it—its warmth chasing the chill away as the door behind them sealed shut with a whoosh.

All three stepped into the room, and a small crack fissured under her boot. There was a sucking noise, and the water on the floor drained into it. She choked back a cry and scrambled sideways, jostling into Hans. He draped his arm over her shoulders, and as they walked farther into the room, he tucked her close.

Roots looped from the ceiling, and both vulk stooped to avoid brushing their ears against the herbs tied up and drying. Oh. Not herbs.

Briony cringed. Small, dried-out, and disemboweled animals hung by their necks, their faces contorted in snarls of pain. Their limbs twisted as if trying to climb away. No organs

—was Baba Yaga a haruspex, using the innards of animals to divine the future? *Don't look at the ceiling*.

Briony squared her shoulders, attempting to appear as fearless as a vulk.

"Hans Volak. Out of Rohant after his self-imposed exile." Baba Yaga rose from where she sat on an antique chair. The seat was a simple cushion, but its back twisted in a swooping pattern, narrow at the base and winging out at the top with an intricate pattern of interlacing wood, inset with a human face in the center. "With his golden-tongued friend and a ... female companion. I'm intrigued."

Baba Yaga was about Briony's height. Wreathed in a heavy black robe, the cowl creased at her neck and mimicked the deep lines etched in her face, especially around the small smile she wore. She had a strong chin and fathomless black eyes that reflected no light from the fire. Her hand stretched out from the sleeve of her robe and gripped the back of the chair, her long nails digging in.

The wooden face in the seatback grimaced, the mouth opening in a silent scream, and the eyes rolled toward Baba Yaga. Briony took a step back and clutched her chest. Hans put his hand around her waist, and she scuttled close, pressing her side against his. The moment there was contact between them, her pulse steadied.

Was Baba Yaga going to explain the rune and why she responded to Hans like this?

The way she craved Hans couldn't be real. It had to result from whatever happened in the cave. Right? Her chest constricted. If Baba Yaga severed their connection, her time with Hans would end.

Baba Yaga patted the chair. "Don't be disturbed. I rarely turn my visitors into furniture. This arrogant prince didn't fulfill his side of our bargain and had to be punished. Only twenty more years as my chair, and he'll go on his merry way. That was the chance he took when he decided not to pay Baba

Yaga what he promised." She scanned Briony from head to foot. "Who are you?"

"Briony Pritel." A drop ran down the back of her neck, and she wasn't sure if it was rain or a bead of sweat. The crone's gaze bore into her, and she grew itchy and hot like the heat was being turned up under her feet.

Baba Yaga turned back to Hans, and Briony sucked in a deep breath.

A small smile curved Baba Yaga's lips, deepening the wrinkles. A flicker of orange appeared in the center of her pupils. Was it the firelight? Baba Yaga patted the chair again. "You're here for help." Not a question.

A log in the fireplace snapped, light flared through the room, then dimmed. There was a faint tapping as a beetle hurtled itself against the small circular window in the kitchen, its hard carapace hitting the glass.

Hans shifted, but his face remained in the same foreboding expression. "Anyone with sense knows to come to you."

Her pulse skyrocketed. She hoped Hans had a plan. Next to her, he stood as always, his face impassive and unreadable. As if walking into a tree hut was something he did all the time. Except his lip twitched up over his eyetooth—only a fraction —and she knew what that meant.

Upon first meeting Hans, his expression seemed to alternate between scary red-eyed snarly face and foreboding get-out-of-my-way expressionless glare. It was difficult to lock eyes with his intense gaze. Those blue eyes pierced like he saw everything, yet remained guarded, keeping his true self off-limits. After a week with him, she now caught the subtle changes in his mouth. In his eyes. She knew when he was pleased, or amused, or tense—like now.

There was a pop and a crackle. In the kitchen, rowan-wood countertops stretched along one side of the room, with a potbellied stove sandwiched in the middle. On top of a burner sat a pan with a burned hunk of something sizzling. A plume of purple smoke hissed from a crack along its surface and wafted through the room. A yeasty, welcoming aroma filled the hut. What? It was like she'd stepped into a bakery.

"My augury stone finally wakes up after I've tended to it for months." Baba Yaga shook her head, and the tension in the room lightened. Until it dissipated, Briony hadn't realized how heavy the room seemed to press on her shoulders. Whatever an augury stone was, it had changed the mood. Baba Yaga pointed. "Sit. All of you."

Cluttered with books and guttered candles, a small table occupied the center of the room, and Hans pulled out a chair for her. She paused and studied the back. No faces. However, there was a wicked-looking knife with a notched blade in the center of the table, its tip pointing toward her. Underneath, a rust-colored stain seeped deep into the wood.

Baba Yaga settled at the head of the table, and the vulk dwarfed both sides, their massive shoulders almost spanning the entire length. Hans pulled her chair next to his until their legs and arms brushed against each other. He hummed a small calming note. It rolled through her, and her shoulders relaxed.

Baba Yaga studied Juri. "You haven't come to plague the creatures of my bog in quite some time."

"Uh, yes, I've remained on the other side of the river."

She waved her hand. "The last time we met, you were after that rampaging, massive gloson that was eating my ternaculas. I grew those plants for months, not a simple task in a bog. There aren't many beasties that dare sneak into Baba Yaga's domain, and that one was crafty." Her eyes narrowed. "You retrieved his scat for me and never asked for anything in return."

Hans choked, and if she didn't know better, she'd say it was close to a laugh. "You didn't mention anything about collecting shit in your tales about your run-in with Big Bluey," he said.

Juri ran his hand over his head. "A storyteller knows what's best for weaving his tale."

Hans's lips twitched. "And what details he might want to gloss over because he got crap on his hands."

Juri's ears flattened against his head. "It was my honor to help the Forest Mother."

Baba Yaga cackled, and for a moment, maybe it was a trick of the light, but she appeared young, maiden-like. "The vae say the vulk use words like a hatchet, with no finesse or charm, but this one has a honeyed tongue."

Briony glanced at Hans. That was true, *he* spoke what he meant without caring how his words landed, but she liked knowing exactly what he thought.

"I replanted the seeds I found in the shit, and my ternaculas flourish now, thanks to you." Baba Yaga pursed her lips. "So, I shall give you a boon for free."

"That's alright." Juri glanced at Hans. "I don't need anything."

"It will help you get what you've always wanted. The one thing you've tracked but never caught."

Juri's yellow eyes gleamed. "The vedogon."

Hans scoffed. "They don't exist."

"Of course they do. Teeth as long as my forearm, scales of the same inky blue as the deep ocean, and venomous spines down their back. They only live up by Ryba, my human village. It's the only rare creature left I haven't caught." He turned to Baba Yaga. "It's okay, Forest Mother. I'll get it one of these days."

Baba Yaga stared at him for a long moment before turning to Hans. "Are you sure that's what I mean?" Juri glanced away, his expression turning wistful. She got the sense there was something else he wanted more than the fish. Baba Yaga clapped her hands together. "All right, introductions are over. Let's talk payment."

Hans studied Baba Yaga; his shoulders knotted with tension. "I have information to offer." Currency was knowledge, and he needed to dangle enough to make her offer her help in exchange for the rest. "Things are happening in Ulterra you haven't heard yet."

One of Baba Yaga's fingernails tapped on the table, a light scratch. "I have eyes and ears everywhere."

Hans leaned back. "I doubt they are as good as a vulk's."

Baba Yaga's lips curled. "That's true. The information you've shared in the past has always been of a certain quality." The fingernail scratched again. "Is that all you need? Counsel?"

Hans waved his hand. "Also, your help with a bit of healing we don't have the skill for."

Baba Yaga's eyes narrowed, and an orange flicker jumped in her pupils. "Healing isn't why people come to me. The vae are better at that." Her gaze jumped from him to Briony. "Of course, after your incident with the king, you wouldn't bring her to the vae to heal her, would you?"

She thought Briony was the one who needed healing. *Good.* He lounged back on the chair. "I think you are the best fit for this type of injury."

Baba Yaga's chair creaked, imperceptible to her ears, but enough to tell him she'd leaned forward slightly.

"I saw someone who should not be immortal cheat death multiple times. And a symbol showed up and floated in midair." Let that whet her appetite.

No one stirred. Only a faint patter of rain against the window trickled through the hut. Baba Yaga leaned forward and pointed at him. "I'm interested enough to offer you an arrangement. When the moons are full, three weeks from today, you will return here and serve me for one year. We perform a blood oath."

Juri growled, so low only Hans heard. He agreed—this was bad. His hackles rose. A blood oath would bind him to the conditions of their pact in ways he didn't understand because he didn't understand magic. There could be aspects to the oath he couldn't predict. "A blood oath? Isn't my word good enough? And I need more than a month to—"

"That's my offer."

He glanced at the face confined in the chair at the fire. It wasn't in a rictus of pain any longer. It stared at Baba Yaga from across the room, its eyes heavy-lidded. Only a year of service was generous terms for the old crone. She could have asked for much, much worse.

Already feeling a weight shackled around his neck, his throat tightened as he tried to swallow. He placed his hands on the table, claws biting into the wood. Whatever Alpha remained inside him roared. Clawed at the idea of subservience to another.

He glanced at Briony and thought of Morana rising from the black fog and trying to kill her. Remembered all the other reasons he wanted the sorcerer dead. "Fine."

"Good." Baba Yaga reached across the table and grabbed the knife. She sliced her palm, and blood dripped onto the table, then held out the knife. He ignored it. Using one of his claws, he nicked his own palm, made a fist, and squeezed. Fat droplets, darker crimson than Baba Yaga's, dropped onto hers on the table, engulfing it. With the tip of her knife, she stirred them together. Baba Yaga chanted a few words under her breath, and the blood sizzled and steamed.

His fur itched like being rubbed the wrong way, and his hackles rose again. The blood on the table burst into green flames, a tinge of copper filling the air, and with a whoosh, it went out. His hand zinged, and the wound sealed into a small white scar.

Baba Yaga speared the knife into the table. "Now, we can begin."

14

HANS DESCRIBED the events of the past week for Baba Yaga. He skimmed over his naked adventures with Briony and summed it up as an intense encounter before a rune appeared. Baba Yaga narrowed her eyes a few times but hadn't interrupted, not even when he discussed the poison and admitted he was the one who needed healing, not Briony.

Hans leaned back. "I watched Morana die a hundred years ago. Then I tore through her neck again in the cave. I want to know how she still lives and how I can kill her." He glanced at Briony. "And why this symbol appeared in the air and spoke to us."

Baba Yaga stood. "Healing first." She unhooked a plait of maroon branches from the wall above the counter. Small lumpy husks rasped against each other as she dug her fingers inside the casings and squeezed out four plump burgundy pods. "Ternacula fruit." She waved her full hand toward Juri. "Everything comes full circle. You saved them, now I save your Alpha." Placing a pot on the stove, she broke each pod in half and tossed them in. "You were hit with a hex—a nasty one, too. Not poison and not a regular spell. Most spellcasters don't mess with hexes because they are just as likely to turn and attack the person casting it."

"A hex?"

"Yes. Clear the table and lie on your back while I finish the paste. I'm too old to kneel on the floor." She pointed at Briony and Juri. "You two, stay out of the way."

The wood table lengthened before him, and Hans stretched on its surface, placing his hands under his head. After waiting for what seemed like an hour, Baba Yaga stood at his right side, holding the pot with the substance she'd created. Snot green, mucous-thick crud gurgled inside like it still boiled. Baba Yaga took the knife from the table and rubbed some of the green goo on the metal. After she finished, she scooped the rest of the paste from the bowl and smeared it over his fur along the wound.

It burned and bubbled. Turned black. The smell of charred fruit filled the air. The mixture seared under his skin and felt like it was burrowing into his ribs as if it was going to gouge a hole straight through him. He flinched and fisted his hands until his claws bit into his palms. Warm blood welled between his fingers.

Pain exploded, layer after layer. His entire side was on fire. Baba Yaga raised the knife and yelled. The knife plunged and twisted, sliding between his ribs all the way to the hilt. Briony screamed. Juri leaped.

The pain stopped. A balm of cool coated the burning, washing it away. The oak hilt of the knife bulged under Baba Yaga's hands, and she yanked it out. When Baba Yaga tossed the knife into the bowl, the hilt was scorched black and twice its size. Hans slapped his hand to his side. No gushing blood. Only the paste flaking away onto the table. Juri scrambled forward to inspect his side, but Briony shouldered him out of the way.

"You're not injured!" she said. He sat up and swung his legs to the ground, and she pressed close, running her hands along his torso, up his stomach, and over his chest. Her face was pale, making her lips pinker.

"I'm not sure. Maybe you should keep checking."

Juri shook his head. "I can't believe what I just saw." He turned and stared at the destroyed knife. "That was a hell of a way to heal you."

Baba Yaga snorted. "Who said anything about healing? I killed the hex. When did you receive this curse? It should have paralyzed you immediately." Baba Yaga held the bowl at arm's length, walked to the fire, and tossed the entire thing in, knife and all. The flames leaped, filling the whole hearth.

"Briony healed me. She had to work at it every day."

Baba Yaga turned, and her eyes narrowed. "Every day or every night?"

What? How did Baba Yaga know Briony could only heal him at night? He opened his mouth to ask, but Briony's hands stroked his side, her rapid breath fluttering over his chest as she groomed the paste out of his fur. "I thought you died," she whispered.

He hummed a low rumble. Who cared if Juri heard? She liked it, so he'd keep doing it. Right now, he wanted her to keep petting him. Every stroke soothed his burned skin. Tingled.

He leaned forward and breathed deep, rolling his shoulders. The poison was gone. No more acrid, sour coating on his tongue, tainting every inhale. Instead, fresh hits of mountain laurel floated around him.

Baba Yaga smiled, her teeth glinting like a vulk's right before they attacked. "All right, that's done. You'll be in top shape when you come to work for me. You," she pointed at Briony, "get me that pouch off the wall. Let's talk about this symbol you saw and check if it really is a rune." A red satchel hung on a hook near the entrance, and Briony held it by its twine drawstring far in front of her as she brought it to the table. The red velvet looked normal, but who knew with this place?

The group returned to the now smaller table and sat. He pulled Briony's chair close to his again. Baba Yaga took the bag, dug her hand in, and scattered what appeared to be sand in a circle, about six inches in diameter, in front of Briony. "You first. Place your hand inside."

Briony's hand hovered, and he tensed. "What is this?"

"It won't hurt. Do you want my help or not?" Baba Yaga snapped.

Hans placed his hand on the small of Briony's back and hummed low so only she could hear. She planted her palm on the table in the circle's center.

The rune from the cave shimmered over the table, and the poem whispered through the hut.

"First, a rune will bind,
But only a bite permanently entwines.
With true love, it must be done,
Or two will never be one.

The vulk they call Shadow,
Content to always be solo.
Return to the great decision of the past,
And decide if that choice should last.

The lightwielder was betrayed,
By those who should have stayed.
To give away her heart,
Everything may fall apart.

It isn't a decision made lightly,
The bonds weave tightly.
Two souls chosen by fate,

Have only a month's time to gain their mate."

IT WAS the same words as before, but as he heard them this time, he didn't reject them immediately. He glanced at Briony. What was supposed to happen between them?

Baba Yaga said nothing. She stood and walked away, brushing against Juri, who sat with his jaws parted, watching the rune shimmer as it slowly turned in the air. Baba Yaga strode across the kitchen to a large cabinet of deep mahogany edged in olive. She opened the doors, and rows of jars glinted along the bottom shelves, each containing a fist-sized mass inside. Upper shelves sagged with books, and Baba Yaga slid a fat tome out and returned to the table.

The book released the scent of rich yet moldering leather when she opened it. The front was so cracked and lined it looked thirsty for oil, but the embossed title, both in the common tongue and in the arcane spellcaster language, stood out in gold. *Runes and Symbols.*

Baba Yaga thumbed through the pages. "It is a real rune. The rune of light and shadow."

Briony removed her hand to lean forward, and the rune in the air disappeared. Hans tilted his head to read. A drawing of the same rune dominated the page. In a tiny scrawl beneath it was an arcane script. Not a language he read.

"A rune. After all this time." Baba Yaga said. "They haven't shown up in Ulterra in many, many years. They're strange things." Across from him, Juri shifted and knocked on the table with his elbow.

Baba Yaga tapped the book. "This rune bound the two of you together."

Hans stroked Briony's back. "We discussed that possibility, and the poem doesn't match."

"Are you saying a powerful ancient force is wrong?" Flame jumped in Baba Yaga's pupils. "The second verse is about you. The humans call you the Shadow of Death, but your kind calls you simply Shadow. It used to be Ice and Shadow. Where Ice went, Shadow was at his side. Even now, you follow him."

Hans stiffened. Those names died long ago. No one dared to use them. "We don't need to discuss that. He's dead, and I'm alive."

Baba Yaga stared, never blinking. "Are you?"

He felt Juri's gaze burning more intently than Baba Yaga's. He refused to meet it. "This isn't relevant and—"

Crack. Baba Yaga slammed her palm on the table, and the entire hut shook as if the chicken feet of the tree stamped. "You want my help or not?"

He nodded.

She pointed at him. "You let your brother take Alpha."

He swallowed. When Hans was six months old, his mother went into the woods and found Zann, six months old as well, orphaned and left to die. She'd brought him home, and from that moment on, Zann was his brother, as close as if they were blood.

What she said was true. Even as children, he'd never wrestled with Zann. Never. In any contest, any challenge, he'd bow out, even though every instinct, every drive, clawed at him to win. To dominate. Instead, he'd channeled his frustration into his fighting abilities until he was second to none.

When the Territory War raged across Ulterra, all the older vulk died, including the current Alpha. Leaving either him or Zann to take his place.

Again, he'd bowed out. He'd felt his brother needed it more than he did. Hans wanted him happy, but as another Alpha, it was hard to stick around, so he'd left to travel alone for a while. That was when he'd lived at the vae kingdom.

He narrowed his eyes. "Are you saying my decision not to take Alpha is the choice of the past the rune mentions?"

"I can't tell you. You'll need to figure it out." She nodded at the circle of sand. "Hand."

Lip curled up over his eyetooth, he slapped his palm in the

circle. An image appeared in the air, translucent and watery, of a leaning mountain lined with a prominent ridge with two distinct notches taken out of it. At its base was a smooth oval section of rock, and centered in its middle, about waist height, was a small indent in the stone. Not noticeable to anyone but a vulk.

A den entrance.

"You need to go there." Baba Yaga pointed.

Hans stared at the image as it rotated. "Why?"

She waved at Hans to remove his hand. She pointed at Briony. "You again. Hand." Briony paled as she brought her hand to the circle.

WHEN BRIONY PLACED her hand in the circle this time, it was different. Baba Yaga's eyes flashed, and they seemed to grow larger like Briony fell into them. The room faded into darkness. Those eyes demanded entry into her every thought, every piece of her life. A sweeping invasion into who she was, and she couldn't break away.

A memory surfaced. It played out in her head and also appeared as an image above the table. It was the fifth year of living with Aunt Petra, and she was eleven. They sat together at the dining room table in the early evening as her aunt read another letter from her parents. They were making a killing in Stok, so they needed to stay a little longer before coming to get Briony.

Her aunt tipped the envelope over. "Where's the money then? If they've made so much, why can't they spare any for you?" Hard brown eyes, a smidge too close together, glared from beneath thick straight brows. No arch for her aunt. There were no curves on her anywhere. Her shoulders were strong and ropey, creating a sharp angle where they merged with her upper arm. Her coffee-colored hair, impeccably clean, was twisted daily into a bun, not a hair out of place.

Briony was shelling peas, a large mound already in her bowl. Her legs twitched as they dangled a few inches from the floor, and her back ached. The chair had no cushion, and the back was so straight there was no comfortable position, even though she sat as her aunt told her to.

Tipping the chair back and putting her feet on the table would be nice. She ducked her head to hide her smile. It would be worth the screaming to see her aunt's face if she did that.

Her aunt rapped on the table. "They're never coming. I'm stuck with you forever."

She leaped to her feet. "No!" A force surged through Briony, wild and heady. The bowl of peas flew across the room in a shower of white light and shot out the window, shattering it in a crash.

Her aunt grew pale, and her spine curled as she cringed back in her chair, her perfect posture forgotten. "Magic! What are you? Some changeling? My brother told me you weren't his child, but he said it didn't matter and to accept you anyway."

Her aunt spat on the floor, her face twisting into something mean and feral. "My brother joined the peddlers because he wanted their lifestyle, and even though it made me a laughingstock here in town, I bit my tongue. Everyone knows how peddlers are. They sleep together in one tent and allow anyone to join their bed. Who knows who your mother laid with to create you?"

She shook her head. "No."

Aunt Petra aimed a bony finger at her. "Magic is forbidden in Rohant, and I won't have you in my house. Especially with no money for your room and board."

The room was blurry. Tears streamed down Briony's face. "That's not true. They're coming back for me. I won't have to stay here." She clapped her hands over her ears and ran from the house.

Her aunt didn't come looking for her, and she slept in the forest.

When Briony returned in the morning, her aunt blocked the door and held a small bag with Briony's things. "I've arranged for you to apprentice with the doctor in town. You'll live and work there. I'm making it clear you aren't kin of mine, and I won't care for you anymore. If you cause me trouble, I'll tell the town about your magic, and you'll be driven out of Rohant. You won't survive in Divorky Forest. The creatures there will prey on a girl like you without a second thought."

They marched into town to Doctor Tucless, and her aunt left her without a backward glance.

Briony stared down at Baba Yaga's table, trying to suck in air, but the harder she tried, the worse it was. Hans jerked her hand out of the circle and pulled her onto his lap. He nuzzled her there, in front of everyone, and purred. She grabbed him as if she would never let go, twining his fur through her fingers.

Her chest heaved. "I remember the broken window, but everything else is a blur. I don't remember shooting light."

His arms wrapped around her. "It's alright."

Her eyes stung from refusing to allow tears to fall. She was a child all over again, watching her parents get in their cart and ride away without looking back. Never to return. The desperation washed over her. The mind-numbing panic.

Gentle, deep hums lapped against her and broke through. She drew in a long breath. Another. Briony sat up straight but remained seated on Hans. She liked his arms around her. "I don't know how I shot light like that."

Hans turned to Baba Yaga. "All right, you made your point. The rune is about us, but why did it appear?"

Baba Yaga studied the book for a long moment. "Rune magic and the way it works is far beyond my ken. Beyond anyone's. But it's no coincidence it happened when Morana returned." Her finger waved from Briony to Hans. "You need to figure out why. I can't tell you that part."

Baba Yaga closed the book. "Morana. It's interesting. How did a peltwalker like her survive Peklo? A magicwielder has no chance down there."

Briony dug into her pocket and pulled out the sodden threads of Morana's bracelet. "She wore these around her wrists. We got one off." The surrounding hut quaked, and the chair holding her and Hans teetered. Baba Yaga grabbed the bracelet, spoke a few foreign words, and the hut calmed and leveled.

The crone didn't open her hand, but she rubbed the bracelet with her fingers and nodded slowly. "It has echoes of power in it. Not the kind a magicwielder has, but an ancient, darker kind." There was a long moment where only the crack of logs in the fireplace and rain splattering against the window filled the hut. "You saw how my hut reacted to this bit of bracelet. My bog has also been jumpy lately. And my sentinels in the northern Kuls have all fled south because deep in the Bodec Mountains, something unpleasant lurks."

Juri stirred. "All the spawn escaping from the underworld have tried to go to the northern Kuls. Do you know what's up there?"

Baba Yaga shook her head. "No. Let's see if this activity is linked to Morana." The crone placed her fist into the sand circle. Above them, an image of a woman appeared. Briony squinted. That wasn't Morana. This woman was golden-haired and willowy. She wore a long red cloak in the image, and her hands glowed blue.

Hans stiffened, his body turning to iron at her back. "I sent her to Peklo, too. She's dead."

Briony turned to see his face. "Who is that?"

"A century ago, Morana had a partner. This spellcaster. She was powerful."

Baba Yaga withdrew her hand and returned the bracelet to Briony without upsetting the tree again, and Briony shoved it back into her pocket.

"If you want to know what Morana's up to, you need to talk to her partner. She isn't dead."

Hans snarled. "She's an enemy. She won't talk to us. Besides, how would we even find her?"

"Your paths will cross." Baba Yaga stood and brushed her palms in two quick motions against each other. "Our agreement is complete, and you've received the help you sought." The door whispered open at the front of the hut.

As they descended the ramp back into the bog, it startled Briony to discover it was still evening. It felt like days had passed instead of hours. They stood on the island staring out at the murk of the dripping bog.

"What now?" Juri asked.

Hans sighed. "I know where we need to go. I recognized where that den was. It's in the Bodec Mountains."

Briony swallowed. "Up where all the evil activity is?"

Juri's brow raised. "And near vae territory."

15

No one spoke as they backtracked through the behaving bog to make camp in the forest. When Briony tried to help with setting up, Hans glowered at her and demanded she sit at the fire to dry off. Juri slipped into the forest to hunt for fresh meat for dinner, and Hans sat next to her and dug jerky out of the pack.

Briony laid her boots by the fire and wrung out her socks. Her clothes clung like a saggy second skin, and her hair lay slick on her forehead. The rain had stopped, but water still cascaded from the leaves above, and the air had turned thick like it sucked up the moisture and only waited for another chance to wring it out on them.

She smoothed her hair and sighed. When it dried out, it was going to be a fright. Absolutely unmanageable. She stretched her feet toward the fire and wiggled her toes. Hans sliced a piece of jerky off with his claw and handed it to her. His large foot, with hooked claws on his toes, landed next to hers, easily double the size.

"Is that aunt of yours still alive?"

"She's not my aunt." Her words boomed across the camp.

"But the woman in my memory? Yes. She still skulks around Vieska. I try not to be anywhere near her."

His eyes turned red. "I am the Shadow of Death. I think she deserves a visit."

Briony turned, and their gazes locked. Realizing he was upset at her aunt's treatment, a tendril of warmth uncurled in her chest. He was the first to ever respond that way. "We have another evil witch to deal with."

He edged closer along the crunchy grass until their shoulders touched. "You still want to continue? I know Baba Yaga said we're bound, but I can figure things out on my own if you want to get somewhere safe and ignore this lightwielding thing. You don't have to look at it any further."

All her life, she'd heard magic was evil and strange. The few splashes of it she'd witnessed in the cave had done nothing to change her mind. If she remained with Hans to figure out their bond and defeat Morana, it would most likely involve understanding the power inside her. Understand what being a lightwielder meant, and she wouldn't be able to undo it.

What would it get her? Newfound knowledge and magic she'd never use, and a greater chasm between her and everyone else. She studied Hans from under her lashes. They were bound by a rune prophesying the opportunity to become mates. Could that be true?

"I'm coming with you. I want to help defeat Morana." Partnering with a vulk who didn't take mates was unwise. Especially one who kept stirring things inside her. She'd just have to guard her heart. Lock it down deep inside. She had an opportunity to see Ulterra and wouldn't squander it.

Hans's pupils dilated. "I won't put you in danger."

"You saw the bowl go through the window, and I'm the one who removed Morana's bracelet. I'm part of this."

He growled. "We have plenty of time to discuss what part you play in the battle."

She raised a brow. "Yes, we do."

They sat in silence for a long moment until he jerked his chin toward their oddly matched feet. "I can't see why a rune would look at us and say we're a match. You don't even walk barefoot like a vulk."

She poked him with her toe. "Barefoot? Ugh. My feet are really sensitive. I step on a pebble, and I hobble for days. I always have shoes or socks on."

"Dainty feet with soft foot pads." He chuffed. "Humans and vulk have never been allies."

Their arms brushed against each other. His dark fur really was pitch black. No wonder he was called the Shadow of Death. "No. We believe the vulk eat us."

He sighed. "It's a relic from the Territory Wars. Our only battle with humans."

She frowned and peered up at him. "Our history books say the war was when the three kingdoms fought to establish how far each realm would spread. There's nothing about the vulk."

He handed her another hunk of jerky. "Eat, or do you need me to feed you?" She liked when he fed her, but she took the jerky and ate. "Your human books have part of it correct. The war was about land, but all the kingdoms wanted more of Divorky Forest. Vulk territory. They fought us for it."

"You were alive during the war? Did you fight?"

"Yes. I was part of the pack, and we all fought to remind humans the forest was ours. Since then, we don't deal with humans, and they stay away from us."

"You were part of the pack, but you aren't anymore?"

His gaze grew sharp. "I live alone and protect Rohant." He spoke brusquely, the softer quality gone. "What about you? Do you live alone?"

"Yes, I live in a small apartment above the tavern. Maybe I could have lived with a friend, but my few friends from school have their own families. The only other way I would have lived with someone else was if I got married, and the two relationships I had weren't serious enough for that."

A low, menacing growl ripped from Hans's throat. Briony jumped and cast around wildly, searching for danger.

Hans's eyes were scarlet. "I find I don't like the idea of men having touched you."

"Wait ... what? That's what you're snarly about?" She sank back cross-legged and tilted her head, squinting up at him. "They're both married now. It was a long time ago."

"Don't tell me their names, or I'll hunt them down and slaughter them."

Was he serious? His eyes were the same deep red as when he fought, his teeth slightly bared. He *was* jealous of the two lovers she'd had.

"What about you? You're one hundred and eighty-six. What if I want to hunt down all the peltwalkers you've been with?"

His gaze returned to blue, and his mouth twitched. "It's been at least a hundred and twenty years, and I was barely a passing interest. Neither of them will remember me. I'd like to watch you storm into the clan and demand to meet them, though. What would you say?"

"Oh." She turned and let the fire lick at her back. Only two females in his entire lifetime? "Well, since it was so long ago, maybe I don't need to track them down. But I'm sure they remember ... your ... being with you." Her face heated, and she ducked her head.

"You think I'm memorable?" His voice changed to its silky, rumbly tone. He shifted, and in one languid, fluid motion, Briony lay stretched on the ground with Hans on top of her, his palms on either side of her head. Hot breath fanned the sensitive hollow below her ear. "Maybe I am to you, but I doubt I made much of a mark on them." His lips brushed her neck. Only a tease. "I didn't do to them what I did to you."

Briony ran her hands up his chest, the muscles taut and strong under her fingertips. "You mean free them from a cave?" The air whispered over her lips, so she knew she breathed, but she was lightheaded as if she wasn't getting any air.

His teeth grazed her shoulder. "Back in the cave I knew magic was around. I smelled it." He licked up her throat, and she shuddered. "There was danger, and I didn't care. I knotted you anyway. It's the only time I've ever done that."

She groaned and buried her hands in the fur at his neck, raking her nails up his nape. He rumbled and nipped. The memory of what it was like when he'd filled her made her stomach clench. "Why?" she whispered.

"I had to be close to you." He stopped nibbling at her neck and drew back. And for a moment—for one fraction of a second—his gaze was unguarded, and she was drawn in completely. The real Hans. She reached out and ran her fingers along his face.

"When Baba Yaga confirmed the rune poem was about us ..." he dropped his head to trace the shell of her ear with his lips, "I was glad."

He scooped her close with one arm under her upper back, and his mouth was on her throat, her jaw. She dug her fingers into his shoulders. His fur was slick from the rain. His ragged lick up her neck burned. Seared. Her blood heated. She groaned, and her head fell back.

A maelstrom swirled in her chest, pounding, making it feel like it wasn't big enough to contain everything whirling around. Whose feelings were hammering through their bond, his or hers? It didn't matter. He was a lodestone, pulling her to him. He purred, silky and seductive, and it rippled over her skin. She gasped and pressed closer.

Another long lick up her neck. "The first time we came together should have been in the forest under the moons. Not drugged in a cave." He panted against her throat; this time, she was the one twisting, so they were face to face. His pupils were enlarging, pushing out the blue. "You would have run through the forest, and I would have chased you. Until you decided you wanted to be caught."

In a flash, she saw herself running, nude, lit by the soft glow of the moons as she glanced back over her shoulder in anticipation. Heat pooled between her legs, and her fingers flexed. "Yes."

The bushes across the campsite rustled. Juri walked into the pool of light from the fire and paused, something slung over his shoulder. "I killed a brace of rabbits—" He jerked to a halt. "Shit. Do you want me to keep hunting?"

Briony crashed back to reality, feeling the prickle of bristly dead grass digging into her back. Hans sat up, his gaze fastened on her throat, and she yanked her coat back down.

Juri stood frozen in place. Hans rubbed his face. "No, we all need to eat."

But dinner wouldn't fill Briony's hunger. She leaned forward and whispered, "I was glad about the rune, too. But you don't have to worry. I remember what you said about mates."

16

COOKED rabbit wasn't on Hans's list of favorite meats. Raw rabbit, either. The meat was too lean and stringy, and he preferred a fattier, fuller taste. With one claw, he carved a piece of the softest part from the loin. Briony had blunt, tiny, human teeth, so best if she ate the plumpest parts.

Instead of handing it to her, he sidled closer and brought it to her lips. Her gaze flew up to his, her eyes wide. Yeah, he remembered what he'd said about feeding her. Recalled what he'd said about courtship. Was that what he was doing? They sat outside in the cold rain, and he wanted her warm, well-fed, and safe. She was his, and he'd take care of her first.

His.

For now. When she'd whispered, she knew he wouldn't take her as a mate, he should have been relieved. There would be no misunderstanding when, after this was over, he returned to his den. To his solitude. Yet even now, something fierce slashed through his chest and raged at her words. Demanded he take her somewhere private and seduce her. Drive her mad with pleasure until she was so sated the words would never pass her lips again.

She studied the slice of meat skewered on his claw tip, then closed her lips around it and sucked it off.

Heat scorched through his veins. His cock was still stiff from tasting her, and it swelled again, pinched from being restrained in his trousers. His claws dug into the hard ground, creating deep furrows in the dirt. He wanted her beneath him, glassy-eyed with pleasure. He needed to take her deep into the forest, where they could have complete privacy, and he could make her his. The real way.

This was no serum pulling them together. He wanted *her*. This human who didn't fear him. Who met his gaze without flinching, stood her ground, and challenged him. Anyone else —he'd rip their head off for that. With her, lust swelled so thick he could barely breathe. He'd known from the start that his desire in the cave was for her. Only her. Her true scent had washed away the thick desire drenching the air. It was only Briony, the real Briony, surrounding him. He hadn't admitted it to himself and hadn't told her.

Hans sucked in a breath and brought another piece of meat to her lips. Her face was flushed, but her pupils weren't dilated.

If they were runebound, why not enjoy it? The corner of his mouth twitched. Perhaps he needed to show her how strong her desire for him was. He sensed it. Smelled it. She needed to understand it wasn't fake and admit how much she wanted him.

Juri coughed. "How about a campfire story?"

Hans turned his head to stare across the fire, lip curled over his eyetooth, and spoke in Vulk, "I have her attention on me right now."

"I'm aware, but I'd rather go pick up Big Bluey's shit than sit here and watch the two of you cuddling all night," he answered in the common tongue.

Briony scooted away from Hans, closer to the fire, and he bit back a growl of frustration. Wisps of moisture curled off her clothes as they dried, as well as hints of sweet vanilla—her lingering lust. Her desire was deep enough to cut through campfire smoke. He almost smiled.

Briony drew her knees to her chest. "Yes, please tell another one of your stories."

Sparks spat into the air, the fire devouring another log. Juri drew a knee up and slung his arm over it. "All right."

His voice dropped into a melodic tone, sounding more like song than story. "When Ulterra first formed, the leaves on the trees remained the gentle green of early spring all year. There was no freezing frost or driving snow to shake them from the branches. No thirst or lack of light to shock them into a darker hue. And most of all, there was only one sun and one moon.

"All those who lived in Ulterra roamed at peace. Even the leshak of the fifteen-foot height and bone-crushing strength, the one who would become the great enemy, lived peacefully in the mountain crevasses and forest hollows and bothered no one."

Briony shivered and cuddled closer to him, and Hans reconsidered being annoyed at Juri for distracting her. She didn't know any of this history, and he liked watching her learn things he'd known for years. Things he hadn't really thought about.

Juri waved his arms. "After many years like this, a great change happened. Instead of one yellow sun, now there were two, with the second sun a rosier red, brighter, and smaller than the original. The light was a living, breathing thing in every shade of color, and that first day, its light flowed through every creature and every plant in Ulterra. Two moons rose at night, and the second moon shone a strange light upon the land.

"All were changed. Even the plants like the great rowan. The vulk became larger with great strength of tooth and claw. Their senses superior to any other. Some beings, like the vae and certain humans with special abilities, learned to interact with the new veins of light, which became the world's magic."

Briony turned to him, her lips parted. "Is that true? A second sun appeared," she snapped her fingers, "like that?"

"That's the story."

Juri scowled at them. Hans knew how much he hated being interrupted. He slung his arm over Briony's shoulder, and she nestled into him like she belonged at his side.

"However, not all kept their new power to themselves. Some because they wanted to prey on others, and some because they lacked control. The leshak gained glowing, green eyes but nothing else from the new sun. They fumed as they watched others scorch forests with their rage or call forth magic with their fingertips. Where was their power? They were one of the largest and most fearsome creatures across Ulterra. They deserved the strongest and best power.

"The king of the leshak, Czart, left his mountain hollow and prowled down to the Divorky Forest. There he met a magicwielder, who became scared and fired a spell at him. Czart's skin of bark and bone deflected the attack, and he laughed. He swooped down, grabbed the human, and held him up by the neck. How dare this measly creature try to kill him? As the last gasp of breath left the human's lips, a shimmering halo leached into the air. Czart opened his mouth and inhaled, and power blasted into him.

"And the first leshak learned to consume a soul."

Briony squeaked. "No!"

Juri leaned forward, shadows playing across his face. "Soon, Czart and the other leshaks roamed Ulterra. No one could kill them. No one could stop them. Until the vulk Wulf. He roared, and the other vulk answered. They came to his side as the first pack.

"Wulf slew Czart in a great battle, and at the end, his dedication to Ulterra sealed all vulk as the protectors for all time, and Wulf became Krol, wearing gold bands around his biceps.

Not only the Alpha of the pack but a king. Far more powerful than any vulk before. No silver weakened him, and no sword could kill him."

Briony gasped. "He was so strong."

"The most powerful of our kind," Hans said. He let his head dip, so his jaw brushed the top of her head.

"He killed the leshak? How?"

Juri stood and paced in front of the fire, claws extending an inch. The corner of Hans's mouth twitched; he'd missed Juri in pure storytelling form. "What happened next has become murky with time. The vae king and Wulf met and formed an alliance to save the rest of Ulterra. Those with evil intent were driven to the underworld and became known as spawn. Others enjoyed the dark places and lived there by choice.

"More complicated were the other immortals. Those overcome by their new power and using it for evil. They were tested, and if they failed, they became cursed, thrown into Peklo by Wulf and the other vulk. Except the leshak. They were too dangerous to live anywhere, and Wulf and his pack destroyed them completely."

Briony practically crawled into his lap; she clutched at him so fiercely. "What happened to Wulf?"

"Wulf lived many thousands of years, reigning peacefully, until one day he walked to the mountains in the sky where the vulk hunt in the afterlife. It's said that because he never died, he can return to Ulterra whenever he wishes, but so far, no one's seen him. He left behind no descendants, and no vulk has been born with solid black fur. Well ... until Hans."

Briony turned and studied him, her eyes wide. "Could you be related to him? Maybe he returned to earth?"

He leaned back. "This is an old legend, with some of Juri's flair thrown in. Wulf died a normal vulk death, and he can't return from the afterlife. We're not related."

Briony shook her head and turned back to Juri. "He doesn't have a story lover's soul, does he?"

Hans's mouth twisted, and he and Juri glanced at each other. She didn't know how awkward that comment was.

Juri raised a brow. "The vae said they saw Wulf walk through the heavens nine months before Hans was born."

Briony's mouth dropped open.

Hans shook his head. "Come on, Jures." The old nickname slipped out, and Juri's grin deepened. "I'm no descendant of Wulf."

Juri stared, his yellow eyes bright from the fire. "You've never tried to find out."

"How? Hold some silver and check if it burns me?"

Juri shrugged.

"Your mother never spoke of your father?" Briony asked.

"No. Never." He rubbed his jaw along the top of Briony's head and stood. Enough of story time. "I'll take first watch."

The quiet of the forest swallowed him. Even the leaves of the rowan remained still. Only the distance hoot of an owl floated through the trees.

His father.

Whoever his father was, it wasn't Wulf. He might resemble the legendary leader, but it was absurd to consider, and he wasn't about to test himself. Besides, Wulf was an Alpha. A leader. That wasn't him. Not anymore.

17

OVER THE PAST WEEK, they'd followed the river north. The Bodec Mountains always looming ahead, a gray smudge against the sky reminding Briony of where they were headed, even if the surrounding forest grew brighter and more colorful. They'd seen cockatrices floating high above several times, but they never came close. Hans remained alert for them, and he and Juri speculated on what it meant that they didn't attack.

It felt like an eerie calm before a violent storm. Like the dark clouds gathered on the horizon, they hadn't arrived yet. Were worse creatures waiting ahead on the path?

The flat terrain now rose and fell like gentle waves, and the air warmed so much Juri shucked his vest and scaled the gorge to jump in the river a few times a day. The rowans gave way to groves of oak and maple, then chestnuts and elms, their trunks as massive and squat as the trees in the bog. Twisty pines, with branches that curled and resembled human limbs, fanned soft needles against her skin when they passed.

A spiky orange flower with trailing lambs-ear-looking leaves bloomed along the armpits of tree limbs. She studied it, trying to figure out what it was and if she could touch it or not. It perfumed their journey with a lemon custard scent, giving her an instant, intense craving for sweets. Hans didn't know what the flower was but told her the nicer the smell, the more likely it killed, so she'd kept her hands to herself.

She was used to being on her feet all day, but the muscles of her calves protested at the brisk pace they kept. On the days she limped by the time they broke for camp; Hans would hold her in his lap and knead her muscles until she turned to putty.

He always stopped, and every night she grew more restless for his touch. She struggled to stay awake, hoping he might join her in the tent, but the minute she crawled onto her bedroll, she'd lose the battle with fatigue and sink into sleep within minutes. Hans didn't wake her; if he slept at her side, he was gone by morning.

The foot of the Bodec Mountains stretched ahead. The mountains around Rohant swooped with smooth rounded peaks like someone stroked them into submission. Here, the Bodecs spiked into the sky in slashes of gray stone.

Hans and Juri conversed in Vulk next to her. She didn't mind when they spoke in their own language, certain they didn't realize they were doing it. She and Hans had continued their question-and-answer game as they walked north, and while he was evasive about some things, he shared many of his travels around Ulterra. If Juri had joined him on his trip, both recounted their adventure, bantering back and forth and even joking. They mixed Vulk and the common tongue often.

Hans stooped and plucked something from the ground. "Here's a flower you can touch." A cluster of small, five-petaled blue flowers waved on a delicate stem pinched between his thumb and finger.

When she took it from him, her hand trembled. "What flower is this? I'm not familiar with it."

"It's a forget-me-not. Not much of a scent to them."

Briony hugged it to her chest.

"Look up there." Juri pointed through the trees to the

mountain, stretching past a clearing full of boulders. On a ledge about fifty feet up was a shaggy white goat shaking its head at them. Long horns twisted above its ears, and it stretched its chin forward and bleated.

Juri rubbed his hands together. "Goat tonight. Haven't eaten a mountain goat in a long time."

The goat turned and leaped onto a tiny perch of rock so small it seemed impossible for it to balance, then it jumped up onto a ledge and disappeared through a crevice. "Well, Goaty got away." She breathed out a quick sigh of relief—she liked goats.

Hans stepped from the trees toward the slope. The ground shuddered, and Briony tumbled sideways. Rock cascaded down, and a boom shot through the air so loud it reverberated in her chest.

Juri put out his arm and steadied her, and Hans's head snapped to the right. "You smell that?"

Juri's expression turned grim. "Oh yeah. It's so strong I can't determine how many there are."

The ground shook again, and Hans put his arm around her waist. "We need to move fast. I'm going to carry you."

"Is that asking for my permission?"

He reached down and cradled her in his arms. "Not really." His jaw ran over the top of her head. "When you can run as fast as a vulk, I won't have to carry you."

Hans launched forward, and she clutched his fur and hung on. The trees flew by in a blur. Kyril was right. When they'd run before, Hans was slow.

The slope descended to a plain of scrubby grass. A jagged gash slashed through the mountain's base, several feet wide, and a stream of spawn charged out of it. There were a few bauk, with their large, blocky bodies, similar to the two that had captured her, but most of the creatures were around four feet tall and lumpy, with leathery skin and matted hair.

Hans skidded to a halt and scanned the forest. He strode

to an elm with a broad branch spreading above their heads. "Bauk are stupid, and the smaller ones—the goblins—barely have a brain. Sit up here." He lifted her into the crook of the tree. "None will get by me, but just in case, the spawn won't see you up here."

She clutched the trunk, hugging the tree, and gulped. "Do I have to be up here? Is there somewhere else I can hide?"

He rubbed his face. "What? What's the problem?"

"I don't like heights. I can't even get on a ladder to go into the attic."

"What? We went up and down cliffs, and you didn't say anything."

"You were with me. I knew you wouldn't let me fall," she said quietly and his eyes softened.

Juri growled. "Hans." Spawn still poured out of the mountain.

She stared at the mass charging through the clearing. "There's so many of them."

Hans tilted his head a fraction, and his blue eyes flashed. "Stay here."

From her perch, she had a perfect view of the valley as Hans and Juri raced toward the mob. At first sight of the vulk, the smaller goblins scrambled over each other to run away, but the bauk stood their ground.

She'd seen Hans in the cave and thought that was impressive. As he leaped into the mass, he was a whirlwind of claws. Heads rolled onto the ground, black blood spraying. The stench rose into the air, thick and putrid, and she gagged.

More streamed through the open crack. Another shudder from the mountain, and the tree swayed. Briony gripped the trunk harder, the bark biting into her palms and the side of her cheek.

Long fingers, tipped by black claws, gripped the sides of the rift in the mountain, and a giant head and shoulders emerged, forcing its way through the small opening. The mountain groaned, and another boom crashed. With one great push, the scaly creature shoved its way through and stood.

A creature, at least twenty feet tall, with hardened reddish flesh, appeared. It resembled something squirmy and disgusting she'd find under a rock, only much, much larger. It had a giant, ant-like head with massive pincers for a mouth, black plates spread along its back and torso, and four legs and two long arms, all tipped with long claws.

It opened its maw and belched out a thin splatter of pus-colored bile, spraying the goblins at its feet. They screamed and fell to the ground, their flesh smoking. Acrid, potent ammonia filled the air. The same stench from the tannery back home when they worked the leather.

She gagged, and her eyes watered.

The screams cut off. The goblins who'd been sprayed twitched, then lay still. With a clawed hand, the giant scooped one body up, shoved it in its mouth, and then stepped forward, the ground shaking at the impact.

Working in tandem, Hans and Juri whirled and slashed, continuing to chop down goblins, and the monster lurched forward, straight toward them. Briony's heart pounded. She had to help! Since Baba Yaga brought forth the memory of throwing light as a weapon, she'd wondered if she could learn the ability. But it was daylight. Even if she could figure out how to call her light, it wouldn't work right now. She had to think of something else.

A brilliant light flashed out of the gap in the mountain. A figure covered in golden armor strolled into the valley. A tall figure, but one that appeared to be a human man.

He shaded his eyes. With the other hand, he reached over his head and withdrew a sword strapped to his back. Then his form wavered, and he ... shifted.

The golden armor barely fit the corded muscles on the elongated and enlarged torso. The bronze skin changed to sleek obsidian. And in place of a man's head, there was now the head of a coyote ... no ... a jackal. Long, lean ears, a muzzle a bit thinner than a vulk's, and glowing amethyst eyes. Not a peltwalker—they changed completely into their animal. This was a hybrid on two legs.

The man—not a man—parried and whirled on the balls of his feet as he swiped through goblin heads. Like he was one with his sword.

She gasped. Was he ...? No. That was impossible. But ... it must be. She'd once bought a book from Only an Obol called *Dangerous Beasts and Legends of Yore.* Inside was the story of a great god who walked the earth with the ability to shift into a form with the head of a jackal. The god Set.

The sword circled in the air, the Jackal-man leaping far higher than a man could.

"Hans, look out!" Briony screamed.

But Jackal-man wasn't aiming for them. He landed on the giant insect monster, drove his sword into its side, and twisted, letting out a battle cry that froze the rest of the spawn. The giant hissed, and its jaws made an awful clacking sound. It tossed the Jackal-man off its back, and Jackal-man flipped, grinning, and landed on his feet.

Swinging his sword and spraying goblin blood, he backed away, clearing a path around him. He darted back and forth at the giant, most of his blows skidding off the hard black scales.

"Come on, wolfie boys," he called in an accented voice. "You distract it, and I'll take its head off."

Hans's claws sank deep under the arm of a bauk, and it slumped to the ground. "You're doing a good job keeping it busy. I'll take it down."

Jackal-man flipped his sword from one hand to the other. "A challenge for who takes the head of the ravec? I accept." The man began weaving so quickly that it seemed, until now, he'd moved in slow motion.

Briony watched another bauk fall at Hans's feet. He picked it up and tossed it at the giant. A ravec? Insect monster snagged the body, and its giant pincers opened. As the giant lowered its head, Hans leaped and landed on its back, scrabbling for purchase as he climbed toward its neck. Blood poured down the ravec's side, where Hans's claws ripped at the unprotected skin.

The great beast threw its head back and shrieked. Juri and the Jackal-man closed in along the sides and slashed anywhere they could. The creature beat with its long claws, grabbed Hans, and tossed him to the ground. It opened its mouth, and its throat convulsed as it worked to spit venom again. Right at all three of them.

"Watch out!" Forgetting to cling to the tree, Briony threw her hand forward, reflexively trying to shoot light at the monster. Nothing happened.

Off-balance, she wobbled. She grappled to hold on to the tree trunk, but it was too late. Tumbling forward, she fell and landed hard on her hip.

With a grimace, she rolled to face the valley, hoping she remained unseen. Set waved his hand. Wind whipped through the forest and down the valley as something she couldn't see slammed into the giant's throat and hurled it back.

The beast spat, and its bile flew back over its own face, the wind's fury a shrieking tumult around the monster. Again, the ravec screamed and jerked backward. The three attackers leaped at it, and the giant fell. As blood flew, Briony glanced away.

Out of the corner of her eye, Briony caught movement from the gap in the mountain. A figure in a long red cloak dove out of the crack in a flurry. A young woman with sickly pale skin and golden hair stood and grabbed a rock from the ground. Briony sprang to her feet. This was the spellcaster Baba Yaga showed them. It had to be. She stepped forward, but several groups of goblins remained between her and the spellcaster, and she halted.

The robed figure slapped at her cloak, clouds of dust

pluming into the air, and surveyed the valley. The rock flashed blue in her hand, and the air in front of her warped and swirled. A resonance filled the air like the echo after a bell rings.

Magic.

Hans shot up from the carcass of the giant and roared. The woman glanced over her shoulder, spotted Hans, then swept her gaze up the valley and met Briony's. As Hans bounded toward her, she walked forward into the swirling air and vanished with a sucking sound.

Hans snarled and roared again, his eyes red. He punched the side of the mountain, and the gap in the mountain sealed closed, smoothing together like it had never been rent apart.

Moments later, all the goblins lay in their own blood on the ground. The valley was a pile of bodies, and the stench of brimstone and ammonia wafted through the air. Briony descended the slope, stepping over the slimy bits.

A horn echoed over the trees and bounced over the mountain. A single pure note.

"Company is arriving." Juri glanced at Jackal-man, now back to his human form. "More company."

18

"WHO THE HELL ARE YOU?" Hans studied the man wiping blood off his sword. No brimstone or sulfur etched his skin, even though he'd ascended from Peklo. His magic during the fight hadn't smelled of sulfur either. There weren't any species he knew of that shifted into a jackal and dealt magic.

Briony joined them as they stood upwind on the slope. His eyes narrowed. She shouldn't have shimmied out of that tree without help. She might have hurt herself.

"You're the god, Set, aren't you?" She tilted her head. "Where's your headdress?"

The man froze, and his eerie purple eyes flashed. "I go by Seth now." He ran his hand over his dark hair. "My headdress is only for ceremony, not for fighting."

"How do you know who he is?" Hans asked.

Her brow arched as if that was a ridiculous question. "I read. He was in my book as a god of Ulterra." She turned toward the stranger. "I can't believe you're a real person."

He smiled. White, even teeth, the canines a touch too long, flashed. "Were you the one yelling warnings?"

She glanced at Hans. "Yes. I tried to help."

Seth grinned again. "Thank you. It was much appreciated."

Briony turned toward the carnage in the valley. "What was that enormous monster?"

"A ravec," Hans said. "They're one type of creature that lives in Peklo. I've never heard of one coming up to Ulterra. They like to stay down in the dark."

The corners of her mouth turned down. "I thought that's what you called it. They aren't spawn?"

"No, we call goblins, bauk, and dokkaebi spawn because all three species try to escape to Ulterra to prey on humans or other immortals. None of them want to remain in Peklo."

"Dokkaebi? They weren't in my monster book."

"Dokkaebi blend in. They prey on humans ... differently. They want wealth, and they use trickery to get it. If you met one, you wouldn't even know it wasn't human."

Briony frowned. "But the other monsters don't want to come to Ulterra?"

"The other monsters are simply monsters. Whether in the underworld or up here, they act the same. Most of them prefer the darkness of Peklo." He scanned the sky. "The cockatrice wouldn't be following us if they weren't obeying orders."

The sun remained behind the clouds, yet Seth's eyes gleamed as if lightning struck. He moved closer to Briony. "You helped me. Let me repay you." His voice had dropped into a deep, almost musical tone.

The same charge in the air Hans sensed when magic was used swirled around him. The hair rose on the back of his neck, and his claws lengthened.

Briony stepped toward Hans and wrapped her arm in his. "No need to repay me. I only shouted a warning." She glanced up at Hans, and he relaxed.

Seth stepped back. "You have a bondmate."

"What? No." Briony flushed.

He turned to Hans, and his gaze flicked from him to Briony, the purple eyes hard, like jewels. "There aren't many, even among bondmates, who are immune to me. You're lucky." He spoke in perfect Vulk.

"Immune to what? How do you know—"

"They're here," Juri said. Pounding hooves echoed through the valley, and out of the forest, kon horses flew down the hill toward them. Larger than regular horses, their wide hooves and sturdy legs let them fly over the peaks of the craggy Zuby Mountains, where their herds roamed in the southern Kuls.

The group of fifteen mounted vae wheeled to a halt in front of him. A silvery-gray horse stepped forward, and the vae on its back tossed a goblin carcass onto the ground at Hans's feet.

"You missed one. You're losing your touch." As the imperial voice spoke, his horse danced on its hind legs and tossed its head, the long mane flying.

Hans sighed. First, a massive rift and a ravec, now *him*. Great day.

He crossed his arms. "And you killed it? You didn't order someone to do it for you?" He pointed at the arrow sticking through its throat. "We better burn this one to be sure it stays dead."

"I want them all burned. I don't want this rot stinking up my lands." The rider nodded to his right, and two vae dismounted and hauled the body down the slope into the valley.

"Your lands don't extend this far."

"Someone needs to protect the Kuls. Most of us don't hide in holes all day. And yes, I shot that one myself." In one swift motion, the vae swung his leg over and landed on the balls of his feet. "When did you leave your lovely hovel, Hans?"

The ascension from princeling to king hadn't changed Caladin much. Maybe he stood a little taller, a little broader from when Hans knew him—back then, he was barely past his teenage years—but he had the same blond hair styled in the vae way with notched triangles shaved at the temple and hair pulled back against the scalp in a braid. Being king, Caladin had two notches on his left temple and one on his right.

He also had the same arrogant mouth Hans always wanted to punch.

There was one change, though. "Nice scar." A dull, white crescent shape stood out against the silvery shimmer of vae skin on Caladin's high, right cheekbone. The corner of Hans's mouth twitched. He'd left a permanent mark.

Caladin's eyes narrowed a fraction. He scanned the rest of the group. "We sensed power used here. Both magicwielder magic and something ... else." His gaze fixed on Seth. "Who are you? What did you do?"

Seth crossed his arms and remained silent.

Caladin's eyes widened. "You're not welcome on my land, incubus. Leave."

An incubus? Hans studied Seth. Briony called him a god, but none of the vulk lore mentioned gods or incubi. What power did he possess?

Seth grinned, but it was like a vulk baring his teeth. He bent low and swept his arms out in a flourish as he bowed. "That's not a problem." He spoke in the same silky tone he'd used with Briony. "I have places to go with people who desire my company."

One of the vae warriors, whose long, brown, braided hair matched his skin, dismounted and stepped toward Seth. "Really, Your Majesty, why not invite him to a feast in his honor tonight? I have a lovely piece on the harp I'd like him to hear."

Caladin raised his hand, and purple lightning sparked at

his fingertips. "Stop listening to him." He pointed at Seth with his glowing hand. "Stop your incubus tricks and speak plainly."

"Cal, cut it out. He helped slaughter the spawn from Peklo." A voice from behind the crowd of vae, soft and feminine, floated over the group.

Caladin glared at Seth. "He's one of the cursed." Caladin was right. If Seth was in Peklo, he was one of the cursed immortals. Wulf himself might have flung this guy down into Peklo, and maybe Hans should toss him back there. After all, he didn't know why Seth was cursed. But Hans wasn't Wulf. He could close rifts, all vulk could, but he couldn't open one. Besides, Seth *had* saved them from an acid bath and destroyed spawn like a vulk.

The horses parted as the largest one yet, pure white, walked into the circle with a female vae on its back. She wore an intricate golden bodice laced over a flowing white shirt, and it looked like she wore a matching silky white skirt, but she sat astride, so they must be loose breeches. Not that he paid attention to vae fashion, but he remembered the vae women wore dresses most of the time. Her hair was braided like Caladin's but with gold thread.

Katisa, Caladin's sister. He'd met her a few times, but she'd spent most of her time with a tutor in another part of the kingdom. He narrowed in on the red-robed figure slung across Katisa's lap, her hands tied behind her back.

Hans snarled. "I need that sorcerer."

"Guess you're out of luck," Caladin said. "She's my prisoner."

Katisa arched a brow. "*Your* prisoner?"

The king turned to his sister. "I told you to stay in the trees."

Ignoring his comment, Katisa surveyed them, then glanced at the mountains, her brow furrowing. "We should move away from this place. Come to the palace. It will be safe to talk there. Even you are invited." She gestured at the jackal.

Hans growled. "We're on the way—"

"If you want to talk to my prisoner, you'll come," Katisa said.

Caladin sneered. "Yes, Hans, what are you doing that's more important than protecting Ulterra?" Caladin pointed at the ravec burning in the valley. "We killed another one of those last week. Where were you?" One of its arms twisted in the heat of the fire as if it came alive and clawed again.

Juri snarled. "Protecting you from the hundreds showing up on the other side of the river."

Hans focused on the spellcaster. If he leaped, he could grab her from the horse, but afterward, he'd have fifteen angry vae surrounding him.

Briony leaned close. "I think we should go with them."

Katisa smiled. "We can prepare a feast for you, and you're welcome to stay the night. You look weary."

Briony squeezed his arm. "A proper bath would be nice. And something to eat other than meat."

The thought of sitting across from Caladin and listening to him at a feast made him want to claw his ears off, but if they joined the vae tonight, Briony would be more comfortable, and he'd have a chance to get to the spellcaster. He put his arm around her. "Why would I want to eat something other than meat?"

She gave him an icy stare, and the corner of his mouth twitched. After all her questions about the vae, he suspected beyond wanting to sleep in a bed and have a bath; she also wanted to see where the vae lived. "All right, we'll come."

Caladin vaulted onto his horse. "You," he pointed at the incubus, "no sweetened words, or you're back in the forest. Find partners the old-fashioned way."

"Look at me." Seth held his arms out and turned. "Look at this face. This form. That won't be a problem." Seth might be right, considering how the vae next to him licked his lips.

Brief introductions were exchanged then they worked together, throwing the corpses into a pile and setting fire to it. They set off for the vae palace, Juri striding with Caladin at the front of the group. Briony left his side and walked next to Katisa and her horse.

He'd caved. Again. Yes, he wanted to steal the sorcerer away and he wanted to know more about the ravec Caladin killed, but mostly he wanted Briony happy. Wanted to see her smile like she had when he gave her the flowers. The white horse craned its neck and ruffled Briony's hair, and she laughed. He paused as warmth bloomed in his chest—her laughter was like a bell. No matter what else happened today, hearing her laugh would be the best part of his day.

The damned jackal loped up to his side, and his moment of pleasure soured. "What do you want?"

"Is the vae, Katisa, married to the king?"

Hans grunted. "Brother and sister, and you don't have a chance."

Seth smiled. "I'm very charming."

Hans growled. "Keep it to yourself, and if you try to seduce Briony again, your head leaves your body."

"If I knew she was yours, I wouldn't have tried. I never go after the bonded ones." He shrugged. "But sometimes they come for me."

"She doesn't want you."

When Seth smiled, it didn't reach his eyes; they remained distant and hard. Like they'd seen far too much. "I already told you that."

"As long as we're clear."

Seth rubbed his hands together. "I'm looking forward to this feast in my honor. It's been a long time since the people of Ulterra celebrated me."

"A feast in your honor? You're lucky to be invited at all."

"You'll see. By the night's end, they'll be fighting for who will feed me my favorite meats. Will they serve venison? There aren't any deer in Peklo, and I miss it."

One corner of Hans's mouth turned up. "The vae are vegetarians." Seth stopped mid-step and swore rather impressively.

Hans strolled on, feeling better.

19

BRIONY WALKED down the white limestone steps of the palace entrance onto the plush lawn of the courtyard inside the inner walls. Once she'd passed through the imposing outer bulwark, clearly built for security, the palace spread before her like a woman delicately spreading her skirts. Arches of limestone and glass swooped impossibly with arching open stairs spiraling up to towers among the trees. More elegant than the rowan, these trees had a light gray bark, almost as pale as the chalky limestone. Their feathery leaves had long delicate fronds that tickled when she passed.

The courtyard hummed as vae mingled beneath the swaying branches. Tables sagged under bowls of food, and the faint aroma of roasted pears drifted on the gentle breeze. A group of vae played violin, harp, and lute. Instruments humans played as well, but vae instruments were more ornate and of material that didn't look like wood.

Briony stepped onto the soft, emerald green lawn, and as her feet sunk into the squishy grass, she wiggled her toes. No rocks to worry about here. After being shown her room and showering in the private bathroom, she'd dressed in vae style, which meant no shoes for a feast on the lawn. The vae offered to clean her traveling clothes and boots, and Katisa lent her this dress for the evening.

Katisa, also barefoot and wearing a soft green one-shoulder floor-length gown that floated around her, tilted her head. "My dress fits you, and you look lovely, but you seem uncomfortable. Is something wrong?"

Briony shrugged. Her dress was golden and nipped in at the waist with a swooping neckline that flirted with the swell of her breasts. It was made of a silky material she didn't recognize. "I don't wear dresses. I prefer breeches."

Katisa's eyebrows shot up. "Really? I figured you were on the run and grabbed those things out of desperation." She cleared her throat. "Not that you didn't look fetching in your breeches, but our breeches are styled a little more ... loose and flowy. And we like color."

Briony laughed. "Where I'm from, we make our clothes for farming and warding off the weather. Loose breeches wouldn't help keep me warm, and they'd snag. I don't own any dresses." If humans had dresses made of this silky material that caressed the skin, she might change her mind, though.

"Are you a plantworker? What kind of farming? I have the black thumb of death. Master Gardener Grigorii won't even let me water one of the lindens." She pointed at the trees with the gray bark. "He says they know. Let's go sit and eat."

Vae sat around the tables or mingled in groups holding glasses. Scanning the crowd, Briony asked, "Where is Hans?"

"The vulk are sitting with Caladin. My brother looks thrilled." At the head of the feast was the central table, and Hans and Caladin sat in the middle next to each other. With his arms crossed, Hans stared left, and the king, wearing a simple crown, scowled off to the right. A few seats farther along, a crowd of vae gathered around Seth and Juri.

Briony and Katisa walked through the courtyard to the head table, lanterns dangling overhead from the branches, casting a gentle, dream-like glow with their warm light. As if she already didn't feel like she'd fallen asleep and woken in a different world. The mingling vae parted before Katisa, giving her a slight nod, and a few vae smiled at Briony as she passed.

Her cheeks heated, and her palms grew sweaty. So many people, all of them staring at her. Then Hans's head snapped forward, and their gazes locked. The music swelled, and she didn't see the crowd anymore; it was just him with his blue eyes glowing brighter in the soft light. The longer he watched her, the more they heated.

Her stomach flipped. She wanted to run her hands all over him until his mouth was on her neck, his hands baring her skin for more. Warmth flooded through her and fanned embers only needing the tiniest of sparks to ignite into flames.

Katisa motioned at the vae sitting to Caladin's right, and he nodded. "And that's Ansel, our counselor." If she'd introduced the other vae at the table too, Briony hadn't caught a word.

Hans stood and pulled out the chair next to him. "Come and sit."

When she sat, he dragged her chair so close to his that the armrests hit. His mouth brushed against her ear. "You're beautiful."

Briony glanced down her face heating. "Thank you." She felt off-kilter. She didn't get compliments and wear dresses. Yet here she was with a vulk who stirred something inside her, and when she was near him, she never caught her breath. Her nerves skittered. "Have you seen the baths here? They're marvelous, and they have hot water like you do. The water came down like rain." She was rambling. Waxing on about bathrooms, of all things.

Hans reached out and stroked the ends of her hair that brushed her back. "There are hot springs here. It keeps the weather warm year-round, and the vae pipe the water through their homes. It's where I got the idea for my den." He stroked her back. "Your hair is down."

"Yes, it's behaving today." Her pulse leaped, and her chest fluttered. "Their palace is sunnier than your cave."

He growled, but it was a soft, chiding one. "A cave is for bears." Hans leaned forward and nipped below her ear. It sent pure fire through her veins, and she trembled.

She remembered what Juri said. "Is yours ... finished?"

His gaze shuttered, and he leaned back. No. She wanted his relaxed, open expression back. Briony shifted in her chair and leaned across her armrest into his space. "Never mind."

He pulled a few dishes toward her and spread strawberries covered in a cream sauce on her plate. "My brother was helping me build my den. When he died, I stopped working on it."

Her hand with its wooden fork paused on its way to scoop food, and she placed it back down. "I'm sorry."

Hans leaned forward and nuzzled his jaw along her head. "Thanks." His nose nudged along her hair. "You smell like a vae."

"I don't think that's a compliment."

His chest rumbled. "On you, it's not bad." He wasn't looking out over the party. Not at the heaps of food or the dancing beginning in front of the musicians. Hans only watched her.

Her chest squeezed. She wanted to crawl into his lap and press close but didn't think that was proper for dinner at a king's table. Although the atmosphere was relaxed, Caladin and Katisa sat straight in their chairs, and their court gathered near them, reminding her they dined with royalty.

A burst of laughter drew Briony's attention down the table. Juri had a heaping plate in front of him and a group of vae leaning toward him as he spoke. He drank from a goblet clutched in his left hand and gestured wildly with his right as he told one of his tales.

Hans pointed at their goblets and slid hers closer to her. "The vae make potent wine, and Juri's a fan. Probably not a surprise. Juri loves most food and drink." His lip curled almost into a smile, his face softening.

Briony eyed the goblet, and her stomach roiled. "I don't think I'm up for wine tonight." She occasionally liked a good pint or a glass of wine, so she wasn't sure why it turned her stomach tonight. "Sometimes it makes me sleepy, and I don't want to crash into bed later."

"I'd like it if you stayed awake too."

Her breath hitched, and their gazes locked again. She didn't imagine the pull between them. The sense that, while he didn't move, he pursued. A wild predator, with his focus entirely on her.

There was a loud snort. "Really, you'd think they'd never seen a somewhat attractive man before." Katisa sat across from Briony and stared at Seth.

Having removed his armor, Seth wore vae clothes in the same style as those around him, yet they looked exotic on him. He oozed pure male sexuality with an edge of the wild. His tousled black hair framed a firm jaw on a face with perfect angles and a penetrating gaze that bore through anyone he looked at. When they met, his appearance dazzled her, but she'd felt no attraction.

Male and female vae clamored for his attention, offering him food, all while brushing against him or stroking his arm. As if they couldn't help but touch his skin. A female vae, her hair in one long, intricate braid around her head, held a grape to his lips and teased him with it before feeding him.

"He's an incubus. That's what happens." Caladin narrowed his eyes. "Did you say somewhat attractive? How about going forward, you describe him as repulsive?"

Katisa's eyes flashed. "Our people have self-control. And I say what I like when I like."

"I'm aware." Caladin waved his hand. "And it's not about self-control. You don't understand the fantasies an incubus induces, and I'm happy about that. Let's keep it that way."

Katisa grabbed a fork and pointed it at him. "Keep your orders for your warriors."

One side of Caladin's mouth quirked upward. "Are you going to stab me again?" Caladin was exceptionally handsome with high slashing cheekbones, a straight, thin nose, and a full mouth, but there was a coldness to him. Something remote. Yet now, as he teased, he thawed and became more approachable. More attractive.

Briony glanced at Hans. Remote as well, but no one would ever call him cold. And she'd seen his passion when he let his true self out.

"I was four when I did that! Four! And you reached to steal my—" She put her fork down and turned to Briony. "Do you have siblings?"

She shook her head.

"Well, then you're missing out on the absolute torment of older brothers who think they know best. It's about a million times worse when they become king."

"No," Hans said. "He was pretty insufferable as a princeling."

Katisa nodded. "Thank you. I agree."

"We have things we need to discuss." Hans leaned forward. "Where did you put the spellcaster?"

"I have her confined to a room, and I bound her from casting."

"How did you catch her?" Hans asked. "I saw her go through the portal."

Katisa sighed. "Why don't we eat first?" A slim vae stepped around Caladin's seat and began serving from the dishes. At Briony's already loaded plate, he tsked. "The strawberries are for dessert."

Hans growled. "We'll decide what we eat and when."

The vae sniffed and proceeded down the table, back stiff.

"Let's talk over dinner," Hans said in his imperial voice.

The one that was just as exacting and demanding as Caladin's. "I want to know how you caught her."

"You know vae magic is different from that of magicwielders?"

Hans shrugged. "They have to create a spark to tap into magic. That's what causes the smell."

Katisa nodded. "Yes, but not only a smell. Every time they access magic, it creates a reaction. Both the smell and a small ripple. We aren't vulk, so we can't smell their magic as well as you, but we can sense the ripple it leaves in its wake."

Caladin leaned forward. "The past few months, we've sensed a lot of magic being cast. We've sent out patrols, and Katisa set up a trap to pull in any magicwielders so we could question them. The magic that's being done … is dark."

Briony glanced at Hans, feeling the tension in his muscles.

Katisa's eyes glittered. "When the spellcaster created her portal, I was close by and sensed the ripple almost the moment she cast the spell. I was fast enough to use my magic to snag her right as she entered her portal."

"What dark magic have you seen?" Hans asked.

Caladin pushed his plate aside and placed his elbows on the table. "I think we're at the part of dinner where you tell us why you're in the Kuls. And"—he pointed at Briony— "the incubus isn't the only one with magic. She has an aura like a vae. I can feel it clearly now."

Briony glanced up at the sky. The moons, only a crescent sliver tonight, winked through the trees. Her magic was active.

Caladin's gaze bored into Briony. "How did you become Hans's traveling companion? No one hangs around with him voluntarily."

Hans growled and slid forward. "Let me speak with the spellcaster. And tell me about the ravec you killed last week. Then I'll tell you why we're here."

The two glared at each other.

"Ah, friends." Seth threw himself into a chair next to

Katisa. The princess wrinkled her nose, then cast a withering stare at the vae gathering at his elbow until they shrank back into the crowds.

Seth waved a hand. "You can't have important discussions without the day's champion."

Caladin and Hans turned their glares toward Seth. "How did you get out of Peklo?" Hans asked.

He flashed a smile at Katisa. "Much courage. Much wit. A lot of sweat."

The princess rolled her eyes. "Really? You probably just strolled out of the mountain."

Seth's brows rose. "I slew many monsters as I followed them through their rift."

"That takes a lot of courage, wit, and sweat?"

"In Peklo, the beasties were all on the move. There aren't a lot of changes in the underworld, so I followed them. One man against many beasts. Quite a feat. Then, when I ran toward the suns of Ulterra, I didn't know if I'd be extinguished or shot back into the bowels of hell. Courage." An expression flashed across his face, too fast for Briony to figure out. "I wore the skin of a bauk over me as I ascended through the vae. Just in case the guardians of the crossing places were watching. Rather witty, don't you think?"

Katisa's lip curled. "I'd go with disgusting."

Seth plowed on. "And it was rather hot in my armor, so I was sweaty. But don't worry, my sweat smells good."

Katisa's mouth opened and closed a few times, but no words came. Seth removed a knife from his belt and speared a baked pear to bring to his plate.

"What do you mean, all the beasts were on the move?" Caladin asked.

Seth glanced around. "Am I feeding myself?"

Katisa hissed. "Yes. Your hands work."

He shrugged and cut the food on his plate. "Over the past few years, spawn activity has increased, and they're more aggressive than normal, but the beasts don't like to leave their dark holes." He waved his knife. "I got reports of monsters attacking in my borough from my people, and I went to check it out."

Katisa raised a brow. "You have people?"

"Of course. I'm the lord of the eastern borough."

Briony nestled farther into Hans's side and leaned up to whisper in his ear. "Do you know what Peklo is like? What does he mean by a borough?"

"No one knows much about Peklo." He lowered his head and kept his face close to hers. "Or the cursed ones."

"How is he a cursed one if he's a god?"

"A god of what?"

"War and Storms," Briony said. Seth turned to her and raised a brow.

"Why were you tossed in Peklo?" Hans asked him.

"Too much sex, of course. I'm an incubus." But it was the first time Seth broke eye contact. "So, can you tell me why the monsters of the deep are all swarming up here?"

Briony watched the silent exchange between Caladin and Hans. In tandem, they nodded and sat back in their chairs, turning towards Seth.

"There's something evil gathering in the Bodec Mountains." Hans told them about the animals fleeing from the northern Kuls, Morana reappearing, and Baba Yaga's suspicions.

Caladin nodded. "Yes, there's death in the mountains."

Seth speared another pear. "I know that sorcerer. Spawn do her bidding. How did she get up here?"

Hans turned to Katisa. "I need to talk to the prisoner. She's Morana's partner."

Katisa sat back in her chair, playing absently with her earlobe. "Can you describe what Morana looks like?"

Briony detailed the sorcerer's hair and face, and when she

got to her old-fashioned elaborate green gown, Katisa's eyes widened. "I've seen her in a dream."

"What did you see?" Hans demanded.

Katisa's gaze was frosty. "*If* I want to, I can perform a dreamcast and show you what I saw." The tension at the table rose despite the lively music and the stars winking overhead.

Caladin's expression turned fierce. Vulk-like. "If you want to talk to my prisoner and get information from Katisa, I want something in return."

The muscles of Hans's arm bulged as his claws tightened on his chair. "What?"

"It's been a long time since vae and vulk joined forces, but we join now to fight this threat. I want my lands safe."

Hans was already shaking his head. "I work alone."

Caladin slammed his fist on the table. "Two vulk won't be nearly enough to handle what's out there. I've seen what's brewing in the Bodecs. You haven't. And if you want to talk to my prisoner or learn what Katisa has seen, you work with me."

"Since when do the vae want to fight?"

"I told you, we sent patrols. One of them never returned." Caladin's knuckles turned white. "I'm fighting."

Silence stretched across the table.

"I'll fight, too," Seth said. "I know you want my skills."

Briony said nothing, but she leaned against Hans's arm and waited, holding her breath.

"Time is short," Hans said finally. "We have twelve days to get this done."

Briony jumped. Over two weeks already gone? Her heart sank into her stomach. Hans would leave when the moons were full. Forever.

Around her was a world of possibility and magic, but she was only a visitor, allowed to pass through for a moment. The same with Hans. She'd become someone he once spent time with. Barely a memory.

Caladin nodded. "The vae are ready now."

"Before we fight Morana, Briony and I have somewhere we need to explore in the Bodecs. We do that alone. It isn't linked to any of this."

"Fine."

Hans nodded. "Then I agree."

Briony let out a large exhale and sagged against Hans. She wanted the vae's help. Even though she had confidence in Hans's fighting skills, whenever someone mentioned what might lurk in the Bodecs, she grew more frightened.

Caladin grabbed his goblet of wine, his expression relaxing. "Good. Let's meet in the morning with a few of my warriors. We'll start planning."

Katisa smiled at Briony. "Since you're staying the night, what about tea before we meet?"

Briony smiled back. "That sounds great."

The rest of dinner passed more easily. Seth melted into the crowd, a throng of vae at his heels. Juri still held his own small court. Waiters brought out one sumptuous course after another until she couldn't eat another bite. The dancing was in full swing, and shadows deepened in the courtyard as twilight passed into evening.

Hans's hand trailed up her back. "Have you eaten enough? The food is only fit for a deer, but they cook it well."

"I liked it, and yes, I'm done."

He bent to her neck, and his breath fanned along her skin. "Do you want to remain at the party? Dance? Mingle with the vae? Or walk somewhere private with me?"

Her breath caught, and she turned until her face was only inches from his. This was it. Did she go somewhere with him where she knew she'd ask for his touch? Or hold herself back and keep them a distance apart?

20

BRIONY REACHED out and lay her hand over his. "I want to go somewhere private."

Without another word, Hans led her along the outside of the feast, staying in the shadows. Glass globes full of flickering light lit the courtyard and the palace, either on the ground or in sconces. Hans led her up the few stairs into the palace, past a few scowling guards, and took an immediate left down a curving corridor. They passed beautiful paintings and tapestries, but she barely noticed. Her focus centered on Hans, with his pine scent wafting around her. He opened a limestone door with a long gold handle; the tip shaped like a wolf's head.

Briony stepped inside and walked to the center of the room. "Oh."

She circled slowly. Arched windows filled the entire back of the room except for a large double door opening into the forest beyond. The floor was a dark stone adorned with a shaggy tan rug under the bed. And it was quite a bed. With dark green blankets piled on top, it took up the entire side of the room. A simple bedside table and a dresser were the only other furniture, but a door opened into an adjoining bathroom.

"When I lived here before, this was my room. The vae tried to make it as den-like as possible. Or what the vae think a vulk den looks like."

She moved about the room, picturing him in the space. "How long were you here?"

Hans prowled after her. "A few years." As if sensing her thoughts, he added, "No one has shared that bed with me." The unspoken word, *yet*, hovered in the air.

The same energy when they'd locked eyes in the cave built between them. Like a bow being drawn for an arrow. In a rush, they came together in the middle of the room. His massive arms circled her, pulling her close, so close she was forced to tilt her head back to meet his glowing eyes.

"No one has given you a serum." He dropped his head to nuzzle her neck. "This time, the scent of your desire for me is real."

"Yes." She trailed her nails down his back, and he shivered.

The maelstrom swirling in her chest was the magnetic pull of *him*. Of their bond. It was hard to distinguish where she ended and he began.

Uncertainty threaded through her lust. "None of this makes sense," she whispered. "But I want you more now than I did back in the cave."

His seductive, silky growl rippled over her skin, and she gasped and pressed closer, rubbing against the soft fur of his stomach.

"The moons are low in the sky, little one." One long lick along her neck. "The vae are busy, and the forest is safe and private. Let me show you how our first time together should have been. Strip. Run through the woods so I can chase you. I'll catch you and make you mine."

Heat pooled between her legs, and her fingers flexed. He licked again. "Okay."

She walked to the double doors and released the laces on her bodice. Her dress pooled at her feet, leaving her naked before his gaze.

Hans's eyes glowed brighter. Hungry. Wanting. He purred, and she wanted to run to him, not away, but she opened the doors and entered the forest.

The moons bobbed low above the trees. The shadows should be impenetrable, making it difficult to see in the thickest part of this unfamiliar forest, but instead of darkness, everything was in shades of gray, as if the moons shone brightly to illuminate the path in front of her. Her feet cushioned by soft moss, she slipped between the tree trunks.

Each footfall pounded on the forest floor, and her toes dug in to propel her forward. Her hair flew free behind her, sweeping her back, and she trailed her hand along a tree, the bark scratching her palm, to leave her scent. With a spurt of speed, she dug in and raced forward.

He was coming.

Something primal unfurled and spurred her faster. An ancient race of male and female. He'd prove he was worthy, and she'd let him claim her.

Her heartbeat pounded in her ears from both desire and exertion. A boulder of limestone blocked her path. She paused for a moment, but it was long enough for an arm to snake around her waist. Hot breath fanned her neck as Hans pinned her against the rock, his thigh wedging between hers to spread her open for him. He bit the nape of her neck, and she groaned.

No. She'd barely made him earn it. When she pretended to go slack and compliant, he loosened his grip and shifted backward a step. Briony twisted free. Sucking in air, she scrambled around the rock and sprinted away.

He released a rich, pleased growl, and she was sure he pursued, but she wasn't slowing to check. Grinning, she dodged around trees, anticipating what he'd do when he caught her, making her entire body tingle.

She stumbled and caught herself. If she fell, he'd be on top of her and inside her instantly. Still, she'd slowed enough that he snagged her hips and pulled her against him. He pressed against her back, hard and eager.

Briony struggled to run again, and he crooned, trying to calm her. The hunter's quarry was in his hands, and he would do what he wanted with her. She thrashed, and he pressed her against a tree, biting roughly at her neck. "Ah," she sighed. The rough bark teased her breasts, and molten flame shot through her veins. It was tempting to give in, but ... no. Not quite yet. His grip relaxed a fraction, and she pushed off the tree in one jerk, slipping free to run again.

This time, she made sure her feet landed squarely on the ground. Hans's breathing behind her became ragged. Heavy with his desire. Briony ducked around a thick elm.

Here.

A circle of pines whispered together around a clearing, and the crescent moons cast a pale glow into a glade. Heat licked along her skin and grew in her blood. She no longer heard his breathing, but she sensed him. Her vulk was here, waiting. Anticipating his approach, she shivered.

A low howl broke the heavy silence. He'd never howled before her, and her skin rippled with arousal at his song. Until she heard it, she didn't notice how hushed the woods had become, as if the forest's soul held its breath. She was his, and he sang it aloud to everyone. Even though she was a human, something in her recognized the ancient call of the wild.

When he stepped into the glade, her heart stuttered, and she stepped backward. As much as her vision had sharpened, he was still all darkness, except for his brilliant blue eyes. And so massive she forgot to breathe. Soon all his power and strength would be focused on her. She trembled with uncontrollable need. She wanted to get tucked under him. Feel his immense body over hers.

Moisture gathered between her legs, betraying her eagerness.

As he stepped left, she stepped right, and they circled each other. His crooning rumble started. They didn't measure each other like opponents. This was a slow spiral, each step bringing them closer together.

<Come to me.>

Did he speak aloud, or had she imagined it? She rushed forward, closing the distance between them, her fingers diving into his fur. He dropped his head, and teeth grazed her neck. With a hard, greedy lick, short and rough, he pushed her head to the side. Briony released a strangled, yearning cry. He nipped the column of her throat, and she arched against him.

Run. Let him work for it. The very air seemed to throb around her, directing her in some timeless ritual.

She whirled, pushing off his chest, and took off again. With a surprised grunt, he followed a beat behind her. Faster than she'd moved in her entire life, she feinted to surprise him. When it worked, she laughed and bounded forward again. Grinning, she pirouetted and ran the other way, and Hans dug his hind claws into the dirt and grappled to follow.

A pleased purring reverberated off the trees, distracting her, and her step hitched for a moment. But it was enough to let him wrap his hands around her waist and pull her to his chest.

With a soft rumble, his teeth nipped at her nape again, bringing them both to the ground. As soon as he had her beneath him on all fours, he pulled her hips under his and pinned her in place. There was no escape this time.

Briony arched, gliding her back against his solid stomach as his legs spread hers wide. "Hans," she whimpered. If she didn't have him right now, she might combust. Even her breath was like fire in her lungs, coated thickly with the scent of his lust. Hers.

When his hands landed outside hers, his upper body caged her in, keeping her securely in place, and she groaned and rubbed her face on his arm. He surged into her. An initial stretch, a brief twinge, then only pleasure. This was what she wanted.

Outside, under the dying glow of the moons, he took her. He used his upper body to hold her, preventing her from shifting away from the power of his thrusting hips. There was a groove against his stomach, his chest, made only for her, and as he pulled them tighter together, they fit perfectly. Merged. She let him show her what only he could do.

He worked himself inside with long, gliding strokes. Each time he withdrew, he dragged his length along the spot that made her spark. Then, as he thrust forward, he let the slow friction tease. Sweat lay slick, and she trembled. She was so close, but he wasn't giving her quite enough to get there.

"A worthy chase, little one," he murmured. He sunk deep. Briony moaned, spasming around him and demanding more.

"I need ..." She couldn't finish. Her neck arched, and she pushed back against him.

"I'll give you what you need." His voice was gruff. Ragged.

His muscles flexed, his claws digging grooves into the earth. He pumped. It was a good thing he held her because she'd lost all control of her limbs.

Oh, heavens ... this vulk. Hans.

How was he hitting things inside her like that? If it was possible, he seemed even thicker. The fullness adding more delicious pressure. It forced her to feel every single inch of him.

She panted as sensation swamped her. It built higher and higher in demanding waves of bliss.

"Hans!" Digging her own fingernails into the dirt, she came. The release centered between her legs, all flame, and heat, but rapidly expanded through her entire body. She bucked so violently that Hans wrapped an arm under her chest to support her. She screamed, and his mouth fell to her neck. She wanted his teeth. Wanted him to bite her. That set off more ripples deep inside, and her hips bucked again.

His thrusts doubled. All she could do was hang on, let him move. And it was masterful. As he angled her, sometimes holding her, sometimes letting her support herself, his skillful cock hit different areas inside her. He wrung every drop of pleasure from her, and she gasped.

When he lowered down over her, his teeth nipped at her neck, and his arm squeezed her tight. His breath came in short pants, the thrusts so controlled before, now deep and urgent. He groaned into her ear and then raked his upper teeth down her neck.

He swelled and pulsed against her, easing his knot inside with short steady presses of his hips. A growl vibrated along her back. It seduced her with its rich tone, and Briony whimpered and pressed backward. A powerful lunge and he joined them fully together. She clenched around him and locked them as one.

She was getting addicted to this. Greedily, she rubbed against him, wanting more, and he rocked his hips.

That was all it took. She exploded into a million fiery pieces again. Briony screamed, her back arching. With a ragged groan, Hans joined her.

She fell into a daze while they were knotted together. She was aware of Hans, repeated rounds of pleasure, and the intertwining bond in her chest pinging as it tied tighter strands around them. She thought the rune may have shone in the glade, but she was too drunk on pleasure to be sure.

When her awareness returned, she lay flat on her stomach on the moss in the glade while Hans kept her warm, lying over her, their bodies no longer joined. He shifted and licked her neck, and a flood of warmth centered around her heart.

Throughout the knotting, he'd licked her neck often, in particular where it sloped to her shoulder, and each time it made her chest flutter.

She rubbed against him and turned onto her back to run her hands through the fur of his neck. His head dipped to her breasts.

When he lapped over the tip of one, a jolt of bliss shot through her, and she whimpered. "They've never been sensitive like that before."

"You crave my touch." He teased the tip, and she bowed off the ground, her hands fisting in his fur. His tonguing was thorough as he concentrated on the nipple while he brushed his fingers along the sides. She writhed under him, gulping in air.

He dragged his tongue over a plump tip again, then trailed down between her breasts. His tongue whispered over the center of her chest where the rune mark lay, and a zing whispered over her skin. She glanced down. Hans used the tip of his tongue to trace the small tattoo of their shared mark.

That wasn't sensitive skin, but molten heat flowed through her as he touched it. "Please, I need more."

Hans stood and drew her to stand in front of him. He ran his hand through her hair. "We'll go to the hot springs and play. Then my bed."

She raised a brow. "You play?"

He dipped his head and teased his teeth up her neck. "Only with you. Let's play some bed games."

Hans took her again in the hot springs, then carried her to his room and began again. By then, she was floating on waves of pleasure as he kept them joined more than they were parted all night.

21

HANS LEAPED FOR ZANN, but just as he was about to close his arms around him, Zann vanished.

He jolted upright in bed, snarling. Where the hell was he? He tensed to leap off the bed, but a hand slid across his chest, and the faint perfume of mountain laurel calmed him.

"Are you alright? Is there danger?" Briony's voice was thick with sleep, and she swiped a lock of hair from her face. "What's wrong?" His heart rate slowed. She lay half tangled in a blanket and half tangled around him. He wanted to roll her under him to sink inside her again.

"It's alright. Bad dream." He leaned down on his elbow and stroked her back. A purr rumbled through his chest. All night he'd purred. Purrs of arousal, purrs of contentment, a slow, even purr to bring her to sleep. If he purred himself hoarse every night to lull her to sleep on his chest, it was worth it because it made her happy.

She'd had precious little happiness.

The memory he'd witnessed at Baba Yaga's haunted him, and the more she told him about her life back in the village, the hotter his rage. Those townspeople treated Briony poorly for no reason at all. He wanted to walk into their town center and roar. Show them what he thought about how they'd treated her and demand they recognize she was good and sweet. Perfect. But most of all, he wanted to give her new memories. Ones where she was happy.

She sat up and blinked. "Do you have nightmares a lot?"

He shrugged. "It's not really a nightmare, it's a memory. The same one, every time."

Briony rubbed her face against his, and her lips whispered against his cheek. Waves of warmth flooded through him from where she touched him. "Will you be able to fall back to sleep?" Her fingers trailed up his neck how he liked, and he leaned into her.

"No."

"Aren't you tired after all our ... you know?"

He nibbled up her ear. "I'd start again, but you need sleep."

She pulled back, bringing them face to face. "You need rest, too. Would it help to talk about your nightmare?"

He sighed. "I doubt it. I relive my brother's death."

Briony wrapped herself closer. "What happened?"

He shook his head. "You don't want to hear this."

Her gaze searched his. "Tell me, Hans."

He broke eye contact to turn and stare into the forest's shadows and took a deep breath.

100 Years Ago

HANS EMERGED from a thick patch of pines to join Zann at the top of a crest. Below them, a small village huddled against the mountain slope. The homes had an orange hue from the fir trees they'd used to craft them. Most humans set their homes low and squat to defend against the weather, but these stretched tall and thin, like mushrooms, along a tall, rough-logged fence.

Buildings tall enough to peek over the outer walls made sense if someone was an archer, though. Or a spellcaster wanting to stand at a window to hurl spells. His hackles rose. "This isn't a simple village of outcasts."

Zann shrugged, and his long shadow stretching across the grass in front of him copied the motion. "Nope, but we knew that when we scented sulfur. There must be a reason they're out here. Usually, the magic folk stick close together." Zann tilted his head. "Necromancers, maybe?"

"I don't think so," Hans said. "The village is laid out strangely, but there are no altars." Necromancers always had altars, and all the necromancer nests he'd found in the past were in dark caves, not out in the forest or nestled in the sunny lee of a mountain. The villagers here had even taken the time to battle the muddy season, laying down sawdust chips on the road, so the reddish clay dirt wasn't churned and choppy. From what he knew about necromancers, they did little else but concoct dark spells.

He studied the main road. There was something odd about it, but he couldn't figure out what. As he followed its straight path up the center of the town, each side street split off in perfect angles, so the town was symmetrical. And there wasn't a human anywhere.

Zann's eyes narrowed. Blue eyes and the same towering height were the only two physical characteristics he shared with his brother. Zann's fur was pure white, leading to their nicknames, Shadow and Ice.

"Let's remind these humans that Divorky Forest is ours, and ours alone. This won't take long, and after, we can go work on your den. I have a week or two to help you before I need to get back to the pack. Tell me you've finished the floor?"

Hans smiled. "Finished it last week." Zann didn't mind hauling tons of stone back to the den, but it was torture for his brother to sit still and shape each one to fit into place. "We can work on the walls and dig out some more rooms."

Zann flexed his claws. "Good. Let's go."

While they loped through the trees, Hans considered the complications a magicwielder might spring if they attacked. Zann's style was to charge in, expecting a vulk's natural immunity to magic to shield him, but Hans had a funny feeling about this village. Something wasn't right.

Looping around the perimeter, sulfur hit them full force. Zann snarled and leaped to climb the fence.

"Zann, wait," he called in Vulk. His brother ignored him and swung down the other side. Hans cursed and checked the homes near the fence. The windows were dark, but based on the smell, someone was here.

He followed Zann over the fence, landing with a soft thump, and dropped into a fighter's crouch. The forest was silent. Even the sheep and goats stopped stamping in their pens.

The gnarled wooden back door of the house closest to them banged open, and a sorcerer stepped out. "I've been waiting for you, Zann, leader of the vulk."

Her red robe swirled from an unfelt wind, and her palms faced forward and glowed blue. She strode toward Zann, ignoring Hans, her long gold hair trailing behind her. The spellcaster was a young woman, but there was no fear as she held Zann's gaze. Held the gaze of an Alpha.

Zann leaped, claws extended to tackle and pin her but mid-jump, he twisted and landed on his feet a few paces in front of her. The visceral growl in his throat softened into a purr.

What the hell? They were Ice and Shadow, the two most feared fighters in all of Ulterra. They didn't stop a fight to gawk at a girl, especially not a dangerous one.

Hans snapped at Zann, but his brother ignored him, fixated on the woman. Her lips parted, and she reached out and ran her hand up Zann's arm, letting the blue glow encase him.

"No!" Hans sprang for her.

Zann whirled in a blur of white and crashed into him, smashing him to the earth so hard his ribs cracked. Pain seared up his side.

Zann pinned him to the ground, claws at his throat. "Leave her. I'll take care of it."

"Pin her hands and get these villagers out of our forest."

They'd never fought, never laid a hand on each other, not even as kids. As his brother's claws flexed over his neck, it was the first time he'd ever felt them. Something broke in his chest. Like another rib cracking, but the pain felt deeper.

Zann snarled. "Stay down." He commanded it, and Hans went limp and lay still. Since he accepted Zann as Alpha, Zann could force him to obey Alpha command, but he'd never imagined his brother would ever use it.

Powerless to resist, Hans lay stuck to the ground, side screaming, as the spellcaster created a portal, took Zann's hand, and led him through it. The last thing he saw was Zann, glowing a faint blue, not glancing back as the portal closed.

It took him five days to stand up. Luckily, the village was abandoned, or even a weak human could have walked up to him and cut his head off. It wasn't supposed to be possible to reject an Alpha command, but he'd done it. No one would ever have that kind of power over him again.

He'd limped from the village and found the pack in chaos. No sign of Zann anywhere.

"What do you want us to do?" Juri asked. The entire pack formed around him in a semi-circle—how they faced their Alpha.

Too long suppressed, his instinct to lead clawed free like a savage beast. He let it come. "We find Zann and kill the spellcaster."

It took months to track Zann to a remote keep far north.

Used as a garrison, the stone edifice in the shoulder of a hulking snow-covered mountain was abandoned when its inhabitants, a northern peltwalker clan, died out.

The frozen ground crunched under his feet as he turned to Juri. "Stay with the rest of the pack until I see what's going on." He didn't know what to expect from Zann, and it was best if he faced him alone.

Warped from exposure to the elements, the wooden entry door twisted around its black steel hinges, but it swung open. Not a good sign. Hans edged through the narrow entryway to the main room. Once hung with weapons, this was where warriors would mingle, train, and lounge. The chamber was one vast, circular expanse with high slits for windows. The stone surrounding him oozed icy air, and his breath puffed out in a freezing mist over his head as he crept through the shadows.

Sulfur burned his nose. It permeated the entire space, choking the air. A large central fireplace, long gone cold, was the only furniture in the room; hunks of crystal rimmed a chalk circle before it.

Inside the circle, Zann and the red-robed spellcaster faced each other. Zann's once white coat was gray from dirt and ash, and the sorcerer's robe was ripped at the shoulder. She held a crystal, and a thread wove from the crystal to Zann, wrapping around his hands and tying his ankles to the floor, binding him in place.

Standing a few paces away from them, her back to Hans, a tall woman with dark hair twisted on her head stood in an elaborate green dress. Morana. "Ah, Hazel, you fail me yet again. My most promising student and my worst. This spell should not be difficult for you. All you have to do is form a connection with him for it to succeed. He's a vulk. They're animals, and they're easily manipulated. Yet you failed. Look at how much he hates you." Green sparks flew from her fingertips. "Guess we'll have to do things the hard way. Bit rougher for you."

The sorcerer began shaking, the crystal bobbing up and down. "Give me more time."

"I've already given you plenty of time, and look! It only made things worse. That vulk gained control and dragged you up here. It took me weeks to find you." She flipped her hand over, and a green ball appeared. "I won't get everything I need, but it may be just enough ..." Morana threw the ball at the sorcerer, and when it reached the circle of crystals, they trilled a high-pitched note, flashed blue, and a dome appeared protecting Zann and Hazel. The ball smashed into it and dissolved.

"Tricky." Morana smiled. She hurled another, and this time there was a brief flash of blue and green, but the green sank through the dome and coated the sorcerer and Zann.

Hazel screamed and clutched her throat, falling to the floor. Bonds gone, Zann jerked, choking as well, and fell to the ground.

Hans edged farther into the room, crouching in the shadows. Let the magicwielders fight and get distracted, and he'd find the perfect time to pounce. Zann wasn't bound any longer. All he needed to do was get him out of here.

Morana raised her arms, and the floor beneath his feet rumbled. Stones fell out of the roof overhead. Starting under Morana, a large crack spread along the keep's floor. Wind whipped through the keep, making her green dress dance. When she pivoted, her dark eyes had turned green.

A cloud of brimstone flooded the keep. From the crack came snarling and harsh guttural cries. A bauk gripped the side of the crack and dug his claws in to get out.

Hans roared and sprinted forward, hurling Morana to the ground. She shrieked and, with a wave of a glowing hand, flung him across the room. His head slammed against the rock wall with a thud.

There was a bigger shudder, and more stone tumbled. This time, it wasn't only the keep but the mountain at its back that quaked.

Morana stood, her glow fading. "Who are you?"

Hans staggered forward and slammed his hand on the ground. The rift to the underworld began to close. A dark shape inside the crack flung the still scrabbling bauk out of the way, and a skeletal hand grabbed the edge and hissed.

What the hell was that?

Morana screamed and threw herself on the ground, her hands grappling at the closing seam in the earth. "No!" She looked up at him with crazed eyes. "Let the rift stay open, or I kill him." She flung her hand out, and a green whip of light lashed around Zann's waist. The red-robed sorcerer groaned and grabbed Zann's ankle.

Rage welled up within Hans like he'd never experienced before. "How about I only kill you?" He stalked forward.

"We're all linked." Morana grinned, and she reached down toward the dark figure. The skeletal hand clutched at her wrist, and a chill raced up Hans's spine.

"Do it." Hans's head snapped around at his brother's words. Zann stared at him, chest heaving. "Do it. Kill her." <I'll help close the rift if she pulls me with her.>

Time seemed to slow. The crack in the earth ripped farther apart as Morana heaved to drag the black figure up into the keep. His hackles rose, and every sense went into overdrive. *Danger.* Whatever that thing was, it was evil—the strongest he'd ever felt—and he couldn't let it get into Ulterra. There had to be a way to save his brother and kill Morana.

Hans leaped and rammed Morana behind her knees. She shrieked and teetered. Flailing her arms, she lost her balance and tipped over into the rift, but at the last moment, she twisted and grabbed the edge.

He raked his claws at the seam. *Close. Hurry and close.* The ground rumbled as it started to seal shut again. Boulders broke through the keep's ceiling and scattered stone and dust through the air. Everything went hazy, and he choked and pawed at the air, trying to see. Where was Morana? Where was Zann?

Through the milky fog, he made out Morana and the flashing green of the magical rope still bound to Zann. Morana and Zann clung to the rift's edge, about to fall into Peklo. Morana shrieked and fell backward, but still, Zann hung on. Hans wheeled around and leaped for him.

"Come on! Take my hand."

"No. This isn't closed. They might open it again." Zann snarled and dug his claws in, and the rift rippled, the earth closing quickly around Zann.

"Leap for it!" screamed Hans. But he was too late. The seam sealed shut over Zann, trapping him in the earth.

Hans roared and charged forward, claws grappling at the ground, but a boulder hit his shoulder and knocked him down.

Juri catapulted into him and grabbed him around the waist. "You need to get out of here. There's a landslide. This is all going under."

The ground heaved and rose like a wave. Juri grabbed him and dragged him toward the entrance. As he left, rock smashed through what remained of the ceiling and obliterated everything.

AT SOME POINT, he'd lain back, and Briony sprawled across his chest, stroking his face. He couldn't believe he had enough words to describe everything that had happened. It had been so long ago, and he'd never told the entire story to anyone, not even Juri.

"I killed my brother." Hans shook his head. "He might have survived in Peklo, but he never made it there. The ground swallowed him, and even if we may have been able to dig him out, the landslide prevented us."

Briony sat up. "No. Morana killed your brother."

He sat up too. "I was Alpha, and I'm a vulk. Possibly the son of ..." He turned and stared out the window. "I should have saved him. We'd been in far worse situations, and I always got us out."

Briony met his gaze, and her bluish eyes blazed. "Hans, no. That's—"

"I failed. End of story."

She pressed herself to his side, stroking his neck and rubbing her cheek against his. As good as that felt, he knew what would feel better, and he wanted to lose himself in her. Let bedding her chase away the memories.

He ran his hand up her stomach and thumbed her nipple, keeping his claw away. She gasped. "Since we're both up ..." His head dropped to her neck, and he coaxed her to lie back.

"Wait—" She pressed her hand over his. Her pupils were dilated, but her gaze focused on his. "I have more to say." She cupped his face. "I wasn't there, but I'm sure you did everything you could. You're punishing yourself for an impossible choice. An impossible situation."

He stilled. "You think I'm punishing myself?"

"Yes. You're keeping yourself in your den, away from everything."

"No. I'm not the Alpha, and a pack isn't for me. I discovered I work best alone. Some vulk aren't meant for a pack and go rogue. It happens."

She frowned. "But your pack didn't take another Alpha, did it?"

"No."

"Maybe that means—"

"Briony. It's all long in the past. My life is the one I've chosen, and it won't change."

She didn't respond, but she dropped her gaze. There was

183

an odd twinge in his chest like someone wrung out his heart. Uncomfortable and unfamiliar.

Hans pulled her closer and nipped at her neck. "I'm not alone tonight, am I?" Honeyed vanilla thickened the air. He laved her neck, and she moaned. She was so responsive and eager for his touch. "Should I let you sleep, or do you want me to keep exploring with my tongue?"

"You can keep going." Her tiny nails bit into his shoulders, and he grinned into her neck. He laid her down and let his tongue meander its way down her body.

22

HER MUSCLES COMPLAINED as she shifted on Hans's lap in the palace dining hall. He'd wrung her out so many times last night that they ached every time she moved, but she'd welcome this kind of soreness any day.

The few vae eating with them stared, but she didn't care. She was the sole focus of a vulk, and there wasn't anything in the world better than that. Was this what it would feel like to be courted by him? The bond in her chest hummed. Before, it was only a faint thread, barely noticeable most of the time, but now it surged.

A young vae wearing the palace sash of the royal staff approached and stood with his hands clasped behind his back, his gaze fixed somewhere over Hans's head. "Princess Katisa has tea prepared and asked me to bring Miss Briony to join her."

Hans didn't spare him a glance. "When she's finished with her breakfast."

She pointed at the food. "You haven't eaten."

"I'll hunt with Juri later. Vae food isn't my style."

She wiggled out of his lap and stood. "I've eaten enough. I'm ready."

The messenger led them through the palace, not up any stairs—thank heavens. So far, she'd avoided the open staircases without railings. There was no way she was using them. Who had towering staircases without safety rails? Didn't the vae fall off?

Katisa sat in a private waiting room tucked in a corner past a long suite of rooms. Vibrant landscape paintings dotted the walls between the large windows, with rich purple curtains sweeping the floor. There were several armchairs of golden wood and white squashy cushions around a matching golden table with a silver teakettle, its long neck swanlike in a pronounced arch.

Katisa nodded at Hans. "Jeral will show you to the sorcerer. My brother will find you there when he's free, and we can all discuss what's happening in the Bodec Mountains."

"I'll know if you need me," Hans said to Briony. The bond in her chest pinged as if emphasizing how he'd know. Since last night, it had been more active, or she was more attuned to it. Would it stay this way until the night of the full moons?

Hans turned to Katisa. "You touch even a hair on her head, and the vulk and vae are in open war." He stalked away, halted, then returned and lifted Briony in his arms and ran his jaw along her cheek. Just as quickly, he put her down and was gone.

Katisa's jaw dropped, and she stared at the empty doorway. "He's protective of you. And he's ... gentle ... around you."

Briony's chin jerked up. "Why wouldn't he be?"

"Please sit." She pointed at the seat across from her.

When Briony sat, the cushions folded her into them, molding around her. Her aunt would have hated the poor posture. She leaned back and enjoyed it.

Katisa sat in the same style chair across from her but remained upright, her ankles crossed under her. She wore a gray long-sleeved dress with yellow handstitched beading on

186

the bodice and neckline. Briony wore another vae garment, but she'd refused a dress. Instead, she wore a simple white tunic, wrapped at the waist, over a navy skirt that fluttered when she walked. They also gave her a pair of woven slippers with a tough leather-like sole that Hans poked with a claw and said wasn't genuine animal skin.

The princess turned her head and stared out the window. "Please don't take offense. It's just surprising to see him act that way." She turned and smiled at Briony. "The vulk differ from you and me. Their capacity to care about someone else ..." Katisa studied her hands. "The vulk are a secretive, private species, and there are things Hans can't tell you about himself and his culture."

Briony leaned forward. "He told me the vulk have no mates. I'm not—" She swallowed thickly. "We'll part soon and never see each other again."

Katisa poured tea into two small cups and handed one to her. The liquid inside was a pale green. "A vulk can't have a relationship. With anyone. You can't take it personally. It's a fault on their side and their side alone." She still hadn't met Briony's gaze. "I'm not sure it helps, but I've never seen him act like he does with you. I've never seen *any* vulk act like that."

Briony knew several girls growing up who she was friendly with, but since she was always working and couldn't go to their houses after school or play on the weekends, their friendships remained shallow. No one was ever concerned about her getting hurt, but Katisa seemed genuinely worried and concerned about her.

"I know he walks alone."

Katisa paused for a long moment and stared into her tea. "Has he told you why the vulk take no mates? Do you understand why Hans can't think about relationships like you and I do?"

Briony sipped her tea. It was fruity, like blackberries mixed with lemon, but the bright, exotic taste turned to watery swill at Katisa's words. "No, he didn't say why. Can you tell me?"

"I've probably already said more than I should. The vulk and vae have worked together for millennia. While we haven't always gotten along, there is a covenant of privacy between our two species, and I can't break it, even if I'd like to. I'm sorry."

Briony's shoulders drooped, and she slumped back in her chair, the tea forgotten in her hand. The bubbles of leftover pleasure and excitement from last night burst, leaving only deadening exhaustion. Even if there was something mysterious she didn't know, it didn't change anything. They were over soon. There was no permanent tie between them. Back to reality.

She forced a smile and took another sip of tea. "Let's change the subject."

Katisa's face relaxed, and she was happy to talk about the vae kingdom and tell Briony more about their culture. She was surprised when Briony told her Hans described the vae festival when the flowers bloomed. "Yes, that's our sacred miagmac flower. I wouldn't think a vulk would have paid much attention."

Briony frowned. Hans always paid attention.

Leaning forward, Katisa poured them both another cup. "I'll be honest. I have two motives for wanting you to take tea with me today. First, I want us to be friends, but I also want to ask you more about your magic. I can sense it humming. It's like vae magic but has a slightly different feel."

"There isn't much I can tell you." She held her hands up in front of her. "All I know is that I can heal with my hands at night." The memory from Baba Yaga's resurfaced. "I've also shot light, but that was only once, and I don't know how it happened."

"Only at night? Are you sure?"

Briony shrugged. "When I learned I could heal, I tried to

use it all the time. After a few years, I realized it was only possible at night."

Katisa leaned back in her chair, tea forgotten. "Does magical discharge build up inside as you use it? In a dangerous way?"

Briony blinked. "If I heal too much, I feel like I've stood outside during a snowstorm without a coat on because I get freezing cold. I've passed out before and had to be warmed up. Is that what you mean?"

The princess stood and wandered to the window, a small wrinkle between her brows. She pointed up at the sky. "Vae magic comes from the small sun. When we use it, we get hot. So hot we always keep special water on hand. Otherwise, we must wait for the sun to go down to recuperate. I'm researching if there's anything we can do to stop it from happening."

"It's not like that for me."

"No, yours is definitely different." Katisa studied Briony for a long moment. "The vae have a ritual to understand our magic when we come of age. If you want to learn more about yours, we could try it."

Did she want to know more about her magic? She'd have to face she had a different father. Face she was different.

She sighed. Memories of her parents were of laughing, tipsy people patting her on the head and telling her to go to bed while they ducked into another tent. Or watching them drive off without looking back. Leaving her behind.

Did her biological father know about her? Her hand fisted. Even if he did, he wouldn't have stuck around. No one did. She'd prayed every day for years that her parents would return. Then she'd hoped maybe her biological father would learn about her, and he'd come and whisk her away from her work at the surgery. After a while, she gave up.

"I guess I'll learn more about my magic."

Katisa's brow furrowed. "You don't seem certain."

"If it can help against Morana, then I want to know, but in the end, I'm returning to Vieska, where I can't use it any longer. I'll need to make sure I know how to hide it."

Katisa raised a brow. "Hide it? Why?"

"I live in Rohant. Magic is forbidden."

Katisa's pale gray eyes turned dark charcoal and swirled like mercury as she stared at Briony. "That's ridiculous. What is wrong with humans? Magicwielders may deserve a ban—they can't be trusted—but not someone like you."

The air crackling around Katisa, Briony sat motionlessly. "O-kay."

Her normal eye color returned. "Why return to Vieska if you can't live as yourself?"

Briony sighed. "I have nowhere else."

"Hm." There was a long moment of silence. "Are you sure about doing the ritual?"

This time, she nodded right away. "Yes."

Katisa turned. "Follow me. We need to get something." A door with no handle stood on one side of the room, and Katisa pressed her palm along the frame, and it swung open with a faint whoosh. Inside was a circular room, with a few high slits for windows allowing in narrow beams of light. Shelves loaded every square inch of wall space, groaning under the weight of books, scrolls, heavy bowls, and jars of powder. Centered in the middle of the room was a hexagonal ebony table. Laid out on top was a map of Ulterra, the edges worn from use.

Katisa went to a shelf, pulled out a crystal bottle, and set it on the table. "We drink a drop of water from our sacred well. The well holds part of a hzievda inside it."

Briony stared at the water. Tiny motes of light swirled as the liquid eddied counterclockwise in the glass. The water shouldn't be moving like that. "What do you mean a piece of a... what? Hzeivda?"

"We built our kingdom here because our ancestors saw a

hzievda—one of the guiding stars—fall from the sky. That's why the waters are warm. The star still lives under the earth here, and a shard remains inside this one well."

Briony watched the tiny flecks of light dance in the water. "What will happen if I drink this?"

"Since you aren't a vae, maybe nothing. Or it will help connect you with your magic and help you understand it. At least that's what happened during my ritual."

"What do I do? Gulp this down?"

Katisa picked up the bottle and withdrew the cork with a small pop. "No. Open your mouth."

Briony opened, and Katisa tipped the bottle until one drop glistened off the small lip. She shook her hand, and it fell onto Briony's tongue.

There was a whoosh and swirling darkness. No more vae palace. She hurtled through velvety shadow until, all at once, everything was still.

She stood in the center of a vast field, golden grass brushing against her skirt. It was morning a moment ago, but here it was inky night, except for both moons shining so brightly there were halos around them.

Briony glanced down and jumped. Her entire body shimmered.

The smaller moon blinked, and a beam of white light shot out, rippled over the grass, and cascaded toward her in a wave. "Zorzye." There was no speaker, only the wind, but the word echoed through the field.

"I don't understand." She spoke to no one, but she sensed she wasn't alone.

Several paces ahead of her, a dark figure rose from the grass. She could see through it to the grassy field beyond, the shadows whirling. Green, glowing eyes fastened on her, and it approached.

Briony screamed and scuttled backward. It was the same creature from her nightmare, and just like then, she couldn't determine what it looked like. Anytime she tried to focus, the shadows enveloping it hid it from view. Was it fifteen feet tall? Twenty? Did it have arms?

A sucking sound, like an indrawn breath, but louder and more forceful. Briony's heel caught, and she fell. The creature pounced. Shadows wrapped around her, icy and suffocating, pinning her arms to her sides. The light and warmth issuing from her skin dimmed. Painlessly, the breath was slowly squeezed from her body.

She struggled and shivered. She was so cold.

No. She wasn't going silently into the dark night. Briony clenched her teeth, and the white light glowing through her flashed. There was a high-pitched scream, and her bonds loosened. Pure white light streamed from her palms. She jerked herself free and blasted the creature. It screamed again. The shadows writhed, bulged, then burst.

She was alone again in the field. Not even a whisper of a breeze stirred the grass. Briony's chest heaved, and she raised her hands. The light glowed and pulsed in her palms.

"Zorzye. One of the lightwielders." The voice rippled around her again.

The field swirled, and with a dizzy lurch, she returned to the palace and stood in front of Katisa again. "What the hell was that?" Briony stepped backward. Her hair hung free around her face, and she reached up to twist it back into the bun at her neck.

"What happened?"

Briony recounted what she'd seen, the attack, and the words that were spoken. "That creature was trying to kill me."

Katisa's eyes widened. "That's never happened before. Are you okay?" She placed her hand on Briony's shoulder, and Briony felt a wave of warmth shoot through her.

She studied her hands. They remained steady, no trembling, but she thought they still vibrated slightly. "I'm fine."

"Did you say you heard the word zorzye?"

"Yes, do you know what that is?"

"Only from our history books because their species died out a long time ago. They wield white light and are linked to the moons." She stared at Briony for a long moment. "If you heard their name during the ritual, it must be significant."

"What do you mean, linked to the moons?"

Katisa returned the bottle and spent a long moment studying her shelves. "Our magic comes from the small sun. Each vae becomes linked to one color of light from the sun and can use that variety of magic. Like green for those gifted with growing things or red for those with warrior magic. When the small sun is in the sky, our magic flows through us. You must have a similar relationship with the moons."

"Can I learn to let the light flow through me? To shoot it?"

The princess turned. "I'd be happy to help you explore your magic and try."

Hans crashed into the room, eyes scarlet and claws fully extended. "What the hell happened? Are you alright? You were panicked. In danger." He stalked forward, hauled her into his arms, and buried his face in her neck.

She cradled his head. "I'm fine. It wasn't real." She gave him a brief overview of the ritual and the creature pouncing on her. "I'll tell you the rest later."

Guards, blades in hand, ran into the small room. Red sparks crackled in the air.

Katisa waved her hand. "Put your weapons down. There's no danger." The guards lowered their weapons but didn't put them away.

Caladin strolled in. "All my guards are leaping through hallways yelling about a crazed vulk." He jerked his chin, and the guards straightened, put their weapons away, and marched into the room where she'd had tea with Katisa. "They don't remember that the vulk always look like they're going to murder someone." The king sauntered to the table and peered down at the map. "What was that all about?"

"Nothing. Briony and I merely discussed her magic," Katisa said.

Caladin waved his hand. "Fill me in later. I have time to have our meeting now." He jabbed his finger down in the center of the map. "Let's get started."

23

HANS PUT his arm around Briony as they stood at the map. She smelled like fresh air. The entire time he'd stood outside the spellcaster's cell to question her, part of his attention remained locked on Briony.

When her terror punched through their bond, he'd thought his heart had stopped. The blind panic and fear left him reeling for a moment. He'd lost control and charged through the palace, only focused on getting to her.

He never lost control.

"How did questioning the spellcaster go?"

"She didn't say a word. All she did was clean her room. Nonstop."

"What?" Briony frowned. "That's strange."

Katisa scoffed. "Magicwielders are devious. It was probably a ploy to ignore you. We can use magic to make her talk."

Briony's eyes widened. "Is that really necessary? What will that do to her?"

Katisa waved her hand. "It won't hurt her. Just bend her will to ours."

"I don't need vae help," Hans said. "I'll get her to talk to me."

Caladin glanced over his shoulder. "He's right. Stay out of it and make him do the work."

Hans pointed at the map. "Show me where you saw the ravec."

The four of them stood so close together their shoulders touched. Caladin pointed at the Bodec Mountain range and used his fingertip to trace a line. "Between these two mountains, there's a deep crevasse. This is where the activity is centered. It isn't a junction between Peklo and Ulterra we know about, and it would be guarded if it were. I think they've used magic to make it one."

Hans used a claw tip to circle around the Bodecs. "What about out here? Near the mountains?"

"Everything within a mile radius has died. When our patrols enter, the stench is overwhelming." His gaze met Hans's. "There are legions of spawn living there. Both goblins and bauk. And there's definitely something big living in the crevasse."

Hans stared down at the map. "Legions?" Caladin wouldn't use that word lightly. How did hundreds of spawn get up here? For what purpose? He tapped on a mountain to the west of the crevasse. "This is where Briony and I need to go. This mountain with the notched summit ridge. How far is it from the spawn?"

"Best estimate? Maybe a quarter-mile."

"Can I get there from along the river and avoid them?" Otherwise, they'd have to head straight into the area where the spawn gathered.

"Yes, there's a narrow mountain pass, but I still wouldn't go alone. Just in case."

Hans nodded. "I'm not interested in getting near any spawn on this trip." Not with Briony at his side.

A scuffle sounded, and Juri, flanked by guards, strode into the room. He held two massive drumsticks, far larger than a turkey or a chicken leg, and tossed one to Hans.

"Thanks." As he bit into it, Katisa wrinkled her nose. Hell, he was hungry. He'd had a busy night.

"Caught a dodo," Juri said. "Didn't know there were any flocks left."

Caladin's jaw clenched. "Oh, you mean you poached one of the protected denizens of my forest?"

Juri grinned. "Flock is too big and needs culling. There were a few baldies in there. They'll peck each other to death if you don't move some of them or eat 'em."

Caladin stared a long moment, then turned to one of his guards. "Have Grigorii check on that." The vae bowed and left.

"What'd I miss?" Juri asked.

"I'll fill you in later," Hans said.

Briony pressed against his side and tugged at his arm. "What about calling the rest of the pack to help?"

He considered it. "Kyril and Ayren may be back at the gorge den by now, but even if Juri or I run swiftly, it will take about two weeks to get them here. We don't have that kind of time."

Caladin crossed his arms. "I know a way to make it there and back within ten days."

"That's cutting it close. They'd arrive only a day or two before the moons are full."

Briony gazed up at him. "The more vulk, the better."

Her fear from earlier still rattled him, and he didn't want her to experience that again.

Legions.

He sighed. She was right. The more vulk, the better. They may not be a pack any longer, but they still could fight as one like in the old days. Lethal and strong.

His lip curled up his eyetooth. "What's the route?"

"There's a secret vae bridge to cross the river," Caladin said. "It will take you directly into the west of Ulterra. We can show you where it is."

Hans turned to Juri. "Take their secret bridge and go to the den. Bring back any vulk there."

Juri's eyes widened, and his jaw dropped. "I'll leave right now."

"I'll send some vae with him." Caladin motioned to a guard positioned at the door, and a few vae peeled off and followed Juri as he left.

"I doubt they'll keep up. Even on kon horses."

"They'll be fine." Caladin ran his hand over the map, smoothing the wrinkles. "Good, now we have more time to prepare for our attack."

Hans turned to Katisa. "Tell me about your dream. What is it you can show us?"

Katisa drew in a long breath and strode to a shelf across the room. She returned with a thick granite mortar the size of a large bowl, her arms shaking as she held it against her chest and plunked it down on the table with a heavy thud.

She retrieved a glass jar and sprinkled some of the contents into it. Purple flame leaped high, and Hans and Briony jumped back.

"Oops. A little too much."

Under their feet, the thin red rug had a few scorch marks. Hans eyed the mortar and drew Briony farther away.

The flame settled into a merry fire, crackling in the stone bowl. Leaning forward, the princess waved her hand over it, and the purple turned clear and translucent. "This dreamcast will show you what I saw. I was asleep, but it was a vision, not a true dream."

Images floated through the flames. At first only wavy blurs, they sharpened into the background of the mountains and the trees peppering this region of the Kuls. A chestnut-haired figure trudged, stopping every few feet to lean over and pant. Smeared with grime, her hair lay matted and tangled around her face.

Hans snarled. "Morana. Younger, but still her."

Katisa pointed. "And pregnant. Almost ready to give birth."

The figure in the image studied a slab of rock in front of her with a rounded stone door. A massive one. Vulk-sized. Her fists pounded against the stone with dull, heavy thuds. "Let me in. I've traveled far to find you."

The door flung open, and a vulk stepped out. Morana and the scenery were so detailed in the flames of the mortar bowl that Hans could even make out the glints of sun on Morana's dark hair, but the vulk was translucent, the color of his fur impossible to determine, and his features blurred.

Hans knew many of the older vulk before they died, and he squinted and tried to place him. Something was familiar about him, maybe the way he walked? But he didn't think he'd ever met him.

Morana threw herself at the vulk, but he sidestepped and caught her with one arm, placing her on her feet at arm's length.

"I couldn't stay with the clan. After months and months, I finally found you. I have to be with you." She tried to pass him to enter the den, but he sidestepped and cut her off.

"Return to the clan. Right now." The vulk's eyes glowed. "You belong with them, not me."

She grabbed her head with both hands, tugging her hair. "No. It's different with us."

The vulk stepped forward, trying to snag her wrist, but she whirled out of reach.

"No," he said. "You know how it works. When you chose to run with me, you knew what would happen if you became pregnant. We discussed it. Your leader discussed it with you."

She shook her head. "But I'm the only one you've ever had a child with. In the thousands of years you've lived, only me. That means something."

He stepped closer. "The vulk walk alone. You knew this when we began. A child changes nothing. Return. Your clan will care for you." While the vulk spoke softly, Morana winced like she'd been struck.

"No."

"Before I left you, I spoke with your leader. Except for him and his family, you have the highest status in the clan. Exactly what you wanted. Return. They are your family, and they'll care for you."

Briony stared at the vulk. "Is that Wulf?"

"No. There are no Krol armbands." Hans was certain. Even though the vulk was hazy, Wulf's dark fur and the gold armbands would show.

"The vulk was wispy in my dream, never in color," Katisa said.

Morana stood frozen, chest heaving. "I love you."

"I'll take you back to your clan." The vulk approached, but she didn't move. When he picked her up, she remained stiff and unyielding. Then she screeched, inhuman in its despair. Morana drew a dagger from her bodice and twisted in the vulk's arms. Both hands wrapped around the hilt she plunged it into the vulk's heart. He roared and fell to his knees.

Briony screamed and covered her eyes. Hans brought her face to his chest; she didn't need to see this. Morana knew how to kill a vulk, even back then. Which meant she'd found a silver dagger—not an easy feat—and brought it with her.

Morana finished her kill and stood over the body.

Katisa waved her hand over the flames again, and the background changed. Gaunt, no longer pregnant, and with hair shorn close to her scalp, Morana lay on a compact crust of snow, yet she was barefoot, wearing only a tattered dress. A thin vapor, pluming in small gasping puffs, showed she breathed.

The snow melted around her, and fog filled the air, turning the hard dirt into mud. Morana drew in a deep, ragged breath. The earth beneath her hands split. She clawed into the ground, and what appeared to be roots tunneled out and wrapped around her wrists as if binding her to the earth.

Morana jerked but couldn't free herself. "What is this? What do you want?" She sank back and closed her eyes. "I'll gladly meet death."

A green glow suffused Morana's body. Her hair started growing in a long wavy cascade to her shoulders. The hollow of her cheeks filled, then her arms. Her dress fluttered, and layers of rich, silky emerald green replaced the ruined scrap. The roots released from the earth but remained wrapped around her wrists. They tightened, Morana's skin purpling. She screamed, but when the roots glowed green, she stopped.

After a long moment, Morana sat up and pressed a hand to her chest. She frowned. "Yes, I hear you." She threw her hand out, tossing a blast of magic at a tree. It glowed, and with a flick of her fingers, it burst into flames.

Standing, she laughed. "Oh, yes." Her eyes glowed green, no longer human.

The flames in the mortar went out. "That's everything I saw. I've consulted every book I own." Katisa gestured at her shelves. "And not one mentions anything about a power coming from the forest like that."

Hans rubbed his mouth. "Baba Yaga said Morana's bracelets held a darker, ancient power. I need to talk to the spellcaster. She's Morana's partner. She knows."

Katisa hauled the mortar from the table and grunted as she wrapped her arms around it and picked it up. Hans sighed and plucked it from her with one hand. "Where do you need it to go?"

She pointed. "Show off. Thank you." Katisa glared at Caladin. "You're my brother. You should have offered. Hans is politer than you."

Caladin's brows rose. "I'm letting you work your arm muscles. Aren't you always complaining you sit too much?"

"I can't believe she killed him." Briony shuddered.

The princess gripped the table. "Even for a magicwielder, she's evil. She killed the vulk she said she loved and was so desperate for power that she let unknown magic bind with her."

Hans watched Briony. Her face was pale, and she hadn't stopped staring at the space on the table where the images had appeared. "Morana cast powerful spells at us without it draining her magic," he said. "She doesn't seem to die. What could she bind with that extends her powers like that?"

Katisa stared down at the table, slowly shaking her head. "I don't know. Magicwielders can learn to hoard their energy stores to cast more spells, but even sorcerers still flag after a time. And no magicwielder is immortal."

"She was left behind. Desperate," whispered Briony, but he still heard.

"You alright?" he asked.

She nodded. "Fine." But she took a step to the side. Away from him.

He pointed at the mountain with two notches. "We'll go here tomorrow. We'll sneak in and out without alerting any of the spawn in the valley below."

"You don't want to wait for the other vulk?" Briony asked.

He shook his head. "No. We'll remain out of sight. No fighting." It was time to find out why Baba Yaga sent them here. The rune sang about past choices, but it didn't make sense that the answer lived in the middle of mountains which held no significance.

Briony hugged herself and turned vacant eyes to the table. "Tomorrow then."

24

BRIONY STARED at the door carved into the mountain and breathed through her mouth. The air stank. As part of being a doctor's assistant, she'd experienced several deaths, and the choking scent around them in the mountains was the same putrid smell that rose from a corpse. An odor she'd never forget. Black clouds snaked across the sky, blocking the sun. The trees stood twisted black and cracked. And this foul air coated everything.

So far, their journey was going according to plan. She and Hans skirted around where the legions camped and stuck to the narrow paths through the mountains. A troop of vae, led by Seth and Caladin, followed at their heels in case the spawn moved unexpectedly.

The large stone door hung by one hinge, a black void gaping behind it. Goosebumps broke out over her skin, and she shivered. Hans jerked his chin toward the entrance. His gaze softened as he peered down at her and held his hand out. "You ready to go inside?"

She clutched it. "Yes."

After a few feet, it was complete and utter darkness inside. She cut off a cry of dismay and peered through the dark for any cracks in the ceiling that might emit a beam of light. Nothing.

Briony gulped. *Great, Hans could see, but she was blind.*

Hans walked to their right, claws scratching against the stone with a slight snick.

"What are you doing?"

"I wonder if there's—" With a whoosh, a torch flared and lit up the entryway. From where it sat in its sconce, a thread of flame shot forward along the wall and lit the torches ahead of them, revealing the den in the flood of light.

Briony gawked. "How did you do that?"

Hans squeezed her hand. "It's vae magic. Most vulk pay for a vae to set up their den with everlasting light. While we can see in the dark, we like the option of having our den lit."

They walked farther, and the narrow entry sloped downward and cut open to reveal a large room. The ceiling arched fifty feet high, and the space stretched far into the mountain to a raised dais at the far end. The walls flowed like water, the gray tones in the stone melding with each other. Stone carvings arched around the doorways with details so intricate any sculptor would weep with envy. Carved facades decorated the walls instead of paintings. It reminded her of a cathedral.

One that was falling apart.

Rubble littered the ground where large boulders and dirt had tumbled from the ceiling. Furniture lay smashed into pieces. Tattered remains of a patterned red rug lay on the floor. It was so quiet that each click of Hans's nails on the floor echoed. Hans and Briony strode up the center of the room, and Hans tucked her to his side. He'd tensed and was on the balls of his feet. Ready to spring.

"Is something wrong?" Even though she whispered, it seemed to echo. Something crunched beneath her heel. Bones. Large ones. One of the mountain goats, maybe?

His head swiveled as he scanned. "I'm not sure yet."

"You weren't exaggerating about how the vulk craft stone. This must have been beautiful."

They were almost at the dais. Seated on top was a chair carved out of stone, its cushions coated in dust. The arms of the chair ended in a snarling wolf's face, and its back looked like extended claws.

Hans stopped a few feet in front of the dais. "This was an old pack den. This room was the great hall, large enough for the entire pack to gather. And this chair"—he pointed— "was where the Alpha sat. They must have lived here a long time ago."

"Why would they leave this place?" It was stunning. Even dirty and in shambles, the opulence and beauty shone through.

Hans was silent for a moment. "We protect Ulterra and were given all the lands west of the river as our own. That doesn't include the Kuls. They must have wanted to leave."

There was a trill, and the rune appeared in the air in front of them. Hans pulled her against him, wrapping his arms around her. The rune twirled faster and faster, and the den grew brighter. Around them, the rubble disappeared, and the rug became whole. The chair glistened, its cushions turning spotless.

And figures appeared on the dais ahead of them.

Hans stepped backward, pulling her closer. A black vulk, almost identical to Hans, leaned against the throne, holding up something in his hand. Next to him stood a male vae. He had dark, straight hair streaming down his back, a thin face with slanted cheekbones, and a triangular chin. His vae clothing was white with gold trim and intricately folded into a wide sash around his middle. Atop his head was a coronet. It matched the one worn by Caladin at the feast.

Hans snarled. "What is this?" Neither of the figures reacted. They remained focused on each other. "Speak." Still, no response.

"I can see through them," whispered Briony. "Is this a memory? Like what Katisa did?" Both figures on the dais were translucent, but their details were clear in the same way the figures appeared in Katisa's dreamcast.

"They don't see or hear us, and it's definitely the past because"—he waved his arm at the room— "the damage to the den is gone. And that's Wulf, even though there aren't any golden armbands. He has black fur and looks like every drawing I've seen of him."

Briony glanced from Hans to Wulf. The resemblance was uncanny. The same large size. Same inky coat. But Wulf possessed a cruelty to his face that Hans didn't.

"Who is the vae? A king?"

Hans nodded. "Yes, but I don't know who he is. He isn't Caladin's father."

Wulf turned his head toward the vae and bared his teeth a fraction. "Can you tell me what this will do, or can't you?" Briony jumped as his voice, almost a snarl, cut through the great hall in the common tongue.

"That heart is from a creature so evil, so foul, absorbing it gives you nothing good," said the vae king.

Wulf sneered. "Taking the strength of my enemy only strengthens me."

The vae stepped back. "No. It will doom you. Doom every single vulk because your actions affect your entire pack and all the future generations."

Wulf shook his head and laughed. "You vae and your whimsy bullshit." He raised his hand, and inside Wulf's fist, a dull green object pulsed. "I killed their king. *This* is my prize. By absorbing this, I'll become more powerful than the leshak." Wulf's eyes flashed red, and he pinned the vae king with his stare.

The vae king's spine stiffened. "That's no prize. Yes, that heart will give you great power, but that power will extend to vulk-kind forever."

"You say that like it's a bad thing."

"It's a permanent decision. It will remove your weakness to the leshak, but at a steep price. Power like that always comes at a steep price. For both you and all the vulk."

Wulf only shrugged.

The vae king stepped forward. "To kill, the leshak consume souls. For the vulk to be invincible against them, you and every other vulk in your pack, every generation to come, will lose your souls. Forever."

Wulf's eyes glowed. He raised his hand and opened his fingers. The greenish mass beat faster. "Who cares about a soul? Does it help me in battle? Does it make me a better fighter?"

The vae drew back. "You don't know what you're saying. Your soul is the fount by which all that is pure and valuable in this life springs."

"Maybe to a vae."

The vae looked stricken. "You killed the leshak with no help. You don't need the heart."

Wulf shrugged again. "The leshak almost killed me. I felt him drawing my soul from my body, but I held on and beat him at the last moment. Others may not be so skilled. This heart will let us sweep through Ulterra and rid all lands of this threat." He raised his head and stared at the vae king. "The vulk will save Ulterra. Now and always."

The vae's shoulders sagged. "You affect the zorzye too. They're your mates, and if you're soulless, your souls won't recognize each other, and the mate-bond won't ever form."

Wulf batted his hand as if flinging the words away. "No vulk has ever taken a zorzye mate. None of us care about that."

"But it's fated, and the zorzye aren't like the vulk. They are closer to the vae in how they need to bond. Without a bond-mate, they will fade from this earth. Their numbers are already dwindling."

Wulf moved to the front of the dais and sat on his throne,

leaning forward and holding the heart in front of him. "Bonding with them would only make us weak. Vulnerable. The vulk have the pack, but otherwise, we walk alone."

The king shifted as if ready to spring forward. "If your soul is gone, so is your humanity. You won't be able to take your human form any longer. No vulk will ever be able to do so."

Wulf grinned, but his eyes remained hard and cruel. "I'm stronger in this form."

There was a long silence, and Briony held her breath.

Wulf growled and the heart in his hand beat faster. "This is for my pack." His eyes flashed red, and he crushed the heart.

A green glow absorbed into his skin, and gold arm bands wrapped around his upper biceps. He stood and howled, his claws elongating.

The vae king turned and walked off the dais toward Hans and Briony. Right before he was about to step through them, the vae and Wulf vanished.

The rune chimed once, disappeared, and the vulk den returned to rubble.

Briony's mouth opened and closed a few times. "Did you know about this?" She turned to Hans. "You must have a soul? Right?"

"All vulk know we have no souls." His voice was flat. Emotionless. "It's one of our guarded secrets."

"But the vae know?" Yesterday, Katisa said Hans lacked the capacity to give her what she wanted. This had to be what she meant. She knew that vulk had no souls.

He nodded. "Yes. It's one reason vulk and vae don't get along. The vae don't trust a beast without a soul."

Briony felt like she'd fallen into ice water. "The rune said, 'return to the great decision of the past, and decide if that choice should last.' It must mean this decision."

"Yes."

She stepped out of his arms and ran her hand through her

hair, pulling strands out of her bun. "I'm a zorzye." After discussing her vision with Hans last night, she'd come to terms with it. Now, being a zorzye had a lot more meaning. "The rune said, 'first a rune will bind, but only a bite permanently entwines. With true love, it must be done, or two will never be one.' It's telling us we can make a different choice."

But when Hans looked down at her, his gaze was remote. It echoed Wulf's with a glimmer of the same hardness.

The night at the campfire after visiting Baba Yaga's hut was the only time he had dropped the guard he kept between them. Back then, she'd thought she'd glimpsed the real Hans and what was really inside him. The way he looked at her now, without a flicker of emotion, she knew even if the rune had given him—given them—another choice, he'd already decided. Nothing was going to change.

She felt like someone had kicked her in the chest. All along, she'd prepared for the two of them to part, but she hadn't truly accepted that there might be an actual choice to lead them on another path. That things could be different. Forever. They could remain together as mates. *She'd have someone who chose her for the first time in her life.*

She didn't want power or status. All she wanted, deep down, was genuine love. All-consuming, sacrifice everything, love. The kind a parent should give and what she wanted in her mate.

But the vulk took no mates.

Her chin shot up a fraction. She wouldn't be the one left behind, wishing for a letter, a scrap of attention, again. Every moment she was with Hans, she had to remember that no matter what their bond did, how tightly it thrummed with contentment, she was never letting herself be abandoned again. She'd leave first.

The ground trembled.

"Shit, we need to get out of here. Now." Hans reached for her.

25

HANS SCOOPED Briony up in his arms. Shit. When he'd first entered the den, the stench was so old he wasn't sure if the creature that left it lay dead or had passed through. Wrong on both accounts. The creature never left, and it was awake and hungry.

He sprinted toward the exit, Briony clinging to his neck. "What is it?"

"Mountain troll." He dodged around a boulder. A roar sounded, and he peered over his shoulder. The troll smashed through a far doorway into the grand hall. Its ribs showed over its bulbous belly as it rose to its twenty-foot height.

"How'd he get in here?"

With all this rubble, he should have guessed a troll got in, couldn't get back out, and had been smashing up the place ever since. "No idea. He's too big."

Briony tried to peer over his shoulder. "How do you know it's a he?"

Hans drew in a breath and leaped over a broken table. "Easy to tell with trolls. His balls hang down to his knees."

"What? I want to see." Briony tried to hike herself up higher over his shoulder.

He kept her in place. "We're running for safety right now. Trolls don't wear any trousers. You won't like it." She didn't need to see dangling troll bits.

They burst out the front door, and he raced to the bottom of the path to join the vae. "Mountain troll."

"In there?" Caladin squinted up toward the den. "How—"

The mountain shook. Rocks cascaded down its face. The top of the troll's head becoming visible as he smashed himself into the door.

With a mighty shout, the vulk door shattered, and the troll tumbled forward on his hands and knees. He stood, blinked at the sun, then narrowed in on the vae and licked his fat lips. He looked like a mushroom, dull gray and lumpy except for a patch of hair on his head and thicker hair from his chest down to his legs.

Caladin turned toward the east. "So much for sneaking in and out. He probably alerted every spawn for miles."

One of Caladin's warriors stepped forward. "A group of us can herd the troll north, back where he belongs. He'll want to chase the horses."

"Do it," Caladin ordered.

Hans kept Briony in his arms as he followed Caladin and Seth into the trees. The group tempting the troll peeled off, shouting and waving their hands, and the troll trundled after them, each step booming through the mountains.

Sulfur wafted stronger with the easterly breeze. The spawn must have been close by. They were already on the trail up to the mountain. Hans sprinted farther into the trees. With either dead trees or bare stone all around him, there was nowhere safe to tuck Briony so he could fight. They wound through the forested hills, down a slope through smoking trees and singed grass. The earth grew warmer under his feet, and brimstone clogged the air. Thorns tore at his fur, and burrs tangled and stabbed. Seth and Caladin raced at his side.

He ran hard until goblin shouts faded, then slowed to a jog. Ahead of him, the forest ended at a ledge. As he neared it, the view below spread before him. Here stood the two tallest mountains in the Bodecs, and slashing a black scar in between them, lay the crevasse. They'd run right at it.

Caladin and Seth joined him, and he dropped Briony to the ground. The four crouched and edged closer to the lip to peer down.

He sucked in a breath. Waves of spawn spread below. Goblins, bauk, and one sleek azhdaya—the two-headed wing-less serpent—mingled along the left bank of the crevasse. In the center of the milling mass stood a tent large enough even he could stand up inside it, with its flap shut.

Two bauk began brawling, trading blows that snapped their heads back. One shoved the other, then kicked it into the crevasse. There was a scream and a long hissing sound. Black mist rose from the split in the earth, and the spawn fell silent.

Brown vines slithered up from the gaping hole in the ground and clung to the earth. No. Not vines. Roots. Roots that writhed and stretched and dug into the ground with a sizzle.

Something emerged from the crevasse, a skeletal hand reaching up. The same hand from one hundred years ago. Nothing stopped the monster from hauling itself into the murky light this time.

Huge elk-like antlers stretched from the sides of its head. A skull with dark gaping eye sockets and a long deer-like muzzle. Fifteen feet high, it wore a black tunic with leather straps lashing across it, arms bare to show the bark-like skin clinging to bone. As the creature turned and scanned the grounds, two green orbs flared deep in the skull's eye sockets.

Hans froze. No. This couldn't be possible.

Briony shrank back against his chest. She trembled, and he wrapped an arm around her. "That's it." Her words were barely a whisper. "That's the creature in my dream. And from the field."

"It's a leshak." Living. Breathing. Returned from the dead. Briony gripped his arm and held on tight.

The leshak strode onto the ground and grabbed a nearby bauk by the neck. There was a long rattling sucking sound, and the leshak's eyes flickered as it opened its mouth. The bauk screamed, and its skin tightened over its bones. It thrashed, but the leshak's grip was solid even with one hand. The kicks, the blows, did nothing.

One last anguished cry and the bauk slumped. The leshak tossed it to the ground, and the body dissolved into dust. The leshak turned, and Hans caught a glint of silver on its head. A crown.

This was the king of the leshak. Czart. He shook his head. No. This was impossible. Wulf killed him.

Yet it had to be. What other leshak wore a crown?

The flap of the tent opened, and Morana sauntered through the goblins. They dove out of her way, creating a wide berth around her. She met Czart and placed her hand on his arm. "You're up early today, my lord." Her voice rang clear in the silent valley.

"I'm restless. You haven't fulfilled your side of our bargain yet." His voice was a low hiss, and Hans's hackles rose.

Morana stepped closer, brushing her chest against him. "The vulk we want is close by, and these spawn will lure him here. Vulk are so predictable. They won't stop until every last spawn lies dead. But if you want me to kill him sooner, give me more power—"

"Have you earned it?" Czart hissed. "No. I granted you waves of power, far beyond the magic your kind uses, yet you still failed to kill him. I need the vulk dead, starting with the Alpha. The true Alpha." Lightning fast, Czart snagged her waist and drew her closer, bending his head to hers. Morana

213

didn't struggle. She clutched at his tunic, and the sleeves of her dress fell back, revealing the one bracelet snaking up her wrist.

The same sucking sound and the bracelet flashed a bright green. The only light in the blackened valley. Morana cried out in pain and shriveled against him as she turned thin and her clothes dulled.

"Your magic gives you an exquisite taste. You're lucky I don't take all of your soul." He drew back and dropped his hands. Morana sagged, chest heaving.

Hans's lip curled over his eyetooth. Pack records described leshaks killing humans eagerly. They didn't sip souls like this. Why was Czart leaving Morana alive? What was their link?

"Thank you." Morana panted, bent over. "Thank you for taking from me, my lord."

"I'm still displeased."

Morana, already diminished, seemed to shrink further. "Let me make it up to you. Give me equal power, and let me show you how I wield it. I belong at your side. Your queen." Morana's hands on the leshak's chest shook so hard even Hans on his ledge detected the motion.

"You belong *to* me." His voice gentled, and he ran one long finger down her cheek, the tip glowing green. An answering glow coated Morana. The flesh returned to her body, and she groaned. A husky sound of pure lust.

"I'll yield more of my soul to you. Just give me more power." The enchanter's voice contained so much desire, that Hans's tongue drew back in his mouth as if he'd bitten something foul. Lust for the leshak? Or for power?

Czart's hand went to her throat, and he stroked up her neck with his thumb. "You know what I do when I take it. You want to experience that again?"

"Yes, I'll submit."

He picked her up and tossed her over his shoulder. "I don't want you to submit. Fight me hard. I want to hear your screams." They disappeared inside the tent.

Silence remained in the valley, all the spawn still frozen, and turned toward the tent.

"I've seen a lot of fantasies," Seth whispered. "But that's new." He sidled forward and leaned over the ledge to get a better view. "Whatever gets your wick wet."

Hans stared at the tent. His heightened hearing picked up whimpers of pain. "Leshak don't play well with others. This isn't a fantasy. It's torture."

"I wouldn't be so sure. There's something deeper between that sorcerer and the tree monster. He may take her soul, but I sensed the depth of her lust. I'm guessing he's giving her a good"—he glanced at Briony— "well, anyway. They might be mates. Of a sort." He eyed Hans. "Humans and monsters, right? An intriguing combination. You'd know all about that."

Briony stiffened in his arms. "Hans isn't a monster, he's Hans. Don't compare him to that thing."

His chest warmed, and he hugged her tighter against him. Not that he needed her to defend him against some jackal, but it still felt good. He growled. "You're an incubus. You don't know anything about mates."

Seth leaned back on his heels. "And you do? A vulk? You don't take a mate either."

Briony stiffened again, and the bond between them throbbed An unhappy pang.

Seth continued, "I've never seen a leshak in Peklo, and I've lived there a long time. Where did he come from?"

Caladin turned away from staring down at the valley for the first time. "They don't live in Peklo. The vulk supposedly killed them all." He pointed. "While you two have been discussing the mating habits of ancient evil beings, things are happening down there."

The ground rippled in the valley. Small hills bulged upward where the valley had been smooth before. The earth shook under his feet, and a pile of dirt near the crevasse heaved upward. With a shower of rock, the top burst open and spat out more goblins, scrambling and scurrying over each other to get out of the hole.

Briony gasped and pressed against him. "Why is the underworld spitting them out like that?"

Hans pulled her farther back from the edge. "They must thin the barrier between the realms here so the spawn can punch through." The hill sank back into the earth, the open hole filling in. As the last bit closed shut, a blur of white leaped upward and landed in a crouch, eyes glowing red and claws out. He launched himself at the goblins.

A pure white vulk. *Zann.*

Hans stood frozen. Impossible. That couldn't be Zann.

"Another prisoner of Peklo escapes," Seth said. "He's a vulk too. Do you know him? He's a bit prickly, but he'll help us. He hates spawn."

Hans shook himself. His brother was in the valley. Not a dream. Or in his nightmare. "That's Zann." He needed to get down there.

"I know," Seth said. "I've done some killing with him here and there." Why hadn't he asked that damn jackal how he spoke vulk?

The mass of spawn surged forward and surrounded Zann.

Hans stood from his crouch and glanced at Caladin. "Protect Briony." He bounded off the ledge in one leap and raced down to his brother.

Hans tore through goblins, swiping his claws left and right to take off heads. Black, oozy blood splattered his arms. Vae arrows whistled through the air, and the bauk in front of him fell.

The tent flaps opened, and Morana and the leshak flew out. Green light shot forward with a high-pitched whistle. It crashed into Zann, and he flew, landing hard on his back, a silvery substance coating him. Zann lay crumpled and didn't move.

Hans roared and leaped forward, but something smashed

into his left temple, and he staggered sideways. Warmth trickled down the side of his face. Blood.

The leshak towered next to him, his arm drawn back for another blow. Hans dove sideways.

Czart's arms spread, and small birdlike creatures burst from his shoulders. Not birds, mini cockatrice. They aimed for Hans's head with their harpy-like talons. A sharp sting lanced through his ear as one of them sliced through it. He swung at them.

The leshak advanced. "The time of the vulk is over," Czart hissed. His green eyes darkened.

Hans slashed his claws through a cockatrice and threw it to the ground. He darted sideways and snarled. "I don't know what hole you crawled out of, but I'll make sure you're truly dead this time."

The skull mouth of the leshak king parted, emitting an awful whine in an imitation of laughter. "You may look like Wulf, but you're much weaker." Czart sucked the air. "I can taste your weakness. Perhaps Morana was more successful than I thought. You'll be easy to kill."

The ground heaved and bulged under their feet, and both lost their balance and fell backward. The valley quaked and shook. Hans flipped to his feet and dug his claws into the scorched soil. Morana was on all fours, her hands green as she focused on Zann.

Hans roared and ran across the field faster than he'd ever run before. He barreled into Morana, and she flew back to the edge of the crevasse, teetering for one moment before slipping over the edge. "Czart!"

The leshak flew past him and dove after her.

Hans picked up Zann, tossed him over his shoulder, and sprinted for the trees. Wind blasted spawn from his path, and Caladin stood on the slope, hewing goblins with his sword. Flashes of purple magic glinted with each swipe. Seth stood on the ledge with his arms out, eyes glittering amethyst and his gaze concentrated downward, Briony at his side. Wind whipped down the valley, but the incubus's hair and clothes didn't stir.

"I'll keep them from following so you can escape." Seth's voice was deeper, and it echoed strangely.

"You'll be able to get away?"

"Of course. No one is faster than the wind."

Whatever. "Come on." He hiked Zann more securely on his shoulder and grabbed Briony's hand. They ran into the woods.

Zann didn't stir, and his chest rattled with each inhale. Dirt mixed with black goblin blood and the silvery substance in Zann's fur. Hans ran faster.

After a half-mile, when the trees began turning green again, he thought it safe enough to pause. He lowered Zann to the ground, and Briony dropped to her knees at his brother's side. She swiped his chest and lifted her hand. It dripped with silver fluid. "We've got to get him clean. Whatever this silvery stuff is, it's turning his skin red, and I think it's still hurting him." She glanced up at him. "Is your skin alright?"

He glanced at his palm, covered in the same syrupy substance. "I'm fine."

Caladin whipped his shirt off and tossed it to her. "Here."

Briony scrubbed at Zann. "It isn't night, so I can't heal him myself. We have to get him to the vae." As Briony slopped away the material coating his brother's chest, Zann gulped a breath of air and opened his eyes.

He struggled to sit up. "Hans?"

Briony swiped the last of the substance off his shoulders and arms. "Take it easy."

Zann turned his head toward Briony, and his eyes glinted red. "You're a human."

"She's helping you."

Zann stood, and Hans looked his brother in the eye for the first time in a century. "What happened?" Zann asked. His brother appeared the same. The same grim determination to battle the world, but maybe his expression held a touch of weariness it hadn't before. And he wore an odd pair of black snakeskin trousers.

Hans couldn't speak. He grabbed Zann and hugged him. It was a human gesture, never done by the vulk, but Zann hugged him back. "I can't believe you're alive," Hans choked out.

They parted, and Zann clapped him on the shoulder. "It's been a long road."

Caladin picked the discarded shirt off the ground and examined it. "This is actually melted silver. We must get out of here and have our healers examine him."

"Can you move?"

Zann grimaced. "I'll manage." He eyed Briony. "Whatever the human did, helped."

Zann couldn't quite run, so they wove through the trees at a brisk walk. Briony tucked along one side and his brother at his other shoulder; Hans glanced at Zann. He was *alive.* Walking next to him, breathing, talking. He filled him in on Morana returning and summoning an army.

"If I'd known you survived the underworld, I would have found you," he said.

"I know." Zann met his gaze, and his expression softened. "But it's impossible unless you use a junction, and the guardians don't let anyone through. I've been trying for a hundred years. Only in the last few months have rifts opened and stayed open for longer periods."

His brother stumbled, and Hans put his hand on his shoulder. Kept it there. "I saw the rock swallow you. How did you survive?" Zann hadn't only survived the rockslide and the rift closing over his head, he'd also lived in Peklo all these years where the cursed, the spawn, and monsters all roamed in deadly numbers.

Red flashed in Zann's eyes. "The sorcerer. Not Morana. My sorcerer. She kept us both alive as the rift closed."

"We have her as a prisoner," Hans said.

Zann bared his teeth. "What? I want to see her."

"Let's work on getting you healed first." He urged his brother to walk faster.

26

Briony wiped a lock of hair out of her face with the back of her hand and leaned against the wall in the palace corridor. Dusk fell hours ago, and the hall was murky, the inside lights not yet lit. It was her first moment to breathe. The first moment to think about everything that had happened since morning. Her shoulders sagged. The adrenaline driving her on ever since the mountain troll showed up had faded. She was so tired she could lie on the floor right here and sleep, but her mind still raced.

Zann was alive. Leshaks existed again. And Hans had no soul.

The same three thoughts circled round and round. She was thrilled for Hans. Ever since he'd seen Zann, their bond vibrated with both turmoil and sparks of pure joy, but she also couldn't get the image out of her head of Wulf sitting on his throne and choosing for the vulk to live without souls.

Briony trudged down the corridor to find Hans and Zann. After a couple of hours with the vae healers, they'd left for food. Vulk food—not vae food—meant they hunted in the forest. However, that was almost an hour ago. They must be back now, and she wanted to join them to visit the sorcerer.

The palace bustled with vae guards as Briony entered the side garden leading to the forest. Thick ferns towering above her crowded around the vae fruit trees, and she pushed their fronds aside as she walked along the stones. A trio of vae knelt and repaired armor on a stone table under a portico. The coarse scraping bounced through the secluded space so loudly she couldn't hear her booted feet tread on the stone walkway. She halted and studied the armor for a moment. The vulk didn't wear armor. From what Hans said, they were naturally immune to magic, and most weapons didn't hurt them, but with Morana so powerful now ... maybe they needed some help.

As she descended two small steps, even over the clamor of the armorers, she caught the voices of Zann and Hans.

"So that's how you ended up with a human hanging around you," Zann said. "Runebound?" He made a low, scoffing sound. About to step into the clearing to join them, Briony froze, her hand gripping the fern in front of her.

The two vulk paced together, their forms visible in glimpses between the ferns. Hans chuffed. "I'll be fine. The rune is offering me a choice. I either take it, or I don't."

"How? What choice?"

Her throat was dry. She shouldn't eavesdrop, but she couldn't bring herself to move forward. Hans told Zann about the vulk den and Wulf, then recited the entire poem. "The rune must be talking about Wulf's choice to sacrifice our souls. Maybe it's giving me the choice to take mine back."

Zann growled. "Wulf gave us a gift. We're the toughest creatures walking Ulterra, immune to the leshak so we can kill them. Who cares about a zorzye? Or a mate? He did the right thing. Look what happened to me? That sorcerer ensorcelled me, and I ..." His voice got tight. "I ordered you to stay on the ground like some dog. I left you behind in the dirt without a single thought. And that was only the beginning of what that female did." Zann snarled, and Briony shivered. Hans snarled all the time, but Zann's rage was so potent she wanted to wince and cower.

"You were bewitched. I wasn't when I made the choice to let you die."

Zann shook his head. "You killed Morana. Or tried to. It was the only way."

Hans growled. "I failed."

"No. You made the right choice, and now, your choice is simple. We need to kill that leshak and a whole heap of spawn. Why the hell would you want your soul when that would weaken you? Because you want a mate? You don't want a mate. No vulk does. Make your choice, and let's move on."

Hans spoke so low she barely caught his words. "You're probably right."

Her heart sank. Back in the old vulk den, Hans's response told her all she needed to know. It didn't bother him that he had no soul. He accepted it. If the rune gave them a choice at a different life, one where they could be together, he wouldn't see it.

Wulf and Zann spoke aloud what Hans hadn't—a mate weakened them. The vulk respected strength. They didn't want vulnerabilities. They didn't want deeper emotions. There was no way Hans wanted his soul.

Enough of listening to this and torturing herself.

Briony sucked in a deep breath, scuffed her feet so they'd hear her over the racket of the vae with their armor, parted the ferns, and strode into the clearing. "Are we visiting the spellcaster?"

Zann bared his teeth. "Yes, but she won't talk. She won't tell you about Morana. They're buddies."

Briony remained behind the vulk as they walked to the prison compound. It was a solitary bank of rooms in muddy stone and moss, blending into the forest until she saw the guards. The spellcaster was in the first cell—a pleasant room with arching windows—even though they were barred. A bed stood on one side of the room with a simple night table next to it. The only other item inside was a rug. A small door opened into a bathroom.

With her back to the door, the spellcaster sat on the bed, not paying attention to their approach. Her hands moved as she worked on something in her lap. Two fluffy misshapen lumps of sheepskin leather had shearling lining bulging out of poorly stitched seams. Briony was no seamstress—it was one skill she'd never taken the time to learn beyond buttons and minor repairs—but whatever the spellcaster was doing ... didn't seem right.

Zann wrapped his hands around the bars, and the magicwielder stilled. She turned, and her eyes opened wide. As if hypnotized, she stood, and the lumps fell to the floor. Bandages covered the tips of her fingers as if she'd stabbed herself with the needle many times.

"Zann," whispered the spellcaster. Then she crumpled in a dead faint against the nightstand.

"Shit." Zann's claws rang against the metal bars. "She's clumsy as all hell. I can smell copper, so she's hurt herself. Again." He turned to a guard. "Get someone to help her. Now!" His knuckles popped as he strained at the bars, bending them outward.

"I can go in there and help," Briony said.

The guards glanced at each other. "We need permission for that."

Zann snarled, and Hans grabbed his shoulder and held him back as he stepped forward. "Let us in, or my brother starts another war between the vulk and the vae." Hans jerked his chin toward Briony. "She's a healer."

A guard flicked his gaze toward the cell. "The prisoner's only a magicwielder. She can't get out of there." The other nodded back and unlocked the door.

Briony rushed to the sorcerer's side. She'd smashed her cheek hard on the edge of the table, and there was a good gash.

She pointed at the bundle on the bed. "Hand me some of the linen." Zann tossed it to her and crouched next to her. She folded it and pressed it hard against the wound. She checked the sorcerer's head and neck, but other than fainting, she seemed fine. "What's her name?"

"Hazel. Is she alright?"

Hazel groaned, and her lids fluttered. The spellcaster had rich green eyes, clear and focused. Good. They lasered in on Zann, skipping right over Briony. "You're alive."

Zann rocked back on his heels. "You're as astute as ever."

Wincing, Hazel sat up and leaned her back against the nightstand.

Briony stood. "Move slow. You fainted and cut your face open."

Hazel prodded at her cheek. "Are you sure? I don't faint."

Zann glowered. "You did. You, the great sorcerer, fainted." He picked up the fuzzy objects on the floor and examined them. "What the hell are you making?"

Hazel snatched them out of his grasp. "I'm bored, so I'm sewing. My feet are always cold, so I'm making fuzzy slippers to—" Hazel struggled to her feet. "Why do you care?" She wobbled, and Zann reached for her, but Hazel didn't notice. She clutched the bed and lowered herself onto it. Zann snatched his hand back and crossed his arms.

Hazel gathered her slippers into her lap. "You're not here to chat. You're here to bellow or snarl. Which one today?" Zann turned and peered out the window, and Hazel's gaze swept over him, her lips parting. The angry glower on her face softened into ... something else.

The moment he turned back, she scowled again.

"I'll bellow today," Zann said. "Tell us what Morana's doing with the leshak and how they're connected."

Hazel's head snapped back as if someone had slapped her, and her expression closed. Her gaze dimmed. "I can't."

Zann stepped closer. "You owe me."

Hazel's chin jerked up. "I don't owe you anything. Get out of here, you oaf."

"Your insults have gotten a lot weaker during our time apart." Briony thought his gaze dropped to Hazel's lips, but maybe his focus aimed lower to her throat. He looked like he was thinking about throttling her.

"I'm sparing you a verbal lashing in front of your friends. Who are these people?" She glared at Hans. "As if I need more vulk around."

Briony introduced herself and Hans, then said, "if Morana succeeds, everyone is in danger, including you."

Hazel pressed her lips together, and now it was her turn to look out the window.

"I knew she'd tell us nothing. She doesn't care." Zann snarled, whirled on his heel, and stormed out. The cell door slammed against the wall so hard, Briony thought the bars would shatter.

Hans turned to Briony and raised his brows.

"You should leave too." She nodded toward the door. Hans studied her a long moment, turned without a word, and followed Zann.

The sorcerer slumped on the bed and sighed.

"Your slippers are ... nice."

Hazel waved her hand. "They're utter garbage. Look." She stuck her foot in one of them, and her toes popped out at the end. "I have no idea what I'm doing. I measured my foot, and I'm sewing sheepskin around the warm stuff I wanted on the inside." She shook her head. "It's not working well. You know, even if I had access to my magic right now, there aren't any spells for sewing, cleaning, or anything useful. Why is that?"

"I can heal." Briony wiggled her fingers. "Well, at night anyway. That's pretty useful."

Hazel's eyes widened. "Can you? I don't sense magic in you."

"My magic is a little different." Briony stared at the

other woman for a long moment. When Hazel had watched Zann secretly, her expression wasn't one of a murderer intent on killing everyone, including Zann. It was an expression Briony knew. Yearning. "You and Zann ... what happened?"

Hazel turned and stared out the window. "I can't discuss it."

"His brother is ... we're ... he's courting me."

Her head whipped back around. "The vulk don't take mates, and they certainly don't court anyone."

Briony smiled. "The vulk not taking mates has come up a time or two." However, Hans had talked about courting. How she'd be his entire focus. His world. Yet she'd only have his attention for another week, and then it would end. Forever. Her smile faded.

Hazel snorted. "The vulk don't care about anyone or anything but killing. I'd stay away from him." She raised a hand to her neck. "The vulk have a way of making your desire to hug them turn into a desire to strangle them." She made a face. "There's a thin line between hugging and strangling. Why is it that the ones who drive you crazy are the ones who are good in bed?"

Briony laughed. "The human men I spent time with weren't so great, and they were also bad in bed, so I'm not sure that checks out." She sobered. "If you help us freely, I can work to get you out of here. The vae said they will force you to talk if you don't."

Hazel grew pale. "You don't understand. If they try to force me, it will kill me."

Briony blanched. "What? How?"

"Because I *can't* speak about it." Hazel's gaze turned imploring. "Please, don't let the vae near me."

"I have no control over the vae. This is their kingdom." Briony studied her. "I'm new to this world, and you're only the second magicwielder I've met, so I could be wrong, but

Morana has an emptiness to her you don't. Are you a necromancer? Do you really follow her?"

Hazel grimaced. "A necromancer? Hell, no. They're hacks with little skill and think they'll gain greater magic if they call on dark forces. Their families rejected them."

Briony stiffened. "That wasn't their fault."

Hazel stabbed her needle into her slippers. "They won't give me real needles. These are blunt. This must be the reason my slippers are so awful."

"Sure."

The sewing paused. "In the magicwielding world, all that matters is how much magic you have. Each family cultivates it and hides what they can do from everyone else. If you are born into a family with exceptional abilities, and yours ... well ... doesn't meet expectations, you feel like it's your fault. Each generation must be stronger. From the moment your magic is tested, your family must choose whether to use you to continue their line or discard you." Her needle stabbed furiously again. "When they cast you out, you believe it was the right thing for them to do."

Briony lowered herself to sit on the bed next to Hazel. "You have a lot of magic. I saw you create that portal. You must have been chosen."

"Zann calls me a sorcerer, but I'm not. I'm a spellcaster. I need a spell, a chalk circle, or an object for my magic to work. My family is a proud and ancient line of true sorcerers. The kind that can whip magic up anywhere and anytime." Hazel glanced around her at her cell. "None of them would ever get snared in a vae trap. I didn't meet expectations, and every time Zann calls me a sorcerer, he's reminding me I'm less than what I should be."

"Your family cast you out?"

"They sent me off to Herskala Academy at eighteen—that's the magic school. They paid for schooling and told me good luck. After I graduated, I was on my own. Totally cut off.

As if I didn't exist. Morana was a teacher there, and she acted caring and concerned. Like a mother should." Hazel's lips slammed closed, and she swallowed hard.

Briony knew what it was like to be left behind by your family. "I'll do my best not to let the vae force anything out of you, but we really need your help. Morana captured me to get Hans's blood, and she's got a massive army of spawn. Hans tried to kill her, and he couldn't. How is that possible? Can you at least tell me that?"

Hazel's hands fisted. "I can't."

"I don't know much about the ancient history of Ulterra, but from what I've been told, having a leshak around is bad. Very bad. I saw Morana with the leshak king today. He's the one feeding her power. Do you know how?"

The sorcerer picked up her sewing needle, turned her back to Briony, and scooted away from her.

Briony sighed and stood to leave, but a slight scratching filled the room.

Hazel had crawled across the bed and was using the blunt needle tip to etch something on the limestone wall. In chalky, wavy lines, a symbol of a spiral curled inside a triangle appeared.

Briony held her breath.

Hazel pointed at it. "I *can't.*"

"What is that?"

The sorcerer only tapped it with her needle and shook her head.

Briony nodded. "Okay." Hazel was trying to tell her something with that symbol. Now she had to figure out what it meant without involving the vae.

HANS FOUND Briony in Katisa's small study at the back of the palace. Books lay heaped on the table, the map pushed off to the side. The few lanterns set in the wall cast shadows that grew and morphed as they flickered over the floor.

He'd spent the evening with Zann, his brother brooding and moody after visiting the sorcerer, even though he tried to hide it. When the healers rounded on Zann and insisted he rest, Hans tracked Briony down.

A disquiet had spread through him ever since they returned to the palace. A whisper to draw Briony close. After the night in the glade, their bond had strengthened, but it thinned again during the visit to the old vulk den. Now it felt fragile like it was going to snap.

Briony leaned against the table and wiped a lock of hair from her face with the back of her hand. "What are you doing in here?" he asked.

She turned to greet him, but her expression remained closed. Not like the usual way she had of looking at him that made his chest expand with pleasure. "I think Hazel's trying to tell me something. I don't think she can speak to us about Morana. Not that she doesn't want to, but she ... can't." She waved a hand at the books in front of her. "I'm checking Katisa's books, searching for this." She showed him a symbol and explained Hazel drew it for her, then shook her head. "I've pored over these books for hours, and that symbol doesn't appear anywhere. Even if these books explain the symbol, I can't read this language, whatever it is. I can only look for pictures."

"It's late. Come to bed and start fresh in the morning." He let a hint of a purr enter the words.

Briony stiffened, and her gaze fixed somewhere to his right. "We need to talk about earlier today. Why didn't you tell me you have no soul?"

He'd hoped to delay this conversation until she lay under him, sated and drowsy. "We have rules no vulk can break. Aspects of our life we are forbidden to tell or show outsiders.

One of those rules is we never discuss the absence of our souls. Why offer information about our strength?"

"You believe it's a strength, too?"

He rubbed his mouth. "I'm about to kill a leshak, a *soul* drinker, so yeah, it's an advantage. He can't kill me by ripping my soul from my body."

"When we were discussing the rune poem and trying to figure out what it means, you should have told me. The poem says, 'two souls chosen by fate.' You don't have a soul."

"That's why I thought the poem wasn't about me. Afterward"—he shrugged— "it didn't seem to matter. It changes nothing."

Briony still hadn't looked at him. "I don't understand why we're runebound. It's pointless. On the night of the full moons, you aren't choosing me, and I'm not choosing you. You've already made your decision." She spoke like she was talking about the weather. "I think it's best if we keep our distance, other than working together to defeat Morana. It will be easier when we part for good."

The beast inside him roared its disapproval. Roared to touch her and soothe her. "We both live in Rohant. After I give Baba Yaga her year of service, I'll be back. We don't have to part forever. We can still—"

"No." Now she met his gaze, and her eyes glittered hard, like diamonds. She stared at him as if he were a stranger. "I won't wait in Vieska, hoping you might come for me. Been there. Done that. And Morana lost her mind waiting around for a vulk."

He snarled. "Don't compare yourself to her. What we have is different."

Her brow raised. "Is it? After a brief liaison, her vulk left and never intended to return. I see little difference."

Red tinged the edges of his vision. "I wouldn't leave you on your own like that."

"What have you been doing all these years? How many

times have I heard, 'the vulk walk alone?' You don't even interact with the pack. *Your* pack."

He snarled and stalked to the door. "You don't know what you're talking about."

"You think you're stronger alone, but you're wrong."

He whirled back. "You've lived alone most of your life."

Her expression remained rigid. "That's right. That's why I know the value of family." Briony took a step forward. "You have a family that wants you, and you're throwing it away."

"Are you talking about me throwing away the chance to return to my pack or throwing away the chance to remain with you?"

She paled. "I want a husband and a family. A real one. But more than that, I want true love. The real kind. Not the kind offered by a rune." She rubbed her chest where the rune symbol lay. "We don't know if anything we feel is real."

He nodded. "Right." His body was numb, his mind buzzing. The words left his lips, but they felt foreign and strange as if he wasn't speaking at all. "Take my room. I'll sleep in the guest quarters with Zann." He strode away down the hall. All he saw was Briony's face, her lips pressed in a thin line, ending things. He didn't know where he walked. All he knew was his feet moved. "Uit." He jerked to a stop. Turned back. Halted again.

No, she'd been clear. While they remained runebound, she didn't want him around. With a snarl, he stalked through the garden and into the forest.

He craved her. He wanted her asleep half on top of him, clutching him like she'd never let go. She was fierce, even while sleeping. And she'd wanted him. Only him.

Not anymore. There wouldn't be any sleep for him tonight. He glanced up through the trees at the thick clouds across the sky. No light in the forest at all. Good.

He slunk into the dark.

27

HANS STRODE past the palace dining hall, but a whiff of mountain laurel halted him. He turned. Briony sat alone, picking at her food.

Ten days. Ten days of polite nods as they passed each other in the hall with only a handful of words between them. Ten nights of tossing and turning, shredding his bed linens in his sleep as he struggled not to go to her. Wasn't it supposed to get easier every day? Instead, he was in a cave, the walls closing in and cutting off his air.

Her cheeks were hollow, and dark circles smudged under her eyes. He growled and marched forward. She noticed him and jumped, her fork clattering to the floor.

When she bent to pick it up, he barked, "Leave it." He slid into the seat next to her and pulled her plate close. With one claw, he speared a piece of melon and brought it to her lips. "You aren't eating enough."

"I haven't been hungry." But she bent forward and ate from his hand. His tension eased. Pretending he needed to shift in his seat, he leaned forward and inhaled. Her scent filled his nose, and the tight sensation in his chest vanished.

The vae messenger, Jeral, assigned to babysit him while he

lived at the palace, stepped into the dining hall and aimed straight for him. Most vae walked with a lilt, almost like they floated, but this vae stomped. "Master Hans, I'm here to inform you—"

"We need different food. Bring Briony some of that bread, the kind made with honey. She likes that. And the yogurt your kind makes. The special one."

Jeral bristled. "That's not for guests."

Hans growled and narrowed his eyes.

Jeral's lips tightened. "I came to give you news, not so you could order me around."

"You can tell me your news after you get what I want. And bring more forks. She doesn't have claws."

Jeral turned on his heel and stalked off.

Briony arched a brow. "You're bossy."

He speared a berry. "Eat."

She plucked it off his claw. "What have you been doing? Where's Zann?"

"He took off early this morning to meet the vulk coming from the den. They should make the bridge today. When Juri sees Zann, he's not going to believe it."

She chewed and swallowed. "You didn't want to join them?"

He hadn't wanted to be far from her, even if they weren't talking much, but he wouldn't tell her that. "I'll see them when they return."

She smiled. "I'm glad they'll arrive today. I need to know how many vulk are going to fight."

His hand paused on the way back to her plate. "You do? Why?"

"Did you see Caladin's sword when he was fighting at the crevasse? He was right in front of me, so I got a good view. It glowed purple while he used it. When I asked him about it, he said the vae use a special metal to make weapons because they can charge it with magic. I asked him if something else

234

was crafted out of the same metal if it would also hold a charge."

Hans tilted his head. Why was vae metal important? "Okay."

Her eyes lit up for the first time. "Well, I had an idea. Why can't we make armor that will deflect Morana's silver spell? We can't repeat what happened to Zann, or she'll hurt all the vulk in the pack. At first, Caladin wasn't sure if it would work if a vae didn't wear the armor, but it does. The metal holds magical protection—at least for a little while. It should last long enough to protect you until we take Morana out."

His breath hitched in his chest. He wanted to pick her up and bury his head in her neck so badly his fingers curled. He tried to speak, but his throat was dry. She wanted to protect his pack.

Jeral chose that moment to return. With clipped movements, he placed down a golden bowl and a slab of bread.

At dinner, Hans had noticed Briony always ate the bread first, so he figured she favored it. He broke off a hunk, scooped up some of the famed vae yogurt, and handed it to her. "It's good together."

"You've eaten this?"

He shrugged. "I tried it. I should warn you, though, the yogurt's probably made from llama's milk or something odd. The vae guard how it's made like gold."

"If we had llamas, I'm sure you'd be eating them, too," Jeral said with a sniff. "The chef's still not happy that your friend killed his dodos. They're his pets, and he's threatening to slice off vulk ears if any of you mess with them again. He's an excellent shot with a bow and lethal with his knife." Jeral drew himself up straighter. "Am I allowed to impart my news now? Or do I have to fetch more things first?"

Hans waved his hand.

"I'm here to inform you of the return of the vulk. They're in the courtyard."

Hans stood. "Why didn't you say that?" The vae messenger turned red and stormed off. Hans's lips twitched. "What's his problem?" Briony gave him half a smile, and his heart lurched.

"Can I come with you to meet the pack?"

He eyed her breakfast. She'd eaten all the bread, and there wasn't much yogurt left. "All right."

Hans tossed open the front doors of the palace and strode past the heavily armored group of palace guards, all of them on alert. He scanned the courtyard and halted. They'd all come. Every single pack member, including Zann, stood in a tight group and stared back at the vae guards.

Wait, no, Juri was missing. Kyril jostled to the front and crossed his arms. "When they heard you were back, they all wanted to come."

Everyone stared at Hans. Some with narrowed eyes, and some, like Ayren, who he'd only met a few times, watched him with a rapt, hopeful expression. The sun broke through the trees and dappled their fur.

Briony called them his family. Until this moment, he hadn't realized he'd missed them. *One claw breaks, but together they prevail.*

Instinct warred and tore through him. His chest heaved. As Alpha, he sensed the pack as if it were a living, breathing entity. Right now, it lay fractured. The need to claim the pack as his own, to fix it, surged hard.

His gaze fell on Zann. They expected Hans to be the son of Wulf. To conquer their foes like Wulf had in the past. Wulf believed in following strength and eliminating weaknesses. His hands fisted. When he was Alpha before, Zann died.

Let Zann take the pack. He'd remain solo. How he was strongest.

"Did Zann catch you all up on what's going on?"

They nodded.

"All right, good. Let's plan our attack."

"That's it?" Kyril asked. "That's all you have to say?"

Hans snarled. "We kill the spawn. It's as simple as that. There's an army of them here, and we're needed."

Kyril bared his teeth. "No explanation of what you've been doing for a hundred years? Or what your plans are after this?"

Hans stared without response.

Juri strolled into the courtyard from around the side of the palace with five fat—and quite dead—dodos strung over his shoulder. Behind him chased an older vae wearing a gardener's apron smeared with dirt.

"You can't just ... kill!" The vae gestured wildly.

"I took the old ones." Juri rolled his eyes at Hans. "We need actual food, not vae seeds and berries. We've been running nonstop the last few days."

A male vae, close to a vulk in width and with prominent forearms on display in a rolled-up shirt, stormed around the side of the palace and notched an arrow into an ebony bow. "Those are my dodos. They aren't here to satisfy your disgusting desire for raw animal flesh."

Hans lived with the vae for years. He'd never seen one look anything other than bored. Even when he fought Caladin, the vae's face remained smug.

Not this one. His crystalline turquoise eyes glinted and turned black, and as he opened his mouth, his teeth elongated and sharpened to points. Wings erupted from his back and curled forward.

Hans's jaw dropped. In all the years he'd lived with the vae, he'd never seen this.

"What the hell?" Next to him, Juri took a step back. He held his hands up. "We need meat. That's all. There are too many dodos. It's fine."

Wrong thing to say. The cook hissed and raised his bow. "Fine?"

Caladin skidded out the front doors of the palace and yelled, but it was too late. The arrow released.

It sang for Juri's left ear, a light-colored blur. Hans leaped and snatched it out of midair, an inch from Juri's skin.

For one breath, no one moved.

Then Caladin leaped off the stairs toward the cook and his wings sprang out mid-jump. The cook cowered, and the bow clattered to the ground.

Unlike a vulk, Caladin didn't yell, but his eyes turned black, and threads of purple lightning sparked off his fingertips. He spoke quietly in the Vae language, and the other vae appeared to get smaller and smaller and his face twisted as if in pain. The vae didn't speak their language in front of non-vae ears often. Hans had only heard it a few times when a vae forgot he was around. Guards surrounded Caladin and the cook, and Hans couldn't see anything further until several guards marched the cook away.

Caladin turned to face him. So, the vae had wings. Not feather ones either, they were leathery like a bat, or a dragon, although Caladin probably wouldn't like either reference. The king's wings were a dusty gold, and they folded and disappeared with a snap.

"Apologies." His voice was lower than usual, and his eyes remained dark.

Hans tilted his head. "Should have taken those wings out when we fought. Maybe you would have stood a chance."

"I didn't have them yet." He grinned, and while his teeth weren't all pointy like the cook's, his eyeteeth seemed sharper. "Next time, I will."

"Good."

Caladin arched a brow. "You caught a silver arrow out of the air. Doesn't silver repel the vulk?"

Hans turned his hand over and studied the arrow. Glinting with undiluted silver, it sat in his hand much heavier than a regular arrow. The shaft and tip were of pure silver, yet there was no searing of his flesh. No pain.

Behind Hans, the vulk shifted and whispered. Hans frowned at the arrow in his hand. The vae were the best archers in the world, and their strength was formidable. Their arrows flew fast and never missed. Catching one of their arrows out of the air should have been impossible. Even more so if it was silver.

A wound delivered from a silver weapon didn't allow a vulk's rapid healing to work. If a silver arrow caught a vulk in the throat, he could die. Silver blades were much worse.

Hans shrugged. "I thought Juri might want both his ears."

Juri rubbed his ears vigorously. "I appreciate that. I'd look lopsided." Juri tossed the dead birds on the ground and peered at the arrow. "How do the vae have these?" Back during the Territory Wars, the vulk destroyed all silver weapons.

Caladin smiled. The polite vae smile of the king was forgotten. This was pure wickedness. He rather liked this side of Cal. "The vulk weren't the only ones to take the silver weapons the humans made during the Territory Wars. We thought it might not be a bad idea to have some around. In case we go to war with the vulk."

Hans snapped the silver arrow in half. "Let's go to your war room and start preparing."

THE MOONS SLANTED long silvery swaths over the private garden as they moved high into the sky. Briony's outstretched hand bobbed in the air as another wave of chills seized her. She bit her lip and focused. Cool air churned against her skin as her magic swirled into a single ball of fist-sized light resting on her palm. It rose several inches into the air and pulsed. Her muscles shook. The chill seeping over her was like a skein of ice forming over the surface of a lake, a slow infusion—difficult to pinpoint—but would eventually freeze everything.

"Good. Excellent control," whispered Katisa. "Know your limits. Explore just how far you can push yourself."

Her vision swam. She glanced up at the moons. A little longer, she must hold on longer. *Use the moons' light, like Katisa said.* Panic beat inside her chest. Tomorrow the moons would be full, and she still hadn't figured out Hazel's symbol. Tomorrow, she and Hans were done for good.

The light winked out. "Damn." Briony slumped, and chills surged full force. She wrapped her arms around herself.

"Here." Katisa handed her a flagon of well water, and Briony brought it to her lips. Water sloshed over her chin as her hand jumped from a fresh round of shaking. As the first swallow slid down her throat, warmth burst through her, and she sighed.

"I was awful. That time I only held the magic for fifteen minutes."

"It wasn't too bad. You lost your concentration." Katisa reached forward and put the back of her hand against Briony's brow. "Your color is returning."

The two of them had trained hard every night. Despite what Katisa said about vae magic only being accessible during daylight hours, somehow Katisa could access her magic at night. Each time she did, she acted guilty, and she raced through her demonstrations. When Briony pressed her on why her magic was different, Katisa clammed up and changed the subject.

Briony handed the flagon back and then stalked to the wide linden tree in the corner of Katisa's private garden. "You're being kind. I'm doing horribly today."

Katisa joined her and put a hand on her shoulder. "Hey, give yourself a break. The amount of control and power you've learned to use in ten days is incredible. Yesterday you wrote your name in the sky. In cursive! Even I don't dare do that. Take a deep breath and try again."

The vae princess was both patient and tough. She made Briony practice her control again and again. All her lessons centered on Briony feeling the power of her magic whisper through her and learning to harness it and shape it. The more she used it, the better her stamina would be.

Healing was the easiest and the one that taxed her the least. She could hold on to her healing power for hours before succumbing to chills now. Something that may be useful in battle tomorrow if it lasted into the evening.

She squared her shoulders and lifted her hand again. After shoving it aside her entire life, it was proving much more difficult to unleash the other aspects of her power. Briony took a deep breath and closed her eyes. This time, a force stirred inside her. From the soles of her feet to the crown of her head, she felt connected to something ... else. The chill that chased her magic was present but far, far off. Not something she needed to worry about.

"That's it!" Katisa's voice seemed leagues away. "Open your eyes and find one leaf. Only one. Use your magic to vaporize it."

Briony opened her eyes. The light of the moons sparkled everywhere. It trailed in the air, played on the leaves of the tree, and washed across the grass nodding in the light breeze. As she breathed in, she absorbed its light.

She frowned. No, it didn't seem right to injure a leaf. She wouldn't do that. There was no ball of light sitting on top of her palm; instead, her entire hand glowed. Briony gestured to Katisa. "Send a blast of your magic toward the tree."

Katisa took a step back. "This is your training. I don't know if that's a good idea."

"My magic isn't for hurting others. I'm supposed to guard them," Briony said. She waved her hand, and a ghostly shimmer coated the linden. "Try to get through my protection."

Without further argument, Katisa shot her hand out, and a blast of light, so dark it was black or deep purple, shot at the tree. Briony focused and held her shield together. Katisa's magic bounced off and dissolved.

Katisa gasped. "I've never seen any vae do that."

Briony lowered her hand, and the light around the tree faded. She waited for the chills to crash into her, but they didn't come. "That felt fantastic."

"How did you know to try defensive magic?"

Briony thought for a moment. "I'm not sure. It's just ... using my magic to attack never felt right. When you wanted me to hurt the tree, I couldn't. I realized my magic was supposed to protect it instead."

"Well, that was brilliant. Let's practice and see how long you can keep your shield up and if you can coat multiple targets." Katisa beamed. "But first, break time."

Briony's favorite part of their training sessions was their breaks. Not because she wanted to stop practicing, but because it was the time she and Katisa talked. She felt like she'd made her first real friend since she'd become an adult.

So far, Katisa told her about growing up as a princess and the trials of having an older brother who'd acted like he was king since birth. Katisa also spoke of her parents, and Briony learned they'd stepped down to let Caladin take his role as king several years ago and now lived with a small community of vae on an island off the south of Ulterra.

At first, Briony hadn't wanted to share about her own life —what was her boring life compared to that of a princess— but Katisa insisted and seemed genuinely interested. Since she wasn't spending time with Hans any longer, it was splendid to have someone to talk with, and every moment with Katisa kept her mind off Hans. She'd avoided discussing anything involving Hans.

"While you rest, I'm going to visit that sorcerer," Katisa said. "We're out of time, and she needs to talk."

"No, wait!" Briony had spent days searching in the princess's study and found nothing about the symbol. She hadn't asked any of the vae for help because she'd worried they'd lose patience and force Hazel to talk, killing the sorcerer. During the past week, she'd learned the vae had no tolerance for magicwielders. Their dislike for them almost bordered on hatred. But Katisa was right. There wasn't any time left. The full moons rose tomorrow, and they'd leave for battle in the morning.

If Katisa did go for Hazel, Briony had just proven she had the skill to guard against Katisa's power. She'd keep Hazel safe.

"Look at this." Briony removed the small scrap of paper from her pocket, where she'd hastily scratched a copy of the symbol. "Hazel gave me this clue and asked me to figure it out, but I need your help. *She* needs your help."

Briony detailed her conversation with the sorcerer and how she suspected a spell on Hazel prevented her from talking and passed the drawing to Katisa. "This is what she drew."

Katisa studied it. "You believe the magicwielder?"

Briony nodded. "She was truly frightened she might die." She pointed at the paper. "This is a clue why."

"So, this is what you've been working on after our lessons?"

"Yes, I've needed to keep busy."

Katisa looked up. "I haven't asked, but I'm going to now. What's going on with you and Hans? I know you don't spend time with him anymore." She smiled. "The vae palace is the center of all gossip."

Briony swallowed hard. "I know what you were trying to tell me when we met for tea. You were trying to let me know the vulk have no souls."

Katisa glanced away. "I'm sorry."

Briony sagged. "He doesn't let anyone in. He wants to be alone." Her voice cracked, and she cleared her throat. Burning built behind her eyes. "I knew that from the first day we met, but with being runebound ... I guess I still had a shred of hope. But without souls? There is none." She shook her head. "I'm going to leave after the battle. If I leave first, I won't have to watch him walk away."

Katisa closed the distance between them and hugged her. A sunny scent, floral like a daisy, wafted from her hair. "For the vae, finding a bondmate is sacred. It's rare and not to be trifled with." She pulled back and lay her hands on Briony's upper arms. "If a rune, one of the most ancient and powerful magical entities, mingled the two of you together, and he doesn't see how special that is? Then you aren't meant to be, or he's a terrible fool. Maybe both."

Briony gulped in a large breath and nodded.

Katisa took Briony's hand. "The vulk chose the way they wanted their lives to go a long time ago. They are who they are." She squeezed it gently. "You don't have to leave. You can stay here. We'll work on getting you happy again."

Katisa gave her hand one last pulse, then lifted the paper again. "Vae magic differs from the piddly magic humans tinker with, and we don't use symbols or spells, but I have some arcane texts that detail human magic buried in my study. Let's go find them."

They bustled through to Katisa's study with its dim light, and Katisa found a few books on a shelf Briony hadn't gotten to yet. She tossed them onto the table with a thud. Puffs of dust drifted into the air, and Briony sneezed. "Sorry." Katisa waved her hand, wafting the dust away. "I have no real reason to open these."

Briony opened one and scanned through it. Lots of complex spells and equations, but nothing that resembled the image. They divided up the pile and flipped through the pages.

"Here!" Katisa dragged an ancient book next to Briony and pointed. Traces of bookworm attack peppered the glue at the lower binding and dotted the paper, but the symbol sat clearly at the top of the page. "It's the oath of silence."

Underneath the symbol was a flowing script, some in the arcane language. "I can't read all of this. What is it?"

Katisa's finger moved across the lines as she read, "It's a binding between two people that guarantees secrecy. If the oath is performed, neither can discuss the event they both witnessed or their discussion. Look"—she pointed at a paragraph— "it can control people. It's been banned since 892 because it almost caused a war."

"Does it say how to remove it?"

Katisa flipped the page. "Yes, here's a list of what we need and instructions on how to undo it." Katisa sniffed. "Great, we get to perform magic like a spellcaster."

Briony read the page. They'd need crystals and chalk and must speak an incantation. Best practice was for the person who invoked the oath of silence to release it, but anyone with magic would do in a pinch. It also directed that the affected person had to perform some of the magic, too.

"Hazel will need to be unbound so she can chant the spell, too." She didn't think Hazel was a danger, but she also didn't know what Hazel was capable of.

Katisa's cool gray eyes blazed. "I'll be there, and her magic is nothing compared to vae magic. There is no spell she can create I can't counter."

Briony bit her cheek to hide her smile. Katisa sounded like Caladin right now. "What is your magic, exactly?"

Katisa picked up the books and busied herself with shelving them. "The color of light of my magic differs from most vae, and I use it judiciously. I required a lot of training to tame it." She turned on her heel, her pale green dress whirling around her. "The crystals we need are in the library. Let's go." Katisa rattled on about preparations for the battle the entire time they gathered the crystals and chalk, preventing Briony from questioning her further.

When they approached Hazel's cell, the spellcaster was on her hands and knees scrubbing the stone floor. The rug lay rolled up in the corner. Her face lit up when she saw Briony, but fell the moment she saw Katisa. "Why is she here?"

"Princess Katisa will help break the oath of silence with me."

Katisa arched a brow. "Is something the matter with our floor?"

Hazel's hair was in one long, fat braid, and she pushed it off her shoulder and stood. "This place is dusty, and I don't like it."

One guard turned. "She asked for soap and a bucket, and

since we didn't see the harm, we gave it to her. She cleans for most of the day, every day, your highness."

Hazel's fingers twitched. "There's no need to discuss my affairs with her. If I had my magic right now, I'd turn you into a newt."

"Don't worry, Tae, if she has the skill to turn you into a newt, which I highly doubt, I'd make sure you got better."

The guard's face reddened.

Briony sighed. Having Katisa here was going to be challenging. "Why don't we enter Hazel's room and work on breaking the spell? Then she can help us." She gave Katisa a piercing glance, hoping she got the message. "Hazel, may we come in?"

"She owns this place, so she can enter whenever she wishes." But she stepped back from the door.

Inside, Katisa set up the crystals in a wide circle on the floor and handed the chalk to Hazel.

The spellcaster stepped inside the crystals, drew an intricate pattern, and then stood in the middle. "Are you going to release the gag you put on my tongue so I can do my part of the spell?"

"Just remember who plucked you from the sky. Step out of line, and I'll give you another taste of what I can do."

"Ah yes, your little magic snare. That was cute. I was distracted, and you got lucky."

Katisa's eyes darkened into swirling gray. "You think you're a match against vae magic? You don't have a clue what you're up against."

Hazel's hands twitched. "If an angry vulk doesn't scare me, you definitely don't."

This was going nowhere, fast. "Okay. Enough." Briony stepped between them. "Katisa, please do the incantation. Hazel, if you want to get out of prison, I suggest you stop angering the vae princess."

Both scowled, and a stony silence fell over the room.

Briony gestured at Katisa, and after a pause, the princess waved her hand at Hazel. A faint silver light shone around Hazel's throat, then evaporated.

Katisa spoke the first part of the incantation, and when she finished, Hazel closed her eyes, and her lips moved, but she didn't speak aloud. Blue light shot out from her hands and filled the circle. The tinkle of the wind through the trees, and the twittering of the birds nearby, shut off. There was a slight pressure, and Briony felt pulled toward Hazel.

"Hazel? Are you okay? Did it work?"

The spellcaster's eyelids snapped open, and her eyes were pure white with no irises or pupils. Along her neck, her veins bulged blue. Briony cried out and ran forward. Her hand hovered at the crystal barrier for a second, eyeing the blue light, then she ignored it and stepped inside with Hazel. She gripped her shoulder and shook her.

Nothing happened.

Beneath her hand, Hazel was rigid and remained staring forward with her creepy white eyes. Briony shook her harder. The dust lifted from the floor to swirl in the blue glow in a slow whirlwind.

"Katisa, what's going on? Did it work?" Briony backed away and glanced at Katisa. The princess was frozen, too. Even her hair was stuck in place as it blew around her face. The guards remained immobile; both turned toward the cell with looks of surprise on their faces. What the hell was going on?

Briony turned back to Hazel and gasped. Morana stood facing Hazel in the circle, wearing her green dress. Up this close, Briony could see each detail of the dress's embroidery, the kind that took a seamstress months to create and cost heaps of coin. She was there in the room ... but she wasn't. Briony could see through her.

Morana smiled with thin lips painted a deep red, but the smile didn't reach her eyes. "Ah, Hazel, explain why the spell hasn't finished yet? And you'll forgive me if I put us in an oath of silence. With you so close to a vulk, who knows what he can make you say or do? We have to be careful."

Briony stepped back toward the door, but neither woman turned toward her.

"Of course." Hazel's voice was funny, and Briony hadn't seen her mouth move. Briony took another step, her gaze darting between the two, but neither glanced her way. She waved. Nothing. Not even a flicker of an eyelash. Whatever was going on wasn't playing out in the present.

Morana stopped smiling. "Why isn't he dead?"

For the first time, there was a flicker of movement from Hazel as she tilted her head to the side. "He's strong."

Morana's face sharpened, her nose and mouth like a hawk's beak. "You're the best spellcaster at Herskala Academy. What I want you to do is nothing. A mere trifle. Use his beastly desire against him." Despite her harsh expression, Morana spoke sweetly, and she stepped forward and caressed Hazel's face. "Stop playing around and get it done."

"It's not that simple."

"My lord isn't patient, and neither am I. The vulk needs to be destroyed. Both of us will get more power when my lord rises. You'll have everything you've ever wanted. But you must take care of the vulk first."

Hazel jerked her head away from Morana's touch. "There's a lot you didn't tell me. Like who your lord is. But I've figured it out, and he isn't about to give either of us power. He'll kill us. Kill everyone."

Morana traced the ropy bracelet around her wrist with a finger. "No, he won't. We're bound, Czart and I. He needs me, and if he kills me, he'll perish. After I kill all the vulk, I'll rule at his side."

"I doubt it. The leshak consume everyone around them."

Morana's eyes flashed. "I promised him this. You'll see, when I complete my side of our bargain, he'll reward me. He'll reward *us*. Finish the spell. Remember who you're loyal to.

You'd be in Coromesto doing simple spells for a bit of coin if not for me."

"You won't let me forget."

Morana's bracelets glowed green, and she shot a whip of green light at Hazel. There wasn't enough time to dodge, and it lashed across her right cheek. Hazel fell to the ground, her hand cupping her face.

"I don't want to punish you, but you know I must. It's the only way to drive you to be better." Morana raised her hand, and Hazel cowered. "Weaken the Alpha with your spell so it can ripple from him to the rest of the pack, and we can finish this. You could have completed this the first day, the first hour, yet you continue to fail me." She slashed with her light again, and it sliced across Hazel's back. Hazel flinched and fell to the ground, but she didn't make a sound. "My lord and I are as one. He's finally giving me what I deserve. Unending power. A true partner. Finish this, and no more pain. No more punishment. I'll give you whatever you want."

Hazel fought to get up to her hands and knees, something clenched in her fist. "You don't know what I want."

Morana raised her hand to send another whip at Hazel, but Hazel shot a blue ball of magic at Morana, and it hit her squarely in the chest. The sorcerer reeled back, jaw dropping. "You attack *me*?"

She blasted a wave of green at Hazel, and it struck her in the back, slamming her onto the ground again. Morana laughed shrilly. "Really, Hazel? You think you can take me out? I'm bound to my lord and he feeds me power. I don't need a spell or a rock"—she sneered at the object Hazel held clutched in her hand— "to focus my magic." She shook her arms, and her sleeves slipped down her forearms, revealing the glowing bracelets in their entirety as they wound up her arms. Her whip snapped and fell again, but Hazel rolled and flung another ball at Morana. It missed, and instead of dissolving at the edge of the crystal circle, it flew past and hit above the cell door with a loud crack.

The entire prison structure trembled and groaned. As if in slow motion, rocks broke off along the ceiling and tumbled inwards. Briony screamed and dove into Katisa, rolling with her to the opposite side of the room as wood and rock crashed into a gigantic pile where the princess had stood.

Hazel remained in the circle, spinning as Morana attacked. She hurled another ball. Another crack as it missed and hit the cell walls. This time, the ground heaved.

Hazel had to stop throwing those things. She had to come out of her dream. Memory. Whatever.

With a sharp inhale, Briony wobbled to her feet and charged at Hazel. She crashed into her, and they tumbled out of the circle in a crumple. The light inside the crystals disappeared with a whoosh.

"Hazel, are you alright?" The sorcerer lay still, partway on her side, her eyes closed, and her face pressed against the rough rock, scrapes oozing a bit of blood along her cheek.

Her eyelids flickered, and one opened a fraction. "I'm not sure what's worse, the pounding head or reliving my time with Morana."

"What happened?" Rock crumbled above them, and the roof groaned.

Hazel didn't seem to have heard her. "She's bound to the leshak king through her bracelets. Remove them, and you break their power, and you can kill them both."

"Will that kill the leshak king?"

Hazel sat up and gripped her arm. "Tell Zann. It has to be him."

"What do you mean?"

"When Morana and the leshak king are no longer joined, both can be killed, but only the Alpha can kill the leshak king. That's why Morana wanted Zann dead. With the Alpha dead, the leshak king has no enemy."

"And you joined her in her plan?"

Hazel shook her head. "Not exactly. Morana told me for years how evil and dangerous the vulk were. That they were only beasts. A menace. She told me the spell she gave me would weaken them so they couldn't hurt anyone anymore. I didn't know it was going to kill."

"You figured it out, though?"

"Yes. I wasn't lying about the spell not working. When I looked up the arcane to figure out why, I learned the truth." She looked away. "The first rule of spellcasting is to never perform a spell you don't know intimately. But she ... forced me."

The building shook, and the limestone shifted. "We need to get out of here." Briony eyed the door, now blocked with layers of rock. "Maybe the window?" It was high and narrow —a tough reach.

"I'll create a portal to get us out." Hazel waved her hand, and swirling air appeared.

"Don't forget the guards!" The two guards lay slumped near the rubble. Muttering strange words and waving her hand, both guards flew through the air and shot through the portal. She and Briony grabbed Katisa's arms and dragged her through after them.

One moment it was rubble and chaos, and the next, the lyrical dripping of a fountain surrounded them as they emerged in the far corner of the vae garden next to the prison. Guards streamed out of the palace, barreling toward them when they saw Katisa and the two guards lying on the ground.

The portal still wavered in the air. Hazel lowered the princess to the ground and stepped back. "Tell Zann to kill the leshak king. You have little time before Morana tries again to kill all the vulk. This time she might succeed."

"Wait, can't you stay and help us?"

"Thanks for releasing me. In more ways than you know. But we both know they'll lock me up again, and that's not going to happen." She shot Briony a quick smile. "See you around." Hazel stepped through the portal and disappeared.

As the guards reached them, Hans and Zann flew into the garden. Hans shouldered vae out of his way until he reached her. "You alright? What happened?" His hands smoothed over her arms, and he nuzzled her neck and face.

"I'm fine."

Next to her, Katisa moaned and sat up. "That sorcerer."

"What did the sorcerer do?" Zann asked.

"Spellcaster." Briony scowled up at Zann. "That's her proper title." Zann raised a brow but didn't say anything.

Katisa dusted herself off. "I can't believe that magicwielder got away."

Briony pointed at the two guards getting to their feet. "She saved your guards."

Zann crossed his arms, and Briony thought his face softened for a moment. "She's skilled. Do you know where she went? We can try to catch her again."

"No."

"What happened?" Hans asked her. She explained the oath of silence and the enactment that occurred afterward. When she finished, the guards fawned over Katisa and practically carried her away. Zann followed them back into the palace, leaving Hans and Briony alone. The trickling of the fountain was suddenly a cavernous noise.

He hadn't stopped running his hands up and down her arms. "You did a good job."

"Hans, Hazel was wrong about something."

"What?"

"She kept saying Zann's the Alpha, and he's the one who needs to kill the leshak king." She shook her head. "He isn't the Alpha. *You* are."

He stared somewhere over her head. "I'm not the Alpha."

Briony placed her hands on his chest. "Even Baba Yaga said it. You're supposed to be the Alpha."

He didn't reply for a long moment. "I'll think about it."

She sighed and glanced toward the palace. "I'm going to get some sleep before we leave for battle in the morning."

He placed his hands over hers. "Come to bed with me."

Briony turned back to face him. Her heart pounded. Tonight, would be their last night together. Did she want to spend it apart?

29

HANS HELD his breath as Briony shifted closer. Sweet vanilla swirled around him. He lowered his mouth to her neck, trailing up the column with his lips. Her skin was so smooth, with her scent the strongest right there—where her pulse skittered below her jaw. He licked it.

Her arms wrapped around his neck.

He nibbled at the spot she liked best, close to the hollow at her throat. "This is you and me. I don't want you because of some rune."

She didn't answer.

"I want you to spend the night with me." He put his lips on the soft shell of her ear. "I need you." He purred a long velvety trill, and she rubbed against him.

"You aren't fighting fair when you make that sound."

"You want me. Only I can give you what you need. Satisfy you." His mouth trailed along her shoulder, and when his teeth snagged in the fabric of her shirt, he growled—a short, frustrated grumble. Hans stepped back and put his hand out. They needed to go somewhere private. Just the two of them. All night.

Briony didn't move. She stared at his hand, gulped in a large breath, and released it slowly. A maelstrom pounded in his chest and made it twist in pain. She wasn't going to join him.

Her small hand slid over his palm and laced into his fingers.

A tingle shot up his arm, warming him and quieting the frenzy in his chest. He closed his fingers around hers like he held a baby bird. Precious and delicate.

He hauled her close and picked her up. Instead of going through the palace, he took the path through the forest to his bedroom. Briony ran her hands up his neck, along his face, her fingers desperate and hungry. Even with the cool air, he was on fire.

He kicked his door open and tumbled with her on the bed.

"You think the desire you feel for me is because of a rune?" He pinned her wrists above her head. "Everything you feel is because it's me. Only me. Not some ancient symbol. I'll tease you until you admit the truth." He loosened his grip. "Unless you don't think you can take it?"

Her pupils dilated. "I can take it. Prove it to me."

He grinned. "Good. I'm not going to let you find release until you scream I'm right."

Her eyes widened, and she froze under him.

He shifted back and released her wrists. "What?"

"You smiled."

"I'm about to see you naked." He tore her clothes off with one slice until only her undergarments remained.

She shuddered. "But you never smile."

He ripped her undergarments off. "Are you ready for me to show you how much you want me? To see exactly what's between us?"

Her pupils dilated. "Yes."

· · ·

FOR THE FIRST HOUR, she cursed. After the cursing subsided, he wasn't sure how much time had passed, but he still hadn't let her find her release. Glistening with sweat, Briony's skin was flushed pink, especially where he'd dragged his tongue over again and again. He'd used a scrap of her breeches to bind her wrists over her head and pinned her hips to the bed with one hand. Briony strained against him, stretching toward his mouth. To reach the climax he withheld.

Not yet. She hadn't earned her freedom yet.

He bent and skated his tongue between her legs again. Rolled it in the way that drove her wild. Her hips bucked and her head thrashed. She was desperate. Needy.

When her thighs began trembling, signaling she was close, he stopped. She whimpered and sagged into the bed. "Please."

He ignored her pleas. How many times had he brought her to the brink? Too many to count. Her eyes stared glassy and pure black. The slightest touch of his tongue and he could drive her to the edge. She was where he wanted her. He owned every breath, every inch of her skin. By now, her every thought should be of him. Only him. His next touch all she wanted. Him inside her, filling her, the only thing in the world that mattered.

He teased his teeth over a nipple, plump and red from the repeated attention. With the back of one of his claws, he brushed back and forth over the other. Having her breasts played with drove her wild. By now, she was so close to an orgasm, a little more of this was all it would take.

He laved hard, and she jolted. "Yes. Please, Hans." She arched, her body quivering as it sought more.

Hans pulled back.

Briony whined and fell back against the bed.

This was how he'd bring her into heat. The idea emerged somewhere deep inside and felt ... right. He was already painfully hard, and picturing her in a real heat that would demand they couple for days brought an unbearable ache. Normally the thought of making her pregnant would send him running in the opposite direction, but instead, the idea had him teetering on the edge of a rut. He needed. Wanted. His desire was so intense the surrounding air should be froth.

He struggled to regain control and sucked in a breath. Reined back the vivid images of them coupling until he got her with child, and of her curled next to him with her stomach swollen. This wasn't the right time. Or place.

He refocused on the needy female under him.

"Okay, I admit it. You're right." Her voice was cracked from screaming. "I want you. Not because of the rune, because it's you."

He placed both hands on her hips and lashed.

Briony arched, and her hands fisted. "Don't you dare stop! Don't you dare ..." She screamed, and her body coiled and tensed. She writhed in her release, sobbing with long, drawn-out hiccupping breaths. He used his tongue until she spasmed under him and tried to twist her hips away. He purred and worked her harder. She screamed again.

More.

Not until he'd wrung every last response and she fell against the bed limp did he stop and cut the bonds at her wrists. Briony's eyes fluttered closed as he stretched out next to her and nuzzled her neck. "Took you a while to admit it." He figured he'd give her a moment to recover, then turn her over and get her wild again.

An eye opened. "You had to earn it."

He rumbled his pleasure, his purr vibrating in his chest. He didn't think she'd have the energy to move, but after several long moments, she sat up, wobbling a bit, and smoothed her hair out of her face.

She rolled him onto his back and scooted close. As her gaze drifted downward, her eyes widened, and she smiled. "That's impressive." She gripped him and pumped. The muscles of his stomach flexed, and he shuddered.

"That ..." He groaned. How was she doing that with her tiny hand? He was lightheaded as if he couldn't get enough air. He propped himself up on his elbows to watch her stroke him.

Briony shifted between his legs. "I want to be on top."

"I don't let anyone pin me. Alphas—" He swallowed. "I mean, vulk, don't allow it."

Briony settled between his legs, and her breath fanned over the tip of his throbbing cock. She was small and harmless. Yet his desire for her, his need, was a fierce and dangerous thing. A power over him that left him vulnerable. But then their eyes met.

She'd trusted him while he'd bound her. It was his turn to trust her. He relaxed and watched her lips, already dewy, wrap around the head as she took him into her mouth and sucked. He collapsed back on the bed, and she hummed a small sound of pleasure. The vibration teased down his length and his hips jerked. Then her pink tongue darted out, and she licked from his base up his shaft. "Should I stop so you can get off your back? Still don't like being pinned?"

"I'm not sure. I might need more convincing." His claws bit into the bed, and he drove deeper into her mouth.

She could take only so much of him. So, she laved along his shaft and then throated him as deep as possible. No female had tasted him before. Used her hands, her mouth, on him. He reached up and released Briony's hair from the binding at her neck, and it tumbled over her shoulders.

When he trickled early releases of seed for her, she lapped it up with soft mewling sounds. Each time, he almost burst into her mouth, desperate to give her more. Desire pumped through the room in heated waves, nearly as potent as during a rut. She licked down to his base, and his knot swelled under her attention. Both her hands stroked him, and she suckled it.

He almost jerked off the bed. "Enough. I need to get inside you."

She crawled up his torso, and her breasts spilled forward, full and lush, as she pressed her hot center along his length. He groaned, and it came out ragged, half a purr, half a tortured moan.

He jutted up, thick and ready. Cheeks flushed pink, she sank down. "Oh. Yes. Finally." Her eyes dilated and grew glassy again, and her head tipped back, exposing her creamy throat.

He'd never had a female mount him. Never seen a female's face when he joined with her, and that was fine because the only female that mattered was the one squeezing him so tightly, he might spend right now.

She rocked her hips, and he gasped. Her heavy breasts, with their puckered nipples, bounced, and he reached up and passed his thumbs over the tips. She writhed harder, and her arousal was so intense each inhale made his blood pound harder.

Carefully, he grabbed her waist and, keeping his claws away, began dragging her up and down his length as he raised his hips and pumped into her. With each thrust, she met him, arching her back.

Briony moaned his name as she clenched and shattered around him, milking him deeper. While she whimpered, he pounded into her. She arched prettily again as she tensed for another release. She was so wet and tight as he pulled her down on his shaft. He was swelling, every inch desperate to lock them together. He wanted her tied to him in this position. Wanted to watch her face when he sealed them together.

Her eyes widened as his knot pressed against her, but she rolled her hips and teased over his sensitive skin. It was bliss. Liquid heat caressing his cock and setting fire through his veins.

Control gone, with a surge, he sat up and wrapped his arms around her, holding her in place. In two desperate plunges, he found home, locking behind her pubic bone.

Briony buried her head into his chest as he buried deep and came with a throaty purr. Arms still around her, he fell back on the bed and nudged his hips, pulsing on the raised spot inside her that turned her to mush. As she rubbed against him, her face remained hidden.

"Look at me." She met his gaze with a tremble. A surge rolled through his entire body, and he drove them both toward another peak.

She turned her head away and closed her eyes. No. Briony wasn't escaping him. Whatever was between them called to him. Demanded more.

He rolled them so she was on her back under him, and his hand dove into her thick hair. Winding it around his fingers, he bent her head back slightly. With their lower bodies clasped together, their gazes locked. Her eyes widened. He pulsed his hips, and she shattered.

All he saw was her as he joined her over the edge. The thread between them, the warmth swirling in his chest, pulsed. Something shifted deep inside. In the place where there had been nothing.

Briony wrapped her arms around his neck and clutched him close, shaking. He licked her throat, her shoulder, anywhere he could reach. His teeth grazed over the delicate crook of her neck, and she jolted. He repeated it.

<You're mine.> It ripped from deep inside him. Clawed its way out. She buried her face in his shoulder and didn't respond. He frowned and wrapped her tight in his arms. Maybe tighter than normal.

They lay like that for a long time. He didn't shift until Briony relaxed against him in the soft way that told him she was asleep.

He ran his hand over her hair and studied her lashes resting gently on her cheek. Were they wet from tears? The rune on his chest flared and flickered a blast of heat through the thread that bound them together. This was his last night with her. The last night with the rune linking them together.

He pulled her onto his chest and wrapped her in his arms.

30

"YOU'VE SHREDDED another vae outfit. They're going to make you pay for them soon." Briony toed the tattered breeches from last night with her foot. Fresh from showering together, she dried her hair, then retrieved a fresh towel from the basket and walked over to him. He'd told her he didn't need toweling, but she enjoyed doing it, and since he leaned into her when she did it, she thought he did too.

"If Caladin's kingdom is this poor, I'll give him some gold so I can continue to rip garments off you."

"I don't think they worry about money." Her brow wrinkled. "Do you have gold? Do the vulk deal with currency?"

He shrugged. "We sometimes purchase things from the peltwalkers and deal with humans or the vae. In the past, our relationship with humans was different. We weren't feared and weren't at war with them, so we traded with them more often."

She nodded. "Oh, alright."

"We dig up a lot of gold and jewels, and we hardly spend it."

She toweled up his chest. "Gold is rare now. Even a small hunk is worth a lot."

He rubbed his jaw along the top of her head. "Does that make me a rich vulk? Maybe I should make sure Caladin finds out, invite him to our pack den and show him ..." With a frown, he trailed off. She paused mid-swipe. He'd said *our* pack den. Like he was one of them.

She resumed scrubbing him dry like she hadn't noticed. "Show him what?"

"Nothing." He rubbed his head and sprayed flecks of water everywhere. "Let's get going—"

She poked him in the arm. "Show him what?"

Hans sighed. "This palace is nice. They did a good job with the limestone, but if gold is really worth a lot"—his jaws parted into a small smile— "our den has threads of it running up our pillars and through our walls. He'd be jealous."

Briony's towel dropped to the floor.

"What?" he asked.

She reached up and traced her fingers along his mouth. "You smiled again. Last night, when you did it the first time, I thought I imagined it." He didn't respond, only nuzzled her fingers.

It felt like he'd invited her to see the real Hans. Something no one else got to see. It started last night when he wouldn't release her from his gaze the entire time they were locked together. She wasn't sure how she survived because she didn't think she took a single breath for ages. Not until her breathing matched his as she felt him tightly wrapped against her, so deep inside her that it seemed they were one. She hadn't known where he ended and she began.

Hans, who purred her to sleep every night and kept the nightmares away. Who fed her the best food off his plate. Savage and prickly, but then he smiled. Or nuzzled her. Or leaned into her caresses, even though he told her the vulk didn't need to be touched. And so clever. He didn't speak often, but when he did, everyone listened.

As she stroked his face, a sensation churned up from a

place inside she'd locked away long ago. One that was fierce yet trembling. Afraid. Her heart pounded, and her stomach fluttered. She shied away from naming the emotion.

Briony snatched her hand back and plucked the towel off the ground, hiding how her hands shook. She dropped the towel in the hamper and went to the bureau for fresh clothes, keeping her back to Hans. How could she have let this happen? She'd protected herself.

There was a soft knock on the door. Briony yelped and ran into the bathroom with her clothes. As she stepped into her breeches, she peeked around the doorframe.

Hans wrenched the door open. "What?"

"I'm here to escort you. The king has armor ready for you and requests your presence in the armory." Jeral stood there. His face was always smooth and polite when he spoke to Hans, but he sighed a lot as if Hans were a trial.

Briony tugged her shirt on and joined him at the door. Her heart leaped into her throat. This was it. Battle.

"Come on." Hans put out his hand. "You're coming too."

HANS DIDN'T RELEASE Briony's hand as Jeral led them down the stairs behind the great hall into the deeper levels of the palace. He didn't want her far away. Down in the armory, the walls were lined in a dark wood, with weapons organized in racks and armor hanging on hooks. Pedestals covered in crushed velvet displayed swords and bows.

The room churned with vae strapping on their gear and prepping their arrows, and in the middle, several weary-looking vae fitted armor on the vulk, scraps of metal littering the floor near their feet. Hans glanced down at Briony, and a surge of pride flashed through him. The pack was wearing the armor she created.

A vae brought armor to Zann, and his brother waved him

away. "I'll be fighting the leshak, not Morana, and I don't want anything constricting me."

Hans glanced at Briony again. *It's your pack. You have a family that wants you, and you're throwing it away.* Her words hit him hard last night, and they'd run through his head repeatedly.

Did he want to return to his dark den alone?

He lifted his head higher. His shoulders straightened. This was it, the time to decide what he wanted to do.

He turned to Zann. "Put your armor on. I'm battling the leshak."

Zann stilled. "The Alpha is the only one who can kill him."

The Alpha, not *an* Alpha. Hans drew in a sharp breath and surveyed the pack. When Zann returned, the fractured turmoil of the pack remained. The pack hadn't clicked together. Like Briony said, it was because the pack was his. He had to lead. He was the Alpha. "That's me."

Kyril bared his teeth. "No. An Alpha sticks around."

Hans snarled. "We have one chance to kill the leshak. If we fail, Ulterra falls."

Kyril scoffed. "Zann's proven he's Alpha. He's the one who has to do this."

There was a flash of light on metal, and he turned. Briony had left his side, and she stood by the back wall of the armory. Next to her, silver arrows glinted, but the flash came from the shirt of heavy silver mail hanging on a hook she'd laid her hand on. A silver hauberk. Created to protect humans during battle, it would fall to a human's thighs, but on him, it would barely fit and sit as a regular shirt. He strode over and snatched it off the wall. No sizzling flesh.

He tugged it over his head and marched back to Kyril, who backed up, avoiding contact with the silver. Hans pounded his chest. "I am the son of Wulf. I was supposed to lead you from the moment I was born."

266

Everything that made him an Alpha flooded his face, and Kyril's ears lay back against his head. A primal beat pounded through him and time slowed. Even the dust motes swirling in the air seemed to pause. "A single claw breaks." He spoke in the old tongue and held up his outstretched hand, then fisted his claws, the tips nicking his palm. "But together, they prevail."

His senses reached outwards. He felt as if the collective pack was a part of him. Felt the fractured pieces snap into place.

Zann dipped his chin in a slight nod.

"Hell yeah." Juri smashed his fist down on the pedestal near him, and it broke and shattered onto the floor. The pack erupted into chaos, jostling each other to surround Hans and speaking rapidly in Vulk. He clapped each one on the shoulder until he got to Zann. He picked up the armor on the floor by his brother and handed it to him. As Zann slipped it on, he lowered his voice and asked, "You alright with this?"

Zann rubbed his mouth. "There's something I've been meaning to tell you."

He'd never seen Zann uneasy like this before. He nodded.

"Over time, as I battled my way through Peklo, some of the cursed began to ... follow me." He shrugged. "You know how it is with Alphas."

Where was Zann going with this? "All right."

"We came together as a pack, and everything felt different." Zann glanced at the other vulk. "I led our pack before because I was obsessed with needing to prove"—he shook his head— "it never felt right. Especially since it drove you away. I didn't realize the difference until I got my new pack, and it felt ... I don't know."

"Everything clicked into place like you finally found a part of yourself that was missing."

Zann nodded.

Hans clapped him on the shoulder. "How many in your new pack?"

"Five." The corner of Zann's mouth twitched. "One of them is a female. She's a kumiho and can turn into a nine-tailed fox. Foxes can't compete with a vulk, but she's a damn good fighter, anyway. Fast and strong."

"Too bad we can't bring them up from the underworld to help us fight today."

Zann rolled his shoulders and pointed at Hans's chest. "You going to wear the silver armor into battle?"

He turned to Briony. "I think you have better armor for me."

She walked to a plate of armor hanging on the wall. Matte black, it matched his fur. When the light hit it the right way, the magic inside shimmered faintly. "Here."

Hans dropped to a knee and dragged the hauberk off. Briony held hers out for him, and he slipped it on and tightened the clasps. It molded around his shoulders and chest like a second skin. He wrapped his arms around her and pulled her close. "Only you would have thought of armor to shield us from silver magic." She melted into him and put her arms around his neck. He hugged her for one long moment before standing.

"The vae did most of the work. They made it and put the magic in place for protection."

"I'll be nicer to Caladin." One side of his mouth turned up into a smile. "Until he pisses me off again."

He turned to the pack. "You'll survive Morana's spells because of Briony. The armor was her idea."

The vulk fell silent as they focused on her, bringing a fist to their chests. A sign of thanks and respect.

"I think it's time to go to the Bodec Mountains and end this."

31

HANS SHOOK HIS ARMS OUT. Day had bled into night, and the dirt had turned black with goblin blood. Corpses fouled the air with their rotten stench, and with each step he took, he crunched on bone. Or worse.

The spawn had fanned out in waves from Czart and Morana, who stood with the crevasse at their back. It took his pack and the vae all day to whittle the legions down until only a small core fighting group remained with Morana and Czart.

With the pack as one again, they were an extension of him. Invisible tethers told him precisely where each vulk fought along the battlefield. He reached out with his mind. <Fade back, join me and wait for the signal.> The vulk melted back into the trees rimming the valley. He nodded at Caladin, and the vae stepped forward to distract Morana and Czart. Hans loped along the forest's perimeter to get closer to the crevasse, scanning the trees for Briony.

She stood with Katisa in the middle of a group of vae warriors, away from the battlefield and ready to help with defense and healing. He exhaled a shaky breath. *Good. She was safe.*

He reached his spot and crouched, waiting for the rest of the pack to join him. The full moons glittered overhead, and their silvery power thrummed through him. Without a glance, he knew the tree at his left was two paces away. He didn't see a flash of green, but a whiff of sulfur told him Morana had cast her magic. With the moons full, his vulk power was at its greatest, his senses strongest.

An arrow exploded overhead. Caladin's signal.

Hans nodded at Juri. Juri pointed, and the pack surged forward, attacking Morana's core group from several sides at once. The tight circle of goblins surrounding Morana and Czart panicked and fled. Seth, leading a troop of vae, pursued.

Hans snarled. "Now!" He aimed for Czart, eating up the ground, the dirt flying under his feet. Cries filled the air as goblin bodies flew. Spinning fast, he plunged his claws into a charging bauk and tossed it to the ground. He flipped sideways and landed on another—a quick stab under the arm took care of it—then he swung his leg upward and used his long, lethal foot claws to dig into the throat of a third. Zann leaped forward with three other vulk and attacked the rest of the bauk, drawing them away from Morana and Czart.

Towering over everyone, the leshak king turned toward him, his massive elk-like antlers with pointed tips like daggers. The leshak's putrid stench, like a carcass, filled the clearing. His eyes glowed, and the skeletal mouth opened as it gulped at something Hans couldn't see.

They locked gazes a split second before Hans smashed into him. His claws scrabbled on the leshak's neck, trying to dig in, but there was no flesh, only hard bone and twisted, bark-like skin with no give.

A fist of bone plowed into his cheek, and his head snapped to the side. Spots danced in his vision, and his ears rang. He swung upward and clobbered the leshak's snout.

Czart staggered backward, then hissed. His bony fingers flexed into claws, and he surged forward, much faster than

Hans expected. A hand closed around his throat, and Czart lifted him from the ground. The leshak swung for Hans's ribs. Hans tensed, waiting for the fist to crush his ribs, but the blow skated off him in a blaze of white sparks. He glanced down. His entire body glowed like a silvery shield coated him. *Briony. It was night now, and she was protecting him.*

Hans grappled at the hand clutched around his neck. It didn't budge. The leshak pummeled with his free hand again and again, but white light flashed, and no blows landed.

With a loud hiss, the leshak smashed him to the ground and slashed with his skeletal hand. Briony's white light flickered, and a blade-like claw made it past and sliced his side from below his armor to his hip. A wet gush ran down his fur. The leshak crowed a high, whining note. Czart raised his foot and kicked, sending Hans rolling. White-hot pain streaked up his side.

The ground trembled and heaved. Wind blasted from the sky so strong it picked Hans up and hurled him back to land hard near the woods with the archers. His side screamed, and he gulped a steadying breath as he scanned the valley.

The wind had tossed Czart backward, and he scrambled to get back on his feet, but the gale strengthened and whipped into a tornado. All the fighters struggled to stand. Inside the eye of the storm, Seth floated several feet off the ground with his arms outstretched.

Back to his human form, amethyst shot through his skin like veins, lighting the incubus from within and making his eyes pure purple. White lightning streaked through the sky, and Seth caught one and hurtled it outwards. It blazed into three bauk, and they vaporized.

Hans stared. All right, perhaps there was a reason Seth was in Briony's book. He frowned as the maelstrom grew hungrier and wider, gobbling up friend and foe alike and tossing them from the battlefield.

A figure cartwheeled through the air toward him. Before

smashing to the ground, he sprouted golden wings and righted himself to land on his feet. Caladin shook his wings out and said, "What the hell is that incubus doing?"

This was not part of their plan. Hans stood and flinched, pressing a hand to his side. Why wasn't it healing? "I don't think Seth was banished to Peklo because of his incubus powers."

Caladin shifted his sword into his right hand. "I'm thinking the same. Besides, if you get tossed into Peklo for being an excellent lover, I'd have been sent there ages ago." Under the splatters of black blood, his lips curled into a half-smile.

"You're the king. Your lovers tell you what they think you want to hear. I'm sure none of it's true." Hans pointed at Seth. "Which one of us is going to take care of that?"

Katisa and Briony rushed up behind them. Katisa stared down into the valley. "What the hell?"

"I told you. He's the god of War and Storms," Briony said.

Caladin sighed. "He thinks he's a god, but there's no such thing. I'll go deal with it and make him rein it in."

Katisa stepped forward. "No. I'll go." Maybe it was a trick of the light, but her gray eyes glittered.

Caladin stared at her for a long moment. "Be careful. There's a lot of bloodlust in the air."

Hans stared at Caladin. Ever since he'd known Caladin and his parents, they'd sheltered Katisa. It wasn't because she was a princess, since Caladin was king and he still fought, or that she was a female as both male and female vae fought as warriors and guards. He'd assumed she was weak somehow, although after catching the spellcaster, he'd questioned that.

Without a goodbye, Katisa sprinted along the tree line toward the other side of the crevasse. Couldn't she fly like Caladin?

Hans turned to Briony. "Go back to safety. Stick with the other vae defenders."

Her chin came up. A sign she wasn't about to listen to him. "You distract the leshak king, and I'll take care of Morana so we can end this."

Hans growled. "You're not going into battle." The idea of her surrounded by enemies, of Morana trying to kill her, made his chest seize.

Briony met his gaze, and her expression grew fierce. "It has to be me. Caladin hasn't gotten Morana's bracelet off, and it's night now. I'm the only one with magic."

Briony wasn't squaring off against Morana. That sorcerer already tried to rip someone he cared about from him. "No."

Wind blasted them so hard Briony teetered backward a step. It roared like a tea kettle screeching in Hans's ears. Leaves, twigs, small trees, and goblin corpses whipped past. "You'll be there to protect me," she said.

"I'll be fighting the leshak."

"Hans, I'm the only one who can do this. Let's finish this." Without waiting for his reply, Briony charged into the storm.

He cursed and bounded after her. Each step was like moving through molasses as the air pushed against them. With a growl, Hans tucked Briony into his side and blocked the whipping wind so they could move forward. Caladin joined them, his sword flashing.

Briony clung onto Hans's waist, then cried out and looked at her arm. Red blood smeared across it. "You're hurt! Let me heal you."

"When you're fighting, focus only on yourself." He shouted close to her ear to be heard over the rush of the wind. "Use your light to guard yourself. Don't look at me, don't look at anyone else. Protect yourself. You understand? You promise this. Now."

Her mouth opened, but when their gaze met, her eyes widened, and she nodded. "But let me heal you first." Briony glanced at his side.

He pulled her tight so her arms remained closed around his waist, and she couldn't get her hands in the right position to heal. "Don't worry about it. Save your strength."

The wind died down, and Caladin shot into the sky. "I'll take care of the rest of the spawn and cover Briony. Tell the pack to follow me." Hans nodded and communicated with them.

Czart and Morana stood a few paces apart from the rest of the fray, and when Czart saw Hans, he stepped forward. Hans let go of Briony. "Go now."

Briony raced from his side toward Morana, Caladin overhead protecting her. Hans crouched, waiting. Brimstone filled the air. Dust and ash whipped his face and stung his eyes. The wound still seeped, and stabbing pain seared up his side with each step. The windstorm obscured the moons, and the landscape was a dull sweep of charcoal. Only the leshak with the milky white bone head and glowing eyes stood out as he reached him.

Czart spread his arms. "Ready for death?" Hans's hackles rose, and his claws shot to their full six-inch length. Czart lunged, and Hans darted to the right, avoiding the vicious kick aimed at his head. He scanned the leshak. There must be some weakness, some point where he could kill him.

Every swoop, Hans danced away, studying, watching. The leshak swung faster and grinned. "Afraid to play, vulk? Feeling weaker than normal?"

Hans stepped left. Could he snap off his hands? "I feel great. Strong enough to kill you."

Czart's jaws parted, and he sprang. A blow hit Hans on his shoulder, and he spun backward. The leshak pounced, but Hans leaped away, and Czart landed on the ground, grasping at nothing.

They circled each other.

"You look like Wulf, but you have something he doesn't."

The leshak king grinned. "Your soul has returned. I sensed it the last time we met. And that makes you easy for me to kill."

Hans stumbled. Was this possible? How? He hadn't retrieved his soul, hadn't made a choice. He rubbed his chest where the rune lay.

Deep down, he knew Czart was right. Twice he'd felt a surge inside. Something foreign but wonderful. Both times because of Briony. His world had stopped when he'd laid eyes on her the first time. Then last night, as she lay in his arms, his world began again.

The choice wasn't to retrieve his soul but whether he wanted to keep it.

Hans growled, dove forward, and raked his claws down Czart's back. The leshak screamed and bucked. Black blood burbled forth, but Hans's claws didn't sink deep. The leshak's skin was too tough. Czart flung his arm out and knocked Hans back. "Soul or no soul, you're finished, and I'll gain all the power I need when I kill you."

Green flashed to his right. Was Briony okay? He turned his head.

With a grunt, Czart hurled himself at Hans. A bone-hard shoulder crashed into him, and he slammed to the ground on his back. His side screamed. Czart swooped, and a foot stomped toward his skull.

Hans rolled, and the skeletal toes missed him by less than an inch. Czart was on top of him in a flash, and a burst of pain blasted across his right temple as Czart hit him. His vision danced. Czart reared back for a second blow. Hans blocked with his arm. A crunch, then fiery agony seared up to his shoulder.

Had Briony taken Morana's bracelet yet? He needed Czart distracted. Vulnerable.

Czart slammed his palm down on Hans's chest, pressing into his armor. He couldn't draw in air. His claws circled

Czart's wrist, but the fingers of his injured arm couldn't tighten. Slowly, the creature leaned over him, its sour breath fanning across Hans's face, and the pressure on his chest intensified.

"I'll enjoy your soul now."

Hans turned his head. Briony was nowhere in sight.

32

Oblivious to the howling winds and cries from the raging battlefield, Morana sauntered toward Briony. She held her palm upright with a green orb nestled in it, looking smug. "Really? You think you can fight me? A human? Didn't I almost kill you back in the cave?"

Briony raised her hands. "You know, there's something I've wondered about you."

"No need to wonder, as I'm killing you, you'll get to see exactly how powerful I am." Morana shot a blast of green light, and Briony spun out of the way.

Briony's magic flooded through her. The moons' light filled her, and her hands glowed. "No, that doesn't interest me. What I want to know is, what happened to your child?"

Morana's smile vanished, and the lines around her lips tightened. She lunged and hurled another blast at the same time. Briony's shield flashed just in time, deflecting the green ball and sending sparks into the sky.

Morana raced forward, and Briony jumped sideways, her shield faltering, and the enchanter snagged her arm. The battlefield faded as a green mist floated around them.

Color swirled around her, and Briony stood on a large

circular platform at the top of a tower. With no railings and no sides. A bluish glow lit up the ground. All around was vast emptiness. Darkness. Only the two moons, like sentinels, shone above them.

Briony darted away from Morana, then scrambled to a halt as she reached the edge. Her pulse skyrocketed. *Don't look down.*

Morana glanced around. "This is new. I've seen almost every fear imaginable, drowning, burning to death, even ghosts, but getting transported somewhere else?" She shrugged. "Oh well, whatever your fear is, you'll be a sobbing mess soon enough." Her mouth formed a menacing smile. "I do enjoy watching others feel my power."

A stream of green light shot toward her, and Briony raised her forearm. Light blazed in the dark as Morana's magic crashed into her shield. Ozone filled the air as the magic, green and white, fought. Sizzled. The force of Morana's magic pushed her backward.

Panic reared. How far was Briony from the edge? Sweat slicked her skin. She was going to fall into nothingness. She dropped her shield and rolled.

Another flash of green light and searing pain sliced across her arm. Morana crowed, and more green trails lashed out like whips. Briony raised her palm, and her light shone brightly. She scrambled to her feet and let it shield her again.

She would die if she didn't do something. Morana's bracelet had to come off. Hazel said it was the only way to break the alliance between her and the leshak king so they could weaken their power and kill them.

Her legs shook. Every cell in her body screamed for her to escape this horrible tower teetering high above the earth. Whether it was Morana's spell digging its hooks into her mind, or her fear of heights, her limbs seized with terror.

Morana grinned. "Ah, there it is. The frozen rabbity look. I was beginning to think my spell didn't work properly."

Morana circled Briony. "Usually, when I cast this spell, the person is instantly overcome by their worst nightmare, but not you. What is it you fear most?" Her voice was like liquid honey. Soothing and relaxing. Sweet.

Briony shivered as images streamed forward. Her parents driving away from her aunt's house without looking back. Hans telling her the vulk took no mates and walking away from her forever.

"Back in the cave, that fool Hoyt cast the spell to summon whatever would weaken your vulk the most. It delivered you. Why is that?" Morana stepped closer. "Something about you weakens him. Makes it so that we can kill him. Tonight."

No.

Briony's arms shook with strain. Being with her gave Hans the chance to take his soul back. His soul wasn't a weakness, and being with her wasn't weak either, because only together could they defeat Morana. Together they were both whole.

Morana waved at the surrounding emptiness. "That's right, there's no one here. No light, no loved ones protecting you. You got dropped onto a tower, completely alone. No one cares about you. Least of all your vulk. You'll die here, and no one will miss you. Having to look after you *is* a weakness."

Briony's hand lowered.

"That's right. Let it go." The voice lapped over her like warm waves. "Your vulk will forget you ever existed. He'll live the rest of his life without ever thinking about *you*. Why would he care? What are you, really? Just some human."

Briony's shield wavered, and cold seeped into her, the magic beginning to sap her strength and her heat. The white light dimmed further.

"Give up and accept how things are. You're nothing. In the middle of a sea of wasteland."

Briony shrank back as the words hit her. She hadn't been worthy of her parents sticking around, never mind loving her. Or her aunt. Always an outsider deemed not worthy of being a true member of the community, forced to serve. Always unloved. She'd been runebound to the one creature in Ulterra supposed to love her, supposed to cherish her forever, and *he* didn't want her either.

Briony stared down at the light faintly streaming from her palms. It flowed from her core. From the essential part of her being.

With a quick shake, she squared her shoulders. She wasn't some pathetic apprentice in a human village that others discarded and discounted. Last night, Hans looked at her. Really looked at her. With no barriers between them and no hiding the intensity of his connection to her. He'd seen her. The real her. She wanted everyone else to see it, too. This was who she was. A zorzye. And she was worthy of so much more.

Briony slapped a hand over the rune on her chest. Magic surged under her fingers and rippled through her body. The tattoo where the rune lay warmed and beat back the cold tightening around her. Like Hans's warmth did. She'd known what she felt this morning but had been too afraid to name it. *Love.* She loved Hans. Even if it crushed her and her heart crumbled, she chose him.

The rune chimed its familiar note.

"Come on, girlie. Just give up," Morana crooned.

Briony stepped backward and dropped to a knee. "You're right."

"Of course, I am." Morana swooped forward, and Briony dropped her shield.

The enchanter cried out in victory and raised her glowing hands. Briony sprang upward, crashed into her, and severed the remaining bracelet from Morana's arm with a slash of light.

Morana screamed. The tower and the darkness whirled, and they flew into the air. With a crash, they crumpled back onto the battlefield.

33

Hans's armor had kept him alive, but slowly the leshak crushed his chest, cutting off his air. With a flip of his hips, he kicked, but the leshak's fingers were like roots on his chest, and he couldn't escape.

"You're mine now, vulk." Czart's eyes glowed, his excited voice raised to a shriek. "You're strong. When I take your life, I'll have enough power to bring back my brethren and rule."

Czart leaned closer, bearing more weight on Hans's chest. Blackness crowded the edges of his vision.

From the corner of his eye, he caught a flash of white. He turned his head. Across the scorched earth, Briony struggled to her feet, something clutched in her hand. Morana lay on the ground, not moving.

She'd done it.

He focused on Briony, and the darkness drew back. Everything around him brightened, growing more vivid. Though he couldn't draw in air, he still caught her scent. On his chest, the rune mark grew hot.

Czart hissed, and his hand on Hans's chest shifted. The pressure on his chest loosened, and Hans sucked in air.

"Enough of this. Time to kill you." Czart opened his mouth.

Let him get a little closer.

As the leshak king tipped his head forward, his skeletal snout yawning open and sucking air, Hans shoved both his hands forward and grabbed hold of the leshak's jaws. His broken arm screamed, but he summoned every ounce of strength left. His weakened hand closed, his arm flexed, and he twisted.

Czart shrieked and reared back, but Hans surged forward and wedged the jaws apart with one last wrench. There was a pop, and he tore the jaw from the skull.

Hot black blood oozed, steaming as it hit the air. The leshak king's body slumped to the ground, twitched once, and was still.

Hans wiped the blood from his face and stared at the body. What was that? Issuing from the Czart's open neck, green light shone across the dirt. Hans bent forward and ripped down the throat and torso.

Lying in the dead leshak's chest was a tangled black pulsing mass. Hans picked it up. The leshak king's heart.

———

BRIONY WATCHED as Hans lifted a bloody mass into the air. The battlefield spun for a moment. He had the heart.

Morana scrambled to her feet, her face ashen. "No. This can't be." She backed away.

Caladin strode to Briony's side, stony-faced and eyes blazing. "You'll come with us." Morana turned and fled. Caladin shot off after her, and Briony followed, her feet thudding on the dead earth.

They slowed as Morana aimed for the crevasse. She had nowhere to go.

"You're trapped," said Caladin.

The enchanter reached the edge and reeled to a stop. She glanced down. "You're not taking me." And she leaped into the abyss.

"Damn it." Caladin launched into the air and dove after her.

At a shout behind her, Briony turned. The pack crowded around Hans. She watched his head bob above the others, then he staggered sideways.

She sprinted, skidding on goblin blood and jumping over lumps of flesh she couldn't identify. When she reached the pack, she barreled through them to where Zann stood with Hans, helping him remain on his feet.

"Let me look at it." Briony lay her hands over the gash in his side. The skin fought being stitched back together, but she gritted her teeth and poured more of her light into Hans. After several long moments, she slumped forward, ice coating her skin. "I've gotten it to stop bleeding, but we need to get him back to the vae kingdom and let their healers work on him."

Hans remained silent. He stared at her as if seeing her for the first time, the leshak heart still clutched in his hand. Briony didn't join the vulk as they supported Hans and practically carried him forward.

She was numb. Now that Hans had the heart, his choice was already made. He'd become the next Wulf. A great Alpha and a great leader. He wouldn't want a mate. She glanced up at the sky. The moons sank toward the horizon; only a few more hours and they would no longer be runebound.

Caladin and a troop of vae came to her side. She turned and scanned the group. Where was Morana? "What happened?"

"I dove to catch her, but she wasn't there. And there was nobody at the bottom of the crevasse." He sighed. "I have my warriors down there checking every hole." He shook his head. "No one could survive that fall. She must be dead, but we'll check again when our magic regenerates in a few hours."

Briony wasn't convinced Morana was dead. The sorcerer seemed resourceful, even without the link to Czart. She sighed, and fatigue crashed over her. The battle was over, and it was time to go.

THERE WAS BARELY an inch to spare with the pack of vulk taking up all the space inside the healing room, but Briony shouldered her way to where Hans sat. He'd refused to lie down and sat in a chair with his armor next to him while a healer applied a paste to his side.

"Krol. Krol Alpha," Kyril said.

Hans said nothing, but he rotated the heart in his hand. No. She couldn't stay and watch this.

His gaze found hers and softened. "We need to talk—"

She shook her head. She didn't want to hear his parting words—saying goodbye would break her. All she wanted to do was make sure he was alright before leaving. "No, that's okay. Get patched up and celebrate with your pack. I'm going to go."

"Wait." He looked down and growled at the healer. "Hurry."

The healer didn't raise his head. "This is a wound from an ancient being. It's going to take a while. Sit there and stop moving."

Juri clapped Hans on the shoulder. "Come on, tell us how you slew the great leshak king and make it as detailed as possible so I can tell this tale for thousands of years."

Briony stepped back into the crowd. Her coach was waiting. She hurried to the front of the palace and walked outside into the haze of dawn. A twinge hit her where the rune lay on her chest, and she halted. With a flash of gold, the rune appeared before her, glittered once in the light, then disappeared.

Biting back a sob, she rubbed her chest. That was it. She and Hans were over. She squared her shoulders and marched on.

Katisa waited, her hand on the horse-led carriage. Fit for vae royalty, it was drawn by one kon horse and adapted for only one or two passengers to make it narrow enough to manage the gorge bridge and mountain pass into Rohant. There was no driver. "Are you sure you won't stay a few more days?" Katisa asked. "We'll be celebrating, and you should join in."

Briony shook her head. Hans would take the heart, and there would be a grand celebration, but she didn't want to watch. Her heart ached already; she didn't think she could take anymore. "There's a lot I need to do back home. I've got some krasa cream to sell, and I'll get the rest of my gold together this winter so I can travel through Ulterra and find somewhere that feels like home."

Katisa raised an eyebrow. "Take whatever time you need, but you aren't languishing in that horrible town all winter. I'll come to get you, and we'll travel together for a while. Or come back here."

Briony tried to smile, but she was afraid it came out more like a grimace. "That would be lovely. Although you may want to wait. You'll get stuck in Rohant when the snow fills the pass and languish in Vieska all winter, too."

An odd gleam came to Katisa's eye. "The weather obeys me."

Briony frowned. "Really?" She'd seen Katisa charge after Seth to stop the cyclone, but she'd been fighting Morana and didn't see Katisa use her magic. "Is that how you stopped Seth's windstorm?"

Katisa's face flushed. "Oh, uh, no. He just needed to remember where he was, that's all. He had battle lust, and I calmed it." It was the first time she'd seen Katisa flustered. There was more there, and when she saw Katisa next, she would winkle it out of her. At least that was something to look forward to.

She hugged Katisa. "Thanks for everything."

"Keep working on your magic. I'm going to test you." Katisa squeezed her tightly back. Briony attempted another watery smile and stepped into the coach. Without a driver, she wasn't sure what to do.

"Tell your horse where you want to go, he understands. He'll stop when he needs to stop, and he gets in and out of the rig himself, so you'll know when he's ready to depart again." Katisa pointed. "The seat pulls out so you can sleep, and there's some food tucked away. Have a pleasant journey."

Briony leaned outside the coach and called out, "Vieska, in Rohant." The door barely shut before the coach leaped forward.

She didn't look back.

34

HANS STOOD. His head felt like lead, and his mouth was so dry his tongue was glued in place. Where was Briony? He grabbed the flagon of water on the table next to his chair and downed it. With every motion, his muscles complained.

The vae healer glared up at him. "Rest."

He poked at his ribs—no more bleeding. "Looks fine."

"No one has treated a leshak injury. Ever. I want you to rest."

Hans ignored him. Had Briony said she was going to go? Go where? He turned to Juri. "Where's Briony?"

"Dunno. She was here a minute ago."

The leshak heart beat sluggishly in his hand. Its power remained alive. As he stared at it, whispery threads hummed through him, enticing him to crush the heart and absorb it. Make it his.

"I need to find her." The pack parted, and he charged into the corridor. He couldn't feel anything in their bond. Ice dripped down his spine. He sprinted down the hall with Juri at his heels.

Katisa entered the front hall, and he slid to a halt in front of her, his claws raking over limestone. "Do you know where Briony is?"

The vae princess stared at him coldly. "She left."

He went numb. No. "What do you mean she left? Where did she go?"

Katisa shouldered past him. "She went home."

He snarled. "I'll catch up to her." Hans tore the doors open and launched down the steps, through the front gate, and into the forest. Mid-stride, he was jerked to the side so violently he lost his balance and almost fell to his knees. It felt like an invisible hand had grabbed his waistband to haul him sideways. What the hell was this? Another spell? He roared and slashed through the air. Whatever held him refused to let him go. He whirled to find out who dared touch him, but nothing was there.

A few paces behind him, Juri leaped forward. "The tree!"

One of the large vae trees next to the road split open, forming an arched entrance. It was a portal door; on the other side, a dark, dripping bog and a chicken footed hut waited. The white scar on his hand throbbed in pain.

Dawn had fully risen. The time Baba Yaga had given him was over, and she called him to fulfill his blood oath.

The air swirled inside the tree. A sucking sensation dragged him forward. Digging his hind claws into the earth, he struggled, trying to get away, but inch by inch, he failed.

A year. He'd be separated from Briony for a year.

Hans turned to Juri. "Let the pack know about the oath and that I must leave. Keep them together. Find Briony in Vieska and tell her I'm coming for her. Protect her."

Juri grabbed Hans's arm and hauled, his claws digging in so deep they drew blood. "I'll bring the pack to the bog. We'll each take a month of service for you."

Hans stopped struggling and placed a hand on Juri's shoulder. "There's never been a more loyal friend." He searched for the right words. "As a pack, we're all brothers, but you're not my pack brother. You're my brother like Zann is my brother. My family."

The tree dragged him back a few more inches, and he scrambled to keep his footing. "I know you'd take part of my blood oath for me, but I'm doing this alone. Not because I don't want you and the pack with me, but because this is mine alone."

Juri shook his head. "No—"

"You're the only one I want to protect my mate while I'm gone. You're my Beta, and I need you here." While Zann would protect Briony, only Juri understood Hans's bond with her.

Juri's jaw dropped. "Me as Beta?"

"Of course. Who else?"

Juri nodded. "All right." His eyes widened. "Did you say, mate?"

Hans let the tree suck him in. As the archway faded, he called, "Don't forget to tell Briony I'm coming."

Baba Yaga's tree loomed above him. Its branches rattled together, twigs spiking out like thorns from the canopy. It rained, like always, and water dripped onto his head and shoulders. The ramp lowered from a dark entrance.

When Hans ascended, the tree began quaking. Limbs thrashed, and the ramp heaved. He dug his hind claws in and dove for the door. Bark skimmed his heels as it slammed closed behind him.

Baba Yaga stood by the fireplace, her hand on the wall. "What did you do to my tree?"

"Nothing I got on the ramp—" He glanced down to find the leshak heart still clutched in his hand. Of course, the tree didn't like it. It was evil, dark magic, the kind that controlled nature.

The whispers returned. Krol. King. If he became Krol, he could fight Baba Yaga's hold on him and win. All he had to do was crush the heart like Wulf had. He'd lose his soul again, but he'd be invincible.

But he wouldn't have Briony.

He could live another century, millennia, but she'd be the only one he'd ever want. The only one he'd claim. Every moment he'd been with her, he'd fought against his feelings and his urge to make her his. He'd pushed her away, and they'd run out of time.

He'd lost her.

A stone lodged in his chest. Heavy and pressing down in the place the bond used to be. His claws curled into fists.

He would never be the same. She wasn't only his. He was hers. There would be no day when he didn't need her. When he didn't want her. He howled, fury twisting into a mournful lament. When he finished, the rain beat harder, and the shadows in the hut covered him like dark smoke.

Baba Yaga stared at him. "Guess you chose poorly."

"We aren't bonded anymore."

She nodded. "Choices were made, and the full moons' night is over."

The stone lodged deeper in his chest. "Is it too late for us?"

Baba Yaga shrugged. "There could be a way, but the two of you had to make choices while you were runebound. It all depends on what each of you chose."

"But there's still a chance?"

Baba Yaga tilted her head. "Do you know what she chose?"

"No." He rubbed his chest. There was nothing there. No hint of Briony around his heart. He'd have to wait a *year* to find out what she'd chosen. A year for her to think he'd never come for her.

That wasn't going to happen.

He lowered his hand and opened his fist. Orange flame flared in Baba Yaga's eyes, and she walked forward as if possessed. "What do you have there?" She reached out, but

Hans held the heart away. His fingers tightened, and a hint of power thrummed through his palm.

"Your tree recognized what this was when I walked in. It's the leshak king's heart."

A small smile curled her lips. "That heart would make you Krol. The mightiest being that walks the earth. You'd even tame death. Every vulk's greatest desire."

Hans watched the heart pulse green as it beat one slow heartbeat. "It was Wulf's desire."

Baba Yaga tilted her head. "For a time, yes. But not always."

His brow furrowed. "What—"

"You become Krol, and you can enter the underworld freely." Baba Yaga continued as if she hadn't heard him. "You'd be the one watching over the realms and judging who is cursed to remain in Peklo and who isn't. You'd be more powerful than you can imagine."

Time stretched as he considered what she'd said. Shadows danced along the wall from the flickering fire. Hans turned toward its warmth and stepped into the light. "Tell me how to unite with Briony and release me from our blood oath, free and clear, and I'll give you the heart."

Her fingers flexed. "You'd turn your back on all this power?"

"I only want her."

Baba Yaga raised a brow and studied him a long moment. "If she didn't choose you, your souls won't join, and she won't become immortal. You may only have her for the next seventy years or so."

"I don't care."

Baba Yaga's gaze pierced through him. "I see."

He glanced at the heart. "You do no harm with this. I'll be watching." He was Wulf's son, and he let his legacy flood into him, let the full power of the vulk swirl through him and around him, until it darkened the inside of the hut with its potency. He noticed the chair with the face watching him. "And release him. It disturbed Briony."

Baba Yaga scowled and opened her mouth, but Hans waved the leshak heart in front of her. "Fine. You've got an agreement." Baba Yaga held up her hand and spat on it. She muttered in the arcane language. A sharp pain lanced through his palm, and the thin white scar shrank away and disappeared.

He dropped the heart into her waiting hands. "Tell me what to do with Briony."

"There's a chance you can bond with her the way a vulk is supposed to bond with his zorzye. The old way. But, if she hasn't chosen you or doesn't love you," Baba Yaga shrugged, "there's nothing you can do."

"You know she's a zorzye?"

"Of course."

He growled. "That information would have been helpful when we came for help."

"No, she needed to learn it in her own time."

Did Briony love him? Would it work? He ran his hand over his head. "Tell me what the old way is."

Baba Yaga smiled. "Kiss her. Your instincts will ignite from there."

Hans stared. "I can't kiss anyone."

Baba Yaga raised a brow. "Can't you? You've had your soul for weeks, and from the moment it returned, you could retake human form."

He lifted a hand and stared at it. Did he really have the ability to take human form again? He focused on his hand, willed it to change, and it tingled with thousands of tiny pinpricks as the fur and claws withdrew to smooth, furless skin. Making a fist, his fur returned. "Wait, you knew I had a soul when I was here, and you didn't tell me?"

"Of course. I noticed the difference the moment I saw you."

"What about the rest of the pack? Them too?"

Baba Yaga's lips twitched in a small, secret smile. "No. There is a reason the runes returned and started with you. You're the Alpha. Your choice opened the door so each of them can find their mate and have the chance to gain their soul, too. They will get a chance to earn it like you did. What they do with it," she shrugged, "that's up to them. Like your friend, Juri, the tracker."

Hans jolted. "Juri?"

Baba Yaga nodded. "He's seen a rune before. Didn't you notice his response when you described it in front of him here? I don't provide free council often, and he would be wise to heed my words before it's too late."

"Why does the rune care about bondmates?"

Baba Yaga's smile fell. "The runes disappeared after the Deciding War. Perhaps this is a harbinger of more tough choices to come or a chance to right wrongs. It's too early to know. I'm not sure about the importance of bondmates, but somehow, it must tie into the balance for all of Ulterra, which brings me to this." She raised the leshak heart. "If there's another war on the horizon, we'll need a Krol of the vulk who can go into Peklo and decide who belongs down there and who doesn't."

A flash of gold shimmered inside the hut. A firefly? In her hut? Not likely.

The gold light grew. It streamed down like a beacon and encompassed him. With a snarl, he lashed out, but instead of a threat ... the ache in his side from the leshak wound faded. Two gold bands wrapped around his upper arms. On both was a crest—a circle with a vulk in profile in the center, snarling toward the sky. The mark of the Krol.

Already excellent, his vision sharpened further, and he could count each leaf on the branch outside the window five hundred feet away. Beyond the hut, past the island, he heard a mouse sneeze.

He ran his fingers over the band high on his right bicep.

Why was this here? He turned to Baba Yaga. "I didn't crush the heart to become Krol."

"The power was yours to earn, and you did." The heart remained in her hand, but it no longer pulsed with a green glow. "That power belonged to you alone, but there are other mysteries inside the leshak heart for me." Baba Yaga waved. "Leave. Go kiss her."

The tree entrance yawned open. He strode to it and leaped over the ramp onto the island. How long would it take him to get to Vieska?

There was a creak behind him. A wobbly figure stepped onto the ramp and fell, somersaulting to the ground in a tumble of limbs. The man grunted and sat up, shoving his hair out of his eyes. "I've forgotten how to walk. I've been a chair too long." The hut closed with a snap.

Hans rolled his shoulders and shook his arms out. "You have plenty of time to learn again as you get on your way." He strode to the path. "Good luck. I'm off to claim my mate."

35

A SCRUM of people crowded her table in the Vieska square, shouldering each other out of the way to get their hands on the last of her salves and creams. Mules and horses clopped down the street, shouts rang through the air as vendors vied for attention, and the faint sizzle of meat from her neighbor, the kebab vendor, kept a constant line of customers. Market day was in full swing.

The clouds overhead hung heavy and oppressive, dimming the light so that the stone edifices and cobbles of the square appeared dull and dingy. So far, it hadn't rained, but the dark slate of the sky threatened it might.

Briony sighed. Despite the flash of the yellow market tents and dyed wool coats in reds and blues, the town was a colorless wash of gray. At least she was busy.

Don't think about Hans or what he's doing. Move forward.

Work kept her distracted from the waves of sadness so intense she'd stop in her tracks, hugging herself as hard as possible as if trying to staunch a wound. The weather only made it worse.

The grill next to her sizzled, and her stomach roiled. She usually liked the smell, but today she wanted to puke. She breathed through her mouth and blew on the tea she'd brewed, its steam trailing off into the chilly air. If she didn't drink this tea, the meager lunch she'd eaten would be all over her neighbor's feet.

Throwing up on them probably wouldn't make the crowds go away. They circled, gawping at her like she'd grown two heads. Nope, no additional limbs, just abducted by a vulk.

Her aunt's pinched face appeared in front of her with its familiar mien of disapproval. "Where have you been? Jail? And why aren't you helping with the surgery? During your absence, Doc Tucless had many problems, and I'm sure he needs you."

Briony almost laughed. Of course, he'd had problems. "I'm back at the surgery, for now, and I work on my own terms."

"That's how you repay his generosity for taking you in?"

She did laugh now. "I've worked for him for seventeen years, most of them for free. I've paid him back many times over."

On her return, Doc Tucless yelled at her for leaving without notice and threatened not to take her back. When he'd finished spitting and sputtering, she told him she would work until the spring, and she'd be doing it her way. She'd get paid what she was worth and work the hours she chose. If he didn't like it, fine, she'd work in the tavern for Owen.

He'd blustered, threatened not to need her, but she saw the alarm in his bloodshot eyes. For the last few years, he'd barely lifted a finger, and when he did, he couldn't keep his hands from shaking. He needed her. After more blustering, he'd agreed, saying he wanted to retire, and they'd work together for the winter and announce it.

Briony focused on her aunt. She pointed at the few jars of product left. "Do you want to buy something?"

Aunt Petra's gaze hardened. "Not from you." Briony had seen that hawk-like expression come across Petra's face many times. It reminded her of Morana. The same predatory, evil look. "No native Vieskan would be taken away by the king's guards and then refuse to tell us what happened. I've kept quiet all these years about your magicwielding ways, but if the king's found you out, I have to say something." Petra half turned to the crowd and let her voice carry. "She's a magicwielder. She should be run out of Vieska."

The two women arguing over a krasa cream fell silent.

A force inside her, a strength, surged up, and Briony straightened. Nausea dropped away. She stared at Petra and let whatever flowed through her veins, making her a zorzye, show on her face. Not her magic, but her true self. "When Tomas fell down drunk on his pitchfork and pierced his lungs, that injury should have killed him, but I saved his life. When Svetlana's baby wouldn't turn, I was the one who saved them both." And she'd used magic to do it.

Petra waved her hand. "Doc Tucless did that."

The crowd murmured. A woman with a round face elbowed a few people out of the way. "That's not true. Doc Tucless arrived an hour after Briony and was too drunk to stand." Tomas's wife caught Briony's eye. "He crowed to everyone about how he saved Tomas's life, and you all bought him free drinks for weeks, but he didn't do a thing. And I never spoke up."

Owen had edged out of his tavern and leaned in the doorway. He slapped his hand towel over his shoulder. "When I got fishhooks in my hand, and the Doc treated me, I had an infection and had to shut the tavern down for weeks. You all remember that?"

"The dark time of no beer," a man in the back said.

"This year, the same thing happened, but Briony treated me, and I was back to new immediately. She always pays her tab, unlike some of you."

"Maybe you need to learn how to fish," called the same voice from the back.

Owen glowered. "Anyone harasses Briony, and they won't be served by me. Ever." He nodded at Briony and returned to the dark tavern.

The murmuring rose, but the townspeople weren't glaring at her. They'd turned toward Petra, their eyes narrowed.

Briony stared Petra in the eye. "If being a Vieskan means tossing eleven-year-old children out of your home, then I'm happy not to be counted one of you. You're a terrible woman, and finding out we aren't related was a blessing. Now buy something or go away. You're not welcome here anymore."

Petra stepped back, her mouth gaping. For a fraction of a moment, she seemed about to argue, then she pulled her hood up and scuttled away.

The crowd returned to life as if nothing happened. Tears built behind her eyes, but Briony bit her lip. She'd sobbed enough since she'd gotten home and didn't want to cry anymore. She'd wept until she thought her heart would break apart in her chest, and it wasn't for this town or these people. This wasn't where she belonged anymore, despite the surprise of them defending her. She missed Hans.

As the sun dipped below the trees and the crowd thinned, Ivan walked out of his shop across the town square, wiped his hands on his butcher apron, and strode over.

"Are you staying for a drink tonight?" he asked.

Her stomach turned over at the thought. "No, I'm going to get some sleep in my apartment." A roaring fire in the tavern, especially on such a bleary evening, usually attracted her, but not today. Although, the idea of sitting alone in front of her hearth at home twisted her insides. The loneliness was a palpable, living thing, so intense she almost started crying again. Why was she crying so much? She'd spent her life holding back tears, but now she couldn't seem to stop them.

The people in the square, watching the juggler teetering on his stilts and crowded around the food stands for dinner, drew back in a collected breath. A tall man with gold shaggy hair and old-fashioned luxurious clothing, including a purple velvet cape, walked through the arched entrance.

But he wasn't alone.

Her gaze skipped over the blond to the man at his side with coal-dark hair. The first man was tall, but this man topped him by a few inches. He had to be almost seven feet tall. Under his plain spun linen shirt in the same style farmers wore, his shoulders stretched with corded muscle. His long legs ate up the ground, and his thighs stretched his worn leather trousers.

His features became clearer as he drew closer. His jaw was firm and angular, and his nose straight. His brow swept up to his carelessly brushed back hair, a few inches long. His lips were full and sensual. And then ... his eyes.

Vivid cornflower blue and locked on her like he saw nothing else. She forgot to breathe. Her heart thudded, flipping in her chest. *Hans's eyes.*

Hypnotized, she remained rooted where she stood. Ivan related town news, trying to catch her attention, but she didn't hear a word.

Hans reached her, glanced at Ivan for a second, and his eyes flashed red.

"Hans. How ... What are you doing here?"

He turned to the shaggy-haired man. "Take this guy and get lost."

The blond man rolled his eyes, turned to Briony, and bowed. "I'm Kole Svarog, the last in the line of the Druk. You kept me from living twenty more years as a chair, and I'm here to pledge my loyalty."

Hans glowered at him. "He won't leave me alone."

"I got you human clothes."

Hans growled. "I could have stolen clothes myself."

Ivan turned to her. "You know these men?"

"Yes. Mostly."

Hans's gaze dropped to the butcher shop embroidery on

Ivan's apron, and his eyes glinted red again. "There's nothing here for you any longer, meat man."

Kole clapped Ivan on the shoulder. "I require a drink. Does this town offer that one with the sweet cherries in it?"

"The kids' drink?"

The blond man slung his arm around Ivan's shoulders, hauling the powerfully built butcher toward the tavern. "Yes, the one that tastes like black licorice. Get that for me, and let's discuss placing a large order of meat. We require much meat."

Their voices faded, and she and Hans stood staring at each other. "How are you here and in human form? What happened at Baba Yaga's? Is that really the man from the chair?"

Hans rounded the table, closing the distance between them. He took her hand and raised it to his mouth. His gaze never left her as he pressed a soft kiss to her palm. A zing shot up her arm from the contact and her fingers curled around his. The achy sense of something being out of place—left.

"I gave the leshak heart to Baba Yaga."

"You did what?"

His thumb swept across her lips. "I knew you were mine the moment I walked into the cave. I'd been half-dead for a hundred years, but you made me remember what it's like to be alive. You made me feel, and you gave me back my soul. You. Not some rune."

It felt like a dream. She placed her hand over his to make sure he was real.

"I want you," he said. "And if you want me, I'm not leaving your side."

"Hans—"

"Every day, I want to be at your side. Every night I want you curled up next to me. If we have a human lifespan on earth together, it doesn't matter. Our souls are entwined, and I won't ever leave you. When you close your eyes for the last time, I'll follow you into the afterlife and demand they let me in because where you go, I go." He put his arms around her. "I love you, and we'll be together for all eternity."

Briony gasped and twined her arms around his neck. "I love you. I chose you."

Hans leaned forward and brushed his lips over hers. Warmth blossomed in her chest. Rising on tiptoe, she wrapped her arms tighter and buried her head in his neck. This was her vulk, and she wasn't ever letting go. Love flowed through her, fierce and hot.

He purred, a throaty, rich hum, and his chest vibrated against hers. Sliding his hand into her hair, he tugged her head back, then slanted his lips over hers.

At first, he sipped, as if memorizing every dip and curve, then hungry, coaxed her to open as he nibbled and sucked.

She drew back and cupped his face. "You're in human form, and you're *kissing* me." She smiled and ran her fingers over his lips.

"The first woman I've ever kissed." He nibbled her fingertips. "The only one I'll ever kiss." He glanced around. "Let's get out of here." He frowned at her table. "What do you do with this?"

"It doesn't matter." She tugged him toward the tavern and the narrow stairs along the side that led up to her apartment. The crowd lining the street and staring at them was a blur as they passed.

Hans growled and picked her up in his arms. "Too slow." She studied his face as he carried her. He was the most attractive man she'd ever seen.

She ran her fingers through his hair, and his steps hastened. When they reached her apartment, he kicked the door open. All that mattered was his lips on hers and tasting more of him. There would never be enough.

He bent and kissed her again without missing a step as he aimed for the bedroom off the kitchen. His lips grazed down her throat. Everywhere his mouth landed, it fanned flames, and her brain frizzled.

He laid her on the bed in the middle of her heaped blankets and cradled her in his arms. Soon his pine scent would coat every inch of her sheets, and it would be perfection.

Hans took his time removing her clothes, peeling them away inch by inch and kissing every patch of skin that appeared. Then he returned to her mouth and lazily plundered in long, drugging kisses. Every sweep of his tongue was potent with leashed passion. She writhed and bit her nails into his still-clothed body; she was hot and desperate. His mouth opened, and he was less controlled, roughly nipping at her lips.

He finally let her tear off his shirt, and she explored the hard planes of his chest, the taut muscles of his stomach and ribs. Considering he was a vulk in human form, he had little body hair, and her hands raced over the smooth skin. His lips found a nipple, and he suckled. She arched and moaned. He teased the tip between his teeth—just the slightest bite of pain —and she writhed.

Hans dragged in air in a raspy breath, and her heart hammered like it might break through her chest. This was bliss. Pure ecstasy.

Her head fell back, and she whined. He switched from breast to breast until her chest heaved, and she trembled beneath him. Then his mouth trailed lower to between her legs. Even in this form, his tongue was wicked. She fisted the blankets. "Hans!"

The orgasm ripped through her, and her back bowed. He kept playing, using his tongue, lips, and gentle sucking pulls to drive her over the edge again.

That was enough. She tugged on his shoulders. "I want you, Hans. I need you."

When he glanced up, his eyes were solid black. Her breath hitched, and a wave of searing heat crashed over her.

He shucked his trousers so fast they flew across the floor.

He slid over her, spreading her thighs wide with his knees. One forearm landed next to her head to keep him propped above her, and the other hand tangled in her hair, tugging her head back. Having him on top of her, desire flooded her more strongly than before.

His lips crashed down on hers as he entered her. *Yes. Yes.* She groaned and sucked his lower lip. Her legs and arms wrapped around him, his bare skin hot and smooth, as he rocked into her in long, slow strokes. It was impossible to have this much sensation crashing through her. Both the building pleasure and the primal possession uncoiling deep within, demanding Hans was her mate. This fierce, incredible vulk was *hers*. Forever. He'd never leave her.

She forgot to breathe and had to break away and kiss his cheek, his neck, to suck in air before returning to his addictive mouth. Every time he sank deeper, she moaned louder. If she kept it up, the village would hear.

Let them. She couldn't get close enough. Press close enough.

A flutter started in her chest. First, as soft as a butterfly's wings, then growing and warming until it pounded as hard as her heartbeat. Hans sucked at her neck, at the slope where her neck joined her shoulder, and she shuddered. He groaned, and his leisurely glides shortened. "Briony." He said her name like it was the most cherished word he'd ever spoken, and she loved it. Each word was a caress, pulling her closer.

He raked his teeth over her shoulder, and she whimpered and raised her hips, her sex squeezing him. The fingers in her hair fisted, tilting her face to his again. His lips crushed hers. Claimed them.

She dug her nails in harder.

He growled and slammed his hips into hers as he thrust. She held on as he worked her, trying to rut her breathless. It was exquisite torture; she was wound tight, desperate for release. She clawed at him, trying to bring him deeper. He growled in short, claiming notes. Everything was a blur, out of control, a whirlwind of pleasure.

It was raw and primal. Hans was losing control and plunging deep ... so deep inside. It was a scorching flame, burning fast and furious, building with clawing intensity.

Hans locked gazes with her and, with one surge, knotted her. The thick bulge kicked as he came inside her, and she exploded into her release. Hans leaned forward and sank his teeth into her shoulder.

Intense heat from his bite punched directly into her chest and pushed the breath from her lungs. The force of his love, of his soul mingling with hers, crashed into her as his bonding bite tied them together. The essence of him, of their joining, swirled once as if to ensure she knew she was his, then settled forever back in place over her heart.

She bucked, and her head fell back as ecstasy rippled over and over. Love swamped her. Overwhelmed her. She murmured his name as she shuddered uncontrollably.

Her chest seared for a moment, and she looked down. The mark had returned to their chests. He'd bonded them.

It was dawn when their need finally diminished. Hans placed his palm across her shoulder blades and pulled her closer, even though they lay pressed together, their legs tangled.

His lips lingered at his bonding bite. "We'll say vows in Vulk in the heart of the forest when the moons are full again. I'll teach you the words. And I want a ceremony. Here. Or wherever you want it."

She rubbed her cheek against his. "You want to get married? In the human way?"

"Yes. Or we can follow the bondmate ceremony of the vae. I want everyone to see you're mine, and I'm yours. Forever." He stroked the side of her face and tucked a strand of her hair back.

Her heart squeezed. "Okay."

His hand skimmed down her body to rest on her waist, and he froze. His pulse rocketed, and his hand went to her stomach.

"What? What's wrong?" But she knew, even before he opened his mouth. Nausea. The heightened sensitivity. She was pregnant.

He drew back to see her face. "My senses are stronger. That plus our bond … I feel … I have to be wrong. Humans can't get pregnant from a vulk."

"I'm not a human, am I?"

He smiled so wide the corners of his eyes crinkled. "No, you aren't. So, back in the cave when we met, your false heat … I guess not so false."

"I guess not." She smiled back.

His smile turned into a wolfish grin. "You're my mate, and you're going to have our child."

Joy shot through her. A family, a real family, all her own. Children. And Hans. His happiness surged through the bond so intensely it tore her breath away. He laughed and crushed her to his chest. "My den needs more bedrooms."

"Yes, it does."

He shifted and kissed her, and it turned deep and hungry. When they surfaced for air, he cupped her face. "I love you."

The bond trilled in her chest, a perfect happy note. He really loved her. And she loved him just as fiercely. She trailed her fingers through the hair at his nape, exactly how he liked it and smiled back. "I'll never tire of hearing you say that."

"Good."

And Hans rolled her onto her back and made their bond sing.

EPILOGUE

One Year Later

HANS EXITED the den and inhaled the fresh mountain air. Winter was late to arrive this year, but the first breath of snow tinted the wind, and the mineral tang would deepen until the storm came tonight.

Not yet, though.

For now, the day remained warm, and the sun broke through the pines to dapple the hawthorn bushes, their leaves still a flame of red. He was in vulk form, yet the birds nearby ignored him as they flitted amongst the bushes to eat their berries.

He gazed down at his son, sleeping in his arms. Rhys hadn't given them much rest during the night but slept soundly now. Drawing the alpaca-lined blanket up around his son's face, Hans settled him into the crook of his elbow, then walked around the corner of his hillock toward the mountain. He wove through the dense copse of trees protecting his home and entered a small clearing before the foot of the mountain. Zann stood at the new pack den entrance, piles of granite at his feet.

His brother turned, and when he spotted Rhys, he plucked the baby from Hans and nestled him against his chest. To everyone's surprise, Zann's most of all, Zann was a natural with babies. It was the only time his brother calmed enough to remain still. "If he's sleeping now, that means he was up all night again. He takes after me. Sleep is for others." He jerked his chin to the left. "I was up all night finishing the second house."

Rhys yawned, let out a small cooing sound, then snuggled against his uncle. Zann had moved back into his old room in Hans's den, first to help Hans finish it and then to help with the new construction. Since he didn't sleep much, he also helped with baby duty so Hans and Briony could catch some extra sleep.

"Where's Kaven?" Zann asked.

"Briony is rocking him to sleep in the nursery. You're right. Neither of them slept last night. Is it a vulk thing?"

It was especially helpful having Zann around because he and Briony hadn't had one son. They'd had two. *Twins.*

When he'd first heard both heartbeats, he hadn't believed it. He still barely believed it, even though he held both sons daily.

Zann shrugged. "Maybe. None of us need much sleep, and we don't sleep at night."

Hans peered up at the sky. "Snow's coming. Are we ready for the winter?"

"Yep. Pack den's all set, and both human-style houses are finished."

With the pack a real pack again, they needed a pack den as a base, but Briony wanted to raise their sons in his den. So, they'd built a new pack den in the mountain at the back of his hillock. Briony also pointed out that the clearing nearby was perfect for human homes, and they'd built two of them in the peltwalker lodge style. Right now, only his mother came and stayed, but maybe someday, more vulk would find mates.

It wasn't odd to consider that anymore.

Initially, he'd figured Kole—the man still hadn't left— would want a house, but he preferred the den. He'd proven useful as he set up trade for the vulk and converted their gold to coin. Briony said one day they may want their vulk village on the peddler maps, and Kole might be able to help with that too.

Trading with the humans helped Hans finish his den, which was now suitable for Briony and their sons. Hot water, vae lighting, and furniture were all things he could get himself, but his mate loved books, and he built her a library and told Kole to buy any books he found. Kole muttered he was a sucker and paying far too much per book, but he didn't care. Whatever made her happy.

"Any word if Blazh and Troy want to spend the winter here in the pack den?" Hans asked.

A vulk needed to run and spend time alone—that was why they had extensive territories. So when a vulk needed solo time, he left. However, Hans was keeping the pack mostly together. It was quiet in Ulterra since the battle, but he still wanted a full guard nearby in case that changed. Especially since, despite searching long and hard, they'd never found Morana's body. Over the past year, they'd searched for her, including in the cave where he'd met Briony, but she wasn't there. Hoyt's body wasn't in the cave either.

Juri, accompanied by Kyril and Finn, were hunting down the necromancer.

One thing did remain in the cave—the breeding bench. He'd decided to take that home and install it in a special room in his den. A room only he and Briony would know about.

Zann shrugged. "Nothing from them, but Finn showed up a few minutes ago. Said he needs to talk to you."

Hans turned toward the den door. "Only Finn? Where is he?" He'd checked in mentally with Juri yesterday, and every-thing was fine.

"Getting a bite to eat, he'll be right back." Zann glanced down at Rhys. "Mother arrives today."

Their mother walked over from the wolfwalker clan near Rohant often. Usually, Zann escorted her, but it wasn't a long walk. In the winter, though, the mountains filled with snow, so she was going to stay in one of the houses Zann had finished.

Hans watched his son snuggle deeper into his blanket. "She always said the vulk were wrong to turn their back on family. She was right."

The door to the pack den opened, and Finn stepped out, scanning the clearing. When he saw Hans, he loped over to join him and Zann.

"What happened? Why didn't Juri say you'd headed back?" While he could contact them as Alpha, they couldn't contact him. Only Zann and Briony could reach him whenever they wanted.

Finn ran his hand over his head. "Juri tracked the necromancers to Ryba. Kyril sent me back to tell you."

"Did you say, Ryba?" Hans asked.

Finn nodded.

Ryba, Juri's home. Well, his original pre-pack home. The place with the human female Juri watched. Hans frowned. The past year Juri was moodier than usual, and he'd refused to talk about his prophecy from Baba Yaga, even though Hans brought it up several times.

Zann sniffed. "He's always prowled around Ryba."

"It's still his home, even though when he turned into a vulk he was supposed to leave it behind," Hans said.

Finn shifted his weight from foot to foot. "Kyril told me to tell you something is brewing in Ryba, and Juri ... He's gotten a bit obsessive about protecting the city. He may need to be commanded to leave."

Baba Yaga's words rang in his head. *Your choice opened the door so each of them can find their mate and have the chance to gain their soul, too.*

Hans shook his head. "He needs to stay. Kyril will keep an eye on him, and after my mother arrives to help Briony, I'll go up there myself." Hans would never command his best friend to do anything. He'd find him and remain at his side until Juri was ready to talk, just like Juri had done with him when he'd left for the Kuls.

Zann cocked an eyebrow a fraction in question, but Hans was certain he was right. Juri needed to settle his past.

Hans took Rhys back into his arms. He pulled his blanket up and cradled him closer. "This one has been outside long enough. I'm going to head back."

He turned toward his hillock. When he walked into the den and entered the nursery, Kaven was asleep in his bassinet, and Briony dozed in the small rocking chair he'd made for her. He put Rhys in his crib, lifted Briony into his arms, and brought her to their bed. It had a lot more blankets heaped on it than he'd ever need—she'd made a nest with his mother's quilt on top—but it was what she wanted, and he enjoyed seeing her warm and snuggled up in them.

He nestled Briony in the center, then curled around her.

The swell in his heart was so strong it might burst. Every night he'd lie next to her. They'd fill this den with their children. He'd hear her laughter, see her smile, and make her weak with pleasure.

She'd made him understand love. For his brother, the pack, his sons, and for her—the other half of his soul. He loved her completely, fiercely, because he didn't know any other way to love.

"How's everything look?" She wound her fingers into the fur of his chest and nuzzled closer.

"Perfect."

WANT MORE?

Can't get enough of Hans and Briony? Get a secret extra epilogue (four chapters!) of Hans and Briony's wedding by going to this special link: https://jocelynmontana.com/join-my-newsletter/

Or use the CONTACT ME page on my website www.jocelynmontana.com

---

Check out Book 2 in the Werewolves of Ulterra series: Fate Promised! Available now.

FATE PROMISED BLURB

WEREWOLVES OF ULTERRA BOOK 2

As a child he promised to marry her. As a werewolf, it's forbidden.

Juri's fight against a necromancer just got personal. Threaten the woman he once promised to marry? Bad idea. Because he's never stopped watching over her. Or yearning for her. Until now he's stayed in the shadows while protecting her, following the werewolf way, but with this threat, he steps to her side. And that breaks all the rules.

Triska has a secret. Not one of the good kinds, either. It's the kind that will one day rear up and change her life forever. For that reason, she's locked her heart away. But then her childhood love leaps out of the forest and back into her life. At one touch, all her carefully placed barriers fall. With one of his sensuous purrs, she wants to hold onto him forever. But she can't.

Every moment with her is stolen perfection. Every moment with him is a gift she can't keep. Ancient magic gives them a second chance to keep an old promise, telling them

'First, a rune will bind, but only a bite permanently entwines. With true love, it must be done, or two will never be one.' But forces just as strong work to rip them apart. They only have one month to decide ... will they choose each other?

Buy online here: Fate Promised
or on my website
www.jocelynmontana.com

I'D LOVE IT IF YOU LEFT ME A REVIEW!

For independent authors reviews are as valuable as gold! Even if it's only a line or two, it helps other readers that love werewolves and monster/human romance find my book.

ABOUT THE AUTHOR

Jocelyn Montana is a fantasy and paranormal romance author focusing on her two series featuring the world of Ulterra. She lives outside of Boston, Massachusetts with her boyfriend of ten years and her chiweenie Marcus, also known as The Dog Who Will Do Anything for Ham.

She loves werewolves, demons, and all sorts of fun supernatural beings. She'd like to thank Disney and their movies: Beauty and the Beast, and Robinhood (animated version) for showing her that handsome heroes don't always look like men.

For her books and updates and to sign up for her newsletter
www.jocelynmontana.com

Hang out with her on Facebook

[f] facebook.com/author.jocelynmontana

[BB] bookbub.com/authors/jocelyn-montana

[g] goodreads.com/jocelyn_montana

ALSO BY JOCELYN MONTANA

WEREWOLVES OF ULTERRA SERIES

Werewolves of Ulterra Book 1: Fate Awakened

Werewolves of Ulterra Book 2: Fate Promised

Werewolves of Ulterra Book 3: Fate Unchained

IMMORTALS OF ULTERRA SERIES

The Dark King and the Thief*

Only available to Newsletter Subscribers. Sign up at www. jocelynmontana.com

ACKNOWLEDGMENTS

Thank you to my writing partners and writing friends: S.J. Primrose, Sherry Bessette, Kat St. Vincent, and John Hundley. You read my story as it was taking shape and helped me craft it to be as compelling as possible. Your patience and insight was unparalleled.

It takes an incredible team to help bring a book into top shape. I want to thank my fantastic beta reader Sue McKerns of Otterville Overhaul and my developmental editor Tanya Oemig for taking the finished story and giving me valuable insight. And a big thanks to my wonderful editor Lynne Pearson for finessing my story and making it the best possible version.

Thank you to my boyfriend Tim. I'm sure he heard more about werewolves than he wanted, but I'll never know because he always listened and encouraged.

Thank you.